THE WINNER MAKER

JEFF BOND

ISBN: 978-1732255203

Cover image by Andrea Orlic

www.jeffbondbooks.com

PROLOGUE

B ob Fiske stalked out onto a glass-bottomed observation box of the Sears Tower, appearing to join the sky. His hair, wild and white, whorled with the passing clouds. His strides were at once rickety—owing to seventy-four-year-old joints—and resolute, each footfall seeming to make gravity, to seize its own plane of air.

He planted the portable lectern before his students with a leathered fist. "Poetry is the evidence of life. If your life is burning brightly, poetry is just the ash."

The entire honors English class, and more than one passing tourist, considered this in reverential silence. The students' faces glowed with a mishmash of excitements. They were out of school on a field trip! They had to recite a poem by heart; would they remember?

Being here with Fiske—Coach Fiske, Fiske the Great, Fiske the Feared—made them feel the way all high-school seniors should at least once during this final, never-to-be-forgotten year: special. Sure that every important thing in life was happening right here, right now, to them uniquely.

Marna Jacobs (left side, midway back) felt all this too, but more pressing was the weight of dual backpacks on her shoulders. *What had Jesse put in this thing, lead?* She shifted to resettle the load more comfortably over her five-one frame.

A voice behind her said, "Ooh, Marna, carrying your boyfriend's bag for him? How old-fashioned. Part of the new vintage motif?"

It was Caitlyn of the perfect cheekbones and 4.5 GPA, a sure-fire Winner when Fiske's list came out.

"Jesse's not my boyfriend." Marna crossed her ankles, suddenly less psyched about her thrift-store oxfords.

"Didn't you two go to homecoming together?"

"We, um, broke up."

"And you've accepted the demotion to pack mule?" Caitlyn said with a grin of ice.

Marna and Jesse were outsiders here, AP English being their only honors class. While the others elbowed for brownie points, Marna tried to fly under the radar—a strategy that had worked until last month when Mr. Fiske had praised her *Brave New World* essay as "refreshing, primitively honest." Now Caitlyn ridiculed her at every turn.

Still, the question was legit. Marna had been standing around waiting to board one of the tower's shockingly fast elevators when Jesse nudged her, asking if she'd leave his backpack on the glass bottom for him. Without waiting for an answer, he'd heaved the pack onto her shoulder. When she'd complained it was heavy, he had said all she had to do was leave it on the glass—then he slipped away as every ligament in Marna's neck and upper back croaked under the burden.

"We're friends," Marna said now. "Friends do each other favors."

Caitlyn sneered around the observation deck. The first student was approaching the podium, stealing a last peek at her crinkled notes. "What's inside, a bomb? You two always were quiet. Maybe too quiet."

Marna squirmed underneath the pack. It couldn't be a bomb. Right? Everyone had gone through security. Jesse's pack had been X-rayed.

She thought. Was pretty sure.

"Marna brought a bomb?" Todd Bruckmueller said, overhearing.

Caitlyn opened her shoulders to a larger audience. "Maybe."

"This is really mean, you guys, I—"

"Let's see!"

Todd, right tackle for the football team, reached for the pack. Marna hunched like a threatened armadillo but couldn't keep Todd from dislodging one arm. They struggled. Marna dug an elbow into the oaf's ribs. He lost his grip, and the pack crashed to the glass floor.

Driven less by loyalty to Jesse than rage, Marna grabbed one strap. Todd grabbed the other. Security personnel moved dimly in the periphery.

"*Enough.*"

The word boomed forth, sucking all air from the fight. Marna first thought Todd had said it—so loud, his meat-pie face right here—before spotting the pair of Illinois State 6A Championship rings against his neck. The rings belonged to Fiske. The septuagenarian had his 230-pound lineman in a half nelson.

"Poor form, Mr. Bruckmueller." Fiske unhanded Todd, then turned to Marna with a wink. "I cordially invite you to Wildkit Stadium this afternoon, four o'clock sharp, to witness your tormentor ascending and descending the east stairs in rapid succession. Two hundred flights or heatstroke, whichever comes first."

Before Marna could respond—*was* she supposed to respond? could Fiske get busted for laying hands on a student like that?—a metallic *clunk* sounded nearby. Jesse's pack began sliding in the direction of the noise.

"Hey, what—what's happening?" Todd said, scurrying back.

Marna instinctively raised her hands. Three guards were beelining her way, fingers pressed to earpieces. Students and tourists alike scattered. The backpack moved seven inches across the glass floor before locking into place with a small, intense shimmy.

Directly below, on the underside of the glass and suspended 103 stories above Wacker Drive, a hook protruded from a squat black cylinder.

A magnet.

That's why the backpack was so heavy. There's a gigantic magnet inside.

The hook was closed, and now a hand—a hand?—emerged from the void to clip what looked like a fat red ribbon onto it. The

3

backpack's fabric strained about the glass in a circle, the magnet inside perfectly mirroring the magnet below.

Marna squinted to make sure this wasn't allergies messing with her eyes. Also, the day was overcast; up here, they were literally in the clouds.

"Oh. My. God."

Jesse.

Suspended upside down, staring at her with that wobbly grin. The diamond-check soles of his shoes visible through the glass, he held on by a short length of the ribbon—which Marna saw was a bungee cord. The rest of the cord dangled far below, lilting now back against the skyscraper, now out over the Chicago River, twisting and kinking, rippling, the greatest part shrouded in fog.

Marna staggered into a row with the security guards. *How did he get up there? Are those magnets seriously gonna hold? Will the guards shoot him, or Tase him? Can you Tase through glass?*

The guards barked into walkie-talkies. When one stepped toward the pack, Jesse felt for something behind his waist and gave the bungee two sharp tugs.

"No!" Marna screamed. "You stupid jerk, *no*! Whatever you're thinking!"

But she recognized the sequence he was rushing through: the harness buckling, the strap cinching, his rawboned fingers jittery but unhesitating. Technical rock climbing was Jesse's thing—he actually taught yuppies at a downtown bouldering gym. He could do it in his sleep.

Marna flattened her whole body to the glass floor, fingers splayed, nose squished. "Why? *What is the point, J?* Stop!"

Into the misty chasm, her words were weak and scrabbling and basically nothing.

Jesse glanced past her. As his wild pupils settled on Fiske, his face took on a dreamy, near-euphoric blush.

The venerable teacher stood with arms folded. Impassive. Like Marna, Jesse had been encouraged by Fiske—had won kudos for his "exuberant prose style," even been assigned an extracurricular joint project with one of Fiske's pet students. In recent weeks, Jesse had even talked about making Winner.

4

"Respect your life!" Fiske called down. "Cherish it. Be the keeper of its sanctity."

He knelt beside Marna and, placing both hands on the glass, glared down. She had a fleeting notion that the Great Man could grab Jesse, that those gnarled fingers were capable of parting glass —or transmuting through, or willing matter around, something— and rescuing him.

The blush heightened in Jesse's face. His eyes pulsed. The sinews of his neck became taut and grotesque.

He plunged. Leading with his forehead, Adam's apple slicing the clouds. He was a falling, twisting, shrinking blur.

Smaller, smaller...very small.

Marna had almost lost the dot when an enormous white tarp exploded upward through the fog. A block-print message snapped into view across its expanse:

LIVE BIG.

PART ONE

CHAPTER ONE

THREE MONTHS LATER

The girl's eyes wanted to quit, shuttering every few seconds, rolling up to oblivion, but Steph Reece stayed with it. She scooted up the bed, keeping the Bob Books early-reader paperback in four-year-old Ella's sightline.

"De..." she prompted, pointing to the title. "De...ah...ah..."

Ella's tongue found the roof of her mouth, which might have been the first consonant sound of "Dot."

"That's it, *you can do it*. Sound it out."

Steph grinned through the pain—her thumb and forefinger had been holding the book still for two minutes—and rounded her lips in an exaggerated, soft O.

Ella's head lolled. Her hair, champagne blonde like Steph's, pooled on the pillow.

"The book, sweetie, focus on the book."

Steph's voice produced only a twitch in her daughter's face. Again, her eyes waned. In another second, she was out.

With a sigh, Steph closed the book. She knew this was an abysmal time to try reading. Ella should be alert, rested, an hour and a half removed from a meal. What choice did she have, though? Both she and Doug had worked late, so dinner hadn't started until 6:45. It had taken a solid hour of exhorting and, in the case of seven-month-old Morgan, airplane-forking, to achieve a balanced meal. Afterward, they had bundled up for a walk (exercise plus nature), eaten raisins and apple wedges (fiber, important for Ella's reluctance to go number two), and by then it had been bedtime.

Now she smoothed Ella's hair off her cheek. Watched the tiny chest rise and fall. At once, Steph felt intense love and equally intense regret. How could you not make time for reading? She considered waking Ella, freshening her with a glass of water, offering some bribe.

Jesus, Steph. Don't be that parent.

She tucked the comforter about her daughter's shoulders and switched off the lamp.

Downstairs, Doug sat with his laptop on the couch. The Bulls on TV, sound off for the kids' benefit.

She took a step for the kitchen.

"Dishes are done," Doug said.

She pivoted for the playroom.

"Toys put away." He looked up with a playful grimace. "Froggy's airing out on the deck. I think he went overboard with hand sanitizer again."

Steph smiled, sauntered over to stand behind him. "Going to be up late?"

Doug shook his head. "Swapping dollars for rupees at seven a.m. sharp. You?"

"Afraid so."

"Oh, right—Nike tomorrow. Big day."

Steph sucked in a breath. "Let's hope."

"You're going to kill it." He eased a muscled arm around her waist. "That whole account is you. *You* made it happen."

She bent to give him a peck, then headed off to the study. The presentation was more or less locked, the partners having signed off at today's dry run, but now she pored over each slide with a red Sharpie, energizing headers, nixing weak bullet points.

Dunham & Prior had never worked for Nike. Three months ago, when Steph had sniffed out their new product launch in the emerging trail shoes market, Rich Hauser—her supervising partner—had said to mock up a deck if she wanted. Be a good exercise. When she'd hustled a meeting with the regional ad buyer, he had shrugged.

Now that they had gotten a meeting to pitch a potential campaign, Rich's tone had changed. During the dry run, he had shown fatherly pride, implying to the other partners that he and Steph had slaved together over the slides when, in fact, he'd only just seen them that morning.

This didn't bother Steph. As a junior person, you expected to do the legwork and have your boss take the credit.

Now, the deck as perfect as she could make it, Steph e-mailed it around. She jotted a note to her direct report, Chad Nimms, highlighting the changes to his section. Rich preferred that she present the whole thing, but Steph—determined to do right in her first managerial role—had insisted on giving Chad the exposure.

Chad immediately texted back, *Love the changes! They can't say no! #SwooshIsOurs*

Steph smiled at Chad's millennial enthusiasm, knowing that Nike, headquartered two thousand miles away in Oregon, was still a long shot. So had been winning the lead in *A Midsummer Night's Dream*, and competing at debate nationals. And the public-school daughter of a seamstress graduating summa cum laude from Stanford.

It was eleven thirty. Doug's footfalls upstairs had ceased long ago. Tattletail was a purring fluff ball on the heating vent. Yawning, Steph powered down her computer. The house chores were ostensibly done, but Steph, unable to let go of the day, began a fresh sweep of downstairs, rinsing water glasses, tidying the girls' art area, tapping back a note to Chad reminding him to study the click-rate backup materials...

Throughout this final burst, Steph felt pushed by a relentless dissatisfaction. At breakfast, she had wanted to have Ella's birthday arrangements finalized. At the beginning of March— today was the fifteenth—she had wanted to have a *Lean In*–style women's luncheon established at work and have begun reading the *New York Times* cover to cover. On New Year's Day, resolution number one had been establishing a foothold in local politics. Her wall calendar, once a slate of clear possibility-rich boxes, was scribbled over with growth percentiles and jottings about Nike— whose pursuit was probably a lark, tomorrow's meeting just a courtesy distracting her from actual paying clients.

Before doubts darkened to despair and she got to the point of writing off her midtwenties for a loss, Steph stopped herself.

You have a rocket ship of a career. (Rich Hauser's words.) Your husband amazes you. Your kids are weird and wonderful, and no brattier than anybody else's.

Today was over, fine. The *Times* would send another paper tomorrow—and there'd be a style section to boot.

She ducked outside to switch off the porch lights. Just past the threshold, her feet tripped on something. A FedEx envelope. Express overnight shipment.

Prying open the tear strip, Steph fished out a single paper. Her eyes took a moment adjusting to the moonlight. When they did, when those first words resolved themselves, her heart lurched. For an instant, she thought she would faint—and Steph Reece was no fainter.

The letter began:

To: The Winners

Steph decided to wait for breakfast to discuss the letter with Doug. He had the big currency swap, so she let him sleep, shouldering the burden herself, her mind drifting back nearly a decade to high school. Those bright, towering emotions. Pride. Elation. Teeth-grinding sorrow. Episodes that lived on forever: a tearful conversation at prom, a might've-been on the shores of Lake Michigan, that first summer with a car when you felt adult and in control of events...even if you weren't. Not even close.

The alarm woke her rudely at 6:10. Steph slogged to the kitchen, where Doug was drinking coffee with his laptop. Two baby monitors fizzed peacefully.

The FedEx sat on the table.

"Did you read that?" Steph asked.

Doug looked past his screen, perplexed, then saw where Steph's eyes were aimed. "Yeah, I did. High drama."

He sipped his coffee.

Steph, ceaselessly amazed by the male need to project unflappability, read the letter fresh.

To: The Winners
   From: Becky Brindle

Hi fellow Wildkits! I hope this note finds you well! I am sending copies of this letter to four of you who were extremely close (and are extremely smart!!) to Mr. Fiske. As you may or may not know, I am a counselor at Evanston Township now and have the unfortunate task of informing you that our old teacher/coach/mentor is in trouble!

   Without going into details, which I hesitate to put in writing, the situation does NOT look good! Please please PLEASE, if you are at all able, join me for an emergency meeting at the school tomorrow at 12:30 p.m. My office is 127b, in the fine arts hall.

Yours Truly, Becky

Steph could hear Becky's voice perfectly, each bubbly concern and breathless single or double exclamation mark. They had seen each other over tapas last weekend as part of a larger group. Why wouldn't Becky have called or texted? Why the trouble of a FedEx?

Last night, Steph had considered reaching out to Becky herself but had decided it was too late. Now she pulled up the contact. "Can I text somebody at six fifteen?"

Doug glanced around his mug. "I've sent thirty-seven so far."

"Right. To Mumbai." Steph, barefoot, knocked his shin under the table. "Think I'd be waking her up?"

"It's a text. If she's asleep, she keeps sleeping."

Steph swiped out a quick note: *Becks, your letter really scares me. What's going on w/ Fiske?*

"Is it possible Mr. Fiske got fired?" she asked.

Doug crimped his brow. "Nah, we would've heard. Probably just another dust-up with Mancini."

Bob Fiske and Principal Mancini had been rivals since time immemorial. Where Mancini was the face of secondary-school convention, religiously frugal, ever banning the latest questionable jacket or hat style, Fiske lived at the vanguard. Fiske had lobbied early for Title IX–style gender equity and mandatory campus nutrition. His passions landed him in frequent standoffs with the administration, and his stubbornness, which he freely acknowledged and attributed to two tours in Vietnam, guaranteed messy resolutions. During Steph's freshman year, appalled by the decision to cut Latin, he had insisted on recouping the program's cost by pushing the night janitor's slop bucket.

Steph distractedly poured Ella's whole milk into her cereal instead of skim. "I don't know. Becky sounds awfully worked up."

"Becks has been worked up since that Naperville field party, first time she tried Boone's."

"Oh, no fair." Steph grimaced mildly. "She's changed a lot since school."

Morgan's monitor crackled. Moments later, after the *suck-suck* of a missed pacifier, she cried. Husband and wife looked at one another wearily. *Already?* Steph began to rise, but Doug waved her back to her cereal.

She checked her phone for Becky's reply.

Nothing.

In another minute, Ella woke too, and the household was consumed by child-processing. Steph and Doug moved deftly between crises, he containing Morgan's diaper blowout with a plastic newspaper sleeve, she finding Ella's missing "sparkly party shoe" upstairs and dropping it to his waiting hand in the foyer. Two Harlem Globetrotters upping the other's game.

Steph kept peeking at her cell. Discreetly—Ella had friends who spent hours on devices, and Steph refused to set that example. She ducked to the hall during teeth brushing and texted again.

Again, nothing.

"Twelve thirty cuts it close," she muttered. "Nike comes at two... I should really be there to meet them."

Doug was snapping Morgan's onesie with one hand, spooning apple / carrot puree with the other. "Lemme handle it, my lunch is wide open. You worry about Nike."

"I should go."

"Come on, babe—you've worked too hard for this. I'll give you the full report. Ten-to-one odds Becks is inventing some big drama in her head."

Steph twisted her purse strap over one knuckle. She knew if she left it to Doug—for whom nothing was difficult, not football or calculus, or parenting around a sixty-hour workweek—he would conclude Becky was blowing things out of proportion regardless of the facts.

It was 7:15. Becky must be awake by now. Steph buckled Ella into her car seat, then dialed Becky on her way to the driver's side.

Straight to voice mail.

She tried reaching Becky throughout the morning without success. What was Becky doing? Was her news so dire it could only be delivered in person? What if Fiske had gotten physical in class, hauled off and hit some troublemaker? Uttered something racial, sexist? Fiske had always been a staunch progressive, but he *was* seventy-four-years-old.

A large part of Steph wanted to leave Fiske's situation, whatever it was, for later. Concentrate on Nike. Check in with Doug or Becky this afternoon.

Except that Bob Fiske had been more than a teacher. More than inspiring, even. The man had paid the first two years of Steph's tuition at Stanford, refusing to abide her mother's decree that all five children receive identical state-school educations. He had planted himself in their cramped living room and argued that Steph's development must not be retarded, that his money had been placed in a named account and would be wasted unless they accepted it. (Years later, she and Doug would wonder about the veracity of that claim.) It was the sort of extraordinary act he undertook for Winners. "Whatever you need, whenever you need it," he'd pledge. "Anything to help achieve the life you're meant for."

At 12:22, slipping into her coat, she found Chad Nimms at his cubicle.

"Nike is on cruise control," she told him. "I've prepped the conference room, touched base with their people. All you need to do is handle Rich Hauser for an hour."

Chad swallowed. "So, so like if—"

"Just if anything comes up," she said lightly. "It won't. But if it does, you know the material. Look him in the eye."

With that—and trying to ignore Chad's shrinking gaze now—Steph blew out for the parking garage. Traffic was light on Ridge Avenue, and she pulled into the Evanston Township High lot at 12:28. Hunting for a spot, she twice had to reverse out of approaches after nearly ramming a short car's bumper. Driving had never been a strong suit, too automatic, a low priority for her overachiever's brain. Steph had caused two accidents in this very lot as a student.

At last she found a spot near the bike racks. Her suede boot had scarcely hit asphalt when the adjacent spot opened up. Her husband's ice-blue Mercedes zoomed in surely as if the letters, *DOUG REESE: 2006 PROM KING/STARTING QUARTERBACK*, were painted underneath.

"Shall we?"

Steph took his arm on the way in, those familiar muscles warm at her side.

The halls were jammed with students hurrying, or not, from lunch to fifth hour. Steph wondered which might be among this year's Winners. You couldn't always tell by looking. Even apart from natural differences from type, Fiske threw plenty of curve-balls: the dropout who will go on to invent the router, the guitar-picking pothead with preternatural gifts for essentializing angst. He'd tapped the daughter of a US congressman the same year as a boy whose adoptive parents were incarcerated on meth charges. The list could be as many as ten, as few as two.

Fiske refused to acknowledge the list's existence on school grounds. Near the end of first semester, new Winners received a cardstock notification by mail—Steph still had hers filed away with the diplomas and birth certificates. Cloaked in such secrecy, the list spawned all sorts of rumors. *Winners get skeleton keys to the school... Fiske hazes them with LSD... There's a retreat in Canada where everyone plays Scrabble and writes haiku and has orgies...*

What if they bumped into Fiske now? Though his classroom was on the opposite side of the school, he commonly stalked the halls—the famed "Fiske foray"—with thumbs tucked through suspenders, head cocked as though counterbalancing an outsized brain. He had been known to cuff bullies or critique a paper over a student's shoulder.

Fiske would be back-thumpingly glad to see them. *Ah, the Royals returned!* What would they say about Becky's emergency meeting? Should they lie?

Fortunately, they reached the fine arts hall without hearing their former mentor's baritone. The counselor offices were located near Wildkit Theater, where Steph had starred as Helena in *Midsummer.*

Becky saw them through the door. "Thank you so, so, so, *so* much for coming!"

Before Steph could ask about the FedEx, Becky—giant chest bouncing like Jell-O—was clutching her and kissing both cheeks. Doug nobly accepted a hug without having his midsection too lewdly mashed by their former classmate's endowments.

"How *are* you? Steph, so sorry for not returning texts—total nightmare getting to day care but of course you guys know the drill."

Becky had recently adopted twins from Haiti, six-month-old girls. It was known throughout their circle that she wanted a husband to fill out the picture. Doug grinned and asked how the Match.com listings were looking. Becky feigned pushing him back out into the hall, an exchange straight out of high school, but her lawn-mower giggle had none of its old zest.

Now Steph noticed a fourth person in the room.

"Hello," Lydia Brockert said upon being discovered. She gave a short wave.

Lydia Brockert? Lydia had been a sophomore when they were seniors, an excruciatingly shy girl who had swept her class awards but been unable to accept for fear of walking across the auditorium stage. Steph had heard she was a psych professor at UChicago now, specializing in anxiety research of some kind.

Steph faced Becky. "Alright, Becks, what's going on? That FedEx really scared me."

Becky urged her to sit, pulling plastic chairs off a stack. "Let's wait a sec. I am expecting one more Winner, supposedly he was getting in by early aftern—"

"Sorry I'm late, all," a familiar voice called from the door. "O'Hare has the kludgiest gate layout in the history of gate layouts. Seriously—I was looking for baggage claim and I swear I almost boarded an Air Bahrain nonstop."

Following the voice inside came a wiry man with quick, intense eyes and dark hair spotted with early gray. He dropped garment and laptop bags in a corner.

"Oh my God, Eric!" Steph rushed into another hug. "I had no idea you were coming!"

The former debate partners stood back from each other. Ten years after graduation, the difference in social caste remained clear as ever. Eric Pinkersby might be wearing Bvlgari glasses and hipster jeans, but the fundamentals were unchanged. Steph taller by an inch, looking upon him with the clear-complected benefice of the lone popular girl in honors class. Eric shifting between insteps, hands comfortable in none of his pockets.

"Aren't you in San Francisco?" she asked.

"The vast majority of days, yes."

Steph smiled but thought it strange that Eric, who, unless something had changed, was on the verge of a lucrative IPO for the high-tech data recovery firm he had founded, would fly cross-country based on Becky's FedEx.

As usual Eric, attuned to every nuance of her face, seemed to read her thoughts. "What's two thousand miles when your sensei needs you? Besides, it's been too long since I've seen Doug Reece. Guy must be bench-pressing sedans by now."

Doug took the smaller man's hand in a crunching grip. "Nice thick layer of callouses, Pinkersby. Good to see you haven't lost your touch with the ladies."

Again, the fundamentals unchanged.

Now Becky pulled her office door closed.

"I know all you smarties lead busy lives, so I'll get to the point. As the letter mentioned—and sorry for the FedEx, it seemed way too important for a text—but anyways yes, this is about Mr. Fiske. *Coach* Fiske." Nodding Doug's way. "As everyone knows, he has been a polarizing figure. We all loved him, but some of our class-mates did not, and it's the same today. Personally, I find him inspiring. Even though I'm no Winner and Mr. Fiske has indeed challenged me at times, I feel he is a huge positive for the school."

She went on several minutes, describing in soap-operatic terms Fiske's relationship with the Brown University English Department—each year he finagled a spot for an ETHS senior—and courageous support for the Student Bill of Rights.

Steph's phone buzzed. A text from Chad: Nike was early. *what should i do???*

She swiped back, *give them a tour, you got this!*, then refocused on Becky. She would've liked to speed things along but did not want to embarrass her old classmate, whose inferiority complex always peaked around Winners.

Doug had no such qualms.

"Becks," he interrupted. "Enough preamble. What's up with Fiske?"

"Oh right." Becky thumped herself in the head, setting her blonde curls bouncing. "Just, like, throw a stapler at me when I get off on a tangent—you guys are the ones with brains."

She took a tall breath, and Steph was sure her friend—well, more acquaintance at this point—would launch into further self-deprecation, dismissing the vocation of counselor or apologizing for her low SATs.

Instead, Becky Brindle gripped the beige table they all sat around and changed everything.

"Fiske disappeared on Wednesday."

CHAPTER TWO

Nobody spoke. Over several seconds, Steph felt the air thicken, becoming heavy at her neck. An overhead heating duct knocked, probably had been knocking. The sound was like thunder now.

"He taught Wednesday classes as usual," Becky explained, "and Principal Mancini's secretary saw him leave the parking lot. Then nothing. Nobody has reached him since."

Steph asked whether anyone had talked to the police.

"Briefly. Because it's only been thirty-six hours, the dispatcher I talked to—"

"Dispatcher?" Steph said. "No, no—we need somebody important. A detective."

"Yes, but as we all know, Mr. Fiske has a history of going AWOL. Remember junior year?"

Eric jumped in. "Yeah, but that was different—Fiske's dad had died, he wasn't himself." His body squared reflexively to match Steph's pose. "Did he talk to anybody about a trip or planned absence?"

Becky said no, not that she knew of.

"Then Steph is right, we go cops." Eric's pinkie slicked the tabletop frenetically. "Now, today. Quicker than a bubble sort on Tianhe-2."

He got back only blank looks.

"World's fastest computer, theoretically capable of 54.9 petaflops? No?"

Becky's full lips curled inward. "I agree we may need to involve the authorities in a bigger way at some point. But maybe we should limit this to a small group at first—a core of people who care deeply about Mr. Fiske—and make sure we have a cohesive plan."

Steph didn't understand. *A plan?* They needed flyers and press and squad cars. Why was Becky wasting time on FedExes and secret tree-house-clique meetings?

And why this particular clique? She, Doug, and Eric made sense—they were Becky's classmates and known Fiske favorites—but Lydia was out of left field. Steph knew Lydia primarily as the little sister of Nora Brockert, a fun-loving member of their class who had drowned senior year at prom. While it was said Fiske thought of Lydia like a daughter, having taken her under his wing after Nora's death, her extreme shyness made her an odd choice for a search committee.

"What's tricky is that Principal Mancini...has not been super sympathetic." Becky squished her palms together. "He told one of the other counselors this is Fiske's second unexplained absence of the calendar year, which constitutes grounds for termination."

"Garbage," Eric said. "He's been looking for an excuse to can Fiske for thirty years."

"I know. And I'm kinda scared that if we go to the police and this becomes some big, like, investigation? Then Mancini will have his excuse."

Steph's phone buzzed in her purse. She ignored it. "Was Fiske depressed?"

"We don't know," Becky said. "He has no real confidants among the faculty. That's one reason I wanted to convene this group, to see if anyone had spoken with him recently."

Eric said he had, just Wednesday, in fact. "I didn't hear depression. We talked about water on Mars, and what answer you'd get crowdsourcing the odds of extraterrestrial life in the Virgo Supercluster."

"Did he mention the Sears incident?"

"Never said a word about Sears. Didn't the school board exonerate him?"

"Completely," Becky said, though Steph had read different in the newspaper. The board had concluded that Fiske bore no direct responsibility for the death of Jesse Weams, who had plunged sixty stories onto the roof of the west antenna tower (actually passing by Doug's office; his firm occupied the ninety-seventh floor) after his magnets disengaged, but said Fiske's "culture of glory seeking, epitomized by his unofficial motto, 'Live Big,'" had created a "fertile environment" for Jesse's ill-fated stunt.

Steph asked, "Had he made any enemies lately? Was he mixed up in some controversy?"

"When wasn't he involved in controversy?" Eric began pacing. "This is what happens when you live by principles. When you refuse to back down."

Doug exhaled at length. "I hate to be the one to say this, but look. If we're being honest, we have to acknowledge that Fiske was impossible at times. Remember how he hung on to *A Clockwork Orange*? Took him years to stop showing that movie."

"So what're you saying, Doug?" Eric asked. "He deserves whatever he gets? We should just forget about him? Let whatever bad stuff might be happening to him right now go ahead and happen?"

"I didn't say that. Any of that." Doug fixed Eric with the same look Ella got for speaking disrespectfully, then addressed the others. "I'm saying we should keep an open mind. There might be some mysterious enemy at play, but it could also be something of his own doing."

Eric: "Your theory's what? Fiske is holed up somewhere in his tighty-whities having a personal Stanley Kubrick film festival, refusing to answer his phone or doorbell?"

"I'll leave the theorizing about his underwear choices to you, Pinkersby."

"Fine, great, hit me with a gay joke. Clearly having never wrestled around with men in pads and colorful uniforms, *I* must be the homosexual..."

As the two men glared at one another, Steph bristled beside

her husband, who generally eschewed locker-room crudeness. Apparently, Eric bought it out in him.

"Let's stay constructive," she said. "Fiske needs us. Bickering won't help."

They brainstormed ten minutes on what needed doing. As Lydia Brockert—who had said nothing since "hello"—fingered her overcoat buttons, the others called out ideas. Did anybody know Fiske's adult children? Becky thought the daughter was at Urbana and volunteered to try the campus directory. Doug said he would search online for car accidents in the West and Southwest, two geographies Fiske had admired. Eric trumped this by setting up, using a flurry of taps and swipes, a Google News alert that would tell them instantly if Fiske's name crossed the newswire.

Doug rolled his eyes.

"And I can talk to Mancini," Steph said. "We can't let him use this as a pretext for firing Fiske."

"Yeah, me too." Eric pivoted for the door. "Go now, catch him in his office?"

Steph glanced at the wall clock. Quarter 'til two. Rich Hauser and the other partners would be setting down notebooks in the conference room, greeting Nike. Wondering where in the world she was.

Principal Mancini could be seen through his office window, the oiled-back bullet o' hair bobbing up and down as he dictated to his secretary. A towering six six, he wore a pinstriped suit and cuff links, and stalked about with seeming agitation, palming his neck.

"Union trouble," Eric cracked, adjusting glasses up his nose. "The Tattaglias must be making a move with the cafeteria workers."

Steph didn't smile. Mancini had been rumored to be "connected" during their time at ETHS, which she figured for a cheap stereotype.

Urging herself up on tiptoes to catch the principal's eye, she felt pulled by competing dreads. The Fiske news was alarming, but the idea of missing Nike—jeopardizing eight months' legwork, destroying her credibility with the partners—was heartbreaking. Chad had texted as they were leaving Becky's office: *About to start, u coming!?* She had quickly called to reassure him she'd be there as soon as possible, that he would be fine, just project authority and focus on decision-makers...

She had not meant to commit to seeing Mancini immediately. Once Eric had suggested it, though, what could she say? She had felt transported back to high school (of course they were physically *at* high school), those competitive classroom melees that Fiske himself had encouraged, slugging it out over Daisy's true nature in *The Great Gatsby* or whether *The Aeneid* merited reading in the twenty-first century. "Argue like your very fate is on the line—your happiness, your station in life. And when it is, you'll be prepared."

She hated to admit it, but the relative success of Eric—and to an extent, Doug, who shuttled around $50 million on any given day—had egged her on too. At ETHS, she had been the chosen one. Transcending the achievers' mishmash of GPA, test scores, and extracurriculars, Steph had had what Fiske once called "an inarticulable providence." People signed her senior yearbook, *Mills for prez, 2028!* and *Pardon me when you make the Supreme Court, okay?*

And she *was* doing great. The youngest account manager in her firm, successful mother of two. Seated around Becky's table of Winners, though, she had felt that familiar dissatisfaction—the urge to do more, to lead.

So she had.

Principal Mancini looked up now and saw them waiting. He ushered them in.

"To what do I owe the honor?" he asked in his gruff but not unfriendly way.

Steph wasted no time. "We're here about Fiske. I understand he's disappeared?"

"Not sure I would use that word."

Eric said, "Hasn't been seen or heard from in two days. Seems worthy of the OED definition."

Mancini looked them over with spent eyes. He had always had a mixed rapport with the achievers of Evanston Township High.

Naturally he took pride in the students around whose necks he draped ribbons, understood the importance of having a healthy number of Illinois State Scholars, but his daily work revolved around the others: troublemakers, average Joes and Janes who needed nudging.

"Bob Fiske is no longer my concern." Mancini nodded past them to his secretary. "I just dictated his termination notice."

Steph and Eric whirled. Miriam, an elderly woman with ball-chain glasses, was entering information into her computer off a form.

"You can't! Fiske has been here four decades—he's devoted his life to this school."

"I can. I did." The principal stood and snapped his lapels as if to go.

"What if it turns out he's been harmed?" Steph said. "Or kidnapped? You'll be forced to reinstate him."

"I'll chance it."

Eric asked what his theory was.

"My theory," Mancini said, "is I don't like theories. Union contract says two unexplained absences in a twelve-month period is cause. End of story."

Steph, experienced in talking peeved clients off cliffs, steered him onto less emotional ground. *When had Fiske's first absence been? Last spring, really? And how had that been resolved?* Mancini's thick brow relaxed as he answered her tactical queries.

"Missed a solid week. Never apologized to me, never explained."

It wouldn't have been the first time Fiske and Mancini had struggled with communication. Fiske was known to schedule impromptu field trips to the Art Institute, to Hemingway's birth-place out in Oak Park. "At times, wanderlust beckons and neglects bothering with paperwork," Steph recalled him saying during one excursion.

She glanced to Eric to see if he wanted a turn. As debate part-ners, they had favored a two-barreled approach on tough judges.

He was staring at his lap.

She said, "Fiske has a lot of support in the community. Sports writers. Evanston City Council. Salesforce, Deloitte—I can hardly schedule a meeting in Chicago without running into another Winner. You'll have an uproar on your hands."

"Maybe." The principal reached into a desk drawer for a sheaf of papers. "Maybe not."

He laid the papers before them. A petition. Hundreds of signatures below the heading, *We the undersigned believe Bob Fiske, on the basis of his callous and blatantly elitist worldview, should be removed immediately from his position as teacher and head football coach at Evanston Township High School.*

Eric said, "I read about this. Started by some friend of Jesse Weams, right?"

"Of course people are reacting emotionally," Steph said. "A kid died—it's awful."

Mancini sniffed. "Ground's been shifting under Bob's feet for a while. Last three years, we've had protests after the Winners list came out. This year somebody egged his car."

Steph asked whether it was possible somebody took their beef too far.

The principal tilted his hand, causing a gold watch to glisten. "Bob's style invited confrontation. Every week it was a new headache."

Steph noted the use of past tense. "Had he made any enemies lately?"

"Oh yeah. Just finished up fighting this gang—this sort of gang we have—over the Solar System."

Steph reared back. The Solar System was a six-foot square section of hallway floor that depicted the sun and planets. "It's carpet. How do you fight over carpet?"

Mancini raised his eyebrows in weary assent. The group called itself Northside Ill; there was debate about whether they were an actual gang or only wanted to be one. Their leader, a senior named Bix, had declared the Solar System off-limits to all non-Ill foot traffic. After a few ugly confrontations, students and teachers had acquiesced and began walking around the colorful illustrations. Not Fiske. When Fiske heard, he reworked all his intra-class walks to include the Solar System, strolling over Mars with his nose in a dog-eared paperback. If an Ill member challenged him, he either ignored them or, if bad language was used, dragged the kid to Mancini. The conflicts grew heated. Fiske fanned the flames, setting up a lawn chair across Saturn's rings during his plan period.

Steph could imagine it perfectly, right down to Fiske's lazy whistles as he paged through his book. "Did you tell the police?"

"Evanston PD has enough on their plate. I didn't figure they needed to waste time filing my detention slips."

Steph frowned. She would have liked to ask more—about this Bix, and Fiske's first unexplained absence, and how much traction the petition had gained—but it was nearly two thirty. If she was going to eke out even an appearance with Nike, she needed to go.

"I respect that Mr. Fiske can be a difficult employee," she said. "But he moved the needle for a lot of students. Certainly for me, and I know for Eric. Give us a few days to track him down."

The principal scratched his well-thatched neck. "Union contract is clear. All he had to do was shoot Miriam an e-mail. As it is, I'm stuck with no sub. Miss Robertson was filling in, but she left." He checked his watch. "Now I gotta walk down, stand there in front of twenty smart alecks, hassle 'em to read instead of play on their phones."

Steph brightened. "Eric can teach it! Sixth hour is still senior English, right?"

As Mancini confirmed it was, Eric's mouth hung open as though propped by a small apple.

"I can?"

Steph felt guilty foisting this on him, but she couldn't go herself. Besides, if he had dropped everything to fly here from San Francisco, what else was he going to do, hang out at the Marriott?

"It'll be a great opportunity for them. To meet one of Fiske's former students, somebody who's having all this success in the real world."

Eric blushed at the praise, causing Steph to feel guiltier still.

She turned to Mancini. "How about it? Three days. If we haven't found Fiske in three days, you take whatever action you deem appropriate."

"One." Principal Mancini raised a single finger—gnarled, broad. "I'll give you twenty-four hours to bring him in. Then he's gone."

CHAPTER THREE

Through the conference-room glass, Steph could see Chad Nimms floundering. Chad was a tall, strapping kid—a skinnier Doug—but now nibbled his lip at the head of the table. His laptop was docked at the presenter's podium. He glanced between it and the 120-inch projection as though worried the two might be different.

Rich Hauser watched from up the table, jaw tight.

Rich didn't trust Chad with clients. Phrases like "wishy-washy" and "lacking gravitas" kept popping up in his reviews. Steph had done all she could pushing back against these critiques but knew if Chad laid an egg here, with Nike, Rich might well stick him in some back office, assigning him cold calls until he quit.

She paused at the threshold. Cracked her wrists, checked the lay of her blazer.

"My apologies, something came up that I wasn't able to move." She breezed to the front, passing behind men thirty years her senior. "Where are we? Ah, perfect—Chad has you into the nitty-gritty."

Steph touched Chad lightly on the back, assuming control of his trackpad. She launched into an explanation of a quadrant graph that plotted Nike against its competitors in the trail shoes category. Merrell, Saucony, Brooks—she cycled through each, addressing its market position and potential strategic responses.

"I don't see our dot," said the regional ad buyer, Nike's Man in the Room. "Where do we play, fashion/performance? Premium?"

Rich Hauser had relaxed as Steph's command performance had taken hold of the room, but his posture stiffened at this challenge.

Steph grinned. "You're Nike." Her eyes did not leave the buyer's as she tapped a PowerPoint key combo. A dozen tiny swooshes materialized. "You play everywhere."

The rest of the presentation went as smoothly. She guided skeptics toward helpful footnotes, offered to hash out particulars offline when discussion threatened to veer off into the weeds. As she drove the meeting, Steph felt the exhilaration of success. A revving in the gut. Adrenaline that grew with every admiring nod. The sensations seemed amplified by the visit to ETHS, where her achievement had begun—where the victories had been clear cut, unmoderated by the adult fog of money and job titles and diverging pursuits. High-school resumes require no interpretation. Valedictorian. Debate nationals.

Winner.

Chad Nimms had recovered two skin tones since Steph's arrival, but his eyes still droned ahead in a thousand-yard stare. Nevertheless, Steph turned his way at the *Online Targeting* section.

"I'll have Chad walk you through our success in digital. He's our subject matter expert."

Rich Hauser's face stormed over, and Chad too seemed surprised to hear his own number called.

Steph prompted, "The newsletter-tracking dashboard is something to see."

"R-right. Correct." Chad rose to the podium, blinked, and began his section as rehearsed.

He did fine. Steph had established authority, and Nike, primed to believe, did not question Chad's core point that Dunham & Prior was an industry leader in precision demo- and behavior-based online targeting.

"And that," Steph said, shutting the laptop on a final wrap-up slide, "is about the size of it. We're thrilled to be talking to you folks, can't wait to get this relationship rolling."

She faced Chad, who had hard copies of three versions of a *Next Steps* slide. Best practices at Dunham & Prior dictated you took the client's temp before making a proposal. If the reaction was tepid, you didn't want to toss out a large number and get laughed out of the room—but the other way, you hated to leave money on the table by presenting conservative figures to an audience that'd gone gaga over your stuff.

"Impressive," the Nike buyer said. "I'll have to steal that nifty scatterplot of yours next time I talk to Portland."

He winked at Steph. She was just indicating the stack of $10 million spend-level slides to Chad when the same voice added, less playfully, "We do need to set expectations here."

A funnel cloud appearing in the conference room's panoramic windows could not have had a darker impact than these words.

"Uh, sure—of course," Steph managed. "What did you have in mind?"

What he had in mind was a lot less than $10 million. A trial newsletter run, $75K to start, focused around prospective *Outdoor Actives* (eighteen to thirty-five, expressed interest in hiking and/or trail running).

"The launch campaign itself will be coordinated by our primary agency, Wieden+Kennedy." The buyer clicked his ballpoint off glossy cherrywood. "Naturally."

Steph squeezed the $10 million slides into a roll at the small of her back, feeling the partners' stares. Blood rushed to her face.

"Great." She willfully relaxed her shoulders. "No, that's fantastic, we welcome the opportunity to start small. Prove ourselves."

After Steph and the partners finished playing it off—"Super, just what we were hoping for"—and got contact info for Wieden + Kennedy, they shook hands with Nike and cleared out. Fortunately, there was a large partners meeting at four, so Steph was spared, for now, the obligatory postmortem with Rich Hauser.

She and Chad watched their visitors board town cars from the lobby.

"Too ambitious?" he said through a false grin. "Did we mess it up?"

"Our foot's in the door." Steph turned with a bracing breath. "Listen, Chad. I want to apologize for hanging you out to dry today. I put you in a tough spot. You did a nice job in there."

He shrugged. "I thought we had it."

"Me too."

The Nike fleet pulled away from the curb, disappearing into traffic. Steph experienced the sudden absence of stress—this momentous meeting weeks in the making, finally over—as yet another pressure. A dark idleness. *Nothing is moving...the gears are stuck...time is passing, and you are standing still...*

She knew this was nonsense, that plenty of accounts needed her attention. Quicken, PetSmart, Chicago municipal's pre-K pitch —they weren't Nike, but they weren't small potatoes either. There was work to do.

Chad, apparently thinking along the same lines, said, "Hey, I heard MetroBuild got through Evanston zoning last night."

"No kidding?"

"Yeah. Apparently, that dude—the one who shows up at every meeting to rant against the shoreline impact?—didn't show. They must be celebrating. Maybe a good time to pitch 'em?"

Steph agreed. They should start pulling together a media plan for the condos, and some B2B/trade-mag ideas for the mixed-use units. The billboard creatives were ready; he could find them on the shared drive.

She did not mention that "the dude" whose rantings had been holding up the development was her former teacher, Bob Fiske.

CHAPTER FOUR

There was nothing nefarious about Steph's withholding her association to Fiske. She hadn't mentioned it around the office out of a kind of embarrassed loyalty. Rich Hauser and others found the "grassroots"—he never used the term without air quotes—challenge to the MetroBuild development ludicrous. Though the proposed high-rise did trump Evanston's current tallest building by six stories, its location by the shore meant it wouldn't affect the skyline, and all agreed the resultant job growth would be substantial.

"Erosion?" the MetroBuild CEO had sneered. "Have they ever looked down the coast of Lake Michigan? It's nothing *but* skyscrapers."

Steph's initial take was similar, but she allowed for the possibility that her thinking might be clouded by the opinions of the bigwigs, whose motives were far from pure. So six months ago, she'd educated herself on the science of large-slab soil erosion. There were some concerns, people worried about downstream effects, but overall the evidence seemed thin.

Without telling anyone at Dunham & Prior, she met her old teacher.

"Of course it's a canard," Fiske said. "The building is a monstrosity."

Steph faced him across a wobbly bistro table of the Unicorn

Cafe, Fiske's favorite joint. "They're calling it 'neo–Spanish Renaissance.'"

"I call it too much glass, which bleeds heat, which necessitates the burning of fossil fuels to maintain office worker comfort."

He looked at her frankly. Since her time at ETHS, his wiry hair had gone an impossible shade of white, Vermont powder.

"I know our client MetroBuild has pursued carbon credits in previous projects. And by other measures—"

"How forthright do you expect *your client* is regarding the environmental damage it inflicts when scheming with the people it pays to write its ad copy?"

Steph crossed her legs, feeling something like mental whiplash. How many sleights can you fit into one sentence?

"Ad copy is just a piece of what we do at Dunham & Prior. We advise on a range of issues. Strategy, community engagement."

Fiske laughed. "Yes, look at us engaging now."

This seemed to break the ice—crack it, at least—and they discussed the project in more measured terms. Fiske conceded the zoning committee had stayed on the sidelines for more egregious developments. Steph admitted she hadn't considered the traffic/congestion issue, focused on erosion. But the city was already planning to widen Sheridan to six lanes, right?

After twenty minutes, Fiske said he would give the data a fresh look.

This granted, he fixed his unruly eyebrows in sharp diagonals —a look he used to flash before unpacking a student's wordy answer. "Tell me, Stephanie. Do you find the work rewarding?"

She glanced around. The cafe had emptied out. "Most days."

"You're at the peak of your abilities. The absolute apex. These years do not return. Sand flows but one way through the hourglass."

There was no responding to statements like this, of course. Steph didn't understand why Fiske was lecturing her. Brad Urquel had ended up in Big Pharma. Alessandra Kaine had turned her federal clerkship into a job with ExxonMobil. Had either Winner gotten this treatment?

Had Eric Pinkersby? It was said Fiske had convinced him to leave Facebook and found Paladin Technologies. *Why?* How many orphans or pounds of CO_2 was a data recovery start-up likely to save?

"I don't see marketing as an end point," she said. "I see it as a beginning."

Fiske nodded. "You were active in student government. President of your class."

"And today's politics, for better or worse, are very much driven by marketing."

"That was your calculus? Means to an end?"

"No, at first...well, my dad was in advertising. That put me onto it."

Steph had no memory of her father, who had died of abdominal cancer when she was three, but her mom always said that: he was "in advertising." Whether creating ads or as an executive (only twenty-nine, he couldn't have risen too high), Steph had no idea. This link to her father, together with romantic TV associations, had given the field an enchanted place in her mind. After majoring in humanities, she had surveyed the bewildering spread of campus recruiters and settled on Dunham & Prior, a Chicago firm in the industry she had admired as a child.

Now Fiske, who knew about her father, palmed his jaw. "It's a powerful thing. A life being ripped off the arc we expect."

"Yes. It—it is."

"Do you know what initiated the Winners list? Did I ever tell?"

Steph flinched. "I heard speculation. But never firsthand, no."

He raked a hand back through his wild hair, exhaling. "It also traces back to loss. My squad mates in Vietnam. So many died, and it—and though the magnitude of the tragedy is well understood, the experience is inexpressible by number. You train together, you prepare for the worst humanity knows together. You learn about their aspirations and plans—those who have plans.

"Then they die. Nineteen years old. Twenty. And everything you've learned is moot. That they played trombone. That their father-in-law expected them to join his concrete business but they were determined otherwise. The information meant nothing to you before, but now...dead...you comb back through memory and you're thirsty for it. Every detail feels vital—a thing to cherish, a thing you insist the whole world remember."

Fiske firmed his top lip. "When I returned home, I began teaching. My students vociferously opposed the war. This didn't bother me. By that point, every rational person did. What bothered me was their utter lack of seriousness about their own lives."

He recalled a cadre of outstanding students his first year, kids who could have excelled along any path but chose to waste their gifts on drugs and apathetic musing. "I wanted to seize them by the shoulders and explain about my squad mates, whose futures had been erased. I tried—a few heavy-handed lectures that only served to make me less relevant. Quickly it became clear that I need a positive message."

His first iterations of what became the Winners list had been clumsy. He tried requiring them to draft a "Life Plan," then to write letters to their thirty-, forty-, and fifty-year-old selves. Eventually he decided to place the onus on himself, pledging to do everything in his power to help them succeed, if only they would pledge in return to pursue success with reckless abandon.

Steph said, "And the rest is history."

Fiske hunched forward gravely. "My point in telling the tale is to impress upon you my urgency—and what I sincerely hope is your urgency—about the direction your life takes. You showed as much promise as any I've taught. And I've taught plenty. Poise. Effortless leadership. Acting, debate. The mentoring program for underserved communities—still thriving, incidentally."

Warmth spread through Steph's body. "I do think about other opportunities. Certainly within five years, I expect—"

"Five years?" Fiske interrupted. "Stephanie, time is our mortal enemy. Time leeches ambition. Never forget that greatness lives inside you. No matter how far off course you stray—no matter what you've done or have to atone for in the past—greatness remains. Greatness is never beyond salvage."

The sockets of his eyes quivered, the blue pupils inside fervent.

Atone?

Fiske was an English teacher; words mattered to him. Steph had a chilling suspicion they were no longer talking about advertising.

Today was the first Wednesday of the month: poker night. Steph had tried talking Doug out of it after Becky's news, but he had insisted. The guys were counting on it—Phil had pushed back an arthroscopic knee procedure to give them numbers. He hated that Fiske was missing, but how did putting their lives on hold help?

She got the girls early from day care, as was her custom on days they would be sleeping over at Grandma's. (The poker banter far exceeded G-rated levels.) Approaching the pre-K room at 4:15, Steph peeked through the door glass.

The junior teacher, seeing her, wrung her hands and went looking for Miss Marilyn.

Uh-oh.

Ella was kneeling by herself, absorbed in a peg-fitting activity. She immediately began shoveling the pegs into their Tupperware when prompted by Miss Marilyn, who reminded her to roll her rug too. Miss Marilyn waited for Ella to finish, then walked her to the door.

Steph smiled.

Ella did not smile back.

"I'm afraid we had another incident," Miss Marilyn said, leading them away from another mom picking up.

"Did she fall off the climber again?"

But Steph could tell from body language that she had not—Ella cowering at the wall, the tilt of the Miss Marilyn's chin.

"Ella, would you like to explain what happened at circle time?"

Ella gripped the hem of her dress.

"You can tell me, sweetie." Steph squatted low. "Whatever it is."

Miss Marilyn glanced back into the classroom where a child had begun wailing. Ella pulled her dress around to chew the hem, showing her underwear.

Steph gently pried the hem from between her daughter's teeth. "I won't be upset. I just want to help."

After a few more prods, Ella started, "Braylon took my seat.

He said *I* stole it, but really I didn't! So I told him he was being unkind and—"

"Ella Grace," Steph said.

"He was being unkind and unlistening, and the teachers say we must—"

"Braylon and Ella both wanted to sit by Jenna," Miss Marilyn said. "I need to go help the other friends, Ella. Please tell your mother how you responded."

Ella faced the wall.

These situations always flummoxed Steph, the child half in the teacher's care and half in hers. Ostensibly she was in charge, but clearly the caregiver had an opinion about what ought to be done.

"Sweetie," Steph said, "did you put your hands on Braylon's body?"

Ella would not answer.

Miss Marilyn's voice turned frosty. "It was a bit more than that."

She had bitten the boy. Steph had feared this from the start, and now, as Ella whimpered a forced confession, the news walloped her. This was Ella's third bite. After the last, Miss Marilyn had made it clear that their spot at Blue Hills KinderCare was in jeopardy. Biting occasionally happened in the two-to-three-year-old room, but pre-K was not staffed to deal with it.

"I am so, so sorry," Steph said. "Dad and I have spoken with her—and I did try role-playing as you suggested—but clearly we have not gotten through. We will do better. I promise."

Thankfully Miss Marilyn rushed back to class before the subject of repercussions arose. Down the hall to fetch Morgan, through the parking lot to her car, Steph burned with shame.

"Jenna hates Braylon," Ella said. "It was *my* spot, she saved it for *me*."

"You had a misunderstanding. I'm sure that made you feel frustrated." Steph slid Morgan's car seat into its base—*snick*—then buckled Ella, careful not to pinch thighs. "But it's never okay to bite."

At home, Morgan batted at fuzzy animals hanging above her play mat while Steph and Ella played a memory-match game. Flipping over pricey, veneered-wood cards, Steph felt no anger toward her daughter. What she felt, oppressively, was disappointment in herself.

Ella was four, nothing more or less than an amalgamation of every experience she and Doug had poured into her. They had made a bratty, biting, non-reading four-year-old. The proof was in the pudding. They had told themselves kids were adaptable, early socialization vital, the quality of care and student/teacher ratios at Blue Hills spectacular. But these were rationalizations.

They spent too few hours with Ella. Day care is day care: kids zoom around with loose guidance, whether the blocks are renewably sourced from Vermont forests or not. When you aren't present to teach your kids how to behave, you get whatever you get.

The time together now did improve Steph's mood. She let Ella pull off her ankle-high nylon and stretch her fingers through to tickle Morgan. Steph tossed her blazer over the couch and sprawled out with them. Giggles washed away her exhaustion. She yanked off her other nylon and tickled them both until they all cried.

At five thirty, she drove them to her mother's place. Returning, she found three cars parked on the street: a Ford F-150, an Acadia with Purdue license plate frames, and a black Jeep Wrangler belonging to Trev Larson—a direct report of Doug's whom Steph disliked.

She parked and slipped into the study unnoticed. As the first Erin Burnett joke penetrated the walls—"She can go *Out Front* on me *any*time..."—she gagged her tongue and opened a web browser.

One saving grace to poker night was that it gave her time to devote to Fiske. She figured her best starting point for tracking him down was the internet, in particular Northside Ill. She first checked social media, and sure enough, Ill was on Facebook. This suggested to Steph they were wannabes—what real gang did Facebook?—but when she found Bix, the leader Mancini had mentioned, any trace of relief vanished.

Ronald Bixley, a senior, looked older than school-aged, thick stubble, a bloated scar running jaggedly down one cheek. His background was the cannabis leaf. In his profile pic, he stood flexing, a faceless girl astride his shoulders and gun in either hand.

Oy, Mr. Fiske. Steph groaned. *Of all the characters to pick a fight with.*

Fortunately, Northside Ill was not big on security settings, and she was able to read several threads without joining the Facebook group. They referred often to meeting up at a place called *Rocks* or *Rockos.* Google Maps found a Chicago-area bar named Rocko's 58th Street Bar. As she zoomed in, her mouse hand shivered.

Englewood. One of the most dangerous neighborhoods in Chicago.

Why would an Evanston-based gang be hanging out on the South Side? She scanned more chatter, half hoping to find something ruling out that location. But when one member of Ill referred to "heading down to the Wood," she concluded that she had hit the mark.

What if Fiske was being held there? She could notify the police, but would they pursue it? According to Becky, Fiske had not been missing long enough to justify devoting manpower to a search.

She could go investigate herself.

Steph had just begun to consider logistics—go solo, drag Doug out of poker?—when noise from the kitchen became suddenly louder. She leaned back from her computer to look through the French doors.

Her husband sat at the head of the table behind a fan of cards. To his left, Trev Larson—a muscle-bound gym rat who always yucked it up around Doug—was hee-hawing.

"I still cannot believe you swung it," Doug said. "I thought your wife said hell would freeze over before she let you get a puppy."

Trev said, "I sat 'er down, had a talk. Made clear my needs."

"You mean you bought her jewelry!" one of the others crowed.

"Nope, didn't spend a dime," Trev said. "On the wife anyway —the pup cost thirteen hundred. Awesome pup. Ten weeks, already knows sit 'n' shake."

"Potty-trained?"

"Eh, work in progress. But I got a system. The wife doesn't understand it, so I hafta take him with me everywhere I go."

"Got her now?"

"Yep. Crated out in the Jeep."

Steph watched Doug push coins into the pot with a brusque shove.

"That's it," he said. "I'm getting one. I refuse to accept a world where you own a dog and I don't."

Someone pointed out that Trev's kids were five and seven, and his wife stayed home. Doug brushed aside these points, which echoed Steph's own thoughts on the matter. They could manage. *Lousy puppy, not a nuclear bomb.*

He was only showboating for friends, she knew. They looked up to him, just like everyone at Evanston Township had. They wanted him to be their Big Swinging Stud, for whom no ambition was too great nor boast too large. So what if he obliged once a month?

A ringtone sounded. Steph's, but strangely muffled. She remembered now that Doug's phone was on the fritz. He must have hers on him. Clicking out of Facebook, she stood. By the time she'd reached the card table, Doug had the phone out and was squinting at the incoming-caller info.

"Up, this one's important!" he announced. "Guy has a huge crush on my wife."

Steph suppressed a scowl, refusing to give him the satisfaction, and snatched back her phone. The screen read, *ERIC PINKERSBY*. She swiped *Ignore*. No way was she attempting a conversation in this testosterone-charged environment. The table was sloppy with change pools—the largest before Doug—and bowls of stale chips, and Trev Larson's dip cup, and clusters of empty beers.

Doug said, "Call him back, say you've got a hankering for pizza and a case of Heineken. And a poker face for Larson."

As the guys roared and Trev blustered up out of his chair, Steph felt a hand on her thigh under the table.

"I think somebody's had all the Heineken he needs." She discreetly swatted Doug off. "How goes the game?"

Craig Jorgenson had his wallet out, unfolding a twenty. "Your husband's taking all our money. I dunno if I can pay my mortgage this month."

"How's that different from any other month?" Trev Larson said.

"Oh yeah, Larson—you're cleaning up. How can you talk? You folded on four queens."

"There were two lousy wild cards, I thought—"

"See, there's your problem," Doug said. "You thought. Next time just keep pushing money into the pot till we stop you."

Trev's face glowed. He scratched his biceps, contorting the fierce calligraphy of a *Semper Fi* tattoo. "Like to see all you jack-offs play poker after driving ten hours straight. I still got seams in my ass."

Craig asked where he had gone.

"Another hunting trip?" Doug said.

Trev spaced momentarily, as though he'd lost the train of the conversation. Five empties sat before him. Steph often wondered whether they could be liable if somebody wrapped his car around a pole on the way home.

"Uh...yeah," he finally answered. "Whitetails. Season's almost over."

Steph felt another touch. Doug's palm higher up her thigh. He could be a horny drunk, she knew, but this was a little much.

Risk was a big part of Doug Reece's personality. It had been central to his high-school persona—the gunslinging QB unafraid to jeopardize his Golden Boy rep by ordering a dozen pizzas from a sub's phone—and was central now to his job as hedge fund executive. Steph could always tell when Doug's firm was engaged in some speculative, high-stakes deal. His eyes shone clearer. He moved differently through the house. It was more than an aptitude; it was a need. With all Doug's gifts, it seemed life was too easy without risk, that he needed some cliff or dagger-at-the-throat to beat back boredom.

Doug had led the football Wildkits for three years. The squad finished each regular season near the top of the Illinois Class 4A rankings but was eliminated both sophomore and junior year in sub-states by Wheaton North. Wheaton didn't field a great team, but they had Cade Ruckert: a beastly defensive tackle who would go on to an NFL career. No Wildkit could block him. Doug spent the majority of those two season-ending losses flat on his back, picking turf out of his face mask.

As seniors, Doug and his teammates made it their mission to deliver Fiske his second state championship. The first had come fifteen years earlier, and there were rumors he could retire anytime. The Wildkits ran undefeated through their schedule, but Cade Ruckert loomed on the horizon. Fiske was trying to whip a hulking freshman lineman into form, hoping his size might impede Ruckert in a sub-state matchup.

Nobody believed it would. In a year's time, Ruckert would be starting for Ohio State.

Doug got wind of a massive party in Schaumburg, which jocks from several schools were expected to attend. He took a half dozen guys from the team on what he called "a little scout trip." Cade Ruckert was there. Doug approached him jovially—*Be a different story this year, bro*—and they began drinking together. Ruckert, whose off-field issues ranged from grades to booster payments to domestic violence, soon invited Doug to partake of heavier stuff. Doug played along, managing to spill or spit most of it.

As the party wound into the early morning, his Wildkit teammates peeled off one by one. Doug refused their offers of rides home. *I got this.* Cade Ruckert got beyond wasted. Doug had so convincingly befriended him and his teammates ("What's it like playing for that old geezer?" / "Dude, I call all the plays, we just ignore him.") that when he offered to drive the five-star recruit home in Ruckert's truck, nobody batted an eye.

The story—as it became known in ETHS lore—ends with Doug running a red light in plain view of a cop, plugging the gas, then after gaining a few blocks' distance, sprinting away and diving behind a row of bushes. The police found Ruckert passed out in the driver's seat; he missed his last month on possession charges; and the Wildkits delivered Fiske state title number two.

The truth, which Doug later confided to Steph, was a bit different. Cade Ruckert didn't pass out. "Guy was an absolute tank." After driving around forty minutes pretending to misunderstand Ruckert's directions through Wheaton, Doug pointed out the window at a dim street sign. When Ruckert turned, Doug decked him. "Took five hard punches to knock him out—and this guy, I mean, he could barely string two words together."

Steph was taken aback by the admission. "You...have you punched many people? In your life?"

"Nope, just the one." Doug grinned. "There was no other way."

Now Steph extricated herself from her husband's happy fingers. The smells were getting to her—she especially hated Trev Larson's chewing tobacco.

"Much as I would love to hear more about seamed asses and whitetail deer," she said, "I have work in the other room. Would you all mind keeping the snorts and grunts to a dull roar?"

The guys made skulking moves for beers. Steph headed for the study.

Doug called, "Babe?"

She turned. His mouth quivered in a faint, apologizing-in-advance smile.

"See if Eric can get that pizza half veggie? Larson's watching his figure. Tell him we'll tip double if he gets here in the next half hour."

Steph snickered. "Last I read, Paladin's IPO was projected to net Eric Pinkersby about $200 million." With her index fingernail, she nudged a stack of quarters. "Pretty sure he doesn't need your guys' sticky change."

With that she left, hoots following her through the French doors.

Eric didn't even answer, *Hello*, launching directly into his tale.

"So I teach the class, completely winging it—do I remember *A Separate Peace*, did I ever even read it? very possibly not—and there's this girl who seems like the class pet, sharpest tool in the shed plus ridiculously attractive, which is irrelevant but just informationally..."

Steph held the phone away from her ear. "Okay, Eric? Slow down."

He did not. "So I'm thinking alright, here's somebody with

insight into Fiske's world. Maybe I'll ask how he's been acting lately. So I follow her to her locker after the bell and ask—just, you know, way casual—if she wants to grab coffee after school."

"You asked her out to coffee?"

"Not *out* out. Just coffee. At the school. They took part of the library and turned it into this pseudo-cafe area, kinda chichi? I didn't think we should talk at her locker out in the open. So anyway, she does show up for coffee." He sidebars, "I killed seventh hour in the computer lab teaching myself Ruby on Rails. Talk about snail-code, yeesh."

He honked a laugh. "Anyway, this girl Autumn seems skittish, right from the start. Glancing around, two hands on the mug. I ask if she made Winner and she says yes but won't hardly say it aloud."

Steph walked to her computer, thinking to check online arrest records for members of Northside Ill. "Perhaps skittish about being asked to coffee by her sub?"

"No no, like I said, it was completely casual. Though I suppose it's within the realm of possibility. But regardless, we start talking, and I tell her that Fiske has gone missing."

"Eric!" Steph exclaimed. "Becky told us not to say anything— she and the other counselors have been telling students Fiske is on vacation."

Eric gave assurances he had explained this and made Autumn promise to keep it on the down low. Steph listened, skeptical. Having been on the receiving end of similar disclosures, she knew that when Eric Pinkersby started gushing—particularly to a female—all discretion flew out the window.

"...her *initial* reaction, after hearing nobody had contacted Fiske since Wednesday, was puzzlement. 'But I just got a text this afternoon,' she said. Which is obviously a huge data point if true. So I ask what he texted, can I see, and she starts to tuuuuurn her phone around"—Eric warbled his voice for drama—"then stops. Makes some excuse and leaves."

Steph said, "She texts with Fiske? Regularly?"

"Didn't get to ask. But see, her response to my news, I feel like, was confusion—not shock. That's significant. She knows something."

Steph closed her laptop, giving up multitasking to concentrate on Eric. She did not trust his fine parsing of this Autumn's reaction. A sixteen-year-old girl, sitting with a twenty-eight-year-old man, hears distressing news about her teacher. How is she supposed to act? Maybe she regretted having admitted to texting a teacher. Maybe she was leery of Eric. In high school, his intense/obsessive style had been tempered by geekiness. Now he was a grown man, a soon-to-be millionaire with gray-streaked hair. Maybe she wondered why he had singled her out.

So did Steph. "Just how attractive was this girl?"

Eric spluttered that, eh, he didn't know, in the moderate to extraordinarily fetching range.

"If she really did get a text today," Steph mused, "after he supposedly dropped off the grid, then we need to talk to her. What was the last name?"

"Gimme a sec, I wrote it down. Actually scribbled it with my stylus, then copied to clipboard, then dragged into Notepad—this Droid UI needs serious refactoring." *Bleeps* and *bloops* over the line. "Here we go. B-R-O-C-K-E-R-T. Autumn Brockert."

Steph, pacing now before a wall of bookshelves, stopped at Doug's collection of vintage *Sports Illustrated*s. "Brockert...as in, Lydia Brockert? Nora Brockert?"

"It never occurred to me but yeah," Eric said. "She did have Nora's, uh, look."

Hm. Steph vaguely remembered, from the aftermath of Nora's drowning senior year, that there had been a second younger sister. *Now she was a student of Fiske's? A Winner?* Perhaps this explained Lydia's inclusion on the search committee.

"Why didn't Lydia tell us her little sister actually takes senior English with Fiske?"

"Because she barely spoke? Because chronic shyness renders her incapable of volunteering information without direct inquiry?"

Steph supposed so. That did not excuse Becky, though. Speaking with Autumn—a current student they had a connection to—should have been action item number one. Again, Steph puzzled over the formation of the Winners group. Why had Becky taken it upon herself to organize in the first place? Was it truly honest concern? What was that she'd said at the meeting—Fiske "had indeed challenged her at times"? Could she have another motive?

"We need to find out when exactly this text was sent, and what it was about."

"I could message her," Eric offered. "I already found her on Facebook."

Steph said she was sure he had but preferred they go through Lydia. That would be respectful to Lydia, and also the girl might be more forthcoming with her own family. Eric agreed, deflated.

She hung up and dialed Lydia, whose contact info she had gotten this afternoon. They agreed to meet at Lydia's—and Autumn's—parents' house on Ridge Ave. A peek through the French doors revealed that poker was still in high gear, Trev Larson slamming his cards to the table as Doug and another player divvied up a large pot.

Texting Eric the address, Steph snatched her coat and car keys.

"Back in a sec," she said, ducking through the game without further explanation.

The Brockerts lived in a sprawling five-bedroom home with yellow shutters and wraparound porch, the type that practically requires a pitcher of Kool-Aid and never-ending games of Duck, Duck, Goose. The house sat farther back from the street than its neighbors, benefiting from the shade of large oak and willow trees. Steph pulled up the drive and wondered if they still had Bo-Bo, the golden retriever who used to romp in and out by the propped screen door. Probably not.

In high school, during Nora's heyday, you would drive by on a weekend night and find cars parked all around the cul-de-sac. A dozen legs dangling from the porch swings, cooler of canned beer tucked behind the yews in case the police showed up.

That was before prom.

Steph and Lydia arrived within seconds of each other. Steph pulled up the circle drive, making space for Lydia's Prius, which edged past the hedge, then reversed a few feet, then cut its wheels and pulled forward, seeking the center point of the pavers.

"Thanks for meeting." Steph gestured around the circle. "Does your sister drive?"

Lydia squinted.

"I figured she might park outside," Steph said. "I don't see another car."

"Oh. Yes, she does. Drive."

The front door opened and out burst a woman. Jane Brockert, the family matriarch and a public relations executive Dunham & Prior occasionally dealt with, rushed toward them in four-inch heels and a persimmon suit, stabbing a cell phone.

"Honey why're you here?" she asked in a single breath.

Lydia placed her keys in the main compartment of her purse. "For Autumn." Her eyes hitched to Steph. "She wanted to talk to Autumn."

Jane's eyes bugged impatiently. She wore her hair in a tight chignon bun. "What about?"

Steph answered, "We think Autumn may have been in touch with a teacher, a teacher who's missing. We're trying to track her down."

Jane Brockert scowled at her phone. "Damn. So am I."

CHAPTER FIVE

The foyer, a generous space overlooked by second- and third-floor landings, featured pictures of all three Brockert sisters. Posed with chins over knuckles on a Caribbean beach. Hanging off various levels of a playground structure, Nora upside down with hair vertical; Lydia lower, gripping with white knuckles. Breathtaking oil portraits that made Steph need them for Ella and Morgan. She now understood Eric's "extraordinarily fetching" comment. Autumn was tall without being gangly, had Nora's headstrong eyes and a lovely bone structure that seemed to make its own light.

"Who's this missing teacher?" Jane asked. "When did they talk to Autumn?"

Steph gave Lydia the chance to answer her own mother, but she passed.

"Mr. Fiske," Steph said. "Senior English."

"Yeah, Bob Fiske—sure. *He's* missing?"

Steph, who remembered being taken aback by Jane Brockert's cutting questions when she had encountered her in adolescence, explained about Becky's FedEx and gathering of former Winners. She summarized Mancini's accounts and sketched only vaguely Eric's coffee with Autumn. He was en route, coming from out by O'Hare, and could say more when he arrived.

Jane listened, eyes sharp. "I haven't talked to her. She didn't eat here." She called into the living room, *"Did Autumn eat here?"*

A man, presumably her husband, called back, "No!"

Back on Steph. "Sometimes she grabs Saladworks on the way to yearbook or lacrosse. Or NOPE, or honors society—hard to keep straight."

"NOPE?"

"Antidrug program," Jane said. "It was DARE in my day. Guess they rebranded."

They headed upstairs to Autumn's room. As they climbed the stairs, Jane enumerated her daughter's extracurriculars, dropping her GPA and class rank, pointing out that she was not only smart but well liked, elected to numerous leadership positions by classmates.

"We call Autumn our Goldilocks kid. Nora was too wild. Lydia here's maybe too intense. Autumn came out just right."

Steph did not care for the parable right in front of Lydia. "I suppose every kid has their own journey."

The girl's room was bright and neat by teenage standards, textbooks stacked, dirty clothes hampered. It seemed governed by an ordered intelligence that recalled the middle sister. Indeed, Steph noticed that Lydia relaxed visibly when they entered.

"She hung them," Lydia said, smiling at a flock of sequined silk butterflies suspended from the ceiling. "The moment I saw that vendor's booth, I thought of her."

Autumn's desk was clear except for a laptop power brick. Steph asked whether she usually took her computer with her places.

"Depends," Jane said. "She'll take it to study at Barnes & Noble."

The doorbell rang. Jane listened for a beat or two, then—not hearing her husband's footsteps—groaned curtly and led them downstairs.

It was Eric.

Steph nodded past him. "You're driving that?"

He twisted toward a forest-green Hummer, snarling in the drive. "Courtesy Hertz, yes. Evidently my autofill checked the

'Will you be traveling through Mogadishu?' box in their booking webflow."

After being filled in, Eric offered to zip downtown and check Barnes & Noble for Autumn.

Jane shook her head. "She'd be with Cassie if she's there. I can call."

While Jane dialed Autumn's friend, the three Winners waited in the foyer. Steph gazed into the dark eyes of the youngest Brockert's oil portrait. Could Autumn have gone looking for Fiske? Steph had found the Northside Ill hangout in ten minutes on the internet; a current student, amid the hubbub about Fiske and the Solar System ban, would know about Rocko's 58th Street Bar. What if she had driven to Inglewood? Confronted Bix and his thugs?

"...apparently Fiske disappeared, did you know?" Jane was saying.

Steph took a step her way, thinking to make a dissuading gesture, but realized it'd be useless. Jane Brockert was not the type to pussyfoot around anything if she was concerned about her daughter.

"He wanted *what*?"

Jane's face suddenly flared. Her neck seemed to stretch and harden over the next minute as she uttered short, fiercely quiet responses. *Yes... Sure... God no...* Her eyes roamed with varying degrees of terror—accusation?—to Steph, to Eric, to Lydia.

What was Cassie saying? Again Steph's mind raced to Northside Ill. Jane had mentioned Autumn's involvement with that antidrug program. NOPE. Maybe Fiske had been the faculty sponsor. What if they had planned some rogue mission together? That could explain the text she had inadvertently revealed to Eric.

Jane ended the call breathing raggedly. She looked to the ceiling, gathering herself, then back to her phone. "I'm getting the cops."

Detective Frank Wright sat behind a metal desk, sports coat rumpled. His half donut of hair slanted left.

"So this teacher, the old guy," he says. "He goes missing first?"

The four of them were bunched on the opposite side of the desk, Steph and Jane—the media professionals—aggressively in front, Eric and Lydia behind.

"Yes," the leaders said.

"Then how do I know this is an abduction situation?"

"Probably it isn't—" Steph started.

"Because he coerced her!" Jane's voice rang around the small office. "He texted her, *explicitly* arranging a rendezvous. Your duty is to issue the alert."

The detective looked groggy. He'd made a point of saying the dispatcher had gotten him in the middle of brushing his teeth.

"Ms. Brockert, I'll be honest. I don't see an Amber Alert here. Max age is sixteen."

"Autumn doesn't turn seventeen until March 12."

He twisted his mouth. "Benefit of the doubt. But State says I need 'danger of serious bodily harm or death.' This guy has no history of violence, no criminal—"

"Did you not listen to her friend? He invited her to meet at the shore. They'd met other times outside of school." Jane planted her palms on Wright's desk, arms ramrod stiff. "He was grooming her."

"But did he coerce her?"

"Of course! Who says coercion has to be physical? That bastard had complete and total power over my daughter."

Wright tipped back in his chair, scratched under his collar.

Steph had tried soothing Jane on the car ride over, saying Fiske would never do anything untoward, explaining what Eric had told Autumn over coffee and theorizing she'd simply gone looking for her missing teacher. Jane had whirled on Eric then, seemingly angry about any grown man engaging her daughter, and he had quickly soft-pedaled. *We talked three minutes tops, seriously, I bet she couldn't even tell you my name.*

"Back up." Wright breathed through his nostrils. "When's the last time anyone saw her?"

Jane answered that Autumn might have stopped by the house in late afternoon, but she couldn't say definitively. Steph thought

Eric should volunteer their ETHS meeting—even bulged her eyes at him—but he kept quiet.

"So she hasn't been outta touch long."

"But that's precisely the point of the Amber Alert," Jane countered. "In a time-critical situation, when you know the abductor's identity, you can stop them."

"It's a lot of speculation."

"No! No, it really isn't. All you have to do is listen to her friends."

Jane had frenziedly called around, pressing Autumn's friends for information. Cassie and others had reported Fiske meeting Autumn off campus throughout the fall and winter. At coffee shops. At least one other time at the shore for what Autumn called "a working picnic." Steph pushed back, saying they could have been meeting about NOPE. Jane had snapped, *"Come on,* nobody works on a school group outside the school."

Now Steph felt she had to speak. "There must be another explanation. An extra-credit assignment, something. It's simply not possible Mr. Fiske would become involved with a student."

"Not possible?" Wright said. "Why? Was he a, uh, confirmed bachelor?"

"No." Steph recoiled at the suggestion. "I mean, I have no idea —but I know he made a point of avoiding even the appearance of impropriety with female students."

She ticked off examples by heart: Wendy Richter whose Valentine's brownies Fiske had refused; the rumored ambush-propositioning by Li Jhan in the teachers' lounge; his insistence that Deandra Pooxler fasten another button of her blouse "to ensure the concentration of more distractible classmates," even though everyone knew the only person Deandra, a Winner and heart-stoppingly cute gymnast, hoped to distract was Fiske himself.

Wright asked what that meant, *Winner.* Steph explained about the elite club and its ambiguous selection criteria. Jane jumped in that Autumn was a Winner, supplying details about her GPA and various honors.

Wright nodded to Steph. "Something tells me you were one too."

Steph confirmed this. She considered mentioning Becky

Brindle and the Winners search group but didn't want to take them off track.

"Here's a question." The detective looked between Steph and a glossy photo of Autumn. "Do all these Winners have a similar appearance?"

"Not at all." Steph motioned to Eric without thinking. "He was a Winner." Eric shrugged haplessly; she quickly added that her husband had been one too.

Wright continued to gaze skeptically at Autumn's photo. Steph felt a flash of anger. She was used to people diminishing her accomplishments like this, assuming she had gotten special treatment. Usually the murmurs were subtle and easily ignored, but once in a while she would catch a stronger whiff, such as the time at Stanford when a guy walking behind her told his friend "that butt and those legs" were why he had lost out on a professor's summer research position.

Rather than respond, Steph changed the subject. "Fiske had recently been involved in a conflict with a gang. Northside Ill?"

She explained the fight over the Solar System, naming Bix and Rocko's 58th Street Bar.

Wright said, "Did a little investigating, huh?"

His condescension was clear, but again Steph didn't rise to it. "I think Autumn went looking for Fiske. Maybe she had information on Northside Ill."

"The gang. That pushes drugs."

"As I understand it, yes."

The detective squinted. "Drug outfits don't generally go 'round kidnapping high-school teachers. It's not high on their list of rackets."

"Bob Fiske was no ordinary high-school teacher."

Wright puffed his cheeks and glanced about as if to say, *No kidding.*

Jane Brockert's four-inch heels tapped impatiently. She had heard Steph's speculation already and didn't care. She wanted the cavalry, and she wanted it now. Steph supposed if it were Ella or Morgan missing, she would be doing the same, steamrolling past whatever factual issues existed in order to marshal maximum resources.

"Okay. Here's what I can do," Wright said. "I need to wake up my supervisor, see what makes sense."

Jane shot forward over his desk. "This has to happen *now* or else—"

"Understood, Mrs. Brockert." He made a slow, flattening gesture for calm. "Trust me, we do not take the disappearance of sixteen-year-old kids lightly."

Trev Larson's Jeep was still parked outside. Steph groaned, pulling around the mud-flecked vehicle, eager to be alone with Doug, to fill him in.

"Hey, babe." Her husband looked over. Poker was done; it was just him and Trev watching the end of a Bulls game. "You were gone awhile. Good times?"

"Not especially." She glanced to Trev.

Doug understood at once. Switching off the TV, he said in Trev's direction, "That clock right, eleven forty-five already? Frankfurt exchange'll be open in two hours."

The hint washed right over Trev, who popped a fresh Bud Light and launched into a vein-bulging recap of poker hands that had "reamed him up the pooper."

"Yeah, rotten luck," Doug said insincerely. "What're you gonna do?"

Trev—a strange combination of belligerent and needy—launched into various drunken non sequiturs, in one breath threatening to waterboard a neighbor whose trees overhung his yard, in the next whining over why some secretary wouldn't text back, *what, he wasn't rich enough? you eat a chick out half a friggin' hour and she can't write a lousy LOL?*

Finally, Doug shoved a leather jacket at his chest.

"Trev: go. Get outta my house. Get sleep so you don't cost me money in the morning."

So Trev left.

As the storm door wheezed shut, Steph—who had conspicuously hung back to avoid any farewell cheek kiss—said, "I really do not like Trev Larson."

Doug walked to the card table, began loading empties between his knuckles.

"Doesn't it bother you how he discusses his infidelity?" she continued. "His wife's been over for dinner."

Doug kept gathering bottles.

"Or how comfortable he is tossing around gay slurs? What if our girls were around?"

"Luckily they weren't."

When Steph scoffed, he stopped picking up and faced her. "Look. If I was choosing friends out of a store display, I wouldn't pick Trev Larson. Alright? But life isn't like that. Guy works for me. He plays poker. I play poker. We don't need to have all the same opinions about global warming, or taste in shoes, whatever, to sit across a card table and enjoy ourselves."

He headed for the kitchen to rinse the bottles. He was wearing his lucky loafers, the ones with holey bottoms he refused to pitch. In this moment, in the mood Steph was in, they struck her as the height of arrogance.

"*Taste in shoes?* So it's a gender issue, this bizarre preference of mine that people we welcome into our home not be complete jerks."

"Didn't say that."

"You implied it." Steph's fists lodged at her hips. "And the driving. There is no way that man was sober. He could kill somebody with that Jeep."

"He's twenty-six years old," Doug said. "Christ, he lives twelve blocks away. These people are grown men. They make their own choices."

"Most of them I can handle, but I just wish you wouldn't associate with Trev. Or if you did, that you did it somewhere else."

From another room, Tattletail mewed. Steph felt her upper lip trembling. Doug's eyes sagged, fatigue and alcohol and marital strife all ganging up.

"I dunno what to tell you, babe. I let you choose your friends. Have I said one word about your date tonight with Pinkersby?"

"Date?"

"Isn't that who you met up with? You ran outta here, barely said a word."

"You seemed occupied telling everyone how your wife couldn't handle a dog."

Perhaps the chronology wasn't 100 percent accurate, but Steph felt the dig was deserved. He looked off to the side with a huff that said, *Unbelievable.*

She continued, "Do you want to know where I was? On my date? The police station."

She related what Eric had told him over the phone about his coffee with Autumn Brockert—omitting her own doubts about Eric's motives—and how they had visited the Brockerts, then accompanied Jane to the police station.

"Eric and I went to vouch for Fiske, to explain that he would never, ever become romantically involved with a female student. We told the detecti—"

"You went to vouch for Fiske," Doug cut in. "Pinkersby went for the free peeks."

Steph was stunned that, after what she had just told him—a missing girl, the possibility of an Amber Alert naming their former mentor as abductor—her husband would choose to focus on petty rivalry. Ninety-nine percent of the time she had no regrets about marrying a jock, but there was that 1 percent, generally when Doug drank, when his inner caveman staggered up from hibernation, when she found herself thinking of all the premeds and mechanical engineers who used to hit on her in college.

"Eric flew all the way out here from San Francisco for Fiske. Like me, he feels an obligation. Like me, he feels an enduring debt."

"What he feels is something puny rising in his boxers."

Steph bolted for the coatrack, shaking her head. Suddenly desperate to escape the stench of stale chips and wintergreen Skoal. "I'm taking a walk."

Doug caught her by a belt loop. "Babe, let's be honest for a sec. Let's tell the truth." He blinked his eyes clear. "Eric Pinkersby is a lackey. He was your lackey in high school, he's your lackey now."

"What is Trev Larson? He takes your shirts to the cleaners. He saves your seat at Buffalo Wild Wings like you're in eighth grade. He isn't your lackey?"

"That's different."

"Of course."

"Trev sucks up to me so I'll promote him. So he can make more money. Buy more stuff. Steroids. Bigger tires for his Jeep." Each phrase punctuated by a heavy, pedantic break. "He's not doing it to sleep with me."

Steph chuckled. "You sure about that?"

They hadn't had a knockdown fight like this in months, since that silliness over radio stations driving to Six Flags. As usual, she felt the substance mattered little and that background factors were the real story. She realized she was tossing grenades with pins half pulled, baiting him out of frustration. With Ella's bite. With the fact that she had come no closer to finding Fiske, and now, with the police involved, the odds of him surviving this ordeal with his job were shrinking.

For his part, Doug had seemed off in the months since Jesse Weams. Not distracted, exactly. Chastened, less sure of his own invincibility? That day, he had returned home ignorant of what had happened; building security would only say the elevators were closed "due to an incident." When Steph had told him the kid died—that he'd been on a field trip with their former teacher —Doug had gulped, steadying himself by a table. Since then, he had adopted a kind of willfully tough stance: the stunt was cowardly, typical of today's coddled, fame-seeking kids. But Steph knew it had had an effect. Didn't it have to, another human being falling to his death outside your office window? And now comes this Fiske caper, dredging up those Live Big competitive juices. Things had simply boiled over.

Doug's forehead tensed as he seemed to consider replying to her quip, then think better. He returned to the kitchen. Moments later, Steph heard a cabinet bang and the furious squeaking of a dishrag.

The couple's anger dissipated over the next hour. Steph did not take her walk, tidying up instead. Her mind stuck on Fiske, what action Wright might take, whether it still made sense to go confront Northside Ill. As she thought, she ordered Ella's stuffed animals atop the toy chest, small to big, fingertips lingering in soft fur. Doug too was taking his time with dishes, the tap stopping often as he drank noisily from a water tumbler—staving off tomorrow's hangover, ever the optimizer.

Finally, their tasks converged at the kitchen island, he wiping down, she depositing a stray milk bottle of Morgan's.

"Ella bit Braylon today," Steph said.

Doug finished the island, moved onto the table. "Which one's Braylon?"

"Younger, wears that *X-Men* coat. Ella says he stole her seat at circle time."

Doug asked if they had been expelled, and Steph said no, not that anyone had told her.

He quirked his mouth. *Could be worse.*

"So what did the police say? This Wright guy—he assumes it's a dirty-old-man case?"

Steph felt encouraged by the question, the fact that Doug recalled the detective's name, had actually processed what she'd told him. "Looks like it. I just cannot imagine Fiske running off with a sixteen-year-old girl. Can you?"

Doug crossed one loafer over the other.

She said, "You can?"

"No, not really. Thing is, though...we don't know Fiske anymore. We knew him what, ten years ago? Maybe he changed. Or something happened."

The tension between them eased, Doug approached from behind and began massaging Steph. It felt amazing—her last deep-tissue session had been months ago—like a vise releasing every muscle in her shoulders. Steph closed her eyes and thought. About Eric's lack of truthfulness at the police station. About Fiske's absence in the spring. About their talk at the cafe—the Winners' origin story, his bizarre use of the word "atone."

She ached at how their lives had diverged. The last day of high school, when she had walked into Fiske's classroom as he was packing up—laying vellum lecture notes into his satchel—and hugged him goodbye, she had been sure he would play an important role in her life. Then came college. And work. And (earlier than anticipated) kids. She always expected to reconnect later, that some common cause or alumni event would reestablish the bond and thereafter they would linger over scones at the Unicorn on Saturdays, discussing novels, filling one another in on personal milestones...

It never happened. Now maybe it never would.

Doug's phone buzzed. A second later, Steph's did too. Not the rattle of an incoming text or the chime of a voice call. Deeper. Insistent. She recognized the tone as something her phone did once, maybe twice a year.

She looked, and inside her a vortex began.

Evanston, IL AMBER Alert: LIC/7KJC97 (MI) 2012 Blue Volkswagen Jetta, CHILD: 16 CAUC F 5'9" 105LB Blo/Blu, SUSP: 74 CAUC M 6'0" 185LB Gry/Blu

CHAPTER SIX

By 7:40 a.m., Bob Fiske was no longer an employee of Evanston Township District 202.

Local news expanded upon the alert with quotes from police and classmates detailing "an inappropriate pattern of communication" between the missing girl and teacher. One report had Fiske "wooing" Autumn at Starbucks. A fringe website placed him at a downstate sex shop, tugging a girl matching Autumn's description by the elbow. As the story accelerated through the morning, the Winners club became a key talking point. Autumn was captioned as belonging to "an ultra-elite cadre of favorites," beside the lacrosse photograph—which could not have been that recent, lax being a spring sport, and was probably chosen for its patrician overtones.

To Steph's trained eye, the fingerprints of Jane Brockert were all over the coverage. The photo, the thematic cohesion, the pace at which details hit the news crawl. Jane was synchronizing all the technical and sentimental forces that propel stories onto the national stage.

Around noon, Autumn's disappearance made the jump. The Facebook group "Please Help Find Autumn!!!" reached ten thousand follows; a prominent infotainment blog plastered the story on its front page; and by two p.m., Fox and MSNBC had taken the bait.

Steph had gotten sucked into a few missing-baby or miners-stuck-in-shaft sagas before. While the mechanics of today's web scouring were similar—the frequent refreshes, eyes swelling at every new search hit—her emotions were completely different. Instead of a giddy rush, each discovery produced chills. The next update wasn't some nugget to be chatted about at the copy machine. It might send her rushing off to search a field, or back to the police station. Or worse.

Given all this, Steph found it impossible to concentrate on work. Chad Nimms stopped halfway through a MetroBuild sample pitch.

"Would you, like, rather hear this a different time?" he asked.

Steph broke off staring over his head. "Sorry, this thing with my old teacher—it's surreal. Pitch looks fine, Chad. Run with it."

Chad hesitated. Usually Rich Hauser reviewed pitches before they went to the client, even minor addenda. But she bucked him up by complimenting the new haircut—"Caesar, love it!"—and he left with a hop in his step.

Steph called Becky Brindle to see if she wanted to convene the Winners again. Becky said she could make a late-afternoon meeting but didn't offer to organize. Steph detected an off note in her voice. Some artificial perk. Fear? Did she think Fiske was guilty, worry about associating too closely with him? Maybe she just had a student in her office or was pumping breast milk for the twins.

So Steph texted/called around herself. Eric immediately confirmed. *Did she need him to call Mancini again? Or ABC7? That piece about Fiske's failed barstool novel in Nevada sounded fishy....* Doug offered to skip his four o'clock. She wasn't sure how Lydia Brockert would be disposed to joining this group, whose original goal had been to help Fiske, whom her mother was bashing on any willing media outlet, but she, too, agreed to join.

Steph got to the Unicorn early, claimed a secluded table with a copy of *Revolutionart* wedged under one wrought-iron leg.

Doug arrived next.

"This is nuts." He nodded at flyers and a makeshift bouquet in the cafe vestibule.

"I know," she said, rising for a kiss. "It's like everybody's reading from a script."

Doug squared his shoulders to the entrance, sniffed. "Is Pinkersby coming?"

"He said he was. Why?"

Her husband leaned close, but his eyes stayed on the door. "I poked around the SEC website this morning—public filings, etcetera. Did you know Bob Fiske was a minority stakeholder in Paladin?"

"Really?"

Doug nodded. Last night after the alert, they had discussed Eric's meeting with Autumn—the fact that it was the last concrete sighting of the girl, his unwillingness to volunteer this to the police. Both had concluded Eric just didn't want the scrutiny with his IPO coming up. The market could be finicky, and naturally he wouldn't want his name surfacing in relation to a criminal case.

"I tell ya." Doug sucked breath through his teeth. "He hops a plane out here, up and goes based on that flimsy FedEx. Yesterday, he was the only one who'd been in touch with Fiske lately. Now he's the last one to see Autumn Brockert before *she* goes missing?"

"What're you thinking?"

"Dunno. But my inclination is that if something dicey is going on, some bizarre plot or conspiracy? Probably involves Pinkersby."

Ahead of the other arrivals, they took out their work phones. Doug kept losing bars—his phone had been on the fritz for months, couldn't hold the network—and asked to borrow Steph's. She finished an e-mail to Rich Hauser, then handed it over.

Lydia Brockert showed next. She ordered a coffee, then shuffled at the espresso counter deciding between waiting or sitting down with her party. A shaggy-bearded barista gestured that he'd bring it out.

Steph asked how she was doing.

Lydia brushed bangs behind her ears. "Passably."

"And your mother—are you, er, in contact about—"

"Mother doesn't know I'm here. She does what she thinks will help. So do I."

The note of defiance surprised Steph. She had thought to offer assurances, to tell Lydia it wasn't fair they should have to deal with this. Not after Nora at prom. This seemed unnecessary now.

Moments later, Eric and Becky walked in together (had they carpooled?) and Steph began.

"The goal here is to quickly reconvene and see what can be done. Obviously, with the Amber Alert, the police think Mr. Fiske abducted Autumn. If there isn't a group like ours out front pushing alternate theories, this is the only hypothesis that will be pursued."

She proposed they again divvy up the investigative avenues, as they had yesterday. Northside Ill, she believed, was their most promising lead. Doug volunteered to hit the Inglewood hangout tonight, and Eric quickly said, *yeah, yeah, count him in, so what if a civilian there was more likely to die than an American soldier in Iraq.*

Steph had just begun addressing the sex shop claim when she noticed Becky's face.

"Are you okay, Becks?" she said.

Becky looked queasy, sour at the corners of her mouth. "I—oh I'm fine, it's just...hard."

"Hard?"

"The whole situation." She glanced sideways at Lydia. "I feel awful."

Steph took her hand over the table. Becky gripped back hard, stifling a sob. She seemed to feel responsible, as though by sending the FedEx she had somehow created the whole ordeal.

It also seemed, Steph felt, that she was buying into the media's basic assumption that Fiske was guilty. That Fiske had done the terrible thing everyone imagined, and might well compound it with more terror.

Looking around the table, Steph saw Becky wasn't alone. Arms crossed. Eyes fell.

"Some unflattering details came out this morning," Steph said. "Honestly, I have no idea why Fiske was meeting Autumn off school grounds. But I do know that when we were students, there was never one whiff of impropriety."

"That's right," Doug said. "Never."

He had been more nuanced discussing the issue last night, but she appreciated his unequivocal support in a larger group.

Lydia began crying softly.

Doug said, "Hundred to one, your sister went looking for him. Freaked out after what Eric told her."

He shot a look at Eric, who opened his mouth to object but thought better.

Lydia sniveled, *"But why isn't she answering her phone?"*

Steph tried, "Maybe it's not charged. Or she lost it."

The rest of her action items, which had felt immensely logical as Steph had crafted them in her office, sounded hollow as she enumerated them now. Who would track down Fiske's cousins in Washington state? Follow up on that green-Camaro tip in Waukegan? Try to get insights into Fiske's recent medical history? (She wondered if that spring absence might have been health related.)

This last item would require tech expertise. She raised an eyebrow Eric's way.

"On it," he said. "So long as the hamster fueling Marriot's half-a-G Wi-Fi keeps chugging."

Eric had always joked neurotically to deal with stress, but this seemed in especially poor taste. *Wi-Fi jokes in front of a woman whose sister was missing?* Steph wondered what could be giving him such brain yips and thought of Doug's revelation that he and Fiske were equity partners in Paladin.

After the meeting broke, she tailed Eric to the sidewalk.

"Care for a research partner, Mr. Pinkersby?" she asked in an affectionately batty warble.

Eric grinned at the reference to their old debate sponsor, Miss Shipley, and they caravaned out to the O'Hare Marriott.

What did Steph hope to learn by shadowing Eric? She could not have said exactly. A peek around his hotel room. Backstory on Paladin—maybe she would bring up the topic and give him a chance to volunteer Doug's info. Eric's bond with Fiske appeared more significant than he had let on in the initial Winners meeting. Could it be they faced some shared financial jeopardy?

They beat rush-hour traffic to the hotel. Eric stumbled out of his ludicrous Hummer, and they rode the elevator up to his room on eight.

"Where do we figure his primary care physician would be?" Eric held his key card against the room-entry sensor. "NorthShore?"

He walked in and led Steph toward his desk, yanking over a second chair. Before he could get to the laptop and minimize its screen, Steph glimpsed Autumn Brockert's Facebook profile in a browser.

"Alrighy then." He rocked side to side, flexing his fingers. "*Hospitals Evanston IL*...top result *NorthShore.org*...patient portal, yes please..."

Eric penetrated hospital security with dazzling ease. One moment they were looking at a username/password prompt; the next, after a fourth try of generic sysop log-ins, they were viewing a flat list of patient hyperlinks. A third of the way down, they found "Bob Fiske." Twiddling his fingers in a *Voilà!* flourish, Eric clicked into Fiske's patient dashboard and navigated them through a series of appointment reports.

Steph deflated, looking over the medical records of what appeared to be a healthy seventy-four-year-old.

"Dead end," Eric said.

She knitted her brow. "I just feel like that spring absence is significant, somehow. I can't explain."

Eric avoided her gaze, fidgeting with the hinge of his glasses.

She asked, "What do you make of Lydia?"

"I dunno. I mean, obviously I feel rotten for her."

"Do you remember what she was like before Nora died? Before prom?"

"Vaguely. She was younger—I know she used to bus over from middle school, a few of my mathlete teammates knew her better. She definitely talked more then."

The whole school, but especially Mr. Fiske, had made a sheltered place for Lydia after her sister's death. Fiske tempered the bombast he typically used to motivate Winners. (Lydia was a shoo-in for the list; besides perfect academics, she had won national prizes for essays and a biology experiment.) The two became inseparable. When Fiske learned that Lydia's research adviser at MIT was burying her under one flagging, thankless project after another, he drove fifteen straight hours to Cambridge and—it was said—cornered the man in the faculty bathroom. Shortly thereafter, she began publishing her own work in journals.

"Do you think Fiske actually threatened her professor?" Steph said.

"That was the rumor. People exaggerate, though."

Steph's eyes washed over Fiske's apparently clean medical records. "Wonder if *she* knows something about that spring absence."

Eric gulped.

Not seeing his reaction, Steph continued, "Except she didn't say anything when I mentioned it. You know what's weird? Her faculty webpage describes her as 'a star on the academic lecture circuit,' but around us..."

Eric's mouth opened and his cheeks hollowed as if he were becoming sick.

Now Steph noticed. "Eric! Are you okay?"

He shut his eyes, composing himself. "I know where Fiske went in the spring."

"Where?"

"San Francisco."

Eric gushed excuses for why he hadn't said anything earlier. *He couldn't imagine how it might be relevant...he'd been embarrassed...Fiske had wanted the trip kept private...*

"I called and told him how cutthroat it was, the whole start-up culture, hustling cash," Eric recounted. "I thought Paladin was done—I seriously expected repo trucks any day, guys in jumpsuits to storm the lobby and start shoveling keyboards into trash bags. So he came. Hopped a red-eye, showed up at my door."

"Like he did for Lydia."

Eric drummed his temple. "Except she was in college and I was a grown-up. Am a grown-up. Whatever."

He and Fiske had strolled Ocean Beach, talking through his anxieties over the crash of white-foam breakers. Eric believed his struggles keeping Paladin afloat meant he belonged in a cubicle, writing subroutines instead of staring down venture-capital sharks. "Nonsense," Fiske had said. It simply meant the sharks he was dealing with were thick and short-sighted.

Fiske's second day in San Francisco, they met with Wess Moran, an ETHS class of '92 Winner. Wess ran Broadframe Capital, a company that had already heard and rejected Eric's pitch for Phase II funding. Wess did not reverse his subordinates' decision immediately, but when Fiske pledged $150K of his own money to defray Broadframe's exposure, the deal was cinched.

"I can't let you do this," Eric had said on the way out, ashamed for not objecting during the meeting. "That's a ton of cash!"

"An investment." Fiske had stared into Eric's face until it settled. "I will bet on you every day of the week, and twice on Sundays."

Telling the story, Eric had moved to the hotel bed. He sat slumped on a creamy duvet, hands between his sleight knees.

Steph sat beside him. "So? Now he's going to make a killing. He was right to believe in you."

"I guess," Eric said, "but it's still a little disconcerting, needing a bailout or pep talk every fifteen months. Sometimes I feel like he props me up, you know? I'd still be chugging on the hamster wheel at Facebook if it weren't for Fiske. Whose success is it?"

She thought about her own meeting with Fiske over Metro-Build. In a way, it had been the same: prodding a Winner to aim higher. The difference was that Eric had taken his shot.

She also thought about that $150K. Where had it come from? Ten years ago, her mother had wondered the same about the Stanford money. *How can a public-school teacher afford something like that?*

"Yours," she said. "It's your success, Eric. Nobody else's."

But this did not lift Eric's gloom. His eyes glazed outside, past the Marriott sign, at ascending and descending jet trails. He had more on his mind; Steph was sure of it. *What?* Was he considering revealing some deeper association with Fiske? Information about his disappearance, or even Autumn Brockert's? Could Fiske have drawn him into some elaborate plot that he was now getting cold feet about?

Steph was deep in speculation when she became aware of Eric's lips on hers.

"Stop!" She jerked back, causing him to fall forward. *"What are you doing?"*

Eric lurched around hunting for glasses. "Sorry—sorry I dunno what I was thinking."

"Aren't you in a relationship?"

"No. I—we broke up. I broke up. Actually yesterday right before I flew."

Steph felt her eyes becoming slits.

"It was on the way to the airport—er, that I did it," he said. "I sorta stopped off? At her apartment? I wanted to come out here with a pure heart."

"I thought you'd been going out with that woman for a while. Ramona, right?"

"Yeah. Well yeah, a few years. But we were too alike. See originally we coded in the same functional group, which was great for a while, but how many times can you refreshingly rag on the syntax highlighting in eMacs? It became a bit of an echo chamber."

This was classic Eric, overanalyzing, unable to take happiness at face value. What was *not* Eric was him trying to kiss her.

In high school, he had been known for harboring supersized crushes, the super-est being upon Steph herself. Steph could not have said how or when she'd become aware of it. They had debated together starting sophomore year, and certainly it had lurked then—chivalrous offers to transcribe note cards, stiff-kneed rides in the back of Miss Shipley's van. Senior year, it became a kind of open secret. To pass time, Eric composed humorous lists modeled on old Letterman YouTube clips, and one was rumored to be titled: *Top Ten Modern Conveniences and/or Appendages Less Dear to Me than Steph Mills.*

When she began dating Doug, the crush went from quixotically cute (Steph's friends cooed at his pain, wanted to "cure him") to a Frodo-battles-Mordor-for-the-ring triangle, with Fiske occupying a bizarre middle space. Apparently, he had advised

Eric to "leave no wish behind in your locker," which Eric took for a reference to Steph. Meanwhile he knew of her and Doug's relationship, had even dubbed them "The Class Royals." Seemingly he had stoked the conflict from all sides, Doug's championing coach, Eric's *Live Big* mentor, Steph's sounding board and de facto counselor. Steph had never quite understood why.

Was it possible he had gotten involved again? Counseled Eric to try...what, breaking up their marriage?

Surely not.

"Tell me, when did this echo chamber start echoing?" Steph said. "You said you wanted to come with a pure heart—so which was it?"

Eric touched his glasses, which remained crooked. "The echo has been, I'd say, more or less consistent. Perhaps the trip here intensified it."

"I am married, Eric. *Married.* Has success gone to your head that much?"

"No no, totally not. I just figured, well, after what Becks told me about you and Doug..."

Steph froze. "Me and Doug what?"

Eric raised one shoulder. "I called her after I got that FedEx. She mentioned your marriage was on the rocks."

For an instant, Steph's pulse spiked as though the statement might be true for being spoken aloud. Then, reassuringly, she thought back on this morning and last night, and the past five years.

"That's ridiculous. She told you that? What exactly did she say?"

"That you guys were considering taking a break. So, I guess, separating?"

Steph looked up to the ceiling, whose textured surface seemed to roil in place. Why would Becky say that? Seconds ago, she had wondered if Fiske were sabotaging her marriage; now Becky? Had Becky just invented it out of thin air to entice Eric back to Chicago? His slapdash trip did make a little more sense now. Why was Eric Pinkersby's presence here so important?

"And based on that information," Steph said, "you *broke up with your girlfriend of three years*?"

He gave a half shrug. "When you say it like that—with that cocktail of incredulity and revulsion—I agree, it sounds bad."

As Steph continued to chide Eric, her mind worked at the ramifications of Becky's lie. Could Becky be having an affair with Doug? Or want to? Steph felt every marital insecurity bubbling up —parenting style, their occasionally mismatched sexual tastes— but none had even been arguments lately, much less crises. They had quarreled last night, sure, but that would have been after Becky and Eric had talked.

"So you didn't fly out here to help Fiske. You came to make a pass at me."

"Absolutely not." Eric squared up her eyes. "I'm here for Fiske. A hundred percent. Now, okay, would I have flown as opposed to maybe dialing in? I dunno. It's complicated. Why does anyone take any given action?"

CHAPTER SEVEN

Steph returned to the office in a funk. Chad Nimms had left a Samsung pitch on her chair; she flipped through and hated the whole thing. Headers, bullet points. Even the gray scale for drop shadows. Most of the decisions she had made previously herself. PowerPoint sometimes engendered a very specialized flavor of self-loathing in Steph, this skin-crawling angst about how many minutes (or hours, or days) she had quibbled over trivialities. The feeling raged now. What over-engineered happytalk. They had rolled out the same Dunham & Prior market leaders, blah-blah, a dozen times this month—why had they needed a new deck? Why had they spent parts of *five workdays* on it?

If there was such a thing as the opposite of Live Big, she decided, it must involve PowerPoint.

Chad ducked in. "Whaddaya say, boss? Good?"

She knew better than to make judgments in this mood. "Let's talk tomorrow a.m.. I need to sit with it."

As he left, Steph flopped the deck closed. Ran two hands back through her champagne-blonde hair.

Eric had revealed in parting that he was booked on a flight back to San Francisco tomorrow. He wanted to stay and help, but the IPO was in twelve days, his i-bankers were screaming at him on voice mail, his cat must be skin and bones by now...he had to go.

To Steph, it confirmed—despite Eric's insistence that actions were complicated—what her husband had claimed: he was only here for her. In this light, the Winners' lukewarm support at the cafe was even more discouraging. Becky, who had organized the group and saw Fiske daily, thought he was guilty. Lydia would go along with any plan offering a ghost of a chance to find her sister. Doug would do his dutiful best, but his heart wasn't in it.

Only one person truly believed in Fiske: Steph.

Am I delusional? Why did she, above the rest, hold so dearly to the ideal of Fiske? Considering this question, she heard a faint echo from the police station—when Detective Wright had asked if all the Winners "had a similar appearance." There had been an implicit criticism there. It had buzzed at the back of Steph's brain, and as she'd absorbed the media hysteria throughout the day, the buzz had grown to a throb.

Because if Fiske was phony, if this elite club was nothing more than another old white male wriggling his way into adolescent girls' pants, then wasn't Steph phony too? Weren't they all? This whole back-scratching society of achievement, entitlement, ego—if you stripped the emperor of his clothes, didn't it all go *poof*?

Her fellow Winners seemed not to feel this. Or if they did, to not especially care. Maybe Steph was stuck back in high school, like any other former big-fish-in-small-pond. Obsessed with memories of her own glory. Maybe it didn't matter to Eric and Doug because they had eclipsed their ETHS identities in adulthood, no longer needed the imprimatur of Fiske's gold star to feel good about themselves.

Steph walked to her office window. Leaning into the frame, she examined her reflection. She saw weakness. Watery eyes, a self-sorry droop in the cheeks.

Enough.

She turned from the window with nostrils flared. She banished every wispy thought from her head. Replaced them with new ones—hard, thirsty. What could be done to turn the tide? Detective Wright, the media, everybody she talked to, had the same bleak perspective. How to change this steamrolling narrative?

She closed her door and sat with her back flush against it, her body a stubborn L. She needed to find Fiske. It was that simple.

How?

Finally, as her shoes were beginning to feel like inanimate bumps in the carpet, a plan took shape. It was illegal, and dubious, and reckless as anything she'd done in life. But it was a plan.

"If Rich needs me, please tell him I'm available on IM," Steph told Chad Nimms on the way out, purse swinging off her shoulder.

Late-afternoon traffic was light. Steph drove with a sort of unhinged ease, winging her car around turns, accelerating through yellows. She whizzed up Clybourn to park in front of a spare, nouveau-industrial building.

Olympia Towers had been part of Evanston's mixed-used rejuvenation of the late 1990s. To Steph, it always felt perfect that Fiske had bought one of the inaugural units. She imagined him reading the Sunday paper on his balcony, unchaining his bike for errands in the type of progressive life his lectures seemed to imply.

Now she locked her car and fixed sunglasses to her head.

The building was fully occupied, which supplied Steph's first lucky break. Three men in suits converged on the entrance ahead of her, making it unnecessary to lie or fumble for a key card she didn't have. She simply followed inside. A doorman lazy-eyed them to the elevator bank. Steph ignored the hissing in her brain —*this is insane, stop!*—and boarded with the men.

"Floor?" one asked, finger poised over the buttons.

Steph considered the choices. She thought Fiske lived on the top floor. "Twelve, please."

The men got off at four, so they weren't there to witness her confusion getting off the elevator. She glanced from side to side, orienting herself. She remembered that Fiske had a lake view ("Nothing unclogs the creative mind like water-kissed air") but couldn't immediately tell east from west. She padded forward, far enough to see around an accent table.

At first, she saw nothing. Tan carpet. A line of indistinguishable doorframes up the hall. Then, telescoping her neck, she made out something slick and yellow sagged across one.

Police tape.

Steph knew the condo would have been searched by the Evanston police. Anything of obvious significance would be gone. There might be some overlooked nugget, though, some file or scribble or list—Fiske was a big believer in lists—that only an intimate would understand.

A clue.

She placed her foot against the door and it gave, having been ajar. She parted the yellow tape with her forearms, careful to avoid contact with bare skin.

The condo was mostly empty. A trestle desk had two orange tags where a computer might've been, and floor-to-ceiling bookshelves had been cleared. Fiske's wall hangings remained—diplomas, coaching honors, *Educator of the Year* plaques—but Steph judged by their skew that the drywall behind had been searched.

She moved inside, tension in the scoops of her knees. A bamboo rug spanned the living room. As Steph bent to peek underneath, she considered what she was undertaking. She was committing a felony. Searching a crime scene without consent or authorization. Her achiever's instinct to *Do Right and Follow the Rules* exerted a strong pull. How could she take this risk?

Doug had once confided that he'd traded stock ahead of a regulatory hearing in a way that technically could be construed as insider trading; he only knew of the hearing's existence, not its substance. Steph had exploded on him...but wasn't this worse? She could go to jail. The stain might cost her everything: family, friends, career.

If not for Fiske, though, the "everything" at stake might've been so much less.

There was Stanford, of course. But it was more than the tuition help. Steph still remembered walking into Bob Fiske's classroom as a freshman—he taught both freshmen and senior English, bookending the honors track—and feeling overrun by insecurity. Locker combo, blemishes, loud senior boys. At the bell, Fiske had arisen from his desk like a whale breaching and recited Lewis Carroll's *Jabberwocky*. She had felt instantly transported, delivered from the institutional confines of ETHS as the poem's giant nonsense world roared alive in Fiske's baritone.

The frumious Bandersnatch tempted...the vorpal sword glistened... Callooh! Callay!...

Steph wanted to learn everything. It was exhilarating, like discovering a new fruit or color she'd never known existed. She understood in those breathtaking, drama-packed moments that high school would be her place. She would thrive.

Now, growling off fear, she raised the lip of the rug.

Plain hardwood.

The living room's couch and end tables yielded the same. Nothing. Steph moved to the kitchen and found a typical bachelor space. Pristine range, a mottled banana, no counter appliances outside of toaster and coffeepot. She poked around the fridge. 2% milk, Dijon mustard. Twist-tied baggies of granola.

It occurred to her that, despite that first move to avoid the police tape, she was now leaving fingerprints everywhere. She scanned Fiske's bedroom (sheets neat but unmade), bathroom (backup rolls of toilet paper lining the sill), behind his washer/dryer.

She tried to think strategically. She needed to *be* her former teacher, to inhabit his head somehow. She swelled her lungs and stalked about. Bob Fiske was a man of discipline. Of order. Steph returned to his bedroom and imagined waking, embarking on his morning routine. She stretched tall at the window overlooking Lake Michigan, recreating that raw, spiraling stretch Fiske favored at the end of class films, then dry-brushed her teeth in the bathroom mirror. She mimed changing undershirts, pulling on pants. Chose a pair of socks from the top dresser drawer.

Into the kitchen now. Meting out granola in a bowl, pouring in milk. Sitting at his bistro table with imaginary newspaper. Reaching for...

Whoops, forgot coffee. Steph walked to the maker and slid the chrome carafe from its cradle. Finding a mug in the nearest cabinet, she raised the carafe and pretended to pour every last drop; Fiske was a coffee fiend, regularly draining a thermos over the course of a lecture. At the height of the motion, she noticed a protrusion on the bottom of the carafe.

She squinted. She ran her thumb along the protrusion. Tape—

and underneath it, a scrap of paper divided into thirty-one squares.

A calendar.

Steph's heart hammered. Mr. Fiske had always stressed the importance of work plans, of defining goals in the concrete language of days and months. "Make a schedule, refer to it liberally. Place it where you will see it every day. Where you've no choice but to see it."

The coffeepot, of course! Probably the police had checked inside and dusted its handle for prints, but nobody'd seen the underside. Nobody had thought to raise the pot up like Steph.

She pinned the carafe upside down to the counter, causing a brown dribble to leak toward the range. She didn't care. Her eyes devoured the calendar. The month/year heading was current. Boxes showed dashed-off reminders about a gift for a colleague, city council meetings.

She hoped the row corresponding to this week might contain her clue...but the only entry was *4th hr quiz* for this Tuesday.

Steph replaced the carafe. Feeling letdown, she moved on to the study where she found an antique file cabinet. She jiggled open the top drawer by brass curlicue handles. The contents were heavily tagged; it appeared the police had scanned everything, then replaced it.

She fingered through. *Fed Tax... Mortg & Insrnc... ETHS Stubs...* Inside each folder she envisioned some smoking gun—records from a Swiss bank account!—but after several minutes wasted on mundane forms, she pushed shut this drawer and pulled out the bottom.

Here the tabs were more interesting, school-related categories like *Test/Quiz* and *Lecture Outlines*. The very back folder, hiding at the base of the cabinet's mahogany throat, especially intrigued Steph.

Lists, Uncategorized.

Steph began picking loose sheets out of the folder, plain typing paper containing lists of anywhere from three to forty-one items. "The mind craves structure, some defenses against its own terrible disorder," Fiske used to say, and here it seemed were his attempts to impose structure on all sorts of wild thoughts. *Musical Instru-*

ments Yet to Be Invented. Great Days for Liberty (US, Society at Large). Books Whose Authors Owe Me Time. Narcotics of Mild Interest. A few of the more sensational echoed rumors Steph had seen online, and she wondered if the police might be leaking.

Near the middle of the file, Steph found a page headed simply, *Disappointments*. The list had eighteen items, from the predictable (*Clinton/Obama presidencies, #16; CTU collective bargaining, #11*) to the mysterious (*Tranquility, #7*). When her eyes reached the last item on the list, number one, she lost her stomach.

Stephanie Mills.

No modifier, or parenthetical, or anything.

The words—her own birth name—blared off the page at her. A half dozen incidents crystallized in her brain. Fiske conspicuously not noticing her in the stands at homecoming, that first year out. The brush-offs he had seemingly given her on reunion-committee e-mails. Their tense exchange over MetroBuild at the Unicorn.

Maybe their arcs hadn't simply diverged. Maybe Fiske had wanted it this way.

Outside, a vehicle door opened loudly. Steph ran to the window.

"No!"

A news van had pulled up bearing the ABC affiliate's circle-7 logo. A reporter and cameraman stepped out to the curb. The reporter smoothed her blazer, gripped a microphone. Her cameraman propped a pair of tripods efficiently and snapped a shade onto the first.

As both glanced up in the direction of Fiske's window, Steph realized she was in their line of sight. She dove to the floor.

For ten minutes, she stayed down, crouched in a ball. Even as her ears stayed tuned for footsteps—ABC7 wouldn't tape a segment from inside the condo, would they?—Steph's thoughts spun at what she had just read in Fiske's files.

How had she disappointed him? It must be about her career again. Fiske saw her as a corporate stooge, prostituting her intellectual gifts for material comforts. "It is possible, even probable, that one who inhabits big houses and drives big cars is in fact, by all meaningful standards, living small."

It occurred to her that if she did miraculously locate and exonerate Fiske, that would change his opinion. Right? Maybe a memoir would grow out of it, a whole Big Life of writing and interviews? She knew this was an unflattering line of thought, venal, but found she needed it now.

Outside, the van's motor rumbled. Steph peeked over the sill. The reporter climbed into the passenger seat as the cameraman fitted equipment into the back. They drove off.

Phew.

Back in the study, she picked up her place in *Lists, Uncategorized. Unprofitable Modes of Critique... Thoughtful Book Reviewers... Gridiron Moments of Joy...* Reading Fiske's chicken scratch was challenging, transgressive, intimate. It made Steph nostalgic for him and freshly sad about his predicament.

She had nearly reached the end of the file when one list made her stop shuffling. *Locales Suited for Contemplation.*

With all the pressure that had been mounting on Fiske—Jesse Weams, the petition—contemplation might well have been his mode.

Steph read down the list, which contained a mishmash of geographic places. There were a few from Evanston Township High, some secret nook in the vocational hall, *The classroom pre-sunrise.* He had made both general entries, *Foreign beaches, any,* and concrete ones like the Unicorn Cafe. She understood every item he had written down, with a single exception.

The entry at the top of the list: *UP.*

CHAPTER EIGHT

The CEO of GigaStorage pitched a decent ball game. A bit familiar for Doug's tastes—you ought to stay with "Miss" and "Mister" until the top buttons came loose—but the guy understood his business. He knew the value prop, cloud tech with the differentiating feature of hardcore security, and their balance sheet played.

"And you all're ready to roll?" Doug said, preempting the closing argument.

"Yes."

"We buy in at $15 million, you're on the air next week in New York and Singapore? Servers ready to scale? I won't hit GigaStorage.com and see 404 errors."

The CEO gave a confident nod. "We just need capital."

Doug eyed him an extra beat. No way in hell they were doling out $15 million in a space as crowded as cloud storage, but $4 million might happen. He scanned the GigaStorage team. Interesting talent mix. Doug recognized the marketing lead as a Carlyle retread, and the young Indian engineer as having been poached from a competitor.

He was about to engage on terms when his cell buzzed.

Steph.

Probably upset about some new smear against Fiske in the

media. He swiped *Ignore* and locked eyes with the GigaStorage CEO again.

Again his cell buzzed.

Steph.

"Excuse me, gentlemen." Doug frowned, backing out of the conference room. "One second."

Double doors swung silently shut behind him. He answered on the sixth ring, just beating voice mail.

"Babe, hey, what's up?"

Listening to his wife's voice on the other end, Doug ambled toward a panoramic window. He placed the peak of his forehead against the glass and braced his hands by a watercooler. In front of him, Chicago unfurled in a magnificent sweep: Hancock Tower, Grant Park and the aquarium, the stately yellow stone of the Board of Trade...

He noticed none of it.

"You did *what*?" he asked at Steph's first pause for breath.

"I broke in," she said. "Not really—I mean, the door wasn't locked."

Doug opened his mouth to speak, but no words came. He found himself staring at the phone like it was some bizarre parakeet or toy of Morgan's spewing gibberish.

Steph rushed on. "Listen never mind that, I need your help with something!"

"I...alright, I guess."

"I found a clue. Maybe. Fiske has this folder full of lists—remember he loved lists? Anyway, I found one called, *Locales Suited for Contemplation*. Number one is 'up.' Does that mean anything to you?"

Doug stepped back from the glass, feeling a touch of vertigo. "Wait, are you actually in Fiske's apartment? Now?"

"Yes! I have to figure this out so I know whether I need to keep looking."

"Steph, if the police catch you—"

"I don't care about the police. I need to figure out this 'UP,' where it could be."

He thought a bit, then began, "How was it writ—" then stopped.

Then thought more. One skill Doug had learned early in business was to play questions forward before you asked—to consider downstream implications, to know exactly where you were preparing to take the conversation.

"What?" Steph urged. "Doug, tell me, tell me what you're thinking!"

He inhaled deeply, gauging her likely reaction. He understood better than anyone Steph's fervor for this case. If he gave an honest answer here, she was going to run with it. She would round up the Winners group again and proclaim a breakthrough, and insist on pursuing it. Insist on *all of them* pursuing it. The horse would be out of the barn. If he answered less than honestly? Probably the group would break up. The cops' investigation would lead where it led, and they'd watch from the sidelines.

A large part of him wanted to go this route. To say he had just been thinking out loud, spitballing. *Up?* Heck, he had no idea.

"How was it written?" he said. "All caps, or was the *P* lowercase?"

"Uh, let me just..." Steph fumbled papers on her end. "All caps."

"U. P." Doug squeezed his eyes. "The Upper Peninsula, Michigan. Where people used to say Fiske had his Winners retreat."

"But there wasn't a Winners retreat."

"That we knew of."

Steph spluttered a minute, reflexively arguing against this sensational rumor—one of several that'd made the rounds on cable TV—before realizing what it meant: hope. After five years of marriage, Doug could almost hear her thinking over the line. Maybe it was far-fetched, and damning if true, but it gave them another play. A way forward.

"We have to go," she said, reversing herself. "We have to find the retreat."

"The UP is something like twenty thousand square miles," Doug said, "so unless you find a treasure map too, we can't hardly—"

"We can. We absolutely can. I'll call Mom and tell her we'll drop the kids by after dinner. If everybody can hit the road by seven thirty, we could make Green Bay before midnight."

"Everybody who? Everybody from that group of people who showed not much interest in helping you out three hours ago?"

"They didn't know about this, that he goes to the Upper Peninsula to think. This changes everything!"

"Does it?"

"Yes. It's exactly where he has to be."

Plenty more counterpoints came to mind. Doug knew voicing them would be pointless. Steph wanted to go. He and the others might give a dozen valid objections to this dash into a landmass bigger than many of the world's countries, but none would budge her. By sheer force of emotion, by that striving, indefatigable goodwill of hers, she would get their butts in cars and deodorant into overnight bags. That was her DNA.

Doug loved her for it.

CHAPTER NINE

The Hummer seated seven so Eric drove. Per Steph's instructions, the Winners group met at 6:15 in the ETHS circle drive. They parked, then ambled uncertainly from their own cars. Steph hustled all into place with a tight grin, then climbed into the passenger seat.

Eric glanced across the gearshift. "So the dead-dino-guzzler here is due back nine p.m...guess I need to extend the contract?"

Steph tilted her phone to show him the drive-time estimate: *6 hours 32 minutes*.

"Right." He dialed Hertz.

As they rumbled away from the school, practice fields fading into dirty-pink twilight, Steph allowed herself to exhale. It had not been easy assembling the group, selling the significance of *UP*, the wisdom of dropping everything and going—even after she had tracked down improvements paperwork for a "SNGL-FAM DWELLING" owned by "B FISKE" on the state of Michigan website. She had cajoled and wheedled and bulled past objections, and made it happen.

Some objections remained.

"Should we at least *call* the police?" Becky asked from the back. "Tell them what you found?"

"No," Steph said. "Wright is biased. If he finds Fiske and

Autumn, no matter what the circumstances, he'll paint the worst possible picture."

"You think? I know I'm a total dummy, but, like, if Fiske is innocent, if he hasn't done anything?"

In the rearview, Becky shivered despite the Hummer's braying heater. Steph had not yet confronted her about those lies to Eric. She looked scared now, hugging the elbows of an *I Love My Sheltie!* sweatshirt, the silkscreen image bunched about her chest. Was she nervous? Had she guessed that Steph and Eric had compared notes?

"There might be room for interpretation," Steph said. "It'd be better if we found him."

This sounded thin, but she didn't know how else to express it. Steph felt rock solid in her conviction Fiske had not abducted Autumn Brockert, but she worried he could be up to something else—something the authorities or public at large wouldn't understand.

They made good time through Illinois into Wisconsin, due north up I-94, one majestic wildwood after another. Eric's skinny forearms framed the wheel as he stared ahead at the road. Mostly —Steph did notice one glance at her legs. Behind them, Lydia closed her shoulders around a spiral-bound periodical. Doug napped.

An hour outside Milwaukee, Steph flinched looking in her side mirror. "Hasn't that black sedan been behind us awhile?"

Eric checked his. "Maybe."

Doug yawned. "Probably just heading the same way."

Steph took no comfort from her husband's remark. "Does anyone else know where we're going?"

"How is that possible?" Eric said. "*We* don't even know where we're going."

"You know what I mean. Did anybody mention it to their family, friends?"

She swiveled around the gunmetal interior, eyes hitching at Lydia—who, of them all, seemed most likely to tell, with a sister missing and mom on the warpath.

Neither Lydia nor anyone else fessed up.

"I'm positive I saw that sedan before. What does Principal Mancini drive?"

"Volvo," Becky answered.

Steph's mouth firmed. The car had not seemed boxy like a Volvo. Who could be following them? Northside Ill? A deputy of Wright's? Some enterprising reporter who had gotten wind of their search party?

Am I imagining things? As they neared Green Bay, Steph felt pressure to narrow the search. She had assured the others they would pin down this supposed Winners retreat en route—it was a long drive—but so far none of her or Doug's cell-phone efforts had panned out. Searches for *B Fiske* had produced no hits beyond the improvements document, and the classmates she'd reached by phone knew nothing about a cabin or vacation place.

"I think he just needed to step back," Steph said to the entire car. "Reboot after this Jesse Weams controversy, do some soul-searching."

Doug's voice from the back: "With a female student?"

Eric said, "We don't *know* they're in the same place." Swiveling from the wheel, hot to take Steph's side. "I think it's entirely possible he got fed up and decided to blow this pop stand. Onward and upward. He is getting up there—maybe petty squabbles with the PTA weren't his idea of Living Big through the golden years."

"Right." Doug wore a sober expression. "But maybe hooking up with one of these adoring sixteen-year-olds was. These girls he'd been turning away forever out of propriety."

Fiske's enduring bachelorhood had always been a source of intrigue. Within weeks of an attractive single female joining the ETHS faculty, rumors would have her attached to Fiske. *They always walk out of the teacher lounge together, did you notice?* Steph remembered a kid once asking Fiske why he didn't have a wife. Instead of brushing off the question as Steph had expected, Fiske had assumed a faraway expression and said, "I have chosen a life true to my ideals." (Doug, during the next passing period: "Translation, he gets a lot of tail.")

Steph was just considering how to respond to her husband's

unhelpful comments when Lydia Brockert spoke her first words since Chicago: "My sister would never have gone."

"Gone willingly, you mean?" Eric said.

Lydia nodded. "Not after Nora. My mother told us, 'You cannot take chances. I cannot lose another daughter.'" She did Jane Brockert in a tough, clipped voice. "Autumn would never put Mom through this by choice."

Steph twisted to see Lydia through the gap between chair and headrest. "But you still believe in Fiske, don't you? There are other possibilities."

The academic sniffled. Her shoulders hiccuped in what might've been a shrug of acknowledgment, or nothing.

Doug reached for Lydia's knee. "Your sister is fine." He waited for her eyes to meet his. "There is a simple explanation, and we—you and me, all of us—will find it."

This claim was far from obvious, but coming from Doug's chiseled visage, it worked. Lydia shimmied at the top of a breath, then relaxed.

"I certainly hope so."

Steph watched Lydia an extra beat. That passage from the faculty webpage kept creeping back to her head, niggling. *A star on the academic lecture circuit.*

The Hummer fell silent. Outside darkness poured into the spacious cabin, whose purple interior lighting Eric was too frightened to attempt deactivating. The combined effect was to separate the occupants even further, tinging shadows, answering unasked questions.

Eric, perhaps to lighten the mood, turned on the radio. "If anyone has listening preferences, feel free to vocalize. I tend toward contemporary adult, though lately I find myself stopping on pop/country as well."

Doug said, "Basically Taylor Swift."

"Oh right, QB1 would prefer some Megadeth. Here—let me find "My Hero" by Foo Fighters so you can channel James Van Der Beek and read a Kurt Vonnegut e-book while pretending to study your playbook."

Doug let the response wither, then said, "I left my dork decoder wheel home."

"Didn't you used to say that circa 2007, *dork decoder wheel*?" Eric said. "Might be time for some new material."

He twisted to say more, but the *BAMP-DE-BAMP-DE-BAMP* of the rumble strip interrupted. A southbound pickup blared its horn. Eric jerked them to the shoulder and back, the Hummer careening on two wheels.

"What *are you doing*?" Doug yelled, arms thrown protectively across Becky and Lydia.

"Sorry." Eric re-gripped the steering wheel. "Good now, sorry —my mistake."

After a few collective breaths, Steph suggested they stop. Eric pulled off at a gas station ten miles on. The women disappeared to the ladies' room while Eric and Doug, still glaring at one another, milled among tabloids and hot dogs glistening on rollers.

Lydia finished first, leaving Steph and Becky elbow to elbow at the metal sink.

Steph scrubbed gritty pink soap in her palms. The tap shut with a *clang*. "Why did you tell Eric my marriage was in trouble?"

Becky froze. "What? Did Eric say, er—"

"He did. I must say it came as quite a surprise, hearing about my own separation plans."

Becky spluttered an apology, *oh God, she messed up, how stupid could she be—*

"Do you have a thing for Doug? Still?"

The whites of Becky's eyes trembled, and Steph worried for a moment some kind of epileptic fit was coming.

"Of course not, it was stupid. I'm just so stupid, and I say things, and I wanted people to come, especially Eric 'cause I figured he's good with tech stuff, we might need tech stuff, and I knew—well, everybody knows he's obsessed with you."

Steph dried her hands. "He dumped his girlfriend of three years."

"He did? Oh, that's awful—I didn't know he was dating anyone."

She was whimpering, pressing her forehead into the smudged mirror. Steph sighed. Laid a hand upon her back. Immediately, Becky turned for a wet-cheeked embrace, snuffling, latching on desperately.

"I should've never sent that FedEx, God if I could just go back—"

"You were trying to help." Steph's anger had passed. She did not seriously suspect Becky of putting the moves on Doug, and after all, Eric had wound up helping with tech stuff.

"No, I made everything worse! It's just—I have my baby girls now, everything is different. But I keep screwing up..."

Her anguish was tough to watch. After partying through high school, Becky had since devoted herself to helping people. She volunteered at Cornerstone Outreach and elsewhere, and of course had chosen the vocation of counselor. She didn't eat meat or fish on moral grounds. When Steph and Doug had heard she was adopting twins from Haiti, neither had blinked. It felt like a natural progression.

The source of Becky's transformation was believed to be an incident that occurred over senior spring break. Nobody knew specifics. Becky had flown down to Cancún as planned with a group. After the first night, she had refused to leave the house they'd rented on Airbnb. She had spent the week sobbing in an upstairs room, hugging her knees in a bay window, gazing out over the Caribbean. Had she been assaulted? Had she drank too much and been involved in an accident that hurt someone? *Killed* someone?

Nobody knew.

"Come on." Steph turned her around by the shoulders. "It's a bad situation. With Fiske. But things will be okay."

"I'm really worried they won't be."

"They will. Becky, they will—you're being too hard on yourself."

"No I'm not, it's terrib—"

"Yes, you are. Whatever this situation is, you can't take it all on your—"

"*Yes I can!* Things are not okay, they're *not going to be okay!*"

The force of these words surprised them both. Steph thought Becky would soften with another self-deprecating apology or drop her eyes to the bathroom floor.

Instead, she repeated through chattering teeth, "Things are not going to be okay."

CHAPTER TEN

The group reached a decision point as it entered the Upper Peninsula proper. Stay on I-41 and bisect Hiawatha National Forest, or cut across by Highway 2 and hug Lake Michigan? Woods or water?

"Water," Eric suggested. "Remember how much time Fiske spent on that Plath poem? *Black lake, black boat, two black, cut-paper people...*"

The others agreed, and so they followed the horseshoe curve of 2 East. In the early-morning dark, Steph sensed the landscape opening on her right, the Hummer's bulk absorbing gusts off various bays and inlets.

She was beginning to have the queasy feeling, not improved by her exchange with Becky, that she had launched them into an ill-considered, under-defined mission. Nothing had materialized to narrow the search. No online bread crumb, no *eureka!* insight from some decade-ago lecture. They were in the Upper Peninsula now, prime vacation territory. Why weren't they checking all these spots right off the highway?

Answer: Because doing so would be hopelessly impractical. Chasing a needle in a haystack. At night. In total darkness.

At two thirty a.m., exhausted, deciding anybody who might possibly be helpful in their search for a cabin—waitresses, park rangers, dock operators—would be asleep, they stopped. Steph found a lodge two miles off the highway, fifteen rooms laid out in the shape of a V. Eric powered the Hummer over gravel to park beside the building's peak, which had lights on inside and an industrial coffee station.

"Needing some rooms?" said an older woman, marking her place in *Reader's Digest*.

While she fished four brass keys from a loose pile, Steph asked whether there were vacation properties in the area. The woman fluttered her fingers vaguely as if saying, *All around.*

Room 7b occupied the far tip of the V, secluded. As Doug shouldered their pack along a dim path, Steph thanked the others and suggested reassembling at 6:45. They muttered agreement. Inside, husband and wife collapsed into bed without showering or unpacking toiletries.

"What were you and Eric arguing about?" Steph asked across the pillow.

"At the gas station?"

"Yes."

When she and Becky had emerged from the bathroom, both men had been red-faced.

Doug sniffed, peeling off a sock. "I asked how he liked the view up front."

She raised up on her elbow, but Doug looked more bemused than angry. It had been wise, she decided, to say nothing about the Marriott. If Doug was willing to call Eric out for a glance or two across the gearshift, how would he respond to an attempted kiss?

"What did he say?"

"Denied it. Then admitted, then denied, then admitted again but blamed the sun visor."

"The *sun visor*?"

"You know Pinkersby—he can reason his way into a paper bag." Doug folded his pillow, laid back his head. "I was mostly rattling his cage. See if he'd spill anything on Fiske."

"Did he?"

"Nah. I pushed him on why he came out here. Said he owed Fiske. I thought he might own up to the Paladin stake, but he never did."

Doug asked what she and Becky had discussed—they'd been in that ladies' room awhile.

"Oh, just..." Steph could not tell the truth without coming clean about this afternoon, and so explained, selectively, "Sort of the same. I wanted to see if she knew more than she was letting on. If she really just randomly organized this Winners group."

"And?"

"I don't know. Becky seems so scared—and I realize this is an inherently scary situation—but still. She told me, 'Things are not going to be okay.'"

"Hm."

"She couldn't stop shaking. It was more than fear for Fiske, almost like she sensed some personal danger. To us. To herself."

Doug stayed quiet a long time. Steph thought he had fallen asleep.

Finally, he said, "Drama. Becks may be a do-gooder now, but she's still all about the drama."

"You don't think she has some larger involvement with Fiske?"

He gave a tired splutter. "I can't imagine what. But never say never."

Steph did not sleep well or long. She tried distracting herself from the Fiske situation by thinking of her children. They were staying with her mother for the second night in a row, which she hated doing. Morgan had made a new vocalization today, a lamblike "bleah." Ella hadn't bitten anyone, but Steph had noticed phonics readers in two of the other kids' take-home cubbies. One, Brooklyn, shared Ella's birth month. When Steph had mentioned it offhandedly, Ella had told her Miss Marilyn didn't send books home with her because she could already read chapter books. "All their books are too *easy* for me, I'm *advanced*."

Steph had fallen asleep with this delusional brag repeating in her head, sneering, begging dislike.

Two hours later, she woke to crunching gravel. Her senses

spiked. She flinched toward the window, then lay still, tensed. Listening.

Another *crunch*.

She slipped from beneath the covers and stole to the window, spreading the blinds with thumb and forefinger. She squinted through the resulting diamond.

Parked beside a dumpster, taillights off but steam swirling off the hood: a black sedan.

Steph's stomach seized. She carefully withdrew her fingers so the blinds wouldn't spank.

They *were* being followed. By whom? Why would a detective slink around like this rather than confronting them? Could it be Northside Ill? Or some henchman from a similar organization?

She tiptoed around a heating unit to the very edge of the window. Nudged the blinds with her head, watched the sedan with her left eye.

One minute.

Two.

Nobody emerged. Nothing inside moved. There were no other cars in this recess of the parking lot—the Hummer was around front—and she didn't have an angle to check the adjacent rooms for light.

Steph's pulse beat slow and even in her chest. Doug lay sleeping ten feet away, but some prideful instinct stopped her from waking him. *You can handle this. This is your mission.*

Finding her shoes at the foot of the bed, she edged outside. Cold stung her face. A vital whiff of pine was tinged only slightly by trash and motor oil. An animal chirped in the distance—or hooted, or yipped.

She stayed low crossing the parking lot. The sedan had no bumper stickers and an Illinois plate—neat, neither personalized nor marked in a way that indicated a police vehicle. She swiveled on her haunches, gravel pricking her palms, and saw one room had lights on.

Were they watching her? The blinds were closed and she saw no gaps. Wouldn't a professional henchman have turned off the lights? Maybe not. Maybe they unpacked like everybody else.

How about an amateur?

Whatever the case, Steph didn't think it wise to simply go knock. She noted the room number and slipped around the back-side of the lodge's V to the front desk.

The same woman greeted her.

"Thermostat cranky on you?" She reached under a plywood desk for a wrench. "Good knock'll do her."

Steph waved her back to her chair. "I was just out getting a bit of air, and I saw a car pull in. A black sedan." She screwed up her face, feigning puzzlement. "With it being so late, I thought I'd check here. Make sure it was registered with the lodge."

The woman eyed her through bifocals, then produced an index card. "Ya, it's registered. Woman named Jane Brockert just checked in."

Relief flooded Steph's brain, but an instant later, questions. Why was Jane Brockert on their tail? Had Lydia tipped her off?

The woman asked if she wanted the room number. Apparently, privacy concerns were not top-of-mind here.

"Thanks, no," Steph said. "I'm all set."

She traversed the V again with brisk strides, approached the room with the light. Its door was freshly sanded and the peephole drilled out. She glimpsed the hem of a full-length women's coat as her knuckles boomed off wood.

Jane Brockert took the merest of peeks out the window, then answered.

"You've been following us for four hundred miles," Steph said. "Why?"

In heels, Jane was taller by three inches. "Because I want my daughter back. I thought you knew where she was."

"We don't."

"I gathered that. My first clue was your friend's eight-point turn outside Escanaba."

Steph shrugged. Eric did not handle the Hummer's girth well, it was true.

"Did Lydia tell you about us? The Winners group? You could have just asked. Nobody would've objected to your tagging along."

"Lydia didn't say a word," Jane said. "I saw that FedEx at her apartment, then I contacted Principal Mancini to pull audio of your initial meeting."

"*Audio?*"

"Every conversation that takes place in the office of a District 202 counselor is recorded. Liability."

Steph was not thrilled to learn Mancini had worked behind the scenes with Jane Brockert. Who else was he "pulling audio" for? The police?

"Well I'm sorry to tell you this, but we have no better idea what's really going on here than we did yesterday or the day before."

"It's no mystery what's going on." Jane glowered. "That monster seduced my daughter."

"No." Goose pimples covered Steph's arms. She refused to cover or ask herself inside. "I promise you, that is not what happened."

"Of course it is! How can you be so delusional? How could we all be so delusional..."

Jane, acting a little fried, berated herself for pushing her daughters into Fiske's lecherous arms. She told of her own adolescence, which had coincided with Fiske's hiring at ETHS and the advent of the Winners club. She had wanted to be one desperately and so packed her schedule with extracurriculars: softball, pep club, the establishment of a student chapter of the Chicago Women's Liberation Union. When the list emerged senior year without her name, Jane skipped school for the first time in her life. Laid facedown moaning on her bed, pouring over her resume for the shortfall that had doomed her. The A-minus in junior trig? Her paltry batting average?

In adulthood, Jane had tried to correct the shortcoming with each of her three offspring. Flashcards and enriched preschool, sleepaway gifted camp, Kumon four days a week, all with an eye on Winner-dom.

"Nora, my first—she fought me." Jane teared up at the mention of her deceased daughter. "She didn't want it, she didn't get it. But Lydia did! And Autumn did! And I thought, *Hooray for me, we made it. The Brockerts made it.* But all we made was a monster. With our hero worship, we told that blowhard he could take whatever he wanted. The rules didn't apply to him."

Her face crumbled at the edges. Her usually precise pronunciations seemed to take on water. "After Nora, I told myself I would never take my daughters for granted. I would protect them no matter what. This is my fault. I propped up Fiske and made him their God."

Steph did not have it in her to argue back. She embraced Jane, stroking circles over her back. She considered telling her about "UP," the group's singular piece of new information, but what comfort would it realistically provide? The cabin was a hypothesis. It might be anywhere, or nowhere at all.

"I wish we knew more. I'm sorry."

Jane nodded thanks. The hands of a pine-log wall clock showed 4:45.

Steph was just stifling a yawn when gravel crackled behind her. Instinctively, she backed away from the door and pulled Jane along.

Seconds later, Doug came pounding around the corner.

"Got it, finally got it!" He held his phone up with two fingers, panting. "Alger County, Michigan."

Jane narrowed her eyes. "What? What's in Alger County?"

"A cabin," Steph said. "We think." She turned back to Doug, whose face beamed excitement. "What did you find, the deed?"

"Yep."

"Address?" Jane asked. "How big a county is Alger?"

"No address, and I dunno how many square feet," Doug said. "But I do know what's there." He looked between the two women, neither of whom had taken a breath since he'd burst onto the scene. "Pictured Rocks National Lakeshore."

CHAPTER ELEVEN

Through the haze of fatigue and displacement, Steph felt a blast of recognition. Her heart began leaping off the walls of her chest.

"Eric! *Becky!*" Steph called into the frigid night. "We know where it is!"

With her husband and Jane Brockert a step behind, Steph raced from door to door. "Let's get going, we have to go!"

Jane roused Lydia; they yanked on coats and climbed into her sedan. Steph stood literally hopping in place, waiting on the guys.

Eric staggered outside in boxers, brandishing a coat hanger. "Where what is?"

"Fiske's cabin, we figured it out!"

His eyes wobbled, then—looking past her to the black sedan—bulged drunkenly.

"Get the keys, *come on*! We're going to Pictured Rocks National Lakeshore."

Steph relayed what Doug had found, and Eric concurred at once. It fit perfectly. Fiske had always raved about the place's singular beauty. "The most visually stunning landscapes on the planet." The week they had read Hemingway's *Nick Adams* stories, which were set there, he had passed around snapshots. The time a student had asked about a pouch of loose-leaf tobacco on his desk, Fiske had said, "For the cliff spirits," explaining that he'd be canoeing in a spot where Native Americans had made offerings in hopes of favorable winds.

Google Maps pegged the drive at an hour forty. Jane was already reversing out of the lot, gravel spewing from her tires. The others powwowed briefly in Eric's room, then climbed into the Hummer, Steph shotgun again, Doug and Becky in back, everybody hustling.

There was a delay as Eric hunted for his phone, tossing a dozen Starbucks napkins from the center console before crying, "Damn you, Droid!" and gunning it back onto Highway 2. Becky ground her palms into one another, looking feverish. Even Doug had dropped his ever-cool facade and was researching cabin spots frantically on his phone.

Eric drove like a madman. He took a wooded hairpin at sixty, slingshotting past a trucker on a blind incline of an undivided highway. Sunrise was an hour away, and many stretches of road through Hiawatha Forest—which bordered Pictured Rocks to the south—had only subtle reflective tape for light. At one point, the Hummer swerved around a fallen branch, causing a duffel bag to fall on Doug's head.

"Let's not die," he suggested.

Eric raised a hand of assent/apology in the mirror, drove on.

Just inside the entrance, beyond a lopsided boulder carved with the park's name, lay the visitors' center. It was quarter past six. A man in ranger olive and khaki came walking around from the back, keys jangling on a thick ring.

Steph rolled down her window. "Can you tell us where we might find cabins?"

The ranger, giving wide berth to the skidding Hummer, looked out upon the brightening landscape. An expanse of hills and dunes were just now revealing their scalloped forms by bleary pink-yellow light.

"Value Inn, over by Grand Marais. Or Hillcrest out M-28. But I'd be surprised if either opens 'fore nine."

"We're looking for a private cabin," Steph said. "Are there any locations in the park where people can build vacation properties?"

The ranger filled his cheeks. "Anymore? No. There are a few spots got grandfathered in, though."

Now the black sedan screeched to a stop behind the Hummer. A door boomed shut, and as the ranger pulled a crinkled map from his vest, Jane Brockert materialized.

"Where're the cabins? *Where?*"

The ranger unfolded his map. His gray eyes lingered at several places. "Gorgeous views from Mosquito Falls. Seven, eight cabins thataway."

Dragging his finger along the trail lines, the man speculated with maddening verbosity about the merits of different spots...the edge habitat at Little Beaver...the invigorating scents of Kingston Lake...Gemini, north or south, last week some fella saw a moose, believe it was North Gemin—

"Do any overlook the lake?" Steph said.

"No, ma'am. They quit building on water—you had to chop down trees. EPA stopped that."

Jane Brockert loomed at the man's shoulder, peppering him. *Had he seen a green Land Rover? Could the Park Service commandeer helicopters?* The ranger took a backward step and refolded his map.

Steph climbed down from the Hummer. "Sir, please, may I take a look?"

He handed over the map. She surveyed it fresh. Parkland areas were shaded green and dotted with terrain markings. Most showed pointy-topped trees, but a few were bare.

"What about there?" She pointed to an icon labeled *Chapel Rock*. "That doesn't look like forestland, and it seems to overlook the water."

The ranger smoothed this section against a placard. His chin shifted.

"Oh, I'm sure Chapel has marvelous views of the cliffs, but nobody's set foot there for years. Unstable. Ever since the landslide in '97. Suppose they coulda built a cabin there, decades back. But you'd be nuts to try those skinny switchbacks now."

Behind Steph, the Hummer's engine cranked alive, and Doug and Eric conferred about directions. Jane Brockert sprinted to her car.

"Thank you," Steph told the ranger. "I think we'll drive a bit and see what we see."

The roads weren't so bad. The grade was steep heading around Chapel Lake and up the face of the peak past Lakeshore Trail, but the dirt ruts felt solid underneath. When they came to a sagging chain with a red *STAY BACK, EXTREME AVALANCHE DANGER!* sign, there was zero hesitation: Doug hopped out and unclipped the barrier with a firm yank, allowing both vehicles through.

They sighted Lake Superior just as the sun crested the horizon, shimmering black, far below the cliffs' vanishing edge. The coastline ribboned such that the famed sandstone formations were visible to both east and west. In a single sweep, Steph glimpsed mauve and olive and gold, serpents and sine waves, the contours of a giant harp.

"This is it," she declared.

A plateau stretched before them, a gap in the woods. It seemed bare at first, only scattered bushes and sprigs of wild grasses obstructing the lake, but upon closer inspection Steph noticed a kink in the terrain. Then, rising from the center, a triangular brown peak.

Shingles.

"Take the left ruts!"

Eric motored that way. The shingles revealed themselves to be the roof of a cabin, small and spartan, made of craggy-hewn logs. The ruts became rocky. A paper cup leaped from the console up front, blurting cold coffee.

Jane Brockert's sedan caught up. At the next bend, as they saw what lay beyond the cabin, the mother's scream penetrated two panes of glass.

"*His car!*"

And there it was, Fiske's Land Cruiser. Dinged up as ever, parked in a dusty patch of chaparral between cliff and cabin. Steph's stomach plummeted from dread and accomplishment and confusion all at once. She felt a pang of skepticism that they had actually found Fiske—it'd seemed such a long shot, had their guesses turned out a bit too lucky?—but the pang passed.

Eric and Jane parked any which way and passengers spilled out. Steph covered ten feet in two strides, immune to the biting wind and her own goose-pimpled arms. Smoke tinged the vital coast air. Pressure bore into her eardrums. The cabin door was locked, so Steph kept moving to a single shutterless window, which had been busted out. As she leaned inside, her neck *plinked* shards of glass.

The place was trashed. Scattered silverware and broken dishes surrounded a toppled butcher's block table. A wall of books, six shelves high, lay heaped in a row on the floor as though someone had ticked them down one by one. A bamboo rug, identical to the one in Fiske's condo, was doubled and tripled over itself like some bucking snake.

Steph was still processing the devastation when Doug blasted through the door. He stormed into each corner of the room, tossing up blankets or anything that might be covering a body.

"Coach Fiske," he called. "*Coach Fiske!*"

Jane Brockert followed a half step behind. "*Baby, where are you! Autumn? Baby?*"

Steph was so eager to get inside she didn't bother backtracking to the door, balling up the tail of her shirt and punching out the remaining shards, tumbling through the window. She landed in a mess of fabric and bent curtain rods.

What she saw made her veins run cold.

A bed. Unmade. Sheets tangled with socks and ripped clothes, and blood.

"That animal," Jane said. "I hope they pump him so full of pentobarbital he froths at the—"

"Jane, *please.*" Steph mastered her own shivering face. "Let's find them."

"That's right," Doug said. "We saw the Land Cruiser, so they must be close."

The others joined them inside the cabin. Becky and Lydia froze a step past the threshold. Eric stalked from one pile of chaos to the next, raking his fingers back through the silver sidewalls of his hair, uttering random disconnected syllables.

"They aren't here, they're gone," Jane Brockert said. "He already buried her."

"Now—no, let's think about it." Steph smoothed a ripple in the bamboo rug with her shoe. "Clearly there's been a struggle, but whoever was involved left. Maybe there was a second car. Maybe someone escaped on foot."

"Escaped where?"

"To the woods. Or the—" She caught the word "cliff" at the top of her throat. "The woods on the other side."

Jane called 911. The dispatcher said her closest responding unit was forty minutes out. Knowing time was of the essence, the group headed outside to check for signs of flight. There were footprints—or knee prints, or handprints—following a scrabbling pattern rather than any clear gait. Jane kept stabbing at dark spots in the dirt and saying, "More blood!", but at least some came from the water bottle clipped to Becky's waist.

They circled around back and found a bonfire. Most of its kindling had been reduced to cinders, but a pulsing-orange core still sent a reed of smoke twisting into the air, dissipating over Lake Superior.

Steph thought of the loose-leaf tobacco on Fiske's desk. *For the cliff spirits.* It occurred to her that they should figure out what somebody meant to burn—clothes, papers?—but in the frenzy for bodies, no one wasted more than a glance.

Finally, they had checked all sides of the cabin, and rechecked inside.

Jane Brockert said, "How long can a person bleed like that?"

Steph looked up with the intention of reassuring Jane, but her mouth would do nothing but pucker.

"Let's split up," Doug said. "If they're on foot, they can't have gone far."

He spread his chest to the landscape, lit now by full-morning sun. To the east, pines towered all the way to the water. To the west, a thin rock bluff buffered the woods.

Eric placed his arm around Becky, who had begun muttering, *I'm so bad, so stupid.* "We can take those woods along the coast."

Doug said he and Steph would head west. "Then Jane and Lydia can go inland."

The two nodded seriously, seeming to agree about keeping the Brockerts away from the cliff. The search teams paired up and tactics were discussed. *Stay near your partner. Be quick but don't hurry.* (A pet phrase of Fiske's from football.) Everyone turned on cell phones and promised to call around with any discoveries.

Jane Brockert gripped Lydia's hand and steered them toward their assigned swath of woods. As they disappeared into the canopy, Steph saw her pull something black and snub-nosed from her purse.

Doug walked ahead, crouched, crabbing open-stanced as through ready for attackers. Steph followed, pulling back boughs to check left and right, scanning the earth for disturbances. Surface roots as big as bricks hid among the velvety needle cover, making each footfall treacherous. Several times she stumbled, then hustled to keep pace. The sight of Doug—his jeans, those familiar sloping shoulders—felt like her only tether against the terrible violence they had wandered into.

Now Doug pulled up short of a clearing. "Quiet."

Steph tiptoed alongside, and together they peered through chest-high ferns. On the far side of the clearing, squirrels scampered up a tree. A frog croaked.

Then nothing.

"Babe, listen, we can't assume anything." Doug pressed her hand. "That much blood...it could be Autumn's or Fiske's. Or both. There could be some third party out here, alive." His eyes skittered about the canopy. "It'd be real easy to lose our bearings in these trees. We have to stay tight."

Steph struggled to match his focus on here-and-now tactics. Her mind reeled. Ordinarily she would have been just starting the morning, coaxing cereal bites from the girls, forcing sleeves over wriggly arms.

As far as this last week had strayed from normal, the gruesome cabin scene was almost too much. *What does it mean?* Steph felt a reflexive urge to weave some elaborate new defense of Fiske —along the lines of Doug's "third party"—but memories of too-red blood stopped her.

Something awful had happened. That was all she knew, and all that mattered.

They searched for twenty minutes. Birdsong startled them; snow crunched; twigs snapped; twice they became convinced they had just completed a circle. When Steph wondered if a persistent rustle might not have the cadence of one human dragging another, Doug hunched low and they clutched each other's elbows, listening. Finally, they decided it was wind swirling up loose pine cones.

Near the rock bluff, more light penetrated the woods. Dew dotted the peaks of holly leaves, and Steph could again discern, through low points in the bluff, the shimmer-black surface of Lake Superior. The vegetation changed subtly here at the woods' edge. Breaking up a row of neighboring pines, a tremendous white birch soared against the sunrise. Without deciding to, Steph found herself stopped and marveling at its fascinating bark: virgin-white shavings curling off the trunk, rough gnarls and horizontal razor slits lending the tree a frown here, a wink there, taking on a different character every few feet. Hypnotized, she followed the bark down, down, down...

An inch before the ground, its color changed.

"Blood!" Steph cried, her pulse blooming in her face and arms.

Doug came without a word and knelt. He touched one of the trunk's red splotches.

"Fresh." He showed Steph his smeared finger.

It required no special tracking abilities to see which direction they had gone. The smooth layer of needles was mangled along a zigzagging path toward the bluff. They followed around the birch, down a sharp depression, then back up a gentle incline. They came to a small pond—a large puddle, really—and saw, on its moist banks, several strips of torn clothing.

Doug examined one. It appeared to have come from a sweatshirt. The pink fabric, semi-stiff, was mottled brown in all but a few places.

"She tried to stop the bleeding here."

"Or *they* tried to stop the bleeding," Steph said.

Her gaze cut between the makeshift tourniquets and gouged mud. There must be forensic information galore here, but they had no time.

"Mr. Fiske!" she called out. "Are you there, Mr. Fiske? Are you *there*?"

Doug swiveled sharply on his haunches as though to object, then reconsidered.

"Autumn!" he joined in. "Autumn Brockert, we're looking for you! Please shout if you can!"

Only swishing leaves answered.

Husband and wife looked at one another. Steph perceived something new in Doug. They'd had rough patches these last days—over Eric, over her stubborn faith in Fiske—but his expression now was frank. Pure. *They were in it together. They would make it through.*

They yelled and yelled. On the fifth try, a noise answered.

Hoarse... If she hadn't been listening for it, Steph would not have picked it out of the wilderness.

"*Mr. Fiske!* Mr. Fiske, where are you?"

She and Doug began moving toward the sound, slowly at first, then—at another faint cry—stretching out their strides. When Doug faltered over a stump, she pulled him on and they ran hand in hand. Steph felt her shoelace come untied. A gust brought the scent of the cabin's bonfire to her nose. Water rushed and needles compressed underfoot and what where those wails in the distance? Sirens?

Steph saw first. Half hidden by a tree. Prone, unnaturally twisted.

A body.

Simultaneous to this discovery of the eyes, Steph's ears received a jolt. Somewhere far in the distance, but not at all faint, a scream.

PART TWO

CHAPTER TWELVE

Detective Wright leaned over the metal table, sleeves rolled. He spoke in a controlled tone, but Eric could see tension in his wrists, as though dual-overclocked GPUs biomechanically embedded in his forearms were pumping billions of *Witcher 3* polygons up the tendons.

"Explain to me, one more time, Mr. Pinkersby. How you and Becky Brindle came to be standing together at the edge of a cliff."

"But see I wouldn't say *together*." Eric winced the word. "I was back a few steps, so I think the more accurate descriptor might be—"

"Spare me." Wright's voice stomped his own. "There's a sixteen-year-old girl out there needs finding. I am not a patient man."

The detective's eyes burned. Eric focused instead on the man's bald forehead. "Let me try from the beginning. And again, some recollections are fuzzy—like when I get to the cliff, right before and after? I'm like a hard disk with a skippy needle, lucky if I—"

"Do your best."

Steadying himself by a cup of precinct coffee, Eric recounted his and Becky's ill-fated search of the woods east of Fiske's cabin. They had started from the edge of the lot and made their way toward the water. They nudged aside sticks. They froze at a sharp stench that turned out to be coming from an overturned compost bucket. Did they speak? Eh, not much. Mostly they just looked and listened. And worried. Did they split up? A couple times when one thought they'd heard something. This was how she got ahead of him at the cliff.

Did you hear that? Becky had asked, whirling. *It was a bark, I think.*

Eric hadn't heard a thing, and before he could say so, Becky was scurrying past the last trees out onto a thin ledge—insanely thin, goat-hoof thin, thin enough to make the warning track at Wrigley seem like Lakeshore Drive—

"Yeah okay, thin," Wright said. "Now what about this bark. Did you see a dog?"

"Well, I kind of thought so—I have this white-ish flash in my memory? Maybe some fur and possibly a collar associated with it? It was off to the side. I dunno, I was a few steps back and right afterward everything went berserk."

"When she screamed."

"Right."

It had been the most arresting, ephemeral sound you could imagine. The very start of a shriek. Had it gone on, it might have oscillated or coiled back in Becky's throat and become a primal, accusatory growl. But it never did.

It just stopped. Disappeared over the cliff with the rest of Becky.

"And then, only after she fell," Wright said, "you rushed to the ledge."

"Correct."

"Not before. You were not standing beside her when she fell."

Eric opened his mouth to answer, but weakness overtook his jaw. He heard an entirely different accusation than what the detective had intended: Why *weren't* you on that ledge, protecting her?

Wright waited respectfully before asking, "How did she fall?"

Eric widened his eyes to clear them. "I—I have no idea. I rushed forward and she was gone. Just physically not present. I crawled on my belly to the cliff—my hands were spasming, I didn't trust myself to be bipedal—and peeked over.

"Nothing. Nothing but rocky surf."

Wright asked if he had checked to the sides.

"No, I—like I said, I saw her at the cliff."

"Said you were a few steps back. Said you were disoriented." Wright worked his thumb over a dent in the table. "How'd you know Becky Brindle had fallen?"

"Well, I mean you guys're the ones that found her body, right? That cliff was so sheer, I must've been looking down an acute angle—"

"You know that now. *Now* you know. Why were you so sure then?"

Eric squished his face and mouth and garbled the first part of a reply.

"She coulda stepped to the side," Wright supplied. "Or back into the woods, no?"

"But I saw her fall. One second she was there, the next she was gone."

"So you did see her fall. Memory's clearing up? Good. That'll speed things up."

Wright's chair screeched concrete. A manila folder had been waiting at his elbow. He opened it. His brow furrowed as he scanned the contents. Eric felt gravity skew underneath him, as though Earth might begin dragging him somewhere any second— fast, sideways.

The sensation had been with him nonstop for the last seven hours, driving back to Chicago, here at the station.

"Coroner already came back with preliminary findings. Miss Brindle had marks on one wrist consistent with being pulled." Wright tapped a spot on the page. "Being violently pulled."

"Really?" Eric wondered how often these CSI types made mistakes. "Because the dog—you know, if it was a dog—the dog was more off in the periphery. Also didn't seem too big."

"We don't suspect a dog."

Eric gulped. Becky's death was barely real—he could still see her *I Love My Sheltie!* sweatshirt, smell her vaguely bubblegum scent from the drive—and now he was being spoken to like a suspect? What bizarre chain of run-time errors had landed him here?

The FedEx.

That fricking Fedex. The whole nightmare had started there.

What an archaic means of communication. Why not bang a gong in the middle of the town square? Eric had texted Becky after receiving it, carried to him by the Paladin mailroom runner two-fingered like some alien artifact, and heard about Steph's domestic troubles. She and Doug were fighting. Parenthood had driven them apart. She wanted to move, possibly out West.

In the time it takes a modern motherboard to cough out 100 factorial, Eric had imagined himself into a Happier Life. He already had a happy life, but Steph Mills (it would always be "Mills" to him) absolutely merited a capitalization of the term. Success at Facebook was great...the Paladin IPO would cover nightly sushi and EVE Online monthly fees ad infinitum...he already had a girlfriend, Ramona, whom he considered fairly spectacular...

But Steph Mills.

He spent six neurotic hours finding his heart. He gazed at images of the two women on his workstation's dual forty-five-inch monitors. He walked the Embarcadero, communing with seagulls. He drank coffee. Much coffee. At one point, he constructed a pros-and-cons spreadsheet featuring eleven cate-gories and fifty-two subcategories and agonized over what scores to assign. Ramona was a clear nine in "Tolerance for *Ready Player One* references," but where did Steph rate? "Dazzlingness of Smile" favored Steph, sure; by how many points, though?

Excel pegged Ramona's Overall Happiness Quotient at 86.3. Steph's OHQ came in at 93.1. Eric was unsure of the significant digits.

So he had marched up six flights of steps to Ramona's Sixteenth-and-Valencia studio. Even with the promise of an SFO-to-ORD boarding pass in his jeans' pocket, he could not escape a parabolic falling in his brain, the sound Wile E. Coyote hears before being crushed by the anvil.

He gritted his teeth. He thought about the thrill of riding beside Steph, thighs brushing, in Miss Shipley's debate van. About prom. He reminded himself there really had been issues with Ramona: his fear they were too alike, that angst he occasion-ally felt at their shared conversational tics, as if hearing his own voice on tape.

She answered the door wearing the topaz eyebrow stud bought during their spontaneous road trip to Vancouver.

He broke the news.

As it dawned on her what was happening, the cute cleft of her chin vanished. Instantly Eric wished for a *Control-Alt-Delete* reboot. That she was so surprised—"Us? You're actually describing us?"—made him question the sanity of the decision. But these words were not unsayable. (After briefly misarticulating his sameness concern, he had defaulted to the *wrong time/place in my life, not sure what I want* breakup script.)

He had never seen Ramona cry. Not when the Facebook module they had slaved over got deep-sixed, not when she'd flipped over her handlebars riding the Miwok and gotten road rash *inside her mouth.*

But she cried now. Keening at first, then angry. Her face jutted at him. "You coward, three years don't say a word? Spineless twink."

He took the abuse in silence until she, feral and growling but helpless against tears, slammed the door in his face.

Eric pressed his palms over his ears against her sobs, the sound of which penetrated the door, and started down the stairs. As he often did in life's challenging moments, he culled his memory for a Fiske quote. The one that came had followed a student's question about what one should seek in life. "Delirious happiness," Fiske had answered. "People and experiences that inspire uninterrupted, ever-expanding awe."

He breathed deeply, patted his jeans to be sure of the boarding pass.

"*Delirious happiness,*" he incanted. "*Delirious happiness, delirious happiness...*"

Detective Wright palmed his stubble. "I figure this case is ninety, ninety-five, percent solved. Leaving aside the whereabouts of Autumn Brockert, we know the biggies. Bob Fiske is laid up across town at Cook County General. He could wake up any second and give us the last five percent. Already got his suicide note, which explains plenty. How he 'surrendered utterly to joie de vivre.' Found himself 'powerless, like those weak giants of literature who could not resist youth's flower.' Sicko had eighteen months of canned food in the cellar."

Eric knew Doug and Steph had discovered Fiske—unconscious, bleeding—and had heard about the suicide note, which they'd apparently missed on that frantic first sweep of the cabin. But this bit about canned food was new. Eric had never detected a nutjob/survivalist vibe from Fiske. The idea that he had been preparing some messianic, Elizabeth Smart–esque captivity came as a shock.

The shocks were only beginning.

"Let me read you something." Wright flipped ahead in his manila folder. "Title of the document is *The Evanston Libertine Club Manifesto.*" He cleared his throat in a toad-like noise. "'We the undersigned pledge to never sacrifice pleasure in the name of convention. To never blunt our desires or passions, nor deny ourselves solely on the basis of un-assented-to social mores.' Who composed those lines, Mr. Pinkersby?"

Eric's heart had begun thudding at the name of the club. "Well, uh...me. I only wrote it for this assignment. Mr. Fiske wanted us to instigate a 'disruptive cultural-political action' for senior English. It was supposed to be subversive so I came up with the idea of a libertine club."

"I see two signatures on this piece'a paper. Yours. And Bob Fiske's."

"Right, right—it was silly, all we did was pledge to recite lines from *The Decameron* in the cafeteria—"

"What is the nature of your relationship with Autumn Brockert?"

Eric scratched at his temple. "We—I—there isn't a relationship. Wednesday was the only time I ever talked to her."

The detective unclipped a stack of papers marked *Cisco Proprietary.* "Internet records here from the Marriot. Lotta guys look at porn when they travel. Not you apparently." He squinted at rows of a microscopic-font printout. "Five hundred eighteen hits on Autumn Brockert's Facebook page. *Two thousand* different searches containing the words, 'Autumn Brockert.' 'Autumn

Brockert photo.' 'Autumn Brockert volleyball uniform.' 'Autumn Brockert smile.' 'Autumn Brockert smile amazing—'"

"Okay, I googled around some," Eric said, "but those numbers are grossly misleading. The ISPs report a hit for every single web-service URL request coming off a page: sidebars, JavaScript auto-completes. Those figures do *not* correlate with button clicks."

"You deny searching those terms?"

Eric opened his mouth and huffed several breaths without making words.

"Researching stuff is what I do," he managed. "Put me in front of a web-enabled device, and it happens. So yeah, I mean, I'd talked to her that afternoon—and I got curious. What else was I going to do at the hotel? I didn't pack a swimsuit."

Wright glanced down the log. "Similar activity for 'Steph Reece.' You some kinda stalker?"

Eric said no, no, no, repeating the word in lieu of explanation. About once a week he binge-searched Steph, not expecting new results, a ritual more than anything.

For his next topic, Wright assumed an irked, boiling expression akin to the television journalist interviewing a pedophile.

"Tell me about *The Man Of 10,000 Crushes*."

"How do you know about *that*?"

"Answer the question, Mr. Pinkersby. Why is a manuscript about a man obsessed with adolescent girls sitting on your laptop?"

"First off, the word 'adolescent' is unfair—the women's ages are left intentionally vague—and second, how did you look at my laptop? That's a blatant violation of my rights!"

"Amazing what latitude a judge'll give when you can place a perp two feet from somebody who fell off a cliff."

Eric's head wobbled on his neck. *They got a search warrant from a judge?*

"Fine, I was working on this book. I always wanted to give writing a shot, and I thought, hey, all this *Fifty Shades of Grey* hype, maybe there's a niche here for a story about a man with intense, complicated feelings about women: a book about pedestals and wish fulfillment, and the psychology of antisocial desire."

Again Wright's expression curdled. Hearing the words with

his own ears, Eric realized his *10,000 Crushes* elevator pitch needed work.

"So what're you implying? Is your theory that *I* was somehow involved in Autumn Brockert's abduction? I acted on some kind of obsession, despite the fact that we'd just met and these searches occur pretty near concurrently with the abduction, meaning I would've had to essentially sprint from the keyboard to do it?"

Detective Wright kept quiet a moment as though hoping Eric would keep talking and incriminate himself. "Tell me what you and Bob Fiske texted about early this morning."

"What?"

"You heard me."

"I didn't text Bob Fiske."

Wright set aside the *Cisco Proprietary* papers, then the libertine club manifesto—stacking them in an ostentatious mountain of evidence—then produced records bearing the watermark of Eric's cellular provider.

"We'll obtain the contents of the texts. You of all people know that, Mr. Pinkersby. Why don't you save everybody the trouble and take out your phone, read me those messages?"

Under the table, Eric clutched Droid to his leg. He knew he hadn't texted today but feared Detective Wright's bag of tricks. Dredging up that manifesto...snooping into the searches and documents on his laptop... Did the police have the capability to retroactively plant text messages? Somehow hack the cell towers?

"I have no earthly idea what you're talking about."

Wright gave a disappointed sigh. "We know you sent the first message. You wanted to warn him, fine. I'll give the benefit of the doubt. Maybe you didn't want the world to discover the old man with boxers 'round his ankles. Give him one shot to run. Hey, I understand. We mighta let you off with being an accessory."

"This is crazy! From what parallel universe are you—"

"But when you shoved Becky Brindle off that cliff in cold blood? You took it to another level, friend. Now we start thinking murder one."

Eric looked into the man's stony face, dumbstruck. Wright's questions had strayed so far from reality that he began to think they were confusing him with somebody else. His knees began knocking in place.

"Becky Brindle was Autumn Brockert's school counselor," Wright continued. "Friends tell us they met often. Autumn confided in Becky. Would've told her things that incriminated Bob Fiske. So she had to go, didn't she?"

"I—that's insane, can we just backup a sec and—"

"What did he offer you? Piece'a the action? Hour or two with Autumn Brockert?"

Now Eric's kneecaps were banging like cymbals. He began to sputter out a denial, but Wright cut him off, pushing up from the table in disgust.

"Why don't you man up and confess. Huh? Salvage one shred of decency."

"Because I didn't push her!"

"Then who did?"

"I don't know, someone else!"

Wright paced back and forth, laboriously rubbing his neck, mouth compressed to a pea. "Autumn Brockert tells her counselor about her little dalliance with Fiske...Becky expresses caution but unfortunately tells nobody...then when they disappear, she feels guilty and cooks up this 'Winners group' to track 'em down...fails to consider, not being a Winner herself, that one of you may be so devoted to the old man you'll kill to cover his tracks..."

As the detective talked through his theory, Eric felt the situation slipping. He groped for some exonerating detail, some overlooked nugget he could point to and cause Wright to smack himself upside the head and say, *Holy smokes, you're right! Get outta here, go enjoy your Saturday.*

He found none.

Wright sat back down, calmly laced his knuckles. "Where is Autumn Brockert?"

Eric said, "I don't know."

"Where is Autumn Brockert? What did Fiske do with her body?"

Eric said again that he didn't know, how could he possibly know—

"Right here, right now," Wright roared. "I don't give a crap

what happened on that cliff. That girl is out there somewhere and if there's any chance she's alive, *any* chance, I will find her."

Each syllable twisted the detective's face. Eric thought inappropriately of that old Billy Joel video, "Pressure," the singer writhing in a chair, palsied, eyes bugged, screaming out the lyrics.

"*Where is Autumn Brockert?*" Wright said, pounding the table.

Eric's cup toppled. Coffee splashed his lap. The outburst startled him, but the physical action of recovering—of scooting back and letting excess liquid drip to the floor, dabbing dry his jeans—reset his mental state.

"Just so I am a hundred percent clear on the situation," he said, "am I being arrested?"

Wright's expression churned in place. "Not at this point."

"So I'm free to beat it, right? Collect my keys from the concierge and drive off?"

The detective folded his arms, gave a grudging nod.

"That's what I'm doing, then." Eric stood with a tall, whistling breath. "If you're going to proceed under the assumption I'm guilty, then I don't particularly feel the need to help."

"Great," Wright said. "Clam up. That's what all the innocent ones do."

Eric headed for the door. His head felt dangerously light, misattached, and his footsteps slapping concrete were rifle shots. The detective's eyes bored into his back—he felt them—and try as he might, he could not suppress the urge to vindicate himself. Every aspect of his life had been thrown back into his face. Traitor, pervert, murderer. No label too vile.

He stopped at the threshold. "You know what Mr. Fiske's greatest lesson was, to me? He taught me that my passions were special. That I should embrace them." It felt somehow important to say this. "He believed the only way to truly honor your life was to trust your passions."

Wright smirked. "Beautiful. How's that working out for him?"

CHAPTER THIRTEEN

E ric drove from the police station to Cook County General on jittery autopilot, buzzing through scenarios. Droid showed no outgoing texts this morning—he had checked immediately from the parking lot. Which meant one of two things: either Wright was feinting, trying to goad him into a slipup, or whoever sent the messages had deleted them. As he drove, Eric voice-searched "recover deleted texts Android," but the top result wanted him to install some specialized app, then perform about eighteen steps to maybe, "if the MIME types break your way," see what got erased.

Not happening.

Presumably the police were in possession of Fiske's phone. *Why hadn't they just read the texts off it?* Maybe they had. Maybe Wright was testing Eric, seeing whether he would confirm or deny. Maybe Fiske had deleted the texts on his end too. *But why?* Since Eric had no idea what these alleged texts said, figuring out Fiske's reasons for concealing them constituted a third- or fourth-degree wild guess.

He was gazing quizzically at his phone when, two blocks from the hospital, it rang.

Justin Isrickov—J.P. Morgan.

Eric hummed briefly from his larynx, warming his voice as he always did before speaking to money men. "Justin. What can I do for you, sir?"

"Eric, glad I caught you! Was hoping to touch base regarding events in Chicago."

"Sure."

The banker waited for Eric to say more.

He didn't.

"Yes, well. I'm hearing chatter from my institutional folks. Concerns about media exposure, your name being associated with such a volatile situation."

Eric wheeled through pylons marked COOK COUNTY, VISITOR PARKING. "It's a little unreal."

"Now, are you—have you been questioned?" Isrickov asked. "Do the police consider you a material witness of some kind?"

Eric huffed. "Oh no, not *question* questioned. I mostly filled out forms."

Blatantly false, but after what this man had told him last week about the fickleness of IPOs, Eric had no interest in describing his encounter with Detective Wright. Any coverage of competing data recovery approaches, or data generally, or even idle hand-wringing about tech valuations, had the potential to halve their offer price.

Network trucks dotted the hospital out-lots. Picketers lined its entrance, signs bobbing along a fence barricade. *Justice for Autumn!!! Fiske's Final Quiz: Where is Autumn Brockert? Stop Teacher Rape NOW.* Eric lowered his head through their chants, then rode the elevator up to floor seven, where Fiske was being kept in a private room.

The other Winners stood around his bedside. Steph noticed him first.

"Are you okay?" She rushed forward. "Did you get held up at the precinct?"

"Yes. Paperwork."

Eric gauged her reaction to this recycled lie. Steph seemed to accept it. Neither Doug nor Lydia looked away from Bob Fiske's impassive face.

Steph asked if he had gotten treatment for his wrist, which he had sprained at the cliff.

"It's fine." Eric shrugged manfully, nodded to Fiske. "Any news from the docs?"

"Same. Maybe tomorrow, maybe never."

"And if he does wake up...?"

Steph's lips twisted. "MRI neither confirmed nor ruled out brain damage."

The four Winners considered the prone form of their former mentor. Eric experienced something like vertigo, seeing him flesh-and-bone after what had felt like a hopeless search, after the day's stunning reversals. The wild hair. The bulbous nostrils, now flaring rhythmically. Turkey-gizzard jowls. Exactly as Eric remembered—except for the eyes, which stayed hidden behind lids.

The suicide note lurked in the room's ether. *I refuse to be cowed by the conventions of Society, particularly one so bereft of standard... Let inferiors judge me; if such a thing as salvation exists, my muse and I shall gain it...*

It sounded like Fiske. Eric never could have imagined this particular content, but the language undeniably fit. The archaic usage, the grandiose dropping of plurals and indefinite articles.

Doug glanced over. "What did the police ask you?"

Eric puzzled momentarily about which word had received stress. *Police*—meaning, why was law enforcement so interested in him? *Ask*—meaning, what asking was there to be done, wasn't the whole thing cut and dried? Or *you*—meaning, they asked me a boatload of stuff, how about you?

"Oh, timeline-type information. Since I was there when Becky fell."

"They're satisfied she fell?" Doug asked with studied cool, cutting his eyes away midphrase. *Did he know?* Had he inferred from the duration of Eric's time with Wright? Or was it possible he had some concrete confirmation?

"They didn't tell me much," Eric said.

"Mm-hmm."

Eric heard a challenge in this utterance, clearly as if Doug were holding him by the hair over a locker-room toilet.

"But I did mention the dog," he blurted without thinking.

Doug reared back. "Dog?"

"Right, I thought there was a dog. Maybe off to the side. When Becky fell."

"Did they buy that?" Doug said, implying by tone that he personally did not.

Eric's breaths accelerated. Steph and Lydia were watching him now too. He felt himself back across a metal table from the law.

Doug. In his mind, the name carried the same nemesis inflection with which Jerry says, "Newman" in Seinfeld. Apparently, it wasn't enough in the view of God or Allah or whoever else ran this messed-up galaxy that Doug Reece got to share a bed with Steph every night—it seemed unlikely they slept in separate rooms as he'd fantasized after Becky's "on the rocks" comment—or command bazillions of dollars of hedge fund flow, or had emerged from the womb with man-grown pecs. He also got to be smart. And apparently an awesome dad. And not really the hothead jerk anyone with his insane collection of gifts would be portrayed as in a cheesy coming-of-age movie. (Eric's favorite kind.)

All the spoils, none of the baggage.

Before Eric's mouth could lose uplink to his brain again, a new sound pricked his ear. A cell-phone ring. Muted, factory default.

Blip-blip-BLOOP.

It originated from a bagged pile of belongings in a beige armchair. Eric stood closest. Through plastic, he could see rumpled pants and a belt, Fiske's wallet, two black shoes individually shrink-wrapped.

Blip-blip-BLOOP. Blip-blip-BLOOP.

He glanced to the hall. Nothing but flecked tile and blue scrubs. "Wonder if we oughta...?"

A look passed around the group. The phone must be Fiske's. Maybe the police had already culled its evidence and replaced it. They must have charged it to gain access.

Blip-blip-BLOOP. Blip-blip-BLOOP.

Only a corner of the phone was visible. Eric tiptoed over, then eased back a blood-crusted shirt by its cuff, exposing the phone's face.

UNKNOWN, read the caller ID.

He shrugged to the others, pulse hot. The protesters' chants outside were audible. Who would be calling Fiske *now*? Some reporter? Family?

Blip-blip-BLOOP.

Afraid of losing out to voice mail, he snatched the phone and swiped. The power in his own finger knocked the phone away. He fumbled to retrieve it. The screen was pulsing, green white to its negative white green, and back, such that he thought he might not have answered.

He raised the phone to his ear. "H-hello?"

Eric shielded the call from the hallway. His thoughts raced to a plausible explanation for why he was answering Fiske's phone—*I thought he might need medication, I'm a friend, I was part of the search party that found him!*—but the voice he heard was dull and uninquisitive.

"The following is an automated notification from the Third National Bank of Delaware, LLC, for account number"—the voice paused before proceeding stiffly—"zero-zero-three, two-nine-one, eight-one. Press or say 'one' to hear the notification. Press or say 'two' for account balance. Press or say 'representative' to speak with a representative."

As he listened, Steph stepped forward as though ready to catch the phone if he dropped it. Doug eyed him from Fiske's bedside.

A loud scrape from the hall. Eric spun, burying the phone in his chest. An orderly entered pushing a cart of folded towels and kidney-shaped basins. She began to speak, but then—seeing Eric on the phone, noting Fiske's untouched washroom—backed out with a nod.

By the time Eric's heart restarted, the automated voice was saying, "...wish to speak with a representative. Otherwise, this call will terminate in five seconds. Goodbye!"

Panicked, he stabbed one on the touchscreen. The line beeped twice before the voice returned.

"On March 14, a deposit of two thousand one hundred and sixty-one dollars and forty-three cents was processed for account number zero-zero-three, two-nine-one, eight-one. To repeat this information, press or say 'one.' To return to the main menu..."

Eric squinted at the phone. *$2,161.43?* What sort of deposit was this? Had Fiske transacted from the cabin? Where had he gotten two grand from?

"Who is it?" Steph whispered.

Eric mouthed back, "A bank."

Steph scrunched her nose—oh, that adorably upturned nose—then gestured, *Could she listen in?*

Together they navigated various menus to access the account balance, $195,765.13, and last ten transactions. The amounts ranged from one to three thousand, except for two which shot up to $12,552 and $9,483. Eric struggled to keep his wits with Steph so near, hearing the moist *pup* of her lips separating. He wondered about the pattern. All deposits. All posted at or around the fifteenth of the month.

Steph asked, "Why the Third National Bank of *Delaware*?"

"Taxes," Doug said. "Corporations in Delaware pay no income tax."

"But Fiske didn't have a corporation."

All four Winners looked up simultaneously. *Or did he?*

"Why do the amounts jump?" Steph said. "Those two were higher by a factor of five—what was different? What sort of revenue stream is that?"

"Gambling," Doug ventured.

"But why so regular?"

"Hits the casino same time every month." Doug raised a shoulder dubiously. "I dunno. Day-trading?"

Eric, in fact, had a pretty good idea what sort of revenue stream. Online advertising. Websites receiving automated payments on a per-click basis exhibit such volatility, spiking whenever a story or blog post went viral. Friends on the business side at Facebook said ad revenues were impossible to forecast for exactly this reason.

Maybe Fiske ran a blog. Maybe he had cultivated some wildly successful alter ego in the arena of politics or online book reviews. It would explain his ability to finance the occasional Winner's education or take such a large stake in Paladin.

Scanning the Winners' faces, Eric decided to keep his insight to himself. The more he thought about it, the more he wondered if somebody here hadn't filched his phone and used it to text Fiske in his name.

There had been opportunity. Right after Steph had confronted Jane Brockert in the motel, but before they sped up to Pictured Rocks, they had briefly gathered in Eric's room. He had not been able to find his cell. "Damn you, Droid!" he remembered yelling. When had he found it? Not until the cabin. It had materialized in the Hummer's center console. Amid the chaos, he hadn't given it a second thought.

The whole dash to the cabin, in retrospect, felt off. How had the pieces fallen into place so quickly? The concept that kept popping into Eric's brain was "caching," the way a computer keeps certain data in short-term memory when it expects to need it again soon. Those Upper Peninsula discoveries felt cached. Ready-made somehow. The question was, ready-made by whom?

The same person who sent those texts.

Both Michigan and Illinois state police solicited the public for volunteers in the search for Autumn Brockert. Blood matching her type had been found at the cabin, and shreds of her clothes in the nearby woods. They believed her to be incapacitated or on foot, somewhere inside Pictured Rocks National Lakeshore.

Badly as Eric yearned to hop a plane back to San Francisco, he knew he couldn't. He needed to help. Accomplice or not, he felt implicated in whatever had befallen Autumn Brockert. Fiske had been his investor, his sounding board, his philosophical anchor. If the old man was dirty, some of that dirt belonged to Eric—for his part in what the talking heads on TV were calling "the cult of Fiske."

So, after a spotty night's sleep at the Marriott, he headed north again.

The drive felt every bit as long as the first time. The Winners traveled separately—Doug and Steph needed to be back for the kids; Lydia rode with Jane—so Eric filled the slog with music, cruising *Seek*, hoping the Hummer's treble-heavy speakers might transport him through some forgotten-but-instantly-familiar melody. He had poor luck despite hitting many of his faves. "You Had a Bad Day." "Hollaback Girl." Anything by The Fray.

Last week, warm tinglies would have been passing down his body. Now? Nothing, as if his emotional nerve endings had been severed.

From the ranger station, dredgers could be seen crisscrossing Lake Superior. Dinghies, fishing boats, a commercial barge three miles out—the police had called in all available vessels. The search was no less intense on land. Volunteers had parked bumper to bumper along the road to Chapel Rock and marched the woods in safety-orange vests. A band of coordinators, identified with pins bearing Autumn's lacrosse photo, distributed headlamps and pitchforks.

In the clearing by the cabin, Detective Wright and Jane Brockert surveyed the landscape.

The latter said, "Why are you bothering with the dunes? You need manpower at the cliffs."

"Cliffs are covered. Everywhere's covered."

"The radius is too small, what if she staggered five miles? What if—"

"Besides it's not my jurisdiction. Detective Orlowe from the Michigan State Police—"

"My baby could be hemorrhaging behind some bush or dying of thirst and you're talking about jurisdiction?"

"Ma'am. I understand you're frustrated." Wright clasped hands over his belt buckle. "Every individual out here, be it law enforcement, volunteers—we all want your daughter found as soon as possible."

Eric, in no hurry to talk more with Wright, sneaked by to a coordinator. The man wagged his finger across a quadrant of the woods on a laminated map. The canopy was airy there; Eric would do fine by naked eye. He donned a vest and joined others walking the area. He tried to use a scientific route, moving in concentric circles, scrutinizing each disturbance in the dirt off his left—similar to how the Paladin algorithm scoured damaged platters for data. The place felt totally different from where he and Becky had been yesterday. The bustle of footsteps, voices, and phones shrank the woods. He walked an hour without pause.

Having exhausted his quadrant, Eric wandered west. A quarter mile outside the predefined search area, he came across a woman on all fours, digging with her fingers.

The woman turned at his approach.

"Lydia!" Eric walk-jogged the last few strides. "Did you find something?"

Lydia Brockert looked down at her own knuckles in the dirt. Eric knelt beside her, and together they cleared another inch of soil. Lydia's fingernails were caked black. Feathery strands of hair stuck to her cheeks.

After a few minutes scrabbling, it was clear they had found nothing.

"I thought I saw silver," Lydia said. "She wears silver earrings."

Eric said, "Why don't we take five?"

"My sister's out here." Lydia took a step farther west. "I can't stop."

"You can, Lydia—maybe it's best you do. A whole lot of people are doing their best to find her. Let's rest."

Lydia set her mouth, but did allow Eric to lead her away to a patch of dappled sun created by a lightning-felled pine. The decaying trunk made a workable bench. Eric tore away mossy bark, brushing clean a swath of heartwood for them to sit.

Eric didn't know what to make of Lydia. She had not been crushed by this ordeal the way he might have expected given her reputation. Her eyes looked keen, voracious—not at all fragile.

But not quite okay either. Her intensity worried him. It felt angry and a little dangerous. How would she respond if the worst came to pass? Eric leaned forward, inviting her gaze, but it was frozen straight ahead. Solid as a 486 choking on Windows XP.

"The police suspect you. In Becky's death."

It took Eric a moment to register Lydia as the source of these words. Apparently, the brain behind the gaze, not so frozen.

"How did you know?" he said.

"Your hands. When Doug asked you, they wouldn't settle."

Eric heard no accusation in her tone, and so told her candidly, "They think I pushed her off the cliff."

"You didn't."

"Question or statement?"

Lydia did not respond. "Becky told me something at the cabin."

He bent to catch her voice, which had fallen hoarse. "About your sister?"

Lydia nodded. Again the eyes were busy, inward.

"*What?*" Eric said. "She was freaked out, I know. I figured it was all the blood."

Lydia began without looking his way. "Certainly, she was suffering acute PTSD. It was rushed. Gibberish. We were all frantic, splitting up to search—I barely heard. Only one word came across definitively."

Now her eyes did shift onto him, and by some inexplicable Jedi mind magic, Eric knew exactly how she would finish:

"Prom."

CHAPTER FOURTEEN

Good God, if every last thing on Earth didn't trace back to senior prom.

The night of May 17 had been circled on Eric's calendar since January, once the admissions crunch was over and senior year a fait accompli. Prom meant the pretend adulthood of limos and boutonnieres (neither of which he'd encountered as a real adult), and liquor, and three-a.m. calls from the cops, and sex—or the pursuit thereof—and unspeakable fun, and Eric believed all these were imminent. He even had a date! Tara Pinney, a sophomore debater he had been seeing for two months. His first girlfriend who did not live in South Carolina or always have to work at her mall job—which was to say, non-imaginary.

The night began poorly. He pumped gas onto his tuxedo pants, then had to endure Tara's mother rubbing baby oil all over his thigh for the smell. They arrived late, filing into the ETHS gym beneath streamers and paper-mache sunflowers. A lousy band was covering the Black-Eyed Peas and only a few theater-crowd kids were dancing. The faculty chaperons, Mr. Fiske and Mrs. Osarzak, chatted by the punch bowl.

For an hour, Eric stood around shouting in Tara's ear. He mocked the playlist and assigned movie roles to classmates—Doug Reece as the cocky-cruel jock from *Some Kind of Wonderful*, the wrestling Halverson twins as Cobra Kai from *Karate Kid*. She chuckled politely whether she heard or not, and the night seemed destined to resemble every sleepy after-party he'd misguidedly attended during football season.

Midway through his fifth cup of punch, Eric went to the bathroom. The nearest was by the janitors' bay, but by habit he walked instead to the forensics hall. Passing Mrs. Shipley's classroom, he did a double take.

A figure was slumped in the door well, sniveling. Some solo nerd? A spurned pep-club girl?

Nope.

Steph Mills. Sitting in a heap, the pleats of her dress splayed about her like a rose-pink moat. Makeup flowed in rivulets from the corners of her pure eyes.

"*Mills, Mills*—hey, come on." He dropped to her side. "What's wrong?"

She squinted hard against a sob. "Everything."

Eric leaned to check up and down the hall. They were totally alone. "Where's Doug?"

Steph shook her head bitterly. "Drinking somewhere. *Blowing it up.*"

The jocks—especially Fiske's players—had been saying this all year, a kind of a catchall phrase to be uttered when somebody dropped their lunch tray or was climbing through the sunroof of a moving car.

"You aren't drinking with him?" Steph was no keg-stand champ, but Eric had seen her with beer at parties.

"Not when he's like this," she said. "He wants tonight to be huge."

"Huge?"

"He has these grandiose ideas about prom—what's supposed to happen at prom. And what I want is irrelevant."

Eric tugged his rented shoes underneath himself to stay off her dress, hesitant to venture too far down this conversational road. When a boy and girl met at such a loggerheads on prom night, didn't it almost have to involve...?

He said neutrally, "People build up prom in their heads. It's crazy."

"I know, I mean I'm the same." Steph wiped tears with her

palm, preserving her wrist corsage. "I had this perfect dinner planned at Oceanique. I wanted it to be special. We doubled with Becky and Jim, and of course they show up trashed. They aren't dating—just another party night. But Doug's right there with them, tipping vodka into everybody's water. He and Jim spelled out 'ETHS' with Vietnamese spring rolls."

"Where is he now?"

"Oh, they were off in the parking lot. Something about a crate of weasels, or greased pig. I tried not to hear."

"Not a chinchilla?"

Steph chuckled wetly at the reference to Mr. Glanville's class pet. "Let's hope." Her eyes cleared as they shared a smile. "Sometimes I just do not understand Doug. He was *all over* me in the car. But once I straightened out my skirt and said I wanted to go in? Some switch flipped in his head. All he cared about was finding his pals."

Eric felt his teeth grinding. Why did she stay with him? After the famous blown kiss to the New Trier cheerleader, and sketchy timing of his hookup with Becky Brindle vis-à-vis his and Steph's junior hiatus, and, more generally, crap like this?

He would ask himself the same question seven years later when, standing at a bus stop in Haight-Ashbury, he received the mass e-mail announcing Steph's engagement. Wait, *what*? He had heard they had rekindled postcollege, but what about those rumors of Doug's "wild period" at Northwestern? Did Steph not care that he had dated eight of the twelve *Women of NU* calendar girls? Or capsized a Coast Guard dinghy with the wake of his frat mate's dad's speedboat?

The answer, of course—both times, every time—was that he was Doug Reece. The Golden Boy. Whose good was so good nobody cared about the bad.

"Where's Tara?" Eric heard through his miffed-at-the-world haze.

"Huh?"

"Tara. Your date?"

He had forgotten. Tara was probably leaning against a wall with crossed ankles, scanning gym entrances for him. One day Tara Parsons—future second-chair violinist for the Chicago

Symphony Orchestra—would enter Eric's pantheon of could've-beens, bestowed with a signature outfit (jean shorts/white socks) and theme song ("Who Knew" by Pink). Tonight, though, sitting knee-to-knee with Steph Mill in a pool of melted chiffon, she could only be an afterthought.

"Uh, she was hanging with friends," he lied.

Steph turned her head askance.

"They got talking about PSATs. Y'know, sophomore stuff," Eric said, then in a rush of bravery: "Hey do you wanna go outside? Get away, go someplace?"

His brain ran forward ten ways at once—staring up at the moon, flat on their backs in the track and field pit; a jaunt downtown ending with a teeth-chattering ride on the Navy Pier Ferris wheel; an unlikely powwow at Denny's with his fellow mathletes wherein Steph was won over by the true hearts of her social inferiors... Any number of geek-rescues-prom-queen (a title she had, in fact, gained two hours earlier) scenarios were possible, if she only said yes.

But she didn't. So they stayed on the cold tile of Shipley's door well.

Eric talked about his father's death, freshman year by heart attack. About drug use he had witnessed, and been frightened by, during his visit to Princeton. About the persistent feeling that all his hard work and academic achievements meant zilch. Had it made him happy? In twenty years, would he cherish his high-school years more than Joe 2.8 GPA, who had spent his weeknights playing Xbox and texting girls? Steph touched his polyester sleeve and cooed about the amazing future waiting for him.

Yeah, yeah, Eric said.

He tiptoed right up to the point of confessing. His voice became croaked, originating from his gut, and a sort of weightless freedom spiraled his head. He cried without realizing it—when a tear splattered his wrist, he looked up to see if it was the school's roof leaking again.

Steph shared doubts too. Surprising ones about her own IQ and ability to prioritize. She talked about her freshman-year relationship with Justin Phyllis, the senior, how foolish and manic and dysfunctional it'd been. As pop tunes drifted in from the gym

—"Breakaway" to Eminem to Gavin DeGraw and everything in between—Eric felt the world teetering. Steph Mills was telling all this stuff *to him*! He listened with liquid eyes, bathing himself in these soulful disclosures. This door well, which they had both trod through a zillion times heading in and out of debate, would forever after occupy a treasured place in Eric's memory.

"Everyone says I'm smart," Steph said as a distant PA voice announced the band would break after its next song. "But only after saying how hard I work."

"I believe that's called 'a compliment.'"

"Not how they say it." She sniffed. "Mr. Fiske is the only one— the only one who ever told me I was special intellectually."

Eric nodded. He wanted with every fiber of his being to say he thought she was special intellectually too—really, truly!—but knew it would sound lame.

"I just work and work," Steph continued, "and sometimes it feels like this massive grind I never even chose. Do you know that feeling?"

He rested his hands on a fold of her dress. There was a body part inside—calf, ankle?—but she did not flinch. "You just go, because you've always gone. It's what you know."

Their eyes locked in a slow, searching dance, and Eric saw plainly that Steph knew. The idle drive-bys of her parents' house. The Top Ten lists he only ever showed his locker mate: *Video Game Franchises I Would Give Up for, Phrases That Would Sound Beautiful from the Lips Of*. All the sleep he had lost lying awake in bed, reliving every glorious second they had shared throughout the school day.

She knew.

Steph Mills leaned close, parted her mouth, and kissed him.

For years afterward, Eric would puzzle over exactly where (lips, cheek, forehead?) and how (passionately, perfunctorily, little brotherly?) Steph had kissed him, because in the next instant, sirens split the air and scrambled everything that'd come before.

One siren turned into many—loud, keening. He and Steph bolted upright. Shrieks came from the direction of the gymnasium. A microphone crackled.

They rushed to join their classmates. Eric's foot was asleep so he hobbled a step behind. As the sirens wailed, his mind raced through possibilities. *A fight? Guns? Some drunk kid pulling out against a red light and getting T-boned?*

Principal Mancini stepped up the bandstand in a tux and half his coat—he kept trying and failing to slip into the second sleeve.

"Everyone remain calm," he called. "Please be calm. There has been an accident, but the paramedics are here and they—"

"Oh God!" a girl shouted, pointing past Mancini.

Then the rest of the students saw.

Fiske had emerged from the gym's visitors' locker-room entrance. He shuffled past the collapsed rafters and over the painted Wildkit, leaving a wet trail. Clothes drenched. Hair clinging like white seaweed to his forehead. Eyes aimed nowhere in terrible incomprehension. The image was so greatly at odds with what Eric was accustomed to—Fiske commanding the halls of ETHS, twelve feet tall—that he felt nauseous.

What happened, Mr. Fiske? Are you okay? Talk to us, Coach Fiske, what's up?

Questions came from all directions. It took several moments for Fiske's haze to lift. Finally, he found himself centered in the dance floor, surrounded by the better part of the student body. The buzz stopped. Mancini watched from the bandstand. The only sounds were water *plops* on hardwood.

Mr. Fiske began to sob. Slow, face-wracking sobs. Eric's fear accelerated. What could this be? What could bring low this Mount of Self Reliance, this teacher who had never projected anything but utter mastery of Life's mysteries?

As details emerged over the next week—that Fiske had discovered Nora Brockert drowned in the lap pool—Eric felt relieved, in all honesty. It was not paradigm shattering to imagine a rebellious girl like Nora meeting such an end. Of course it was sad, of course he felt ripped apart when her mother spoke at a school assembly, at which the sophomore sister Lydia never raised her face from quivering hands. But it didn't topple his worldview. It was tragic, awful. Sometimes the world was tragic and awful.

That night, though, Bob Fiske sobbed with the intensity of one who does not understand the world. On a dance floor that had seen all sorts of regrettable moves, Fiske crumpled and stomped and tore at himself. The gym remained silent, lending a kind of helpless, existential backdrop.

Finally, having exorcised as much anguish as he bodily could, Fiske surveyed the crowd. His eyes didn't pause conspiratorially on Winners—as they sometimes would in lecture—and his chin's tilt showed no hint of superiority.

He took them in with a single, weary sweep. Then left the building.

CHAPTER FIFTEEN

"*How?*" Eric bulged his eyes, attempting to clear out the memory. "Did Becky say how prom was involved?"

Lydia shook her head.

"Was it something with Nora?"

"She didn't say. Mother was pulling me away into the woods."

"Wow." Eric wobbled, then righted himself on their shared log. "Prom."

He wanted to probe but didn't think it wise to delve too deeply, prom having been so traumatic for Lydia. He sat dumbly for several beats before finding a topic to fill the void.

"When Fiske went up to MIT," he tried, "people said he threatened your professor. I was always curious—is that true? Did he really?"

Lydia's black-edged fingernails dragged up her slacks. "I have no idea."

"He never said? Just dealt with the guy, spared you the details?"

Her head whipped up, so quickly Eric felt a flash of fear.

"That's right," she said. "He dealt with it. All by himself. I didn't need help, but he gave it anyway."

She proceeded into an account of the incident that differed greatly from what Eric had understood before. At the time of Fiske's impromptu drive to Cambridge, Lydia had already corresponded with the psych department head about her advisor's unfair deployments. She'd had meetings scheduled with other professors and assurances she would be free to join another group. Two of the papers she would later publish solo had been preliminarily accepted by journals.

"He knew all this," Lydia said. "But it didn't matter, did it?"

Eric stuttered, "Yeah I—I guess."

"He wanted his big fight. His Homeric confrontation."

The skin of her broad, pale forehead seemed unnaturally tight. Again, Eric found himself at a loss, wondering whether this was revisionist history, anger about Autumn's disappearance reflected onto the past, or honest truth. It was undeniable that Fiske strove for white-night heroics when it came to these Winner-in-need situations. Last spring, when he'd flown out to San Francisco to save Paladin, he had set up the Wess Moran meeting without saying a word to Eric.

What does this mean? Clearly Fiske and Lydia did not have the mentor/mentee rapport others assumed. Did this imply anything about his relationship with Autumn? Thinking through the events preceding the disappearances, Eric had been nagged by the possibility Autumn had enticed Fiske, lured him to some nefarious end. The media image of Autumn as Helpless Adoring Pupil had never squared with his own impression. Over coffee, she had seemed shrewd—"Why does your company need to be in San Francisco, or even California?"—and self-aware, and if his interpretation of certain seventh-hour flirtations had not deceived him, more-than-platonically invested in a boy her age.

They walked back to the cabin. Volunteers glanced up from their stoops, perhaps recognizing two principals in the case, whose media coverage had only intensified in the last twenty-four hours. Jane Brockert broke off haranguing an official with the outline of Michigan on his epaulet. Joining her mother, Lydia gave Eric a last cryptic look.

He watched them go, considering.

Did Autumn know that Fiske had discovered her older sister's dead body a decade earlier? She would have been six, seven years old. Would Jane Brockert have told her? Or shielded her from the trauma? Probably shielded. Still, what if Autumn had heard a rumor? The unofficial-official story had always been that Fiske unsuccessfully tried CPR...maybe Autumn didn't buy this. Maybe she had discovered fresh evidence.

But this didn't compute either. Autumn Brockert had not seemed naive over coffee, but neither had she seemed a diabolical psychopath—which she would've had to have been in order to conceal this vendetta from her family and orchestrate such elaborate revenge. Also, the crimes themselves, physically, were a stretch. Overcoming Fiske. Yanking Becky off the cliff. She would have needed an accomplice.

That boy from seventh hour?

Lydia?

He decided to poke around the cabin. There were no volunteers here—the cabin belonged to the professionals—but a perimeter wasn't being enforced so he could move freely, even peer inside through crisscrossing tape. Two technicians in surgical gloves stepped over carpets and overturned furniture, tweezing fibers into bags.

As she was zipping up a sample, one technician caught Eric's eye. He hustled off and, trying to look natural, ambled around back of the cabin. An ash heap was marked off by tiny flags.

In a blink, he remembered the bonfire they had seen but not lingered on yesterday. The police had combed the remnants; tags were visible on some unburnt papers and a cereal box. He tried remembering if there had been other items yesterday. Keys? A thumb drive? Surely anything like that would have been confiscated.

Eric sidestepped the flags and bent low to check the cinders. Most of what remained were charred documents. A stack of graded quizzes...credit card solicitations...a flyer with a smiling treble clef...

There was, near the bottom, a block of papers held together by a fat binder clip. At first, Eric saw just the clip's shiny metal. Then, nudging ashes with his shoe, he noticed the papers. They were barely recognizable as such, a blackened mass of pulp with only a few wavy-crisp edges defining the stack.

He wedged his toe underneath and tried separating the pages.

His shoe passed through without resistance, releasing a puff of soot.

The top sheet alone was legible. Its upper-left corner contained a name, *Vance T____* (the fire had taken the last letters), and its upper-right read, *115,000 words*. The font was large and blocky, monospaced like an old typewriter might produce. Spaced halfway down the page, underlined and all-caps, were the words *ILLUSORY GREATNESSES.*

A title.

Fiske had often talked about wanting to write a novel. He believed composing a story from start to finish to be one of the great endeavors available to Man. "Crafting characters and themes; synthesizing a cohesive symbolism; and then writing the thing, paragraph by paragraph, line by line, word by blasted word: name me a whiter whale." He would casually reference an outline kicking around his head or joke about repackaging Russian master plots in zombie/vampire YA skins.

Had he finally done it?

Eric's head buzzed at the possibility, and with the questions it raised. Who was "Vance T____"? A pseudonym? What sort of a title was *Illusory Greatnesses*? It sounded high-minded and wispy, Fiske to the core, but how would a story fall out of it? *Would* he write a story, an actual yarn with twists and big moments, or would a novel of Fiske's revolve around ideas? Did he plan to publish it? Was it even finished?

But the biggest question by far: Why was it sitting in a pile of ashes? Had he read through and decided it was all garbage? Had he faced sudden, paralyzing doubts?

Eric thought about yet another piece of advice Fiske had given last spring. He had just handed over a copy of *The Man of 10,000 Crushes*, explaining it was rough, probably tripe, bunch of emotions and situations his brain had puked out via keyboard, whatever.

Fiske had fluted his lips seriously. "It's none of that, Eric. What it is is sacred." He hefted the pages between them. "Every word is an expression of yourself. An artifact of your soul."

And Eric knew, recalling this, that Bob Fiske would never have burned his own manuscript.

Eric returned to Chicago feeling jumbled, feverish. Between the manuscript and revelation that prom factored in (at least according to Becky, by way of Lydia), it seemed likely the truth was more complicated than indicated by Fiske's suicide note.

Could it be fake? Was somebody trying to suppress *Illusory Greatnesses*? Then why involve Autumn Brockert? Unless Autumn was herself the suppressor. But did that really jibe with a long-con revenge theory? The clues were disparate and without a clear organizing principle. Every time he tried shoehorning them all together, one squiggled out of place.

Underlying all, sinister and steady, was an intuition that the whole mess involved him. That he was in jeopardy, would pay a price if the truth failed to out.

Droid rang as the hotel came into view over the trees. He checked the screen.

EVNSTON PLC DPT, FRANK WRIGHT.

He considered letting it ring but decided he couldn't risk missing some break in the investigation. "Hello, Eric Pinkersby."

"Where are you?"

The question pounced from the phone's speaker.

"Driving," he said. "In my car."

"Near your hotel?"

Eric paused, the detective's breath heavy over the line. The Marriott sign loomed two stoplights ahead. "Why?"

"I think you know, Mr. Pinkersby. I think you know exactly why. Cisco got back to us today with the contents of your text message to Bob Fiske."

"I told you, I never sent a—"

"*They found out about Pictured Rocks. Heading your way, ETA 45 minutes.*"

Eric muttered a few indecipherable words, panic exploding his ability to make sense. In the haze of prom and *Illusory Greatnesses*, the alleged texts to Fiske had been written to ROM and wiped from Eric's short-term memory. Vaguely, he had hoped they would fade away, the cops would find a logging glitch or decide they didn't matter.

Now it was undeniable: someone was framing him.

Wright continued, "I'm still in Michigan, but we got a black-and-white waiting outside your hotel. If you go there directly and surrender, we take you in easy. No cuffs, no popping flashbulbs."

Eric felt dizzy. "Listen, I honest to God did not send that text. But I have a lead for you. A couple. Prom was involved—senior prom. Also I found a manuscript in that bonfire behind the cabin."

"Uh-huh."

"I think Fiske finished a novel. I think somebody burned it."

"*Illusory Greatnesses*?"

"Yeah, how did you—"

"We saw, Mr. Pinkersby."

"Then you know! You know he wrote a book, which changes everything."

"We found burned checks too. Copy of the *Racing Form.* Nobody here figures horse-fixing was a motive."

"But—but aren't you going to follow up and see if—"

"We're confident of the facts. Come down to the station and we'll talk books if you like. We can talk about your book. *Man of a Thousand Crushes.*"

"Ten thousand," Eric corrected automatically. The traffic light turned. His foot raised off the brake, and he began drifting toward the hotel.

"Come on in," Wright repeated. "You got information? We'll take a look. We'll consider it. Just come in. Trust me, you do not wanna do this the hard way."

Now Eric was a block from the Marriott, driving fifteen in a thirty-five, traffic streaming past, chrome and glass blurring in his periphery. As he cleared a Kroger on the right, the check-in circle drive became visible. Waiting under the awning, just as Wright had said, was a police cruiser. That instantly recognizable Crown Vic, shield on door, red/blue sirens up top. Motor running.

He turned left.

"I don't think so."

Over the line, baffled silence.

"You don't *think* so?" Wright finally said. "This situation is not voluntary, Mr. Pinkersby. I am doing you a favor—a very big favor—by allowing you to surrender. You got a livelihood and a reputation to uphold. I don't want to damage those but I will, you don't gimme a choice."

Eric considered a few responses but decided none would help his cause. So he hung up.

Damn, he thought, accelerating. *Damn, damn, damn. What madness is this?*

CHAPTER SIXTEEN

E ric drove twenty minutes, distancing himself from the Marriott. Detective Wright called three more times. Each call Eric ignored. Like a squirrel wary of traffic, he avoided highways and major thoroughfares. His logic was at once decisive and gauzy. First, he concluded he should run for Canada, then that it was enough to lay low until the police figured out their mistake, then that he could still surrender at the Marriott: for all Wright knew, he had been downtown and driven straight there.

When a ragtop-ful of kids flashed thumbs-up at a stoplight, it occurred to Eric that the Hummer was conspicuous.

He turned down the next alley. Ditched the Hummer by a dumpster, walked back to front through a shoe store, exited onto Ashland Ave.

Inhaled deeply. He was now a fugitive, possessing only the clothes on his back and contents of his pockets. Thirty-five dollars. Droid. Keys to the Hummer, which he presently pushed through the slotted mouth of a USPS mail drop to no clear benefit.

Crap.

Last weekend, literally seven days ago, he had been drinking Negronis on the skydeck of Elon Musk's place in Pac Heights. Batting around the feasibility of space elevators. On the cusp of ungodly money from the Paladin IPO. He shuddered to imagine the conversations Justin Isrickov would soon be having with those "institutional folks" today. The California teachers' union was going to be *thrilled* about entrusting its members' retirements to an accused murderer.

What hope did he have of proving he hadn't killed Becky Brindle? They had the texts. His admitted presence at the cliff. Those apparently unassailable marks on Becky's wrists. Who wouldn't send him up the river?

Wright wasn't being a bastard. He was being a perfectly predictable agent of law enforcement.

Crap.

Eric reached back in memory for other times he'd been up against it. With Paladin. When his jerk boss at Facebook had taken credit for his optimization that shaved ninety-three milliseconds off page load. Each time he had skulked around a few days, letting stray thoughts coalesce to a plan, then picked himself up out of the dirt.

"In life you have one, and only one, true advocate," Fiske would say. "Yourself."

Eric walked into the first Starbucks he saw—roughly twenty-five yards away—and ordered a triple espresso. Gulped half in one swallow, the rest on a stool near the exit. He began again to wrestle the case's conflicting info shards before realizing this was the wrong approach. He had been focusing on the top of the stacktrace, twenty thousand feet in the clouds, instead of debugging at the source.

What was the fundamental driver of his problem?

Becky's fall.

If he could crack that mystery—how/whether she had been pushed, who might have done it—he had a fighting chance. He didn't need to solve the Kennedy assassination.

Code small, code careful.

Moment by hazy moment, he returned mentally to Pictured Rocks. He seized upon each detail—tree bark, flashes of color—and tunneled in, stretching the image wider like a pizza-maker rolling out dough, working the outer edges for information, for those nuggets his brain had saved to disk without fully indexing...

He worked and worked, and focused, and thought, and refocused, until he had something.

Droid still had Ramona's number in Favorites. Eric tapped the icon and raised the phone to his ear, leaving Starbucks, preferring to place his call from the sidewalk bustle of Rogers Park.

She answered, "What in the world has compelled you to call me?"

Eric dodged back from the phone like it'd bitten off his earlobe. "Can't you just answer 'hello' like a normal person?"

"I have caller ID. Every modern mobile device has caller ID. What's the point of pretending I don't know the identity of whatever douchebag is attempting to contact me?"

Eric flubbed his lips, already regretting the call. "Ramona, I'm not fishing for drama. Really. I'm calling as a friend."

"That's not surprising, given your emphatic opt-out of the alternative, higher-commitment association we previously enjoyed."

"Please, can we just—"

"At least *I* enjoyed, for the most part, despite your hopeless devotions to LISP and eMacs. Apparently you found me annoying. No wait, how did you phrase it? 'Focused on my own neuroses to an oppressive, joy-killing extent'?"

"Which, as I laboriously pointed out, is exactly like me. The whole breakup was on me, my issues."

"Don't coddle me. I need these personal critiques. How else will I improve?"

Eric rubbed the bridge of his nose. "You win: I'm awful. Listen Ramona, I'm in some trouble. I need help. I need somebody who knows dogs."

For once, Ramona was silent.

"The police—I dunno if you've been following the news—but the police think I pushed this woman off a cliff. I didn't. Someone else did. And I'm pretty sure they have a little white dog."

"Oka*aay*."

"Just listen. Right before Becky fell, I saw this dog. Totally out of place, this cute little dog running around the forest."

"Interesting." Her flat Portland accent sapped the word of all meaning. "So what is it you want me to do? ID the dog? Draw a police sketch?"

"IDing would be perfect." Hearing a scoff, Eric added, "I'm fully aware this sucks, okay? All my options suck here. This is the absolute least-suckiest available one."

He told what he remembered. The white-ish flash (fur?), a black button (nose?), gray streaks about the forehead and sides—this last visual clue having been teased from deep within his subconscious. When Ramona said nothing, Eric filled the void by expanding on these scant details, guessing at a size (*eighteen inches?*), saying the markings and head shape resembled a wolf's. *A miniature wolf's? If that made any sense to her?*

"Look, I'm desperate," he said. "Any ideas you have, anything at all."

Ramona asked, almost grudgingly, "What about the paws?"

"Uh...yes. It had paws."

"No, *the size*. Were they in proportion or did they seem too big for the body?"

Eric squeezed shut his eyes, focusing, tweezing at threads of memory. "I'll go with big. Yeah, no—they were big. It seemed sort of unsteady."

This was a gross extrapolation but Eric didn't care. He just wanted to give her some positive information, something to nudge the situation forward, or sideways, anyway but where it was currently heading.

Over the line came a series of thoughtful *tocks*, which Eric knew to be Ramona's thumb ring against the outside of her cheek.

"Sounds like a malamute pup," she murmured. "Were the ears triangular?"

"Yes!"

"Pointed up from the skull?"

"Yes, yes!" Extrapolating further but whatever. "They stuck straight up like arrows!"

"Okay. Then yeah, you saw an Alaskan malamute puppy. Adults weigh eighty-five, ninety pounds, so it must've been a pup."

Eric uppercut the air in front of him, then shadowboxed the facade of a Vietnamese banh mi joint. He strutted coltishly another block before losing enthusiasm near an upscale pottery boutique. So...the white-ish flash was an Alaskan malamute puppy. Assuming valid extrapolations, et al. How exactly did that help?

"Does anybody maintain a registry of purebred puppies?" he asked. "American Kennel Club, would they have a list?"

"Of every Alaskan Malamute pup in existence?"

The tone in which Ramona asked made plain Eric's stupidity.

He sighed and was about to segue off the call when she said, "AKC does keep a registry of breeders, though. Malamutes are fairly rare. It's conceivable you could check local breeders and figure out which placed litters recently."

"Where? Where?" He switched to speaker and opened Droid's browser. "AKC.com?"

"Dot org," Ramona corrected.

In seconds, he had tapped past the busy homepage and down a few unhelpful nav paths, then—finding no registry at AKC.org itself—stumbled upon a list of breed associations, which contained a link to AlaskanMalamute.org. Here he quickly found listings...*124 entries...filter by country...USA...filter by state...IL...loading, loading...*

Six hits.

"Woot!" he cried. "There's only six, perfect. Awesome. I'll start calling right now."

"*Excelente*," Ramona said. "Best of luck escaping the yoke of national infamy."

Eric had punched four digits of the first breeder's number before his brain processed the edge in his ex's voice. "Hey, thanks, Ramona. Thanks a ton—I completely owe you."

"Not at all, no worries."

"Maybe we could, uh, I mean, once I get myself out of this mess, it'd be great to meet up. Maybe tea at Burma Superstar, or try the uni at—"

"Spare me," she cut in. "Last night I screwed a cricket player from Mumbai. He does frontend UI for Oracle."

"Oh."

"Figured I'd celebrate our unanticipated breakup with some wild cubicle sex."

Eric, waiting at an intersection beside three teens on bikes, coughed away from the speaker. "Well, uh...great talking to you."

His mind snagged briefly on the mental image, accompanied by horribly stereotypical Bollywood sitar music, before returning to the breeder list.

Breeders, judging by the hour's phone experience Eric accrued with them, were a quirky lot. One woman yelled at him for calling rather than contacting her via her website form. Another lectured him on bloodlines, the importance of muzzle breadth, the ability of a "true Malamute man" to gauge a whole lineage by one dog's stance.

In the end, of four Chicagoland breeders Eric spoke with (two others had disconnected numbers), only a husband/wife team by the name of Beyers had placed a litter in the last six months. Way out in DeKalb.

How was he going to get to DeKalb?

The El rumbled by overhead, advertising itself with a *wheeze-clang* approach to a nearby station. Tempting—and not just for its romantic echoes of *While You Were Sleeping* and *Risky Business*. Those smelly, crowded trains meant anonymity, a way through whatever dragnet Wright was constructing.

Could you even take the El out to DeKalb, though? Public transit inside the city limits might be anonymous, but in the burbs? Not so much. He would likely have to connect to a remote bus line outside of rush hour. If his photograph had been circulated to transit employees or blared on cable news, any bus driver could do him in.

He needed a car.

Searching *best way to hotwire a car* produced a bounty of methods. Some assumed extraordinary knowledge of electrical wiring. Others wanted you to blast the steering column with a power drill. The easiest still required tools Eric didn't have, so he walked until he found a hardware store.

He cruised the aisles, praying there was no checkout algorithm for catching hotwirers—the way he had heard chemical retailers programmatically nab basement drug cookers. Okay, item number one: slotted screwdriver. Easy. Item number two: insulated gloves. Also easy, $4.99, hanging from clips off a cardboard display. Item number three: wire strippers, which took more consideration as the store stocked several types. When Eric checked Droid for clarification, his eye happened upon an asterisk in the article's title. He scrolled down.

Please note this method, as with all hotwiring methods, only works for cars built prior to the late 1990s. Newer vehicles contain security measure that make hotwiring difficult if not impossible.

The webpage date, printed just below: *June 2002.*

Piss.

PISS!!!

How many twenty-year-old cars were sitting around parked on the North Side of Chicago?

Eric's head flopped forward. He tossed the screwdriver into a bin of bolts. Dropped the gloves to the floor.

He was out of his depths. Way the hell out, Mariana Trench out. A few years back, Eric had tried coding a cell phone MMOG in a weekend. Not some text-based puzzler. Oh no: an actual World of Warcraft–lite, blockbuster game. He dove headfirst, modeling the characters server side, writing his game loop in iOS and Android emulators simultaneously because of course the game needed to be cross-platform at launch.

What silly, wasteful arrogance. The mechanics of drawing a 3-D game world baffled him, and even after he capitulated to using a game engine—a shortcut he'd refused to consider when cracking his laptop Friday night—the project proved a boondoggle. He spent all day Sunday making a red dot (playerX) cross a blue screen (theWorld) when you jiggled your phone.

Then, of course, his overreach had only cost him a weekend. Now it meant precious minutes as the police were hunting him.

Back to the drawing board, he searched for other ways of procuring a car. There was urban legend stuff about lifting one off a dealership lot, somebody in Colorado who could start Acuras using bobby pins. One poster claimed to be stranded in a hostile country facing persecution; after the requisite *yeah right, pal* replies, someone suggested looking under fenders and wheel wells for a hidden spare key.

Eric perked up. Now this had promise. It was simple and intuitive, involving neither sonar nor inside knowledge of Henry Ford's numerology.

Worth a shot.

He left the hardware store and walked Sheridan, peering along chassis underbellies. He noticed a bump below the fender of a Mazda and dark spots near two other cars' front tires, but upon closer inspection, none resembled the oblong key holders he was hoping for.

Droid rang as he was waiting to cross Leland Ave.

EVNSTON PLC DPT: FRANK WRIGHT.

At the same time, a black-and-white cruiser slowed through the intersection. The cop dragged the steering wheel in a lazy turn, head swiveling.

Eric dashed behind a bus schedule. Did they have his location? They must be zeroing in on his phone, triangulating pings from different cell towers...and here he'd been surfing away like some tween hungry for One Direction gossip.

(Oh no, no, no, no time for you, soaring "Story of My Life" chorus!)

Panicked, he shut off Droid. Full power down. He joined the mob waiting for an approaching bus, then slipped away as the others boarded, keeping the accordion behemoth between himself and the cruiser. Then ducked into a Sprint store. Strolling between smartwatch and tablet kiosks, parrying salesmen, looking out the windows for police.

After five minutes, seeing none, Eric headed back outside.

He decided to shift his search for a spare key to side streets, which had just as many parked cars but fewer watchful eyes. He ambled past a church and several apartment buildings, craning his neck. He tripped over a hydrant. Stepped in a slushy pothole that dirtied his jeans to the knee.

Finally, on a midnight-blue sedan in a private drive, he found it: a metallic pillbox set inside the left wheel well. Eric only saw one edge, but that straight segment in an otherwise round cavity was enough. He strode forward, and, yep, the box contained a key fob.

He glanced up the block. Sucked in a breath. Tapped the doors unlocked.

The car, a Toyota Corolla, unlocked. He stepped in. His first grand theft auto.

Yee-haw.

CHAPTER SEVENTEEN

Eric felt liberated by the smaller vehicle after two days driving the Hummer, confident of its dimensions, snapping off go-cart turns. The owner's possessions did creep him out. Reading monocle. Newspaper. Furr's Cafeteria receipt. The first dozen blocks he kept glancing in the rearview, expecting some grandpa chasing on foot, some Larry David-cum-Terminator-1000 shaking a liquid metal fist at him.

DeKalb was a solid two hours away. Exiting I-88, he followed a dusty two-lane due south to Lynch Road. He was leaning out the window squinting at the half-rotted numbers of a rural mailbox when the first howl came.

"Roo roo, roo roo. Roo! Roo*oooooo!*"

He whirled. He had been looking at the wrong property, a stately ranch with a pillared porch. The dogs lived across the street at a dilapidated earth-contact home peeking out from the base of a hill like Oscar the Grouch from his trash can. Siding cobbled together from irregular shingles and swaths of corrugated metal. A van in gravel between rusted Fieros. A pack of adult Malamutes massed at the fence line, ears flat, eyes dead-level serious.

Unlike Ramona, unlike Becky Brindle, Eric had no love for dogs.

He cut the wheel and barely made the Beyers' drive without

falling into the shoulder ditch. Dogs surged up the sides of the Corolla, nails heavy on the glass. One yipped around to the front and refused to move.

Eric revved the engine.

The dog growled and worried its paws deeper into gravel, full-on Tiananmen Square. Eric eased off the brake.

"Down boy," he tried through the windshield. "Just here to ask a few questions."

When the bumper brushed Tiananmen Dog's coat, the rest went ballistic, jumping halfway up the hood, racing laps around the car. Eric instinctively locked the doors and wrapped both arms overhead.

He stayed in tornado-drill position until a whistle sounded from the house. A scraggly man emerged swinging a pair of buckets. The dogs ran whimpering to the man, who carried the buckets to a trough and dumped their schloppy contents.

Eric parked, then joined the man a safe distance from the ravenous dogs.

"Mr. Beyers?" he said.

"Winston," the man corrected.

He extended his hand, and Eric, trying to ignore the brown morsels on his work gloves, shook it.

"My name is Eric Pinkersby, we spoke on the phone earlier?"

"As I recall. What can I do for ya?"

One dog had eaten its fill and now rushed up to Eric and the breeder, lips smacking. Winston edged his thumb along its lower jaw, causing the dog to close its mouth and mew. When Eric tried the same, it snapped.

"*Duke!*" Winston said, then turned for Eric's reply.

"I believe I may have found a puppy that came from your kennel."

"That right? What makes you think she's ours?"

Eric was prepared for the question, having poured over the Beyers' bare-bones website and consulted further with Ramona. "She has the snow nose, which I know your dogs tend to show. Also a little sable in her undercoat markings."

The words couldn't have felt any hollower coming out. Still, Winston stroked his chin.

"Hm. Possible."

"I just—you know, obviously feel terrible for the owner and was hoping you could help me track them down."

"Bring 'er?"

"The dog? Oh no, no. She's, um, home. At my home. Where I live."

The breeder kinked his brow. "Why didn't you bring her?"

"Because I wasn't sure, uh"—Eric fingered the seam of his pocket—"how she'd do riding in my car."

Winston Beyers regarded the Corolla. "No Cadillac, but I imagine there's room enough."

"True. But my interior, it's vinyl—I dunno what all fabrics she's accustomed to."

The man kept looking at the stolen car, mistrustfully, it seemed to Eric.

"Anyway," Eric pushed on, "I assume you keep records on the folks who purchase puppies?"

By degrees, Winston moved his gaze back to Eric. He held his visitor's eyes for a tick, then disappeared back into his ramshackle home. Probably going for his shotgun.

Now Duke returned with two friends, all three of their noses homing in on Eric's crotch. He withdrew a step, then stiffly held his ground. *Remember: dogs feed off fear.*

Did they? He should confirm on Snopes. He'd never understood these animals, how people could stalk right up to one they had never met and offer their fleshy forearm. How're you supposed to know the tame ones from Michael Vick's dogs?

At last, after Eric had squirmed away from so many sniffs his insteps were becoming sore, Winston appeared with a spiral journal.

"Last litter whelped in July. Outta Yasmine, sire Moonhawk."

He showed Eric the page. Listed in neat, amply spaced handwriting were eight names.

"Saw Georgia the other day, so it's not her." He gestured to the house, where his wife stood on the welcome mat with a handset. "Like us to call the others?"

"Oh, don't bother," Eric said. "I can take it from here."

"Sure?"

"Positive." Whipping out Droid, copying over contact info. "I'd like to surprise them."

This made no sense—why? wouldn't he have to reach them by phone first?—but Winston Beyers did not object. Eric returned to the Corolla and pinned his phone to the steering wheel, scouring the list. Several were nonstarters. Three in Western Illinois, one Indiana. (He was working off the assumption, possibly erroneous, that Becky's murderer hailed from Chicago.) The rest he called from the road.

Yes, hi, sorry to trouble you. I'm from the National Alaskan Malamute Society, and we're conducting a color survey...

A woman from Glencoe had a sable, as did another in Hyde Park. Bob and Janice Hopper of Schaumburg had a predominantly white puppy, but the quavering voice that answered sounded like a seventy- or eighty-year-old man's.

Which left a single possibility: Janine Rhimes of Orland Hills.

It was late by the time Eric reached Janine Rhimes's neighborhood, another two hours' freeway zip bisecting outer Chicago suburbs. First-floor windows were dark. Nothing seemed afoot. Juvenile trees lined the streets at regular intervals, nursery tape still around their trunks. A booth and automated card reader, but no physical gate, marked the subdivision entrance; Eric drifted through warily, expecting spikes to pop the Corolla's tires at any moment. None did, but those mounted boxes surely snapped his picture.

He took a while finding Yardley Court, navigating by handwritten directions. (He had banished Droid to a pocket on fresh triangulation concerns.) At one stop sign, he jumped when a line of shadows rushed across the street, but relaxed on noticing that the last—stumbling in the middle of the intersection—carried three rolls of toilet paper. Kids TPing their friends.

Now he made the left, then 0.3 miles to the right, then another right in 0.2...squinting at the green sign, which was not at all perpendicular to the road—did that say *Yardley*? Yes! Yes, it did...now checking mailboxes for numbers...1382, 1384...some frilly, illegible calligraphic number...1402, *whoops*, back her up...there, 1392!

The house was a two-story saltbox. A pair of kids' bikes faced each other on the porch, whose railing still featured a string of Christmas lights.

Eric had felt guardedly hopeful after speaking with Janine Rhimes. Her puppy was indeed white. She did have a husband—Eric didn't figure the pusher for a female—but attempts to tease out his occupation and/or background had failed. ("Why does the National Alaskan Malamute Society care whether my husband works in law enforcement?") Eric believed if he could get eyes on the dog, perhaps learn something about the family circumstances, a theory might suggest itself.

A long shot? Clearly. At this point, that was the only kind available.

Now Eric mused what sort of person might have killed Becky Brindle. If the perpetrator lived here, it could not be the parent of a counselee: these children were grade-schoolers and lived far outside ETHS territory besides. What if Becky had had an affair with the husband? A jealous wife? Maybe he should put Janine Rhymes back on the table. But why would she have chosen to do it up in Pictured Rocks?

He was strumming the Corolla's gearshift, contemplating sneaking up the side of the house, when a patrol car appeared in his mirrors.

Crap!

It inched ahead with only parking lights. The beam of a flashlight wagged first from the driver's side, then passenger's, then back again.

The cop was a block and a half away. Eric did not like his chances in a car chase and knew that if he waited much longer to try escaping on foot, he risked being seen.

Quietly as his fingers could manage, he opened the door. Lowered his feet heel first to the pavement. Shouldered the door closed a centimeter at a time, then took off in a hunched tiptoe-run for a yew hedgerow.

Five endless seconds later, he threw himself to the ground. He lay still a few beats before crawling forward to a gap in the prickly cover.

The cruiser kept coming. Its driver swung wide of the Corolla, flashing his (a mustache and white or Latino face made Eric think male) beam into the back seat. He did not linger, though, continuing another block on Yardley before turning left.

Eric exhaled. He did not have many thoughts in his head—coherent ones, anyhow—but felt strongly that he should get farther off the street, and fast.

The house next to the Rhimes' had a *FOR SALE* sign and no cars in the driveway. He ran that way before his mind could counter-argue, elbows flailing, ears screaming with wind. He stutter-stepped at the porch—where the hell was he going?—then dashed up to the front door and tugged.

Locked.

Of course it's locked, you idiot. It's for sale, not a flophouse.

He sprinted back down the porch, taking the last step short and narrowly avoiding a face-plant, and veered around back of the house. The yard fell off sharply after a corner chimney. Eric's knees were rusty hinges as he lunged down the grade. He passed underneath a raised deck, breathing hard, and stopped to kneel at the base of a four-by-four post.

From here, Eric could see the back of Janine Rhimes's property. Swing set, keg-barrel smoker. There was a utility shed near the fence line. *Do I run over and check for weapons?* If this person was collaborating with Fiske, could Autumn Brockert's body be buried here? Maybe he should go looking for fresh dirt.

The patrol car cruised by several times, always just before Eric mustered the courage to break cover. They were definitely searching, the flashlight zagging out either side, and he feared the radius was getting tighter. He reassured himself with the thought it was just the one policeman. If the authorities knew he was here, a fugitive in the ultra-publicized Autumn Brockert case, wouldn't it be *Smokey and the Bandit*? Sirens and flashing blue lights?

Now the patrol car eased to a stop behind the Corolla.

He's running the plate!

Sure enough, the mustached cop stepped out of his vehicle, bent at the Corolla's bumper, and scribbled in a flip-over pad, the notation taking approximately the right amount of time for a seven-digit plate number. His only hope was that Larry David / T-1000 hadn't reported the car stolen.

Not likely.

Eric clutched the four-by-four post, landscape pebbles stabbing his knees. He felt a moment of relief when the cop slipped a ticket under the Corolla's windshield wiper, then panicked anew realizing the cop had not run the plate yet. *You moron, like his pad has some magical link to the database?*

He needed to move. Now. This second. He needed to get off Yardley.

There was no fence between the deck he was hiding beneath and the next property. Eric waited for the cop to drive off, then sprinted through the backyards to the cover of another deck.

These neighbors were home; mud underneath a play structure looked freshly trodden. Fortunately, they had a large, two-tier deck, and Eric felt pretty good about his hiding spot, recessed by a few stairs, nestled between a storage ottoman and woodbox planter.

He peered back across the lawn at Yardley. The patrol car did not reappear for five minutes.

Prone, going on twenty-six hours without sleep, he struggled to keep focus on the very real danger he faced and found himself drifting...drowsily considering the play structure...looked fun...a Folgers tin, probably full of screws and nails...eyelids heavy...these sweet, comfy woodchips...

"WE HAVE YOUR LOCATION! SURRENDER NOW. STEP FORWARD AND SURRENDER!"

The order had bleated from what sounded like a bullhorn, and close. Eric popped to his knees—awake in a heartbeat—and whipped his gaze from side to side.

To the left of the Rhimes' home, two running cops. Faces pinched, pounding over grass. Moving diagonally this way.

Eric felt every nerve in his body flare. He considered busting into the house. There would be kids inside he'd scare half to death, and what would he do with the parents? Take them hostage? How? With what? No time to ask Droid *that*.

Out of ideas, he tensed to a ball and prayed for invisibility.

He began to wonder what kind of cell he would get. He imagined that if you ran, they treated you as badly as the law allowed. A naked toilet in the corner, urine—or worse—seeping to a center drain. Cellmates with menacing gold-tooth grins and neck tats, rocking up from a cement bench to greet him.

Eric braced, and prayed, and braced some more.

Nothing happened. No gun leveled at his eyes; no hands gripped the scruff of his shoulders. The sound of rushing boots receded.

He peeked. The cops were moving away from him, flashlights trained on a brick-red house in the same block. They disappeared behind a boat trailer. Scuffling noises carried through the neighborhood. Then one cop emerged with a half-empty bag of toilet paper rolls.

"Five hundred bucks a tree," said the other, shoving a high-school kid from behind. "Hope you been saving up those allowances."

CHAPTER EIGHTEEN

E ric slept fitfully, a series of catnaps interspersed with web searches about Janine Rhimes. (The Great TP Scare had convinced him he was being paranoid about triangulation; for the police to track him in real time, they would need warrants and packet sifters and all sorts of jazz you couldn't summon with a snap of the fingers.) He learned that Mrs. Rhimes had been married eight years and recently served on the Kirby School District board. She had received a commendation from U of I for hospice work. She may or may not have finished a half marathon in the top decile of her age/gender group—the results page listed a *J. Rhimes*, but thirty-two to thirty-seven felt too old for the rest of the bio.

Not much to go on. The hospice stuff didn't read *VINDICTIVE MISTRESS KILLER*, but who knew? Circumstances changed people.

The horizon was still black when the sound of a door seal roused Eric. He found his glasses in his shirt pocket. An elderly woman stepped onto the deck carrying a tuft-faced dog. As she lowered the little goblin to the ground to do its business, its hyperactive eyes found Eric. He leaped off the deck into a bed of sharp rosebushes.

He swallowed a *Yow!*, flattening to the ground. The dog whimpered overhead, to which the woman scolded, "Now, now, what would you do with a chipmunk anyhow?"

Finally, the dog gave up the scent, peed, and was taken back inside.

Eric was considering his next move—return to the vacant house, check on the Corolla?—when the rumble of a garage door sounded from 1392 Yardley. He bolted out into the yard for a better view, risking exposure to any number of neighbors, and knelt by a stone birdbath to watch.

That's it!

Urging down the driveway, tugging against a thin red leash, came a white fur ball with big paws and pointy ears. When it sniffed the sidewalk, Eric got a clear look.

The close-set eyes, fluffy muzzle. It jibed with his memory, or at least the mental image he'd arrived at after the jostling of Wright and Ramona and his own desperate imagination.

Janine Rhymes's presumed husband trailed the puppy, jerking it away from plants and a wiffle ball. Eric spotted a tie knot above the collar of his coat, wingtips below his pants. A formal occupation, then. Not a laborer, not a teacher, unless some sort of stuffy throwback. Did this make him less of a suspect? Not necessarily. A security professional might wear a tie.

Eric moved closer, leaving the cover of the birdbath. He was out in the open now and visible to any early riser looking out their kitchen window. He didn't care.

The man walked a few sidewalk panels past the neighbor's drive, then turned back. Eric squinted at the face. Ruddy. Goatee. Late twenties? Light hair that might curl if allowed to grow. Vaguely grumpy, but maybe that was just annoyance with the dog.

Eric inched even closer.

He was physically on the Rhimes' property now. He strained to make something of the man's features, feeling the effort in his temples. The guy was built. Turning up the drive, he yanked the straying puppy off three of its four paws with a mere forearm twitch.

Had Eric seen him before? In a crowd? Out the Hummer's

side-view mirror? He let the face waft through his innermost thoughts...

Nada.

The dog and its walker disappeared back into the garage.

What should he do? What *could* he do? Make a citizen's arrest? Call Detective Wright again? Wright wouldn't give a rip. Eric's theory was no more believable now than when he had babbled it yesterday, right before running.

The Puppy Theory was dead. Had there even been a puppy? Hell, he didn't know anymore. He felt so tired and down and frazzled that nothing was certain. Maybe the white flash up at Pictured Rocks, which had spawned this whole nutball chase, had been a cloud.

He slumped to the ground. His jeans' butt sank into three inches of mud.

Then, in the middle of his darkest dread, a fresh rumble sounded from 1392 Yardley. In another moment, Eric saw what Janine Rhimes's husband drove.

PART THREE

CHAPTER NINETEEN

Steph considered keeping the girls home from school Monday. After the nightmare the Brockerts had endured, were still enduring, all she wanted was to cuddle on the couch and read *Frog and Toad* and tell her children they were the most precious people in her whole world and always would be, no matter what they became, no matter how big or small their lives turned out. She wanted to grip Morgan's tiny feet and piston those chunky legs until she giggled. To make Ella a healthy breakfast—who knew what she'd conned Grandma into feeding her—and chat forever about horses and fairies.

In the end, though, Steph decided normalcy would be better.

"This was just another weekend with your mom," Doug said. "Same as our Cozumel trip. They'll sense if we make it into a big deal."

True. And she did need to get back to the office. Gordon Foods was demanding a campaign review today. *We're unsure about the value prop of these exorbitant outlays,* they had e-mailed, a phrase containing at least four words you never liked hearing from clients. Rich Hauser wanted to plot a response at eight a.m. sharp.

Morgan woke on schedule, but Ella slept late. Steph let her. With Doug gone early to tend a Swiss derivatives swap, she set the baby up on her mobile mat and prepped cereal and OJ, and lunch/bottles for Blue Hills, and e-mailed Chad Nimms her thoughts on Gordon—shifting every possible task forward to maximize Ella's sleep.

Finally, the clock reading 7:31, it was time to wake Sleeping Beauty.

"Sweetie." She stroked a hair from the corner of Ella's mouth. "We need to get moving."

Ella shifted away, instinctively tugging the blanket to her chin.

"Time to wake up, Ella. Breakfast is ready."

The girl's small, perfect body stiffened in a stretch. Eyes fluttered but did not fully open. *"Pancakes...Mickey pancakes...with blue M&M's for the eyes..."*

Ella crunched back to the fetal position with a drowsy smile. Steph would have to congratulate her mother; adding candy to pancakes was truly raising grandparent-sugar-loading to new heights.

Eventually Ella was coaxed downstairs and ate a passable amount of Kashi cereal. Steph topped Morgan off with another ounce of milk, wrangled both into jackets and boots. That old feeling of industry was returning. The comfort of tangible, well-understood challenges.

Steph was no wallower. Sophomore year when she and Eric were eliminated from debate regionals, she had politely refused his offer to "volley out the pain" on a Best Western tennis court to some Lifehouse. She preferred cauterizing wounds with action.

Still, this wound would be large. The fact of Bob Fiske's being a fraud had gobsmacked her like the birth of a child, or college ending; she saw it coming but remained helpless against the scale of change. Riding back to Chicago in a squad car, she had resisted memories of the cabin and groped for conspiracy theories. When Wright had read her the suicide note, she had felt parts of her body physically churning against themselves, grinding, as though she were a turtle belly-up on its shell.

Her Winner's mind had needed to keep at it. *Never quit. Never fail.* For an hour or more, she'd struggled, triangulating thousand-to-one odds, before Doug took her hand.

"You gave him every chance to surprise, babe." His voice kind, deflated. "To be that great man he promised us. He failed."

Doug was right. The time for defending had passed. To

proceed otherwise would be to dishonor the Brockerts, a family suffering so much worse than the revelation of a false idol. She had visited Fiske at Cook County with the others, and she supposed if he woke from his coma, she would hear him out. But no more blinders.

The girls stood before the door to the garage, outfitted and prepared for on-time departure, when Ella remembered something.

"I hate blue." A quarter inch of blue fabric could be seen between her mittens and coat. "Want to change. Change shirts."

Her lower lip pooched out in baby-talk mode. Steph checked her watch. Rich Hauser expected her in his office in twelve minutes. "There isn't time, Ella. These clothes are perfectly fine. Let's go."

"No. *Not* go."

Ella crossed her arms, then, catching fresh sight of the blue, began a pathetic mewling as if the color itself was bleeding boyness into her wrists. Steph unclenched her teeth with effort.

Remember, she's missed you. She's only looking for attention.

"Alright." Steph stripped off the coat, eyes bright like a lunatic's. "Walk extremely fast upstairs and choose a different shirt, then come right back."

"So when I come back down," Ella said, head askew, "also go *exteemely* fast?"

Steph's eyes brighter still. "Yes! Correct Ella, everything extremely fast!"

The girl did hustle upstairs, hunt around—dresser slides clanged through the ceiling—and hustle back. Morgan squirmed in her car seat. Steph's phone buzzed in her purse. Finally, her eldest was back at the door to the garage.

"*Mom!*" She bowed one leg, inspecting her instep. "My boots —I never saw the bottoms were blue."

Steph pushed into the garage. "You're fine, please get in on your regular side—"

"You never told me! Why would you ever *dare* to get me *blue* boots, Mom?"

Ella was looking down at her feet with such anguish that Steph felt, through a knot of infuriation, something release inside.

Some valve. She exhaled at length, tapped a text to Chad—*u and Rich start w/o me*—and bent to wipe her daughter's cheeks.

"The color of your boots is not important." She squared the girl's shoulders. "Understand?"

Ella did not understand—not then, not ten minutes later as she was being buckled into her spot in the SUV. Steph neither plowed through Ella's illogical concern, hiking her full wail through the garage, nor caved by pulling down last year's Olaf boots (which would've bent toes but worked)—either of which would have gotten her to Rich Hauer's office by eight. Instead she spoke to her daughter in placid, reasonable tones until all oxygen had burned out of the conflict.

Finally Ella, spent, lifted her arms in the universal *Uppie* pose. Steph smiled.

"I love you, sweetie." Hoisting a child in either arm, marveling at their weight. "Now let's have ourselves a good day."

The hands-free rang as Steph was turning left from Ridge onto Walnut. She glanced away from oncoming traffic, which was impossible to see with this UPS truck sitting in the intersection.

The dashboard flashed: *Incoming caller: ERIC PINKERSBY.*

"Mommy, Oliver told me and Katie his pee-pee can go out of his underwear," Ella announced from the back. "Is he lying?"

Steph leaned against her window to see whether it was safe to make her left turn. "Nobody's pee-pee needs to be going out of their underwear."

"So he's lying?"

This Oliver, a towheaded boy who came across regular enough in Steph's brief classroom-door observations, had made claims recently on subjects ranging from his own pee-pee, to girls' pee-pees, to why "daddy drinks" tasted yucky, and on and on.

"It's complicated, sweetie. Let Oliver worry about his own pee-pee."

The call kept ringing.

Steph ought to ignore it. Late last night, a newswire story had surfaced referring to Eric as "a person of interest" in the death of

Becky Brindle. One website had gone so far as to call him a fugitive. Creepy things were being reported—about his obsessive internet searches for Autumn Brockert and "other unnamed females," about some pornographic memoir or manuscript.

For the life of her, Steph could not imagine Eric playing a part in Becky's fall. Eric: the boy who'd written a poem from the point of view of mice being lowered into the cage of Mr. Glanville's snake, who'd begged out of seventh grade dodgeball on bruising concerns.

Then again, how many counterpoint memories had she conjured of Fiske these last few days?

"Oliver says you hafta start smoke sticks with fire," Ella continued. "But I thought fire was too dangerous. Is he lying?"

The light turned yellow, then red. Steph held up traffic waiting for the UPS driver to clear the intersection, then completed her turn.

She winced at the chorus of honks. "Does Miss Marilyn hear these conversations?"

The hands-free stopped as she explained that smoke sticks themselves were dangerous, that Ella should never go near them. Steph wriggled her nose odiously. Just as the bewilderment on Ella's face was lifting, the hands-free rang again.

This time she answered.

"Steph! Oh God, you picked up—thank God you picked up," Eric's voice gushed. "Are you home? Please tell me you're not home."

She thumbed the car's speaker volume lower. "I'm in my car, dropping off the girls."

"Good! Great. Listen, you have to go. It's Doug—you have to go. Take whatever's in your car right now and go, get far far away."

Steph reached into her purse for her phone, switched off the hands-free. "Eric, what are you talking about? Where are you calling from?"

"My car. Well not exactly *my* car, not the Hummer I had to ditch the Hummer."

He spoke so fast that ends and beginnings of words were blending.

Steph asked, "You have another car?"

"Yeah picked it up yesterday around Lincoln Park, Corolla." Before she could probe, he continued, "Okay where can we meet? Someplace Doug wouldn't know to look, how about the IHOP—"

"Wait," she said. "Just stop for one second. What are you trying to tell me?"

"I'm telling you that Doug, your all-American Mr. Everything jock-rock-of-a-husband, Doug, is behind the whole thing."

Steph's lips cycled through many different shapes before managing the words, "What whole thing?"

"Becky, Fiske, Autumn Brockert—devil knows how far it goes. Meet me out and we'll talk, I'll explain."

Steph blinked now, twice, and realized she had just missed the entrance for Blue Hills. "Look, I have a client meeting I have to prepare for. We need to get the deck ready."

"*Deck? Client meeting?*" It sounded like Eric was speaking through froth. "This is urgent! I tell you your husband's a murderer, and you need to go make bar charts in PowerPoint?"

"Eric, you're not making sense." She lowered her voice. "What basis do you have for calling Doug a murderer?"

He launched into a wild account of the previous night, veering back and forth in time, raving about a fluffy white dog and text messages, and liquid-metal Larry David, and five hundred dollars a tree and sprinting between decks and being ready to give up...but then he backed out of his driveway and it was a black Jeep.

A black Jeep!

Just like the one parked outside her house last Wednesday!

Steph had backtracked to Blue Hills and, as her former debate partner delivered his grand revelation, was mouthing, "Thanks," and handing spare clothes to the parent volunteer in Morgan's class.

"Did you hear what I said?" Eric demanded. "Doesn't it scare the bejesus out of you?"

Back in the parking lot, kidless, she removed her hand from the mic. "What scares me right now, frankly, is you. How do you know a black Jeep was parked outside my house last Wednesday?"

The fervor drained from Eric's voice. "I was just...well, driving by. Happened to be in the neighborhood."

Steph only had to remain silent a moment before he confessed.

"Oh okay, I was watching you. It was a Wednesday night, my parents don't live here anymore and I'm stuck in a hotel, and Z100 is playing The Fray's concert album in its entirety...so yeah, for old time's sake, I parked outside your house and spied. My bad.

"But look—the black Jeep! One of Doug's poker buddies, right? It cannot be coincidence. Doug is framing me for Becky's murder!"

"Eric, calm down. Relax." She reversed out of her space, pulled into traffic headed toward Dunham & Prior. "Why would Doug frame you for Becky's murder?"

"Hell if I know! Maybe he's still mad about our kiss. Did you ever tell him?"

"Kiss? What are you talking about?"

"Prom! Remember? Outside Mrs. Shipley's classroom?"

The desperation in Eric's tone—the breakneck, circular certainty with which he argued—caused Steph to hold the phone away from her ear. Was he suffering a breakdown? One commentator had speculated based on passages in that memoir or whatever (*The Man with a Thousand Lives?* or *Wives?*) that Eric could be manic-depressive. Even schizophrenic.

"I can't meet you now. Not possible. I have this eight o'clock, and the client meeting after. There is a chance I could do lunch."

Eric said she ought to know that his situation was not exactly leisurely. His stolen car (well, *joyridden*, officially, since he had not forced entry) had been ticketed last night, and he didn't know whether Larry David/T-1000 had reported—

"Lunch," Steph interrupted. "That's the best I can do."

He sighed and agreed. *The Skokie Blvd IHOP, 1:15.*

At Dunham & Prior, Steph rode the elevator straight to fifteen, not stopping at her office on the way to Rich Hauser's. He and Chad were poised over a printout.

"Aha, here she is—our celebrity!" Rich pulled a third chair up to his desk. "See if you can explain in English what I'm looking at."

Chad gave her an apologetic look. *Presenting statistical material to clients/senior execs in an accessible way* was one of his top development objectives.

Fortunately, outside of Rich's "celebrity" reference, the meeting did not touch on Fiske. They got right into the meat of the issue with Gordon, whose VP of marketing claimed to be seeing "zero impact" ten weeks into a $15 million brand-awareness campaign. Both Rich and Chad were flummoxed. Gordon's mentions per day had surged after the October launch but flatlined since. The share-of-voice story was no better, with Choice Foods still dominating the segment.

"I pulled the contract," Chad said, "and technically they're locked in through May."

Rich rolled his eyes. "Technically I was on the hook with my first wife 'til death blah, blah, blah, but when a thing quits working, you find a way out."

Steph suggested they probe some second- and third-order metrics. Logging into their analytics provider's reporting tool, she punched up Gordon's share of conversation, a newer measure that required the user to bound the analysis with keyword parameters. Steph tried a few combos before producing a strong upward trend line for the last two months.

She returned to her office and flowed right into deck preparation. Gordon's team would be on-site at eleven. She worked two hours without coming up for air. The earlier phone conversation with Eric flitted about the edge of her brain, half dream, half wrong number.

At quarter of, she was sending slides to the printer when Doug called.

"Hey, babe, did you sign Ella up for spring soccer yet?"

"Uh...no." She hunted for the *Print* icon, sent ten copies to the LaserJet. "Was I supposed to?"

"No, she just mentioned it last night at bedtime, and I couldn't remember if you had. I'll do it online."

"Thanks."

"No prob. Anything else? Morning going okay?"

"Yep," she said automatically. "Yep, going well."

They hung up. Gathering pen/notebook and heading to retrieve copies, Steph realized she had not told him about Eric's accusation. Why? She hadn't meant to deceive or omit. It had just happened. Did she subconsciously fear he *was* involved? No. Surely not. Had she not wanted to betray Eric, make him sound ridiculous? Maybe because she would look bad by association?

Thankfully, Gordon soon overshadowed these doubts. Steph met Chad at the printer—she had parceled out a straightforward section for him—and after praising his effort, melded slides and led the way to the conference room. Gordon arrived with a team of seven, all men, all in dark suits.

"Gentleman," Rich Hauser began. "What's this I hear about cold feet? I thought everyone was on board for knocking Choice Foods into next fiscal year."

Before the words left his mouth, Steph saw it was a stupid utterance. It was well known that some at Gordon disliked using big-city agencies over their own marketing people. (Company headquarters was Des Moines.) Bluster was a bad play.

The Gordon CMO was fit, silver haired. "We are. But your punches haven't done much."

"No? Steph showed me some numbers this morning that looked encouraging."

With a plastered grin, Rich volunteered his place at the overhead. Steph strode forward feeling the visitors' hard gazes. Up the table, Chad kept biting callouses on his palm. She clucked at him to stop.

"Evaluating campaigns in the early going can be problematic." She advanced to the first graphic. "Our plans follow a precise order, and quite often the multiplicative effects take time showing up. That said, I believe our metrics support the conclusion that Dunham & Prior is moving the needle for you all."

Steph talked through a half dozen data plots, educating when Gordon showed interest in snazzier metrics like Sentiment Score. "Sentiment" reminded her of Eric Pinkersby's runaway emotions this morning; she quickly dismissed the thought. Steph assured Gordon that all signs pointed to a coming inflection point in brand awareness. "You're right at the cusp," she said, curling her fingers along the slope of a projecting graph.

"If we downsize some of these large print buys," the CMO mused, "do we jeopardize the uptick?"

Rich Hauser welled up his chest and, Steph knew from experience, was preparing to sermonize on the continued primacy of print, that stake in the ground, no matter what the dang bloggers—

"You would," she jumped in first, "but I do believe there's room to optimize the spend. Possibly go leaner in print but double down in the online space."

The partners liked to hold campaigns to a minimum 40-percent-print threshold, but Steph knew they would rather capitulate than see Gordon dock its spend: a tragic result she did now manage to avert.

After handshakes all round, Steph and Chad walked out with Rich Hauser.

"Yikes, that was a close shave," he said. "Steph, you're a lifesaver."

She moved aside so they could walk three abreast with Chad in the middle. "Thanks. Chad's stacked-bar chart made a huge difference."

Rich furrowed his brow, not remembering. He was an avowed "big-picture guy" who only worried about details when one blew up a pitch.

"Haven't lost a step, have you?" He chuckled. "I worried with all this hullabaloo going on, we might lose our big gun for a while."

She forced a smile. "Not at all. I'm quite relieved to be back."

"And we're relieved to have you back." Rich palmed his elbow thoughtfully. "This goes without saying, but if you ever need anything from the firm in terms of support, just say the word."

"Sure."

They had arrived at the elevator bank where Steph and Chad normally split off. Rich was still regarding Steph curiously, though, so she waited, standing with crossed wrists. Chad muttered an, *Uh, okay bye,* then shuffled onto the next descending car.

Once they were alone, Rich steeled his expression. "You haven't let this nasty business drag you down, Steph. You faced it head-on. I like that. It's the sign of a winner: the ability to turn adversity back around on itself."

Steph felt queasy about the reference, intentional or not, to her status as an ETHS Winner. Rich was her official Dunham & Prior mentor, and sometimes offered this type of generalized feedback, unasked.

Just to say something, she observed, "It was an ordeal. I can't imagine anyone feels good coming out the other side."

Rich shrugged. "I'd wager MetroBuild feels slightly better off today."

And off he strode with a wink.

CHAPTER TWENTY

S teph paused in the IHOP vestibule to peer through the door. Eric wasn't sitting at the counter or any of the tables in the dining area. She moved inside, smiling off the hostess, and checked the booths.

There he was. Alone, up against the wall in the last booth. Hair ruffled. Shirt smudged. In the brief time she was able to observe without being seen, he reset his glasses on his nose twice and crossed his legs three times.

When their eyes did meet, he shivered as though waking from a drowse. Steph made her way back to the booth.

"Eric, you look miserable. Did the police do this? Are they interrogating you?"

He grimaced. "I sorta declined to answer their questions."

"So are you a fugitive? I read one report saying you were a fugitive."

"That...would not be completely inaccurate."

"How'd you get so dirty?"

He looked at his reflection in the back of a spoon, flinched at the image. "Oh yeah, I dug around the backyard some. I thought they might've buried her there."

"Who?"

"Autumn Brockert."

"No, whose back yard?"

"That's what I need to know!" Realizing he had spoken loudly, Eric hunched low and glanced nervously out the window. "Listen Steph, we have to figure this out. Which one of Doug's buddies drives that black Jeep?"

"Okay, back up," Steph said. "How many black Jeeps do you suppose there are in the city of Chicago? Hundreds? A thousand?"

"Nah, green is more common. That mossy, pseudo-military shade? Or khaki brown. If it were green or khaki brown, fine, we'd have to consider coincidence. But black? No way."

"Did you get a license plate?"

"No."

"Any bumper stickers?"

"None that I saw."

"Parking sticker? Permit for a garage?"

Eric shook his head.

"Did you at least get a look at the driver?"

"Briefly."

"And?"

Eric made a thin, keening noise. "He was, you know, average looking. Goatee, short hair. Built pretty well."

Steph tried remembering if Trev Larson—owner of the black Jeep Eric must have seen Wednesday night—wore a goatee. She didn't think so. She also didn't think "average-looking" fit Trev very well. Whenever she saw him, she thought of Porky Pig.

"Have you told the police?" she asked.

"There's not exactly an open line of communication there. Besides which, I already know what Wright would say. His mind is made up: I'm an obsessive psycho who can't control his emotional urges, who chucked Becky off a cliff either intentionally on Fiske's behalf or in some fit of rage."

This seemed a fair guess of what Frank Wright thought and, Steph had to admit, a not-wildly-unbelievable pass at the truth, given the media reports.

Eric asked where she was staying tonight.

"At home," she said. "Where else?"

"Anywhere. An underpass, the back seat of a car. A hotel."

"I can't run off to a hotel—I have two children. I have a husband."

"A husband who's a *murderer*." Having spoken loudly again, Eric took a furtive glance around before continuing, "A husband who's *never* been good to you—whether he's ditching you on prom night or screwing calendar models at Northwestern. You're blind to it! He's never taken you seriously during this ordeal with Fiske, and you are a brilliant and beautiful and phenomenally awesome person who *should* be taken seriously."

Steph turned away from his intensity. "Doug takes me seriously. Do we come at situations from different perspectives? Yes. Are there moments when he frustrates me? Or I frustrate him? Of course. Usually when in-laws are around. That doesn't make him an insensitive brute...and it certainly doesn't make him a murderer."

Her and Doug's romance had more kinks than people understood. Classmates reconnecting on Facebook years later would probably see family portraits at the botanical gardens and assume they'd traveled a straight line from high-school-sweetheart-dom. In fact, they had never been exclusive during college, and even after ending up in the same city postgraduation, neither had pursued the other. Doug had hopped between loft-apartment parties as a single, newly flush financial analyst. Steph had been focused on her career at Dunham & Prior, happy with the occasional dinner date or girls night out.

When their paths crossed again—at a loft-apartment party on girls night out, in fact—the spark was immediate. They began dating. It was far from clear, though, that marriage and 2.5 kids were in their future. Doug insisted on keeping his own place and was working overseas for months at a time. Steph felt no great hurry herself. Doug was familiar and safe and effortlessly great as ever, but their lives had just begun.

Then you peed on a stick.

Steph's mother had given birth to Steph's eldest brother at sixteen, and though there was never any overt dogma in the house, she felt terminating the pregnancy would be a slap in the face. Ungrateful somehow—even if her mother never found out.

There was also, in some corner of Steph's mind, a sense that taking the easy way out would diminish her. She had so many advantages over her parents: money, education, another seven years' life experience. If she couldn't make the same sacrifice, having such means at her disposal, what did that say about her character?

Doug reacted like a prince. He paused for a second, two at most, then broke into a broad grin and cradled her in his arms. That embrace alone, tender as a brushstroke, was enough to make her want him forever.

They booked a venue and rushed invites through the mail. Marriage at twenty-three was unusual among their Stanford and Northwestern friends, but they embraced their trailblazing role, strategizing over school districts, beginning a rotating couples' dinner club. They had succeeded in everything else; why should premature domesticity be different?

When Steph miscarried six weeks later, it barely mattered, so thoroughly had they adopted the new goals. Doug laid his forehead against hers at the OBGYN's office, and they cried together. The idea of canceling or delaying the wedding was never discussed. Fifteen months later, Ella was born full-term.

"So because you haven't stumbled upon a set of bloody knives in the garage," Eric said now, "he's innocent? The black Jeep is irrelevant?"

"There's just physically no way he could be involved. I was with him *the entire time*. We were never separated by more than a step or two at Pictured Rocks."

On top of which—Steph was not going to divulge, at the risk of stoking more wild theorizing—she had done a little investigating this morning after the Gordon meeting. There had been no unusual transactions on their joint account, no unrecognized numbers (Trev Larson or otherwise) on the Verizon log.

"Explain the black Jeep," Eric said. "Explain that coincidence."

"You can't explain coincidence—that's what defines the word. How do you explain Fiske's suicide note? Are you going to tell me Doug is behind that too?"

"Maybe." His face buzzed, erratic, strung out. "It could've been faked."

Steph leaned both elbows into the table, chin in hands. "The pieces just do not fit. I've looked for different explanations as hard as anybody—you know I was Fiske's biggest advocate—but I'm sorry, this Doug theory is off the reservation. What possible motive could he have to kill Becky? Plus Wednesday night, the night Autumn Brockert disappeared, both Doug and this supposed black-Jeep-driving accomplice were *at my house*. Right? You *saw* them. How could they be involved?"

Eric had no answers.

"Let's put cards on the table, Eric. This crush of yours..."

Steph forced eye contact, waiting for his to limp their way around to hers. "You can't see clearly. There is a myth here you want to believe. A story you've built up over the years where I'm in this awful predicament, and Doug is some ruthless creep, and you're the only one to save me. Now you find yourself under extreme stress—from the police and whatever else—and you return to it. You fall back on your dream."

They looked at each other over cinnamon-chip pancakes. The call sign of an easy-listening station sounded over the dull IHOP speakers, followed by the first strains of a Mariah Carey song.

Eric grinned weakly. "Is that so terrible?"

CHAPTER TWENTY-ONE

Steph got home at six thirty. The girls were already at the table, Morgan bibbed and belted into her high chair; Ella on her knees in the big-girl chair, picking napkins one by one from their holder. The day-care sheets were pinned to the hall corkboard: turkey wraps for lunch, no accidents for Ella. Both jackets hung neatly off the French door handles.

Doug was dicing pork-chop meat, divvying out kid portions. "Hey babe."

He twisted from the cutting board to give her a squeeze. Steph started to serve herself.

"Already made yours," he said, nodding to a plate on the island.

"Oh, thanks." She carried the girls' milk and utensils over at the same time and took her place beside the high chair.

Dinner conversation started slowly—Ella kept unfolding napkins until they got taken away—but soon hit a more or less normal groove. Miss Vicky had raved about Morgan's emerging pincer grip. Ella had done works with Katie and Sam but not Amelia. *Never in her whole entire life!* was she doing works with Amelia. Steph and Doug shared a smile with their eyes. She talked about the Gordon meeting. He recounted a conversation with her sister, who'd called the moment he walked in the door and delivered a fifteen-minute diatribe on the backwardness of North Dakota politics.

"She was the one who took that job," Steph said. "Remember what she told us? 'People are authentic up there.'"

"I know," Doug said. "I chose not to remind her."

As she topped off the girls' applesauce, Steph felt fresh guilt for what she was not telling Doug. Here was a man who did his fair share at home, had already banked enough for college and any graduate school the girls might choose, who supported her emotionally. Considering the range of possible male outcomes, Doug Reece was a statistical anomaly. These last six months had been rough on him too, from the Sears jumper all the way to Fiske, but he'd never let it show. Not once snapped at the kids, or lashed out at her, or anything.

Still, she was in a box. If she told him now about lunch with Eric, he would probably—rightfully—be angry she hadn't mentioned it sooner. How would he respond to Eric's accusation? Would he laugh it off? No. That was asking too much, even of Doug. He would be furious. He might even try to find Eric, and that could end badly for everyone.

Doug asked how she had liked the curry on day two.

"Huh?"

"The curry," he repeated. "I saw it was gone from the fridge—I assume you took it for lunch?"

"I did, yeah," she said. "It was, um, not bad. Pretty good."

"You heat it up together with the rice? Or separate?"

"I *did* heat them together," she said with too much emphasis. "Worked well."

Of course the curry was still sitting in her office mini fridge. Now she had told an outright lie on top of the omissions.

After dinner, they tried the sled hill down the block. The season had passed, but the hill was shaded and held its pillowy scoops late. Calm winds and mid-thirties temps made for the best conditions a toddler parent could reasonably wish for. Ella shrieked with delight on the purple disk, coming up grinning after a faceful of caked snow. Morgan participated a good half hour before waving off further runs.

"Wanna watch?" Steph asked. "Mommy just hold you?"

She pooched her lip and nodded. Steph held her baby to her chest, rooting for kisses in the folds of crinkly fabric, while Dad and Big Sis finished their fun.

If she closed her mind to Eric's ranting, and the heartache that grew every hour Autumn Brockert remained unaccounted for, she could almost imagine life returning to normal.

Bedtime hummed right along, aided by the exercise and fresh air. After bath and brush, they split up as usual, with Steph taking Ella tonight. She read two *Pinkalicious* stories, then prompted Ella liberally through a *Bob* easy reader before returning to the ever-popular stick-thin protagonist for *Pink Around the Rink*.

Finally, Steph hit the lights and climbed into bed for a snuggle. She asked about Ella's day at school and received the expected nonanswer. Floated the idea of going to the children's museum Saturday, then had to explain at length the difference between week*days* and week*ends.*

"Mommy, do you love us so much, even when you're not here?" her older daughter asked.

Steph shimmied to bring their faces close. "Of course. I love you always."

"But do you love us so much?"

"Yes. I love you so, so, so, *so-ooo* much."

Ella rubbed her eyes, little wrists knobbing into her sockets. "Okay. That's what Daddy said, I just wanted to double-check."

She was always "double-checking"; that was Steph's term of choice when sniffing Morgan's diaper or making sure the stove was off.

"Were you worried, baby? I'm not gone that much, am I? You know I always love you."

"I know."

Steph would have liked to probe, to understand how the subject had come up and learn the root cause of her anxiety. But that would've been selfish. Ella was tired. She needed sleep.

Steph whispered good night, pulling her hair back to kiss her cheek.

Downstairs, Doug was loading the last of the plates into the dishwasher.

"Easy?" he said.

"Not bad, only three *Pinkalicious*. Yours?"

"About the same. She wanted more bottle, but I convinced her to settle for Happy Bee." Morgan's favorite pacifier featured a picture of a grinning bumblebee.

The triumphantly unburdened parents watched a bit of TV, flipping between HGTV and the Bulls, passing a bowl of olives and Gruyère on a cutting board. Steph got into a show about real estate in the Caribbean, and Doug told her to just leave it when she offered to switch at commercial. "It's second quarter, I'm not staying up." So they followed a couple from Washington state through three gloriously sun-drenched haciendas before heading upstairs.

Doug was out before Steph had the electric toothbrush back in its cradle. She briefly curled against him, then switched on her nightstand lamp and tried reading herself to sleep. It didn't work. Page after page, Grisham or Murakami or Jack Welch—she waited for her eyelids to sag, for words to disassociate into the germs of a first dream, but they refused.

Around midnight, a sour note crept into Steph's thoughts. That conversation with Ella. *Did she love them so much, even when she wasn't there? That's what Daddy said.*

It was sweet of Doug to stick up for her, of course, but felt out of character. Too meek. Doug never coddled the girls. He believed fussing over kids' anxieties reinforced them. If you just patted their back, told them it was no big deal, over time, the attitude rubbed off and they grew up resilient.

Maybe Ella had been crying, forced his hand. Maybe he hadn't phrased it that way at all. How much stock could be put in a four-year-old's recall?

Steph rolled onto her side, knee hiking up the mattress. Watched the minutes of her digital clock. Doubled one corner of her pillow.

A sudden grip around her thigh startled her.

"Still up, babe?"

Steph's breath returned. Yes, she said: she was having trouble sleeping. Doug mumbled a question about everything being alright but dropped off again before receiving an answer.

It's nothing, she decided. *Stop overanalyzing.*

Finally, she did sleep.

It was a light sleep, though; at 2:40 she awoke at the faintest crackle from Morgan's monitor. Reflexively, she stalked down the hall, grabbing a spare pacifier in case Happy Bee was lost in covers, and tiptoed to the crib.

By the night-light's soft wedge, she watched her baby snuffle and wheeze in place. *How beautiful were they when they were asleep?* She backed out of the nursery with soft, flat-footed steps.

Now she had to pee. Not wanting to disturb Doug or the girls, she used the downstairs toilet. She squatted and picked the first magazine she saw off the tank. Shaquille O'Neal was on the cover in a purple-and-yellow uniform Steph did not recognize, looking unbelievably young. She checked the date: 1991.

One of Doug's vintage *Sports Illustrated*s.

When plastic coins and a pretend five-dollar bill fell out from within the pages, she understood. Ella had been doing her "money buying" and must have raided the den for merchandise.

Finishing in the bathroom, Steph considered leaving the magazine out for Doug—he would see it in the morning and put it away how he liked. Besides which, it was so late. The hall clock read 3:02 a.m.; she would be lucky to eke out five hours' sleep regardless.

As it generally did, on matters small and large, Steph's focus on excellence won out. *Don't shirk. Do it now.*

She walked the *Sports Illustrated* back to the den. Sure enough, a chair had been pushed up against the bookcase, and the fourth-shelf magazines lay in a lopsided heap: Ella's idea of picked up.

She set the O'Neal cover atop the others, tapped the sides and bottoms until the stack was neat, and placed them back upright. She tried pushing them flush into the bookcase but couldn't. The bottoms resisted. The stack kept fanning forward stubbornly. She re-tapped the edges and tried again, twice, before noticing the obstruction at the back of the shelf.

A stick? Some kind of board, or bat?

She reached into the shadows and pulled out a wooden dowel. Rectangular, eighteen inches long. There was a hole drilled in one end and, attached by heavy-gauge wire, some kind of key.

Steph had never seen a key like it. No teeth, just a single prong with a deep groove running down one side. The base made a T with the prong, a shape for one to make a fist around. It was powder-black and might've weighed five pounds, substantial in her hands. She could not imagine what it opened.

Until she read the dowel's magic-marker label.

WILLIS TOWER, 97TH FLOOR WINDOW WASHER.

Steph gagged forward. The periphery seemed to fall away precipitously and she felt as though worms were leaving her eyes and ears, being yanked, her guts spiraling out in grotesque ribbons.

Doug had lied. She did not understand why, or about what precisely. But she knew.

Her phone was charging in the kitchen. She staggered there on loose legs, feeling her way, and ripped it from its wall plug.

She texted Eric: *are u there? need to leave house and meet somewhere right now.*

She sat on the bare hardwood clutching her phone. The house felt suddenly huge, the cabinets across the room a million miles away, the girls—*oh God, the girls*—impossibly far from her clammy hands. The refrigerator hummed. The ice maker coughed.

When Tattletail rubbed her shin, Steph jumped half out of her skin. The cat scurried away but soon came purring back, nosing Steph's bare toes, eyes orange in the darkness.

Thirty seconds later, her cell buzzed.

ETHS tennis courts. be there 10 min :-)

She texted back *Ok*, then tried standing. She tottered sideways and braced herself by the counter, allowed some blood to return to her head.

She couldn't leave the girls. Whether Doug was a murderer, she didn't know—knew virtually nothing about her husband at this point—but her children were not safe here. They were coming along.

Thankfully there was laundry in the dryer, so she managed pants and a sweatshirt without risking the noise of dresser drawers. She crept upstairs, then—doing a quick calculation about which order gave her the best chance—slipped into Ella's room.

"*Sweetie, we need to go,*" she said at her daughter's ear.

Ella groaned, shifting from a fetal position to facedown on her tummy. Steph tapped her shoulder and brushed hair off her face, whispering that they were taking a little trip, a little nighttime adventure, *that's right, Sweetie, no, you can wear your jammies, that's fine.*

"Can I bring Purple Rhino?" Ella asked, pulling the stuffed animal from the sheets.

Steph shushed her voice lower and said, *"Yes, you can bring Purple Rhino—"*

"And Baby Cinderella too?"

"Just one, sweetie. Please choose one."

"But Baby Cinderella will be sad! She hates it when Purple Rhino gets to—"

"Fine." Steph jammed both under her armpit, helping Ella around her bedrail and down onto the carpet.

They walked hand in hand to the nursery. Morgan always cried waking up; Steph's idea was to scoop her out of the crib, shove a pacifier in her mouth, and hustle her into the car seat before her brain processed anything. It might work. It *had to* work. They absolutely could not be heard—if she had to clap her hand over Morgan's mouth and muffle her screams all the way outside, she would. Failure was not an option.

The hallway seemed longer than a football field. They passed the linen closet, Jack & Jill bathroom, door to the guest room. Tattletail walked ahead with tail high, peeking back like a timid advance scout. Ella yawned but kept moving. Steph held on to her small hand urgently, her grip as strong as it had been through the deadliest parking lot.

They were a step from Morgan's door when a voice stopped them.

"And just where are we going on our little adventure, Mommy?"

Doug, in boxers, taking up three-quarters of the hall. Holding the baby monitor by its hook and grinning: a tight, airless expression that only an adult would know to fear.

CHAPTER TWENTY-TWO

E ric could hardly manage the biomechanics of parking. In this
lot he'd navigated hundreds of times before, even with not
another car in sight, there was too much noise in the neural path-
ways between brain and muscle. He tried parking up against the
school but didn't find the brakes in time, bumping brick. He
revved forward and reapproached, and mismatched his wheel cut
to the orientation of the yellow lines, such that he spanned two
spaces. He decided he didn't care—the ETHS parking Nazis must
sleep, right?—but his foot missed the memo and jabbed the accelerator anyhow.

He finally cut the engine with one wheel up on a divider curb.
Okay cool it. Okay breathe.

In, out. In, out.

*Okay. Steph Mills is coming HERE, imminently, to meet YOU, in
the middle of the night. Are you running away together? Has she been
harmed by Doug, or harmed Doug herself?*

*What music is appropriate? Usher too provocative? How about silky-
cool John Mayer?*

He had successfully exposed Doug. That much was clear from
Steph's text. If not clear, at least implied. You did not bolt your
husband's bed to meet his rival unless you had experienced a
profound change of heart.

It felt surreal to Eric, who had imagined it so many times

under so many different scenarios. Steph coming to her senses after a pressured make-out session, or forgotten anniversary, or being stood up at her favorite restaurant. (To his knowledge, Doug had done none of these.)

Now it was happening. Actually. Nonfictionally.

He stepped from the lopsided car and walked to the tennis courts. Two cheap rackets, the kind you toss into a bin at the end of phys ed, leaned against the fence. He picked one up and began twirling it, venting nerves, the electric-tape handle soothingly rough in his palm.

He twirled a good while, then checked his phone.

4:03 a.m.

Half an hour since her text. And they lived ten minutes away.

Eric had been able to get here right away. He'd been sleeping in the Corolla outside the chemistry complex at Northwestern, where postdocs booked time on specialized instruments for all hours of the night and his car wouldn't raise eyebrows. There had been risk staying in Evanston, but he had felt it justified in order to be available if Steph contacted him.

Now, phone in hand and with nothing to do but wait, Eric did what he normally did when no productive activity occurred to him: checked Facebook.

All the usual gunk. Somebody snapped a double rainbow on their Yosemite hike; somebody else ate brandade with Meyer lemon and chilled pea soup at Azizi. (Eric thought we were done posting pics of entrees at restaurants, but apparently not.) He liked a Larry Ellison facial-hair joke. He blocked further updates from a Stanford girl who'd apparently become addicted to a word-puzzle game.

A message popped up over his newsfeed: *why are you pissing around FB with cops on your ass?*

Ramona's profile image, fern-haired Bill Murray from *Kingpin*, pulsed for an answer.

Eric pulled up the AP wire. *SUSPECTED ACCOMPLICE STILL AT LARGE IN BROCKERT CASE.* He scrolled down and learned that the police believed him to be in the Chicago area—the Hummer had been recovered and identified—and considered him "a danger to the public."

Crap.

He swiped back to Facebook and, before responding, was allowing the twenty second *I-wasn't-actually-doing-Facebook-it-was-just-open-in-the-background* interval when headlights appeared around the corner.

He put Droid away. The car was a blue SUV. Steph's. It came barreling across the lot like a mine cart screaming through some Indiana Jones cavern, teetering, wheels whistling. *Definitely Steph's driving*, Eric thought as he edged closer to the Corolla. The SUV roared to within ten feet, then fishtailed to rest. A rubber smell burned Eric's nostrils.

The headlights went black, and a leg dropped out of the driver's side. A leg and a foot.

Neither belonged to Steph.

CHAPTER TWENTY-THREE

Doug Reece carried a gun at his side and glowered and seethed and had crazy bedhead and a coat collar folded half into the sweatshirt underneath. He slammed the SUV's door behind him, the noise exploding the early-morning air. He stalked toward Eric with none of that graceful ease he had oozed a decade ago on the football field: he was a jerky, raging ghoul.

"Couldn't leave well enough alone, could you?" he called ahead. "Millions waiting for you in San Fran, but you had to run back here, keep sucking up to the prom queen."

Before Eric could make sense, Doug had closed the gap and jacked him. Somewhere in the nose/cheek region; the whole middle of his face began throbbing. The cheap tennis racket clattered away behind, and something—or things—fell out of his pocket. An open-handed blow to the chest sent him sprawling. Doug pounced on top, knees pinning his arms.

"This did not need to happen. You could have kept your life— we would've let you."

Eric struggled to free his hands and wormed his neck back and forth, trying to present a moving target. Punches landed hard against his ear, to the top of the head, then glancingly off his Adam's apple. He looked past Doug's shoulder and saw—blurry, his glasses were nowhere—the SUV rocking in place.

Somebody was inside! Wait...*was* somebody inside, or was that rocking an optical illusion of his own head's thrashing around? What had Doug meant when he said "we" just now? Could Steph be involved? Had she gone home and told him all about their IHop conversation? Had they schemed how to lure him to an isolated location, at this strange hour when there'd be no witnesses?

No. Couldn't be. In that case, why would Doug pop out of the car instead of Steph? Unless she couldn't bear to commit such treachery face-to-face. No, they must have had a fight. Doug's anger was too raw. Whatever was happening tonight had not been part of some measured plan.

"Is she dead?" he asked between wallops. "Did you kill her?"

Doug wiped spit with the back of his wrist. "Who, Autumn Brockert?"

Eric stopped himself from saying, *No, Steph,* but Doug caught the hesitation.

"Pathetic *dork*," he said, punctuating the word with his fist.

They were in a dark enclave of the parking lot, dumpsters blocking the nearest light. Eric barely saw one blow before the next landed. As he shrank into the blacktop, something sharp dug into his thigh, probably his keys, and a long, inch-wide object kept getting between the back of his head and the pavement.

The handle of a tennis racket.

"You thought you were in a movie, we were all in the movies." Doug's lips quavered against his teeth. "You were the nerd, I was the jock. And Steph was Molly Ringwald. Except the nerd is supposed to be smarter than the jock, Pinkersby. And despite your glasses and silver-fox hair, and pipe-cleaner physique, you are *not...*"

Gripping Eric by both ears.

"*...anywhere near...*"

Rearing back his face.

"*...smarter...*"

Inhaling, the veins of his neck hollowing.

"*...than me.*"

Doug rammed his head forward, and the world momentarily became the inside of a paper bag filled with slow-bursting fireworks. Eric kneaded his aching forehead but kept his arm moving nonchalantly higher, toward the racket.

"Is that why you framed me?" he said. "Because of Paladin? You couldn't stomach being less successful. Nobody gets to be better than Doug Reece."

Doug scoffed. "Duct-tape a bunch of junk hard drives, that makes you big-time?"

Eric fought to protect himself while probing Doug's motives. They insulted back and forth, but Doug—hot as he was to crow about his superiority—would not be goaded into spelling out his evildoing like some James Bond villain. He didn't bite at the mention of "his pal with the black Jeep" and only chortled when Eric wondered whether he'd had the decency to let an innocent sixteen-year-old like Autumn Brockert keep her life.

With that gun looming somewhere and his face feeling like a peach dropped down several flights of stairs, Eric decided there was no time for sleuthing. He had to escape. The racket was reachable, but he didn't think he could grab it and manage a solid swing before Doug reacted. He needed a distraction. A second or two of space, something to throw his attacker off.

"Know what Fiske told me once?" Eric slipped his fingers around the handle. "He said you were a fraud. Said Jamaal and the offensive line carried you your whole career. Said every paper you ever wrote was trite. He only picked you for Winner because he figured you might manage to bluff your way through life."

Either from anger or confusion (Fiske had never said any of this), Doug's face pinched. Eric brought the racket forward, swinging with the frame-edge leading. It caught Doug hard across the brow, the impact billowing up Eric's arm to the collarbone. Doug staggered, eyes closed, feeling blindly around the point of contact.

Eric bolted. He spotted his glasses ten feet away and ran, scooping them in full stride, fumbling them onto his face as his lungs gaped for oxygen. He raced around a corner, in a courtyard now, skidding over grass, falling and then scampering up, hearing Doug's footsteps, wondering who was in that rocking SUV.

He yanked the first two doors he passed. Neither budged. Mercifully, the third was propped by a broomstick. He dove inside, pulling the broom with him, and hunched against the wall. The knob had a push-button lock. He reached up to stick it in.

"Where a-*aaare* you?" came Doug's voice through the door. "We still have business here, Pinkersby. Stuff to straighten out."

Eric squeezed his knees together, bones touching through the denim of his jeans. He didn't dare flip the lights, but it seemed he was in a janitors' closet—sharp solvent smell, wheeled buckets. Doug's footsteps grew fainter, fainter, until they couldn't be heard at all.

Probably he'd gone ahead to the next courtyard. Or back to the parking lot.

If he had gone ahead, Eric could make a break for it. Run to the Corolla and peel the hell out of here. Of course that meant leaving behind whomever was in the SUV: most likely Steph.

What would Doug do to her? Having just seen—and felt, first-hand—the violence of his mood, Eric did not want to imagine. What if Autumn Brockert was inside too? He could wrap up the whole case with a bow.

But no. There was zero chance he could spring her/them *and* make the Corolla before Doug caught on. None. Discretion was clearly the better part of valor here; he should drive to safety and call the cops.

Then he realized in a blast of relief that he didn't need to drive anywhere. He could call from here! He plunged his hands into both pants pockets at once for his cell...

His fingers only found lint.

Now Doug's voice returned. "Hey, look what someone left behind. A phone. And it's got this darling gray-and-pink case. Wonder who the owner could be?"

Eric could not hear footsteps and so figured Doug was in the parking lot. He firmed his back to the wall. (Cursing the Amazon photo that'd made the case's edge trim appear more red than pink.)

"Did he put a password on it?" Doug continued. "Nope, sure didn't. Fantastic. Here, I'll just unlock...now get over to Messaging...looks like he sent a text to a person named *Steph Mills*—I guess he fantasizes she didn't change her name when he jerks off."

Eric's leg kicked involuntarily, toppling a bucket. The noise echoed around the closet. Cloudy-brown water sluiced out, soaking his shoes and the seat of his jeans. He hopped up and righted the bucket, scooched to a dry spot.

"*ETHS tennis courts. Be there ten minutes,*" Doug read, apparently off Droid. "Then he closes with a smiley emoticon. Precious."

In the gaps between words, Eric sensed Doug concentrating intensely on something. Was he bent over checking underneath doors? Cupping his hands to windows to see inside?

"I love that it's three thirty in the morning, and you're being asked to drop everything and come like a little-bitch dog, and you're still taking the time to show my wife—to the maximum capability of the English character set—what an obsessed, subservient peon you're willing to be."

As the malice in this voice grew, so did its nearness. Now Eric heard every pop and slurp of his mouth. He leaned to raise one butt cheek off the ground, the moisture itching like crazy. His shoe squeaked.

He froze.

Outside, there were no sounds for a moment. Then Eric thought he heard a careful step, the smallest crackle of sole over grass. Then another. Then breathing just outside the door.

What should he do? The door was locked, and like all ETHS doors it was heavy. That thick, institutionally colorless steel. Could he ride it out? Bunker down and wait for...what, daylight? Wouldn't Doug find another way in? Even if he did manage to last until—

TOINK.

The sound and simultaneous jolt to his spine interrupted Eric's thoughts. He hopped up and faced the door. Another *TOINK.* The door bowed in the middle. *He's breaking in!* He must've brought a hammer or found a rock.

With the third blow, a high-pitched *zing* sounded from within the knob. Eric didn't wait around to see whether the lock held. He burst through the interior door and out into some hall, legs wild, feet slamming tile, not knowing if Doug was behind and not about to turn and look.

He veered around corners, taking them wide, feeling to make sure of his glasses. The halls were pitch black. Eric had only a fuzzy idea where he was—the shop hall, that new athletic wing? —and even less clarity about where he wanted to go. Out to the Corolla? To a safe hiding spot? Someplace where he could dial 911 on a phone, maybe the administrative offices?

His pace lagged as he considered, and now he did hear Doug, not close but moving his direction. Several classroom doors were open. After a four-second spaz over which seemed safest, Eric threw himself into the nearest.

Motion-detector lights blinked on.

"Hm. Wonder which one he's in?" said Doug up the hall.

Eric stood in the dizzyingly bright classroom, looking around, fingers digging his hair. It was an econ room, Venn diagram of asset classes over the blackboard, stock-ticker printouts on the walls. The students' desks horseshoed around the teacher's; desperate to do something, anything, he began shoving them two at a time against the door. The desks were bulky and he had terrible trouble making them stack.

He got maybe seven finagled into a crude pile before the siege began.

TOINK...TOINK...TOINK...

Eric hunted for a weapon. Picked up and set down a stiff ruler, a jangling set of keys on a lanyard. Metal pencil sharpener. What the hell good would any of this be versus a gun?

TOINK...TOINK...

He had to get away. He ran to the window and saw that the classroom overlooked the lot where he and Doug had fought. Lucky break. There was the Corolla parked crookedly on the divider, and the SUV, which might or might not have been rocking—perceptions of subtle, far-off motions were impossible to trust the way his body was heaving.

He checked his jeans for keys. Still there! He might make it, depending on how quickly Doug circumvented his barricade. He felt awful leaving Steph or whomever, but there was no alternative—he couldn't do anybody any good if he were dead.

Eric tried thumbing open the window, but the scoop-shaped lock barely budged.

TOINK...TOINK...

He rammed his palm against the lock several times, putting his shoulder into it. Finally, the sash came loose of its frame with a depressurizing sigh. Eric pushed the glass out, hands plunging into frigid air, and peered down.

The drop was ten or twelve feet. He hiked one knee through the window, then tottered precariously for a moment—facedown, balanced on chest and crotch—before swinging the other through. He lowered himself as far as possible, arms outstretched, clinging to the edges of brick by his fingernails, and released as Doug came crashing into the classroom.

After an instant's free fall, he landed on one foot then cart-wheeled the rest of the way, swinging back against the bricks. His nose and elbow throbbed from the impact, but Eric popped right up—highly motivated by the clattering of desks overhead—and sprinted for the Corolla. He tripped on a sprinkler head, tree limbs raked his jacket, his knee hyperextended over black ice...through it all, he ran.

Doug ran too. Gaining now, a bellows of hard, even puffs closer every second.

No way Eric could hold off QB1 in a footrace. He had misjudged the distance; the Corolla was twice as far as it had seemed from the window. He ran and ran and ran and reached and strode and gulped, and begged for speed, and lassoed the car closer in his mind.

Five yards away, a hand seized his shoulder.

"*Enough*," Doug growled, stopping him roughly. "You're done. This is done."

Eric flailed ahead for the Corolla, as though just touching it might magically transport him. But Doug had him. He produced a length of twine and bound Eric's wrists behind his back, forcing his arms into unnatural angles, jerking the knot. Nylon fibers gouged Eric's skin. As circulation to his hands stopped, they became limp, tingly meat.

Doug shoved him to the ground, then bound his ankles too.

"Now let's have some fun." He held Droid in one hand and a second phone in the other. "Gimme a sec, I need to get myself in the right mind-set. Put on my lackey hat."

Looming over Eric, he wiggled his shoulders and sniffed effeminately. *"Your husband is a pig. He doesn't love you like I do,"* he said, tapping out letters. *"Run away with me now, today. Yesterday."*

Eric, looking up through swollen eyes, grimaced hearing his own rhetorical tic.

Doug switched phones, then did Steph in a clipped, priggish voice: *"I have a family, Eric. Could never leave them."*

Back to Droid: *"Forget convention, forget society. Follow your heart."*

Doug considered the phone at arm's length, his square jaw working side to side. "Maybe another emoticon here. How about one of those winky smiles, semicolon for the eyes. You must do those, yeah?"

When Eric refused to answer (he did use the winky face, generally to soften overbold compliments to women), Doug switched to Steph: *"It's all in your head. Sorry but there is nothing between us."*

Droid: *"How can you say that?! What about kiss? Remember? U can't say that meant nothing."*

Doug read the confusion in Eric's face. "She told me the next day in chem II. I imagine she's forgotten it since. You didn't make much of an impression, Casanova."

He continued on Steph's phone: *"Don't know what else to say. Love my husband and kids, you need to deal with that."*

A shifty glint came into Doug's face as he began his next phony text.

"I won't deal with it. Can't." He put a slight quaver into Eric's voice—desperate, unhinged. *"Just meet me like we planned. ETHS, 4 a.m. Must talk this out."*

With that, he put away the phones. Then from an inner pocket of his jacket, he produced the gun. Black and muscularly compact.

Panic gushed through Eric. A dozen pleas crashed together at his lips. *"No,* don't! Please stop! This is crazy—think it through. I won't say anything, please, *please* just put the gun away."

Doug's head ticked back and forth as he slipped on plastic gloves. "Game over, Pinkersby."

He advanced the gun and Eric braced, squeezing his eyes, fish-flopping away from the muzzle in a way that only exposed the back of his head.

The gun did not fire. Instead Doug slipped it between Eric's tied hands, rubbing his index finger on the trigger and forcing his palms around the handle. Then it was gone—before Eric could even conceive of resisting.

"Hey, what're you *doing*?"

"No: What are *you* doing?" Doug backed away deliberately, holding the gun by two gloved fingers.

"Wait—don't kill her!" Eric said. "Kill me instead, let her live!"

"Oh, you get yours. We'll stick to the classics—standing over the corpse of your beloved, you'll find yourself overwhelmed with grief and give it your best Romeo."

Eric convulsed against his ties, bucking, flailing. He managed to get to his feet. Doug drove a shoulder into his solar plexus, flattening him back to the asphalt.

He screamed. Anguished screams, for help or for Steph or to entice intervention from some omnipotent, heretofore-unbelieved-in deity.

Doug stuffed a glove so deep into his mouth that lamb's wool tickled his tonsils.

"I would let you say goodbye, give you one last chance to deliver some ass-kiss soliloquy." Doug, grimacing, wiped a last set of prints onto the gun. "But it's late. Very damn late."

He paced off toward the SUV. Watching his arms crank, that arrogant gap between sides and triceps, Eric felt keenly aware of the unfairness of the universe. You could do everything right, make the high-minded choices, eschew morally bankrupt shortcuts, and still get stomped. You could follow every rule and wind up in the penalty box. He didn't know if things squared up in an afterlife—he supposed he was about to find out—but down here, man alive, the breaks were brutal.

Doug was halfway across the parking lot when the SUV's headlights came on.

CHAPTER TWENTY-FOUR

The next thirty seconds passed in a blink.

The SUV vroomed alive, barreling into Doug before he could dodge. The bumper slammed his thighs and flipped him up onto the hood, then roof—*plink, plink*—his chiseled body pinwheeling weightlessly. Eric's only conscious thought was a phrase he had heard from video game developers, "ragdoll physics." Both shoes flew off. Doug's jeans sheared in half, the contents of its pockets spraying across the parking lot.

He rolled down the liftgate and landed in a clump. He did not move.

Now the SUV braked hard, back end rearing up like a cornered cat's.

Steph leaned out the window. She was panting and her eyes wouldn't settle. *"Are you okay?"*

Apparently realizing he couldn't answer, she hopped out and pulled the glove from his mouth.

"Yeah, I—yeah, yeah." Eric smacked his tongue on the roof of his mouth, recovering saliva. "He had a gun. He was going to frame me."

She backed out the knots in the twine, freeing him. As sensation returned to his hands, Eric forgot his aching face and allowed himself a moment of joy. He was alive—and Steph Mills was the one who'd saved him. Her green eyes were perfect almonds of concern. The skin between her mouth and nose, that perfect quarter inch, quivered with every good emotion in the human palette. All she needed were wings and a halo.

"Is this your phone?" she asked, picking Droid off the asphalt.

Eric pried a swath of denim from the case's camera cutout and checked the screen. The glass had spidered at one corner, but the display underneath seemed fine.

He looked up to Steph, then across the lot to where Doug lay motionless. "So should we, um...?"

"Go," Steph said. "We're going."

"Is Autumn Brockert inside?"

"What? No, I—*Autumn Brockert*? My kids are inside and they're horrified!"

And they were. Eric heard their cries as he circled to the passenger's side, muffled screeches through the windshield. He opened the door, and noise caved his eardrums—spiraling wails, hysterical questions from the back seat.

"Why is Daddy mad?"

"Mommy Mommy, did we hit a deer again?"

"I want go home! Go home go home go home *go home*!"

Steph jammed the SUV into gear and drove, out of ETHS, west on Church Street. She muttered assurances, reached back to soothe Morgan's knee. Nothing helped. Eric could feel her struggling to project calm, biting her lips, mastering rickety breaths.

They had driven a half dozen blocks when the older girl squirmed out of her five-point harness. She lay horizontal, bare tummy sticking out of her PJs and legs furiously kicking air.

Steph pulled over. "Ella, Honey Bear, we have to stay in our car seats."

"*Why did you run over Daddy? Is he okay? Why aren't we checking on Daddy?*"

"Daddy is...fine. Sweetie. He's fine, but we have to leave him for now."

"I want Daddy, *Daddy*! *Go back get Daddy...*"

The younger joined in with a primal scream, which made the older scream that that was too loud and begin clawing ineffectually at her little sister.

"Why don't we go visit Grammy?" Steph said, boosting Ella

back into her car seat. "She told me she made snickerdoodles, and if you're good, I bet she'd let you have a glass of chocolate milk."

This at least spaced out the protests. Steph climbed back to the driver's seat.

The grandmother lived just a few minutes away. Eric faced forward, but his eyes in their throbbing sockets kept drifting to Steph. Her wrists showed marks similar to his, and a red streak bisected one cheek. Her pants were torn. Through the hole, her thigh was pale pink.

"What did he d—" he began, but she stopped him with a look.

By the time they reached Steph's mom's house, Morgan had cried herself to sleep. Eric stayed with her while Steph walked Ella up the porch. Grandma answered the door with a smile and accepted Ella's face in her nightgown. If she was surprised or confused, it didn't show. She and Steph spoke briefly, then Steph returned to extract Morgan, unpacking her chubby limbs, easing the baby onto her shoulder. She walked bow-backed up the drive and handed the package to her mother.

Back in the car, Steph faced Eric. "Is he dead, you think? Did he look dead to you?"

Eric said he had absolutely no clue. "Should we go back and check?"

"No!"

Steph seemed surprised by the vehemence of her own reply. She sunk back into the driver's seat, grinding palms into her forehead.

"I don't know." Her voice hoarse, suddenly tired. "I don't know what we do. I guess we tell the police, right? Let them sort it out?"

Eric thought back over the last forty-eight hours. His flight from the Marriott. Diving for cover at the sight of any longish/wide sedan. One night sleeping on deck boards and another in the back seat of a stolen car.

"Yeah. We call the cops."

They decided to collect themselves first in the parking lot of a nearby Walgreens. Grandma was having trouble coaxing Ella away from the window, and Eric thought they should spend a little time getting their story straight besides.

En route, Steph gave him a rundown of her ordeal, how she had discovered the Sears Tower window washer's key behind the *Sports Illustrated*s, then failed to sneak away with the kids. Doug had read their texts about meeting at ETHS and said, *Mommy's right, girls—we are going on a little nighttime adventure.* He had even managed to play up the gun and nylon twine as part of the game, making silly-spooky eyes, saying they might come across *zombies!* and better be prepared, and *ooh look*, Mommy had already turned into one.

"I saw the car rocking while he was punching—er, when the two of us were fighting," Eric said. "How did you get free?"

Steph nodded at his seat belt. "The buckle has a sharp edge, but only a small part is exposed when you're clicked in. I just kept rubbing."

They pulled into Walgreens. Two cars were parked in a back corner, possibly employees. Steph cruised through the pharmacy drive-thru and parked several spaces away. Over neighboring apartment buildings, the sky was lightening, soot gray with a hint of strangled pink. It was 5:40 a.m..

Eric asked, "What do you think Doug did with that Sears key? Did he push the kid?"

"No, the kid jumped. He rigged up that magnet, he strapped on the chute himself." Steph ran two hands down her face. "Doug must've helped him scale the building. Let him out of his office window, something. But why?"

"Because he knew the kid would die."

"Okay—I can accept that, given what we've lived through tonight. But still, why? What does that kid—I can't even remember his name, maybe Tristan—have to do with Mr. Fiske? Or Becky?"

"So are we saying Doug *is* behind all this Fiske stuff? Did he tell you?"

"He didn't tell me a thing."

They faced each other in silence. Eric felt a mishmash of emotions: elation at being alive, fear about what came next, empathy—but also excitement—for everything Steph had learned about her husband. He struggled to conjure up a best-case future, trying on a life where he stepped right into Doug's shoes (following his arrest and the successful rescue of Autumn Brockert from some basement cell)...or kissed Steph goodbye on a tarmac, followed by an extended, Skype-heavy courtship from San Fran...or *Us Weekly* covers featuring split images of them strolling different white-sand beaches: *Will They or Won't They?*

Of course, any of these presupposed one very large break.

"I'm still a fugitive," he said. "My status with the police...do you think it changes?"

Steph laid a hand on his arm. "It must. It has to."

She offered to make the call to Detective Wright. Doug was her husband. She should handle it. Okay? Agreed?

Eric nodded.

They dialed on his phone—hers was lost, presumably back at ETHS—and listened to it ring once, twice. Three times.

Just then, a background chime began. Not his ringtone or a new-text alert, but that hollow, frightened-leaky-faucet *blip-blop, blip-blop, blip-blop* of his AP newswire app. He tapped a red exclamation mark on Droid's cracked screen and read.

"Hello, Wright speaking," came the detective's gruff answer.

Steph's mouth opened, but Eric clapped his hand over before any sound escaped.

CHAPTER TWENTY-FIVE

The words could not be real. Steph read the first paragraph four times—Eric's shaky grip made the screen a moving target—before catching the gist. She gave a dazed nod, and he dragged the article down for her to finish.

"Here, there's video."

He tapped, and Victoria Keane—scandal-following tele-journalist extraordinaire—appeared, standing on some street corner in a maroon slicker.

"The case of Autumn Brockert, long thought solved or at least well understood, appears anything but on this early morning, as police say this woman, Stephanie Reece"—a glossy headshot from the Dunham & Prior website flashed—"and her alleged lover, Eric Pinkersby"—a pale still from the police station—"may be the true villains in the disappearances of Brockert and their own former teacher, Bob Fiske.

"Police are searching for Ms. Reece and Mr. Pinkersby, as well as a third individual, Trev Larson, who may also be involved. Details are sketchy—this latest development has come to my producer's attention within the last five minutes." Keane raised a paper in the wind. "According to sources, the authorities are in possession of incriminating text messages sent between Mrs. Reece and Mr. Larson: messages that provide chilling insight into how and when the elaborate hoax developed."

Steph felt her core dissolving, sickened by the memory of Doug asking to borrow her cell. "Keep losing the damn network." *How long had he been saying that?* Since June or July.

"...unclear at this point what motives are at play," Victoria Keane continued, "but we do know Ms. Reece and Mr. Pinkersby were members of Fiske's so-called 'Winners.' And as the entire country has witnessed over the course of the last week, these individuals accept no obstacle in pursuit of their goals."

The video blinked out, replaced by a trailer for the new *X-Men* movie. A note along the bottom read, *Your video will resume in 30 seconds.*

Steph's thoughts whorled. "This is insane! I can't even...I mean, it's just too crazy..."

"Why is Victoria Keane reporting at six a.m.?" Eric said. "How did she get the scoop so fast?"

They both stared out the windshield. A third car had parked beside the two others, and now a young woman in Walgreens blue crossed the lot and entered a side door. The sun had cleared the roofs of the adjacent apartments, but the temperature in Steph's SUV dropped with every second they sat without the motor running.

The answer to his question was obvious: Doug.

"He's alive," Steph said. "While we were dropping off the girls, he was calling around. He planned everything out ahead of time."

Her entire world was broken. Everything she counted on or believed in. From the moment she had found that strange key attached to a wooden dowel, her life had become unrecognizable. A rush of anger, betrayal, violence.

On the way to the tennis courts, bound in the passenger seat, she had hissed across the console, "You can't get away with this. Doug, turn around—those are your children in the back seat!"

"They won't be hurt," he had said.

Steph swallowed her fear at this unsettling answer, focused on the kids. "They'll know. Whatever you're doing here, *they will know.*"

She spoke in low tones to not upset the girls—had been suppressing her own terror since being discovered, even playing along with Doug's zombie tie-up game to spare them the sight of their father physically overpowering their mother.

"I'll make up a story. Ella still thinks dragons steal your Halloween candy if you eat more than two pieces the first night, remember?"

He said it nastily, seeming to drive home the suggestion Ella might not be too bright, a constant source of anxiety for Steph. At ETHS, he ferociously re-cinched her knots; forced a pacifier into Morgan's mouth—the zombie jig was up, both kids were hysterical; and stormed off to confront Eric with a gun in his fist.

Who *was* this man? Doug never showed anger, which made the fury pulsing off him then so disturbing. How long had this been building? Months? Years? Had *any* of her marriage been real? Made him happy or given him the slightest satisfaction? It was like learning your bank was a Ponzi scheme or termites had eaten your foundation. Sudden, gut-crunching devastation.

After the *X-Men* trailer, Veronica Keane returned with details of the search.

"The fugitive couple was last spotted in Evanston, in the vicinity of Evanston Township High School. Police believe they may be armed and advise anyone who crosses paths with them to steer clear and phone the authorities at once."

She went on to report that Trev Larson's whereabouts were unknown, and police efforts were focused on an area bound loosely by McCormick to the west and Sheridan to the east. The shot zoomed back as she gestured circularly behind her.

It took Steph and Eric several seconds to resolve the building behind Victoria Keane, but when they did, both sat bolt upright.

"The fire station," Steph cried. "That's two blocks away!"

Eric buckled his seat belt. "Go, we gotta go."

Steph inserted the key but stopped short of turning it. In the distance, visible between a stoplight and *Walgreen's Pharmacy* sign, a police cruiser turned up the road. Slow. Prowling their way.

"Maybe we should surrender," Eric said. "It's our word against his, right? There must be plenty of physical evidence of what he did to us."

"No." Steph pocketed her keys, gaze steady on the cruiser as though it might pounce if she broke eye contact. "Doug will have all his bases covered. We need evidence of our own."

What that evidence might be, or how they would go about getting it, she had no idea. But she was done being outmaneuvered by Doug.

Clearly, driving around in a car registered to Stephanie Reece was a poor idea. They opened their doors quietly and shimmied through missing pickets of a privacy fence, huddling in the shadow of the apartment building.

Eric stood in puddled oil. "Now what?"

The first thing Steph did was call her mother and alert her to the fact Doug was alive. Steph didn't see Doug going after the children—they would only be a hindrance—but after tonight, all bets were off. *Dad still keeps a shotgun, right? Good. Get it out.*

Next, they needed to put space between the cops and themselves.

"The Dempster El stop is close," Steph said. "Five or six blocks."

"And where do we go from there?"

"Anywhere."

She looked up and down the alley, realized that she had to pee. Bad.

There was no decent cover, so they just headed for the El. The streets were residential, and Eric started out taking one house at a time, moving only when the coast was clear. The morning commute was only getting heavier, though, and Steph soon yanked him out from behind a carport and led them into foot traffic. She wore a sweatshirt and his face looked like hamburger— not your prototypical eight-to-sixers—but they walked briskly with purposefully stiff backs, and nobody stopped them.

Steph paid cash for two single-ride tickets. The CTA worker eyed them through the turnstile, thumbs in his Day-Glo-yellow vest.

"Sir," he called from his booth. "Sir, do you need medical attention?"

Eric kept shuffling for the tunnel, but Steph gripped his arm. The last thing they needed was a chase.

"Oh, it's nothing," he said. "Bike accident. I always take that driveway too fast."

He knocked himself clownishly upside the head, and Steph did an exaggerated eye roll. The man's tongue shifted in his mouth.

They joined the crowd through the tunnel, passing under the tracks, then up to the platform. Steph staked out a spot beside a billboard. In the distance, visible through leaf-bare treetops, police cars surrounded Walgreens.

Eric shielded his words with his body. "You think the CTA guy called the police?"

Steph pinned her knees together. She really had to go. "If a bulletin gets sent around with our descriptions, and he sees it? Not good."

Luckily a Purple Line train came chugging around the bend within seconds. People mobbed forward to wedge at bifold doors. Steph and Eric took a bench near the front, the type that sits perpendicular to a single. Eric folded and refolded his legs to stay out of the other riders' space.

"Motel?" he muttered into his collar. "South Side maybe. Lay low, figure out a plan?"

It occurred to Steph that Eric was the authority here, having been on the lam three days running.

"Sure." She bit her lip against the tears softening her upper face. "A motel."

The train moved off. She watched the police in the Walgreens lot fade and Evanston vanish in the whir of a passing car, and felt again that the world had shattered. Everything was a lie. If Doug could tie her up like that, and be willing to use a gun, then it had all been a lie.

To what purpose, though? She felt keenly that it was about *her* somehow, that escaping life with her and the girls must be at the root of Doug's plot. Why he had involved Eric and Becky and that kid who jumped off the Sears Tower, and (possibly, or not?) Fiske and Autumn Brockert too, she didn't understand.

Have I been that bad a wife? I let him have his poker nights. I didn't nag or overspend. Was never stubborn about holiday travel. We had sex regularly, and fine, there were a few places I wouldn't go, but what woman says yes to every last request?

Now a conversation came back to her about what they would do if the other died early, in something like a car wreck. Doug had started with the obligatory *of course I couldn't carry on, would never remarry* answer, but when pressed, said he guessed he would scout out a different city, start fresh in a new country or on the West Coast. He would take lots of time doing nothing. Reading. Learning to surf. (Apparently the kids had also perished in the hypothetical tragedy.) And his eyes—it seemed to Steph now, in memory—had gotten a little too bright, his fingers a little too spry up and down the handle of his coffee mug, as he'd mused about apartment life and what sort of luck he might have on Match.com.

The Purple Line ran to Howard. There they transferred to Red, bumping across the platform, faces down. Four CTA security guards milled about, but, Howard being one of the rougher stations, Steph didn't feel conspicuous.

They boarded a middle car and took hand straps near a group of rangy youths.

"Can we take this all the way down?" Steph asked.

Eric nodded. Garfield or Sixty-Third should be far enough. They could scout motels from the platform.

It took a while for the train to move, doors closing and opening, closing and opening, cold air blasting in each time. The youths—big, loud sixteen- or seventeen-year-olds—shouted at one of their group to back out of the way, but the doors kept splatting even with both the kid's feet clearly inside.

A chime sounded, and at last they jolted forward. The train was less than ten seconds underway when it stopped.

"Pardon, folks," the conductor's voice called over the intercom. "Need to return to the station for a moment, have y'on your way shortly."

The youths jeered and slapped windows. Others groaned. As the train reversed, wheels squeaking, gears grinding, Steph glanced back and saw more uniforms on the platform. Two policemen had joined the transit cops. Six altogether now, shoulder to shoulder.

Pointing at their train.

"Uh-oh," Eric said.

Steph clutched her strap so hard she felt the stitching in her knuckles. "We have to get off."

"How? They'll notice somebody getting off."

She grabbed his wrist and started for the doors anyway, lips firm. The youths were in the way. She nudged through an outer layer before hitting a solid wall of coats and puffy sleeves.

"Excuse us," she said. "Sorry, excuse us please."

They turned around, and one, seeing Eric's face, said, "Damn, somebody gave you a beatdown."

Eric touched his glasses. "Little misunderstanding was all. We straightened it out."

"His ass straightened it out. Yours got whooped."

"I—well, it went back and forth. I wouldn't say either of us won, per se—"

"Eric," Steph cut in. "We need to go."

But they weren't going anywhere. The train had stopped, and now a policeman or transit cop was waiting at every door. The one at Steph's and Eric's car held a small paper in the crook of his wrist. As the doors opened, he glanced at the paper before stepping inside.

The youths surrounding them blanked their faces and stood tall, defiant. Steph saw an opportunity. She pulled Eric close and kept their bodies inside the circle. The transit cop eyeballed the kids but never lowered his gaze to check the interior beyond. He then moved on to the rest of the car, alternating between riders' faces and the paper—which, Steph saw now, had photos of her, Eric, and a person in army fatigues who must've been Trev Larson.

She did not breath. Her bladder pulsed.

"What did y'all do, Rihanna and Chris?" one kid said, hushed. *"Dust somebody?"*

The others nudged Eric, pinballing him off Steph and themselves. One offered a fist bump. Eric, fixing his glasses, got the kid back with a hesitant open palm.

The transit cop pivoted at the end of the car, forearm heavy on the end-door latch, then came back through. He peeked under ball caps and asked one woman to lower her newspaper. Squinted at a slender man seated behind a pole. Stumbled on a briefcase. Steph worried the kids' joshing might draw his attention, but they cut it out once he reached their side of the car again.

Finally, the *wing-wong* chime sounded and doors opened. The transit cop took a last sideways look at the youths, then stepped off.

CHAPTER TWENTY-SIX

They switched to Metra at Union Station. The commuter trains had few security personnel, a double-decker layout with plenty of hiding nooks, and—a huge point for Steph—bathrooms. She rushed to a stall. Safe inside its steel walls, taking her first full breath in hours. When she emerged, Eric was sprawled upstairs with coat draped over his head, looking like a sacked-out college kid. Steph made sure their tickets were visible to a passing conductor, then lay down too.

They slept.

Washington Heights was the end of the line. They rubbed their gummy eyes and disembarked. Three blocks from the station, between a laundromat and a liquor store, they found a motel. The clerk put away nail clippers as they walked in.

"Reservation?"

Eric asked, "Do we need one?"

The clerk brushed his clippings to the floor. "Name?"

When Steph didn't answer straightaway, Eric said, "Bill and Janine Thompson of Columbus, Ohio. Quick road trip to see the natural beauty of Wisconsin!"

The clerk blinked once, then began writing in pencil. Over his shoulder, a bracket-mounted TV played cable news. The sound was off but Steph could read the closed-captioning.

COMING UP NEXT...MY LIVE INTERVIEW WITH THE MAN

WHO NOW FINDS HIMSELF IN THE CENTER OF THE AUTUMN BROCKERT CASE...HUSBAND OF ONE OF THE FUGITIVES AT LARGE THIS MORNING...DOUG REECE.

Steph angled her face away in case the broadcast flashed her photo next, but the clerk was paying no attention, ferreting through magic marker–labeled key rings.

Eric went on to fabricate an address ("1011 Sunnyvale Drive") and explain—arm stretched across but not daring to touch Steph's shoulder—his strategy of driving through the night in order to beat city traffic. *That* was why they needed a room at this odd morning hour.

The clerk said, "Gotcha ace," and thumbed directions to their room.

Room 206 was the size of a large shed, with black mildew at the ceiling corners. As Eric scrubbed his wounds in the bathroom, Steph collapsed onto the bed. Her body felt brittle, used up. A husk.

She flopped over to reach the nightstand remote. Found the channel that'd been playing in the lobby.

"Thank you for joining us in this difficult time," began Victoria Keane in a faintly upper-crust accent. "I understand you sustained several broken ribs and a fractured leg?"

The camera cut to Doug in a wheelchair, sitting with elbows awkwardly hemmed in. His chin was bandaged, and a gash showed in the part of his hair.

"It's only hairline." He smiled and winced. "Thanks for having me."

"Clearly, Mr. Reece, you have been involved in some manner of altercation. What can you tell us about the events of last night and how they relate to the Brockert case?"

Doug—drawing deep, rattling breaths—recounted how he had discovered his wife's plot. It was the silliest thing. His four-year-old daughter had been bugging him to look at some picture she had "drawed" on her mother's phone, and so, waking to use the bathroom at midnight, happening across Steph's phone on the vanity, he'd started tapping.

That was when he discovered the texts. He returned to bed to confront her. She became enraged. *Why was he poking around her phone? This was stupid, very stupid of him.* Before he understood the full ramifications of what he'd stumbled onto, she pulled a gun.

Victoria Keane, whose celebrity had been created by the loss of her own son to a Vermont prep-school hazing incident, listened with knuckles pressed to lips.

"Then she bound you."

Doug nodded. From a slight tremor in his neck, Steph could see this part of the lie irked him: the idea that his wife could overcome him.

"Yes," he said nonetheless. "She forced me into the car, then forced the kids into the car. The looks on their faces, how they screamed...it was beyond...I—I don't know if I can ever forget that."

"She was taking you to Evanston Township High. To rendezvous with her lover, Eric Pinkersby?"

Another tremor at the word "lover."

"As I understand, they planned to kill me and disappear with the girls."

"But you escaped."

Doug nodded, shifting in his wheelchair. "I chewed through my ties, then ran to the school and hid. I got myself into a janitor's closet. Eric Pinkersby found me and blasted out the doorknob—he was absolutely insane. Possessed. I feel as if I understand now what my dear friend Becky Brindle must have been facing on that cliff in Michigan."

"Indeed," Keane said. "So Mr. Pinkersby flushes you from the school. Then?"

"I'm in the parking lot, and I see my wife behind the wheel of our car. And I think..." Doug's eyes dewed. "I thought she'd had a change of heart. Maybe she had remembered our seven years together, remembered that I carried her over the threshold of our first apartment, how Ella would only sleep propped against my shoulder those first days in the hospital..."

"But I was wrong. She hit the gas."

"She ran you down?"

"Yes. I rolled up onto the hood, then the roof. Like a coin loose in the dryer."

"And they thought they'd killed you? Your wife and Eric Pinkersby?"

"I assume. I kept still, hoping for exactly that. They stood around talking a while, then drove off with my children."

Victoria Keane folded her arms in disgust.

Steph burned inside. She supposed this should come as no surprise. Doug was great at everything; why wouldn't he be a great liar? She was so accustomed to having Doug's gifts at her disposal, though—benefiting from his advice, finding comfort in his strength—that it was bewildering to feel them aligned against her.

Bewildering...devastating...*infuriating.*

Eric, back from the bathroom: "He's inhuman! Seriously, it's airtight—this story explains away every piece of evidence they're going to find."

Onscreen, Doug accepted a tissue to dab his face.

"And—you know, in all honesty, Victoria, I hope this is a simple case of adultery. I hope I'm mistaken about there being this larger plot. If my wife prefers another man, I...that's hard, but I can accept it."

Victoria Keane said, "The text messages are quite damning."

Doug said he knew.

"*Yeah, you frickin' know!*" Eric blurted. "*You faked them! You fed them to the cops!*"

"And also," Keane said, reading off a tablet mounted to her desk, "we are just now learning that police have found your wife's fingerprints inside Bob Fiske's condo, as well as closed-circuit video that shows her entering the building's lobby two days after Autumn Brockert disappeared."

Doug dropped his head.

"Now there has been a third person implicated today," Keane continued, "Trev Larson, about whom we've heard conflicting reports. One eyewitness account has him fleeing on foot after a confrontation with police. We're being told he remains at large." She looked to Doug. "Mr. Larson was a colleague of yours, I understand. A friend?"

"So I thought," Doug said. "We played in a regular card game.

He would come over and, you know, he and Steph would flirt a little, but I figured it was harmless."

Steph was off the bed now, her toes clawing the motel carpet. *On top of being a murderer and kidnapper, now I'm a slut too?*

"Betrayed," said Victoria Keane. "By those you loved, and best trusted."

Doug waved off her sympathy. The motion threw his wheelchair momentarily out of balance. He righted himself with a game grimace. "That may be true, but I got off easy. What makes me truly sad is to think of Autumn Brockert. Of Coach Fiske.

"I keep thinking about something Coach told me years ago, when he found out Steph and I were dating. Coach pulled me aside after practice and said, 'I think the world of Stephanie Mills, but know this: Her ambition will be limitless. She will live a great and effective life, but Home and Husband will not quench her thirst. She'll demand more. And get more. And demand more again.'"

Keane asked, "How did you respond?"

"I was seventeen, I didn't care about Home and Husband." Doug chuckled joylessly. "But Coach was right. I worked and worked to make it enough for Steph, and to my eyes, we had a heckuva life. A brownstone ten minutes from the beach. Stainless-steel fridge. Two healthy kids. More money than we could spend."

"It was never enough."

"No. No, it never was."

He went on to describe their "hyper-ambitious" life together, how Steph pushed for new titles at work (*and he didn't?*), the outsize importance she placed on their four-year-old daughter's reading ability, on and on. These characterizations irked her, but she understood Doug was simply portraying her in the worst possible light. The Fiske anecdote bothered her more deeply. It sounded like Fiske. Doug had never told her about this rather presumptuous piece of advice, but then she supposed a spouse wouldn't.

Did Fiske actually believe that about me?

"In terms of establishing motive," Keane said, "because we're all struggling to understand—just as you are, Mr. Reece—how much do you know about your wife's dealings with MetroBuild?"

"I know she worked for them. They were a client of her advertising agency."

"Indeed." Victoria Keene snapped another supporting document to her desk. "My producers have discovered inflammatory exchanges in the minutes of recent Evanston City Council meetings, wherein Bob Fiske makes an impassioned case against a large development deal between the city and MetroBuild. Were you aware of this?"

"Somewhat." Doug tensed as though reluctant to go on, but of course he did. "MetroBuild was Steph's biggest account. She mentioned several times that Coach was holding up the project. They had a lucrative marketing campaign in the works, but it couldn't run until the city council gave the green light."

Victoria Keane allowed this to hang in the air a moment, then said, "Later in the hour, I'll be interviewing a partner at Steph Reece's firm who claims to have e-mails assuring him that Ms. Reece would 'take care of' her former teacher's vocal opposition."

With a sickened pang, Steph recalled Rich Hauser's bizarre comment yesterday. (*Was that really just twenty-four hours ago?*) "I'd wager MetroBuild feels slightly better off today." Probably Doug had e-mailed using her phone.

Unbelievable. He was so good, had been so thorough in assembling his trap. It must've dominated his non-working thoughts. He must have been dreaming up incriminating details while he changed Morgan's diaper, and mowed the lawn, and massaged her back on the couch.

Keane began a question about Autumn Brockert's possible whereabouts, but Steph switched off the TV with a thrust of the remote.

She and Eric stared at the blank, gloss-brown screen.

"If only we'd picked up your phone," Eric said. "At the tennis court."

Steph's eyes stayed on the screen. "Or backed up. Ran him over again, harder."

A million bad actions flooded Steph's mind. She wanted to light those lucky, holey loafers of his on fire. Throw his Urlacher jersey off the Clark Street Bridge. With him inside. Despite Eric's assurances that larger issues were at play—what about Sears, and Becky Brindle, and Fiske's fake suicide?—right now it felt personal. As if she and Doug stood naked in their bedroom in front of the world, screaming, clawing each other.

A chime sounded. Eric crooked his brow, then looked down to his pocket.

"Facebook." He fished out his phone. "A message from...huh. A user whose name I do not recognize."

"Not a friend?"

Eric shook his head. Steph circled the bed to look over his shoulder. They read the name together and experienced roughly the same three seconds of confusion before their eyes got wide.

The name of the Facebook user who'd messaged Eric was *MARNA JACOBS.*

CHAPTER TWENTY-SEVEN

E ric assembled his indeterminately-labeled *Dark Roast* with
difficulty. His trench coat took a rivulet of 2% milk down the
sleeve, and his vinyl Sox cap kept falling into the sugars—wearing
it street sideways made for poor stability. Their disguise options
had been limited. The only general merchandise store within three
miles of the motel had tiki torches and e-cigs in the window, the
type specializing in whatever fell off the back of the truck. After
quasi-successfully forcing a lid onto his large Panera cup, Eric
walked his tray through chatting students to Steph's booth
in back.

"What time did we tell her again?" he asked.

In noir lipstick and mascara, Steph was a dead ringer for
Kristen Stewart.

"Eleven," she said. "It's eleven fifteen now."

Eric took a sip—timid, true to its urn's label—and glanced at
the nearest table of students. Asian tweens with coats unzipped,
simultaneously laughing together and engrossed in their devices.
Did the one kid keep looking up? In the skullcap? Had he recognized Eric from the news?

Nah. Come on, *the news*? Nobody under eighty watched the
news. Unless their photos had somehow gotten pinned, or Insta-
grammed, or liked fourteen thousand times, they were off these
kids' radar.

They were safe.

Well, not *safe* safe.

Eric asked, "What assurances do we have this girl won't turn us in?"

"None," Steph said.

Marna Jacobs, friend of the Sears jumper, would not reveal over Facebook messaging why she wanted to meet. *i might know something*, was all she'd say. He and Steph figured they had no choice. They needed answers, and given what Steph had discovered behind those vintage *Sports Illustrated*s, it seemed reasonable to believe Marna's puzzle piece—whatever it was—might fit one of their gaps.

At quarter 'til noon, just as their table sitting was becoming conspicuous, a petite girl wearing a peacoat and black-felt bowler cap entered. She ordered nothing and began scanning the dining room. Before Eric could decide whether to beckon her over, she spotted them.

"Those disguises aren't, um, great," she said.

Eric adjusted his Sox cap. "Thanks a lot."

Marna removed her own cap and placed it on the table. "I have to ask, before we start. You didn't shove that counselor off a cliff, right?"

Eric said no, he hadn't.

"And you"—turning to Steph—"didn't really beat up your husband? He has, like, a hundred pounds on you."

Steph nodded.

"Okay. Okay, that's what I thought." Marna exhaled. "When I saw him on TV—your husband, Doug—I knew he was the bad guy."

"How?"

"For one, he's a jock. I never trust jocks." She fingered a turquoise thumb ring. "But also I recognized him. I'd seen him before with Jesse."

Eric and Steph locked eyes, then asked at once, "*Where?*"

"Hanging out. At the climbing gym downtown, right before Jesse's stunt."

Eric said, "Hedge fund big shots don't *hang out* with sixteen-year-old boys. What did they do?"

"Talked mostly," Marna said. "I remember Jesse saying, 'This guy is *sick*, he understands how Fiske *thinks*.' Making Winner was Jesse's obsession—he was ravenous for anybody who could help. Doug told Jesse to Live Big and not be intimidated by these nerds in class. Told him he had cojones, the stuff Fiske actually cared about."

Sniffing back tears, she recounted Jesse's story. Eric already knew the broad outlines, but several of Marna's details surprised him—the way Fiske's withering praise for an essay had hooked Jesse ("Intriguing—a young man with mouthwatering insights in the pot but no means of getting them to plate") and the role Doug had played in stoking his ambition.

It seemed Doug had laid back initially, booked Jesse for a half-hour climbing lesson and just shot the breeze. *Oh yeah? You're ETHS too?* Not until the third session had he mentioned Fiske, revealing that he had been a Winner and understood the old man —having played the achiever's game in high school, and now with the perspective of another decade's life experience. The two had met outside the gym at least twice. Coffee, Froyo. Doug had looked over Jesse's *Atlas Shrugged* paper.

"I didn't think anything of it," Marna said, "but when I saw him on TV this morning, in the middle of all this Fiske stuff?" Her eyes slit. "It felt wrong."

Steph looked a bit undead, in dark makeup and with that stony, boiling-under-the-surface face Eric had seen so much of these last twenty-four hours.

"I found a key." She explained the wooden dowel and its *Willis Tower* label.

Marna's jaw gaped. "Oh my God! *That's* how Jesse got up so fast! He was an amazing technical climber but not that amazing— I *knew* he had help."

"My husband worked on the ninety-seventh floor." Guilt throbbed Steph's voice. "Jessie, your friend, could have taken an elevator right to his office."

The tweens at the next table were quieter now. Were they just packing up or eavesdropping? Had one of them left already? Gone ahead to find a cop? Eric tried listening in but couldn't make out a thing.

Giving up, he asked, "But why help? If you're Doug—why goad Jesse into jumping?"

"To kill him!" Marna said. "Because he was trying to kill him!"

"Right, okay, that's right." Eric flattened his fingers soothingly to the table. "What I meant was, *why* kill him? What's the payoff for Doug?"

"Just, like, laughs." Marna was compressing the sides of her bowler cap. "Why do jocks yank a geek's underwear up over his head after gym?"

"No," Steph said. "Doug takes risks, but not unnecessary ones. He gained something from Jesse's death."

They rumbled around the subject ten minutes, draining their coffees, wringing the cuffs of their jackets. Did Jesse have incriminating information on Doug? No, Doug had been a stranger to him. Had Doug just wanted to make Fiske look bad, create a backlash that cost him his job? *Why?* Did Doug have some decade-old ax to grind?

Eric's supercharged imagination drove the speculation. He asked Marna to dig deep for any possible connections between the principals. Biting a knuckle, she recalled that Jesse and Autumn had been partners for an extracurricular project in senior English.

Hm. Eric gathered up empties, headed for the coffee station. What if Jesse had discovered the relationship between Autumn and Fiske during the project, threatened to expose them? And then Doug...what, wanted to keep it under wraps so he could do them in himself? A preemptive, cover-up murder?

Financial gain from shorting shares of whoever owned the Sears Tower, in the event the skydecks had to close? Publicity for Doug's hedge fund if the floor of Jesse's shortcut became known?

Man, these limbs were getting longer and thinner by the second.

"Did Jesse find Autumn attractive?" Eric asked, sliding fresh (well, fifty-five-minute-old fresh) *Dark Roasts* to all. "How about a love triangle? Forget Doug for now—let's understand Jesse and Autumn."

Marna shrugged, but her turquoise ring was pressed hard into her thumb, turning the skin white. "Probably. I mean, half the universe did."

"Did she ever reciprocate?"

"She talked to him. Didn't have a choice, Fiske made them be partners."

"And they got along okay? Did they ever meet outside of school?"

"Did he dump me for her? Is that what you're asking, if he dumped me for a hotter girl?"

Eric, who thought he had been treading discreetly, wheezed back from the table. "Look, we're in the dark. I'm looking for anything—attraction, intrigue. Conflict. Anything. What kind of project was it? Were they writing a paper together?"

"Jesse never said."

"What was the assignment?"

"It wasn't for class. It was outside of class."

Eric looked to Steph, both their faces piqued.

"So Fiske puts two students on a secret project together...one jumps to his death...the other goes missing...Doug plays a role in both..."

Before he could extend the associations, Eric glimpsed—up the block, through the frost-print *Panera* of the window—that tween in the skullcap. The kid was beckoning a cruiser, motioning for the officer inside to roll down his window and glancing back toward the restaurant.

"*Police,*" he whispered. "*Let's go, out the back!*"

The three hurried out to a side street, past a yeasty vent, past a display of frame-corner samples. Speed-walking, hugging the building face. Eric's Sox cap fell off; he stuffed it into his trench coat. The side street fed into a busy thoroughfare, whose first storefront was a Chinese grocery.

They scrambled in.

"Farther back," Steph said, leading Eric and Marna by the wrists. They squeezed past wizened ladies picking through a bin of chicken feet, wriggled between rice cookers and a freezer of mochi balls. Eric banged knees with a man carrying an entire hog carcass over one shoulder.

"*Ow*, pigboy," he muttered.

Steph veered them into an aisle of bean pastes and scraggly, tendriled herbs. Eric sat and, once they had confirmed there were no sightlines to passing traffic, let his head flop back. He smelled liquefying cabbage.

We're hosed.

Coming and going, forward and backward. The cops had their location. Soon a fleet of squad cars would descend, and they'd be paraded before the media, providing the necessary distraction from the fruitless search for Autumn Brockert. They would be grilled about the location of her body and claim innocence. Eventually, her remains would turn up in some ditch or downstream Lake Superior, and the mountain of evidence Doug had shammed against them would be plenty to convict.

Then it hit him.

Steph recognized the light bulb over his head, gripped the collar of his trench coat. "What? *What is it?*"

He smiled into her warm breath. "I know what Autumn and Jesse's secret project was."

They stayed at the Chinese grocery another five minutes, ambling now up to the produce, now back to a tank of large pink fish, ready to dash away but never having to. Apparently, the tween in the skullcap had not managed to get the cop's attention, or else failed to convince—they did not see another cruiser. When the coast felt reasonably clear, they walked another six blocks to hole up at Barnes & Noble.

(Thank God for the bland anonymity of chains.)

At the revolving-door entrance, Steph thanked Marna and wished her luck.

"I want to help," Marna said. "I wanna nail this jerk too. For Jesse."

Eric crooked an eyebrow at Steph—a third might come in handy—but she was having none of it.

"Go to school, Marna. You are a hundred percent innocent as long as you leave now. We'll nail him."

Marna opened her mouth to object, but Steph was already

walking her forward, nudging the girl's shoulders along—a move she must've perfected on squirming toddlers. Marna's vintage boots clacked reluctantly, but she kept moving. They watched her to the El stop.

"Alright, she's gone," Steph said. "Now tell me about this secret project. What were Autumn and Jesse working on?"

Eric tapped the spine of a hardcover. "A manuscript."

As they rode the escalator to more secluded sections of the store, he told of finding the charred manuscript behind Fiske's cabin. *Illusory Greatnesses.* The pseudonym, "Vance T____." His conviction, based on Fiske's encouragement about his own manuscript, that someone else must have started the blaze. He had almost forgotten in the hurricane of cops and dogs and black Jeeps, but Marna's revelations had brought it back.

"It also explains the money, potentially," he thought aloud.

Steph perked up. "The deposits. From that bank in Delaware."

"Right. I figured the amounts might be online advertising, from some blog or website, but now I'm thinking royalties. If Fiske has books in print, he would be receiving automatic payments that fit the pattern—regular, with occasional spikes depending on promotions."

Eric typed *Vance T* into Droid, hoping Google autosuggest would supply the rest of the pseudonym, but all the mighty algorithm gave back was "Vance Travers," a minor character from *Assassin's Creed IV: Black Flag.*

He backed out of AssassinsCreed.Wikia.com, wondering who the hell maintained these sites, and tried searching *Vance T author.* Nada. He tried *Vance T novel* and *Vance T writer novel*, tapping the screen with that weak sensation that always comes when sending Mountain View, California, a bunch of junky terms that didn't have a nanobyte's chance in the cloud of finding diddly.

Until they did.

"Check it out!" He steadied the cell phone for Steph against a block of psychology texts. "I typed in *Vance T author novel download*, and look—here, look at the first result."

It came from a website selling books. Not Amazon or any of the giant used-book sites but a website devoted to self-published works. The right navbar was ads, and the left hawked supplemental services—editorial, cover art. The center section contained a list of titles matching the inputted search terms. Seven belonged to the author "Vance Tietjens."

"Ford Madox Ford," Steph said. "I forget which book, but Tietjens was one of his characters."

"'The most tragically overlooked novelist of the twentieth century.'"

Fiske must have said it a dozen times while lecturing on *The Good Soldier*.

Steph's eyes poured over the screen. "Are these books published? Self-published? There's no *Illusory Greatnesses* on the list."

"I think you download them." Eric pinch-zoomed on the hyperlinks beside each title. "Yeah, you can either do an e-book or print-on-demand."

They clicked into the synopses and read, heads together, strands of Steph's hair falling intimately across Eric's shoulder. The books featured high-school-age protagonists and racy plots. *Scandal, sex, back-stabbing: Tietjens proves once again that intrigue is the only constant in the halls of Wissenbaum High.*

Steph said, "Didn't that drama instructor at Evanston Township sell spots in *Our Town*?"

The synopsis they were looking at described a music teacher taking bids for first-chair violin.

"The year before we got there." Eric clicked ahead to *Anything for Billy*. "And didn't some mom sleep with an assistant principal? Trying to get her kid off after a drug bust?"

Except for one—*The Last Impressionist*, about a freshman painter's hazing by an underground painting clique—Eric and Steph were able to identify the kernel of each novel in some sensational ETHS rumor. And the hazing, they reasoned, could have originated from a football incident they weren't privy to. The fictionalized versions always changed a key piece of the story—gender, the team or student organization—but the crux was recognizable.

Steph stood with mouth open. "So, Mr. Fiske is...an author?"

"Yeah. Pretty successful too." Eric brought the phone closer to read. "This last one sold almost forty-thousand copies."

A voice over the intercom announced a kids club reading beginning in five minutes. They decided to move back downstairs. Eric bought the first Vance Tietjens novel on his phone for $3.99. He read the up-front pages on the escalator as children streamed up the adjacent stairs.

The book's publication date was 2003. The acknowledgments contained a single paragraph thanking the author's parents and two others: Mary-Ann McCallagat "for her diligent editing" and Davey Reichert "for reading, for reacting, for injections of absurdity."

Eric showed Steph the page. "Wasn't Mary-Ann a Winner back in the eighties?"

Steph nodded slowly. "Sounds right. I don't recognize the other name."

"Me neither."

"Why 2003? Why wait twenty years to publish?"

"Maybe he tried and couldn't. When did all this e-publishing start? Probably around 2003."

They downloaded the second Tietjens novel, which also had a publication date of 2003 and mentioned two former students in the acknowledgments: Craig Foote, a Winner; and Anabelle Adams, the well-known goofball who founded the *Wildkit Lampoon*. Both had been at ETHS later than McCallagat but well before 2003.

"So Fiske has students help with these manuscripts," Steph said. "And Autumn and Jesse..."

"Were helping with *Illusory Greatnesses*," Eric finished. "His latest."

They settled in a sleepy aisle of biographies and, in low tones, talked out the rest. Whatever happened in *Illusory Greatnesses*, it must incriminate Doug—incriminate him in a big way. Somehow Doug learns of the manuscript's existence. Learns that Jesse Weams and Autumn Brockert are involved. He engineers the ill-fated bungee jump, then takes out Fisk and Autumn with the *teacher-runs-off-with-student* ruse and thinks the whole mess is done. Until Steph discovers his window-washer key.

That would explain his extreme anger that night. He figured he was in the clear, had achieved his cover-up without upsetting his life. It explained the manuscript, the trickle of deposits, why Autumn Brockert had been in such close contact with her septuagenarian English teacher.

Didn't quite explain Becky Brindle. But the fog was clearing.

"We have to find out what he did."

Eric squinted.

"*Doug*," Steph clarified, biting the *g*. "We need to know what he's hiding. Without that—a motive, a solid reason he would take the extraordinary step of framing his own wife—we'll never prove our innocence."

Eric donned his metaphorical tinfoil hat and again tried getting inside the head of his nemesis. Having seen Doug's eyes in that parking lot, glowing as the blows rained down, he felt like a broad range of atrocities were on the table. Theft. Fraud. Rape. Obviously murder.

Their only clue, really, was the title of Fiske's book: *Illusory Greatnesses*. Eric sprouted scenarios forward from there. Doug wanted to obliterate the Central Suburban League passing record, so he took steroids. (Except he was never that huge.) Doug wanted to ace the SATs, so he slept with the monitor. (Except he could have gotten into Northwestern on grades/sports alone.) Doug bumped into a man with horns in the Chipotle bathroom, came out soulless but with godlike powers over every person, animal, or object he came into contact with. (Possible.)

Steph, too, kept drawing a blank.

"If you, his wife, don't know about it," Eric said, "then most likely nobody does."

"Except Fiske," Steph pointed out. "And Autumn Brockert."

"Right. One's in a coma, and the other probably has seaweed in her lungs."

Steph's face changed, and Eric instantly wished he could take it back. *Seaweed in her lungs?* What was wrong with him? It had just popped out, a knee-jerk attempt to be funny and smart and colorful with language. Could he not go three seconds without trying to impress Stephanie Mills?

Idiot.

But Steph wasn't upset. She had an idea.

"Actually," she said, brightening, "there is one more person who might know."

CHAPTER TWENTY-EIGHT

They compiled a dossier on Trev Larson. To the initial background he already had on Janine Rhimes, Larson's wife, Eric added names and addresses of relatives, the unit he'd served with in the military, and various other web nuggets available thanks to the helpfully unique given name "Trev." He scribbled notes on the back of a flyer, forking up lukewarm pad thai with his off hand. They had relocated to a Noodles & Company.

"This ain't half bad." Eric tapped the clicker of his pen. "We have the guy's social circle. We know his interests, everywhere he worked. There's a lot to go on here."

Steph was adjusting an auburn wig. They had changed disguises in case the Panera sighting had been reported around. Now she looked like Amy Adams in *Enchanted*, Disney ringlets about her collarbone.

"A lot the police will know too," she said.

Eric was dubious about the police's ability to marry Trev's LinkedIn and RallyPoint profiles, or dupe Ancestry.com into coughing up the whole maternal branch of the Larson family tree, but knew saying so would sound petty.

"The police are focused on Autumn Brockert—Larson is secondary. They may not be looking as hard for him."

Steph twisted her mouth. "So where do we think he hides? Up north in Michigan?"

"No. Remember, he came back. I saw him drive to work. He's in Chicago."

"Okay. Where? With a relative?"

"Or a friend."

Eric inputted what contact info they had and punched up a map of Greater Chicagoland. The drop-shadow pins spread from a cousin up in Racine to two former squad mates in Dwight, and everywhere in between. Eric's cell phone screen dimmed. He hadn't been able to find the right type of charger on any of their disguise/drink runs, and his battery was down to 9 percent.

"He'd stay out of Wilmette and Glenview." Steph pointed to a cluster of pins. "Too close to the investigation. What's that brown star out in Kankakee?"

Eric zoomed in, tapped the icon. "That would be Carl Thume, his personal trainer."

"How did you get that?"

"Facegym. People post about their workouts. Reps, sets. Stuff like that."

The skin around Steph's eyes crinkled. "I could see Trev Larson doing that."

"Could you see him holing up with his trainer?"

"Maybe. He was always sucking up to Doug, all buddy-buddy, *bro* this, *bro* that. Some macho personal trainer? It's worth a shot."

They finished eating and headed out. After stopping at CVS to tweak their look—they would tell Mr. Thume they were reporters —they picked up a beater Eurovan from an independent rental-car place that required only a Mastercard imprint.

On the way to rural Kankakee, an hour south, Eric read aloud from the internet. It was amazing how quickly the press had found people willing to trash them. A UI designer Eric had once shared a cube border with told CNN about phone calls he used to overhear, Eric telling somebody in angry whispers to *stay away, HE was going to kill the boss!* (He'd been talking to guild mates about World of Warcraft.) Steph's college roommate claimed she had "daddy issues" and had hooked up with multiple professors.

Eric glanced over.

"One. I hooked up with *one* professor," she said. "He was twenty-eight, nontenured."

Deep in the subcortex of his brain, Eric felt fingernails scrape chalkboard. Steph's list of sexual partners was widely thought to be short. Doug, obviously. The senior-when-they-were-freshmen, Justin Phyllis, who would go on to tour briefly with Imagine Dragons. And now this upstart prof. (Tweed, wavy bangs, Ben Franklin specs.) Lucky punks whom fate had placed in position to sleep with Stephanie Mills. His own profession was 90 percent male. Outside of one halting encounter with a Taiwanese manager, Eric had tallied a big fat zero in the fall-into-your-lap column of hookups.

Carl Thume's house lay off a fifty-mph country road, at the end of a long, straight drive. The surrounding acreage might have been farmland—flat, treeless—except for the lack of tractors or tillers or any barns to hold them. The only equipment Eric saw, as the Eurovan puttered up alongside a pickup with side mirrors as big as elephant ears, was related to fitness: iron chin-up bars, a dip station, a sled holding two boulders.

It was freezing, but Thume had only a screen door. Eric knocked the frame.

A man holding a power shake answered.

"Yeah?"

"Hi, we're here to ask a few questions about Trev Larson," Eric said. "My colleague and I are with a small paper from Peoria."

He had been worried Thume would recognize them, but that seemed unlikely. What he could see of the home's interior was spartan, no TV, no reading material. The man wore close-fit sweatpants and a sleeveless undershirt.

"This rap on Trev is nonsense. Ex-military make easy scapegoats." His left biceps fired, causing a bald eagle to flare its wings. "Press find out some ex-soldier's suspected of a crime? Boy, they eat that up."

"Rest assured, sir, we have no such bias. We're just looking for background on Trev."

Carl Thume swigged his power shake. "Trev Larson is a decent, honorable man."

"I have no doubt, Mr. Thume. That's exactly what we hope to illuminate here, with your assistance."

The trainer took a while swallowing. "Want your scoop, hm? Make your name off Trev."

Eric shook his head. "Not at all. We're here because every side of the story deserves to be told. We want to tell Trev's side."

"Mm-hmm. Standing up for Trev. *The honest man in glasses*, right?"

He capped his power shake and folded his arms like some brainless orc at the castle gates. *The honest man in glasses?* Eric didn't get the reference.

Before he could stop himself, he'd muttered, "Were you two openly affectionate or still in the closet?"

Carl Thume's face tilted and began taking on a green tint.

"Forget Trev Larson," Steph said, stepping forward. "We're here to talk about you. About how your innovative training methods molded Trev's physique."

This calmed him. His skin stayed white and none of his clothes burst.

Steph continued, "Nobody's telling this story. We read a little about you, Mr. Thume, about your fresh approach to bodybuild-ing." Thumping every "you" and "your." "I understand you don't allow clients to wear headphones or listen to music during workouts?"

"Distraction is the enemy."

"And you paper over your windows?"

"Duct tape." Lower lip lapping the upper, prideful. "Zero natural light."

She asked a few more ingratiating questions, recasting his caveman ideas as genius in a way that only a marketing pro could. Eric glanced past the man's balloon-ish shoulders to look down the hall. Two doors, both open. No clutter, or backpack, or anything. The screen door had been open when they walked up; Thume could've done some quick tidying, but he didn't seem the type to hurry on another person's account.

Once the trainer felt at ease, Steph asked where his studio was located.

"Studio?"

"Gym, sorry," Steph said. "Where is your gym?"

"Downtown."

"In the Loop?"

Carl Thume's body turned, a few degrees askance. "Do you have a constitutional right to know the location of my facility?"

Steph held up two hands as though braking herself. "Certainly not, no. We're only gathering information. Of course if we were to do a write-up, a piece talking up your methods, it's possible our readers would be interested. And if they knew where your gym was located—"

"I got clients."

"Well, right, but presumably more clients means—"

"Presumably nothing. I'm done talking."

And the orc was back, scowling, biceps snuggled together over his chest.

Eric said, "Now with these clients, do you charge by the hour or does it depend how kinky—"

"I think we have what we need," Steph cut in, leading them away to the van. "Thanks so much, Mr. Thume. Have a great evening."

Carl Thume stepped back inside, letting the screen door *clang*, and eyed them down the drive.

Eric waited until they were up to speed on the country road to say, "He's there."

CHAPTER TWENTY-NINE

I t was not difficult to find Thume's gym. Eric searched the
city's database of municipal deeds and got back only two
results: the property in Kankakee and another with a listed type of
COMM_WAREHOUSE on West Polk. He typed it into Maps and
saw that it was indeed in the Loop, in an industrial block adjacent
to a tangle of El tracks.

They hopped back on I-57. The sun was low in the sky by the
time they reached the madness of the Stevenson Expressway.
Steph braved the Eurovan's poor sightlines, guessing at lane
changes—Eric closed his eyes and prayed as she merged onto Dan
Ryan—but managing to get them to West Polk. They followed
GPS to a dead-end lot of unmarked warehouses. Here there were
no meters, but a few cars had parked against the curb.

"You have arrived at your destination."

Eric frowned at Droid and checked its battery. Down to 4
percent.

They climbed out and walked to the nearest building,
numbered 1023. They needed 3671. They checked the next, and
the one after, then circled behind to the next row of warehouses
and saw the enormity of the complex. Three city blocks of feature-
less gray buildings.

Wind howled off the stone faces. Eric tensed against the sting.

"What kind of signage is this?" He nicked a column of brass

plates beside a closed garage bay. "*V. Industries? N.P.O.E.?* Where did the numbers go?"

They kept moving, which helped with the cold, and kept scanning for 3671, or some mention of "Thume" or "gym" or any fitness-sounding term. One building had its door swinging open. They slipped inside and tiptoed around until the roar of a front loader chased them off.

When they emerged, the sky had gone full dark.

"This is hopeless," Eric said. "We could be here all night and never find it."

They were standing in an inner courtyard. Not quite road, but no benches or tables for eating either. The pavement sloped gently to the center like it might've once contained a fountain. A strip of Bubble Wrap tumbled past. There was an unpleasant odor here, greasy, faintly moldering.

Steph gritted her teeth. "This feels like Trev Larson. We're in his domain."

That phrase—"in his domain"—triggered a thought in Eric's head. What was that app he'd heard about the other day? He had been talking with investors at some launch party, and this guy walked up and started pitching. Apparently, he'd mashed up Google Maps with the GPS footprints of several common video-chat apps, then tossed a UI overtop. It allowed you to pull up a map of all cell-phone users within about a quarter mile who had Skype, iChat, or Google Hangouts installed.

"Is Larson at all techie? Any chance he would have video chat on his phone?"

Steph shifted in place. "I'm sure he has a smartphone—everybody at Doug's firm does. Why?"

Eric told her about the app, and they both agreed it was worth trying. After a few quick searches, he came across LookyLoo—*that was it!*—and downloaded/installed it. The app opened with a lighthouse-sweep graphic and cheesy, owl-hoot sound clip. Moments later, a map appeared with one pulsing circle, representing Droid, and twenty-seven blue or red pinpoints.

"They're all on top of each other," Steph observed. "Is that a party? A rave?"

"No, that's just where the cell-tower is pinging," Eric said.

"That's as close as the app can get without making direct contact. You need to initiate an actual video call to resolve their precise location."

Steph made a face exactly like the investors at the party had when the app's inventor admitted this shortcoming. "What good is that?"

"If we can get him to answer a video call, his icon will move to the right spot."

"Why is he going to pick up on Skype when the whole world is looking for him? And wouldn't the call be coming from your phone? With your Google ID?"

Eric rolled his tongue around his mouth. Even if Larson were here, even if LookyLoo worked as described—neither was a given —there were challenges.

"That part I can get around, the ID."

He logged out of Google, considered for a moment, and then, smiling, created a brand-new account. It took time, entering phony contact information, providing a secondary e-mail account he had access to. (A long-abandoned Paladin address did the trick.) Steph walked ahead to nearby buildings, looking for taped-over windows as Eric worked. Finally, he got through all the screens and chose a password. Then restarted LookyLoo.

They scrolled through the list of IDs. Unfortunately, there was no *TrevLarson*, or *TLarson13*, nothing like that. Most IDs were clear first/last name concatenations. These they ruled out. That trimmed the list from twenty-seven to seven.

The first was *CHIBEAR34*. Steph did not know whether Trev Larson was a Walter Payton fan, but the odds of him choosing a jock-ish ID seemed better than one of the other six—which were just random, incomprehensible alphanumerics. Eric tapped the *Call* button.

Steph leaned close to see. Their breath converged to a single stream through the cold.

A Skype window opened. After two outer-spacey rings, a dark picture emerged. The exposure changed radically, a bright flash followed by dim outlines of a person as the camera wavered between focal points.

The person was a man. He wore a trucker's hat with a frayed bill, and no shirt.

"Hullo. Hullo? Sweetness here." The picture stopped at his navel. His hands were engaged in something below that point. "You from the website?"

Eric ended the call and wiped the screen with the cuff of his shirt.

The next three pinpoints didn't answer. As they moved down the list, he began to worry. About police. About the van—a few blocks away, but after all that getting turned around, could they even find it? About the usefulness of this whole exercise—the odds Larson would have his cell on, that he would be down here in one of these warehouses at all. Maybe his trainer was just a jerk. Maybe he would've stonewalled if they had asked him about his favorite color too.

A user named *mont2trip* picked up on the fifth ring. The audio came before the video.

"Carl, is that you?" said a pinched voice. "What happened? Why are you calling?"

A second later, a man with a buzz cut appeared onscreen.

Steph gasped and looked disbelievingly at Eric. He gestured to his phone's Notification and Status bar, which showed his active Google ID: *carlThume_003*.

Trev Larson appeared to be sitting in his Jeep, roll bars visible behind either ear. His cheeks were taut. His eyes bore into his phone's screen.

With a gathering breath, Steph squared herself in front of Droid's camera. "Trev, this is Steph Reece. I'm in hiding just like you. We need to talk."

Meanwhile Eric crouched out of the shot and, holding the phone up with the thumb and forefinger of his right hand, used his left to shrink Skype and resize LookyLoo to fit the remaining sliver of screen.

The pinpoint labeled *mont2trip* moved away from the cell-tower clump.

"Carl? This isn't Carl? What happened to Carl?"

The connection was poor. Steph's image kept freezing in the outgoing-video inset.

"*Steph Reece*—this is *Stephanie Reece*," she repeated. "It's important that we talk."

As Trev Larson continued to be baffled by the disconnect between Steph's words and the ID *carlThume_003*, Eric watched the map with consternation of his own. Larson's pinpoint had moved quickly at first but was now drifting, teetering around a point not far from their own pulsing circle.

"Doug's wife?" Larson finally managed.

"Yes, yes!" Steph said. "Doug's wife!"

"Is he with you?"

"No, Doug framed us. That's why we need to talk. We need your help to understand why."

The image of Trev Larson zagged sideways. *He isn't driving, is he?* When it stabilized, he waited several moments before answering. Eric began to wonder whether he had understood or even heard Steph.

He had.

"Why in the world would I help you?"

Even over the static, the derision in his voice was apparent.

"Because you're in the same boat," Steph said. "Doug hung you out to dry."

"No, he didn't."

"Yes, he did, Trev. He made it look like you and I engineered this whole thing."

Above the LookyLoo map—which still had Larson wandering about lazily—Trev Larson's image disappeared, then reappeared, then a noise sounded and Larson peeked back over the headrest. Then he mouthed something the audio didn't pick up.

Steph asked, "*What?*"

The sound came back: "I said, *you're lying.* We pinned everything on Fiske and the geek."

"What geek?"

"That geek with the crush on you. You guys went to high school together? Now he has gray hair—"

"Yeah, geek's right here." Eric jerked the phone down to his face, glared into the front cam. "*What did you monsters do with Autumn Brockert?*"

Larson rotated his face like a stumped dog. "It's the geek. Hm."

"Is she dead? Did you guys toss her in the lake? Or drive back and bury her here?"

In debate, it sometimes worked to barrage your opponent with invective, to try unnerving them into some admission or unplanned revelation. "Rattling the cage," Ms. Shipley had called the technique. As he shouted, Eric used his off-camera hand to direct Steph's attention to the LookyLoo window. Larson's pinpoint had settled. If the map was correct (and he was going to eviscerate their Play Store review score if not), Larson must be in a warehouse to their immediate left.

"I'm telling you squat," Larson said. "We have a plan and I'm sticking to it."

"'We' have a plan? No, *Doug* has a plan," Eric said, "and you are collateral damage. He's already zipped up the body bag. He's chambered the bullet and told Old Yeller to sit—whatever, pick your metaphor."

"You're wrong."

"Yeah? Go find a TV. Every newscast in the country has you as Boogeyman number one, or number one *a*."

"That's the media."

"The hell it is! It's Doug—he sold you out."

In the lull that followed, Eric could feel Trev Larson's conviction wane. Would he fold and come clean? Would he help them? Eric didn't know. There was a thick chucklehead layer to overcome.

"Hey," Steph whispered, a few steps away now. "One of those, you think?"

She waved at a row of warehouses to the north, twenty yards off their courtyard. Eric gave a tight nod, aware that Larson could see him, and gestured for her to walk ahead, that he would watch the LookyLoo map and let her know if she was getting warmer or colder. (Well, he made walky-walk fingers and bugged his eyes excitedly; how much she understood was anyone's guess.) Steph started toward the row of buildings.

"Doug will get me off the hook," Larson said. "Doug has a plan, I'll be fine."

Unreal. I'm dealing with Lennie from Of Mice and Men.

Eric decided to change tack. "We know he had you burn a manuscript at the cabin. And wipe some hard drives, right? What was in that manuscript? What was it about?"

Another noise sounded behind Larson. He tried to swivel, but his shoulder snagged the seat belt, so he unbuckled and tried again. He glanced back. Twice. When he faced forward again, his eyes were scattered.

"I—how—how would I know?" He glanced back a third time. "It wasn't critical to my mission. I burned the pages. I degraded the hard drives and flushed them."

This had the unfortunate ring of truth. Trev Larson was an incurious man and might well have executed Doug's orders without asking questions.

Up ahead, Steph had reached the garage bay of the first warehouse. She looked back to Eric. He stepped sideways and watched their pulsing circle in LookyLoo to see how it moved, how its arrow tilted vis-à-vis Larson's pinpoint.

No, Steph was not quite on a direct line. He waved her to the next building.

Eric said, "Flushed them where?"

Larson considered, then seemed to decide there was no harm in gloating. "Millennium Park. Nastiest, scuzziest public crapper you ever saw."

Eric's throat lurched involuntarily. He thought he knew the spot. During a young violinists' concert sophomore year, he'd had to use the underground restroom next to Pritzker Pavilion. An inch of standing brown water, bowls without tanks—steel but definitely not stainless.

This sucked. They had gotten lucky finding Trev Larson, but it wasn't doing them any good.

"Confess," Eric tried. "You and Doug Reece did this. Go tell the cops. Go tell Autumn Brockert's parents where they can find their daughter, give them peace. Aren't you a marine? Do the right thing."

He did not expect this to work. The feed from *mont2trip* stuttered, then froze. When it began moving again, the camera angle had changed as though Larson had switched his phone to the opposite hand or balanced it differently on the dashboard.

Eric continued, louder, desperate, *"Do you honestly think Doug gives a rat's ass what happens to you? What a joke. Pathetic. I mean seriously, how much abuse does a person have to endure? How bad does it have to get before you quit being someone else's lapdog?"*

Across the complex, Steph had reached the next warehouse. She pressed her ear to a windowless gray door. Tried the knob. It twisted. She ventured a half step inside, then stepped back out with a questioning look.

Again, Eric moved to see how his pulsing circle responded in LookyLoo. This time, its arrow pointed directly at both Steph and the onscreen representation of *mont2trip*. He flashed her thumbs-up.

Steph beamed—a smile that lit the dark night, filled his chest with roses.

Trev Larson was sitting sidesaddle, sticking his keys in or pulling them out of the steering column.

"You tell me," he said.

Then, a *crack*. Possibly an engine starting, definitely coming from the building Steph was now running into.

CHAPTER THIRTY

Steph sprinted for the sound, following the hot tickle in her nose. Through halls and doors, up and down steps—three at a time, across concrete floors and a narrow, carpeted locker room. Arms pumping. Mind ahead. Her kneecap blasted a rack of dumbbells and she didn't stop, absorbed the blow twistingly and kept on.

Mirrors. Machines. Smells of sweaty rubber and chalk. The space was dark except for faint baseboard spotlights. She paused to flip a row of switches but only managed to start huge overhead fans whirring. Her breath felt like it was being pumped into her body by some outside force—urgent, powerful.

"Be careful!" she heard, far back, feeling a puff of air that must've been Eric entering. "I think I saw him reaching for a gun!"

Steph paid no attention. She hurtled weight belts and loose Nautilus attachments and rammed through a turnstile, thighs burning, and toppled a tin of snub-nose pencils. She passed an area of storerooms with red-flashing keypads. Her steps slowed into a large open area with high, sloped ceilings...then another *crack*, and she dashed off toward the noise.

Around two more bends, she reached an interior parking lot. The air was different. Charged. Thick. *Where is that black Jeep?* She paused to listen but heard only Eric plodding behind.

The parking structure forked, one path leading to the second floor, the other to the basement. A dozen or so spaces were visible along either ramp, all handicap or otherwise specially designated.

No Jeeps.

Then she heard. Not much—a faint scrape, possibly the sole of a shoe landing or briefcase sliding into a trunk. It had come from the basement ramp.

She took off. Motion-triggered lights ticked on in her wake, turning her periphery grime yellow, but it remained dark ahead. Cold air poured in by some open bay. Eric yelled about calling or waiting or stopping.

Steph ran. Like her whole life was inside that Jeep—her former life, the one with a home and job and husband who hadn't tried to kill her. The downslope multiplied her speed. Her shoes sailed ahead, one flight after another, bottoming her stomach like a roller coaster.

She passed the handicap spots. Approached a bend. Two fuzzy circles appeared on the concrete curve.

Headlights.

He does not get away. I will stop him. I will find out why this is happening.

Steph made the bend in two strides, then saw it. The black Jeep. Sitting crookedly in the middle of the aisle, tires opposing frame, steam billowing off the hood. The windshield looked black from here.

Ten feet away, her shoes crunched. *Glass.* A trail of it coming from the driver-side window. She kept sprinting, her soles pulverizing whatever they met, an acrid smell in her nose now, bitterness in her throat.

There was a figure in the driver's seat. Its dark shape resolved as she came nearer. Broad shoulders...buzz cut...

Trev Larson.

The window was half gone. Without a thought, Steph plunged both hands through the remaining shards. Pain shot though her knuckles, but she kept reaching. She got hold of Larson's seat belt, then the shoulder of his coat, then maybe an ear—anything to prevent him from driving off.

But he wasn't driving anywhere.

They drove fast. Pushing the van as hard as possible without attracting police attention, seventy mph out 290—the first highway ramp they saw, through the west suburbs, away. Far away. Traffic was light. Steph watched out for semis and weaving drunks over her blood-caked fingers.

"How about this rest stop?" Eric said.

"For what?"

"Sleeping. I don't think we risk a hotel."

She had not even thought about stopping, much less sleeping. She kept seeing Trev Larson's cleaved head and feeling his hot, sticky blood as she had smeared it, along with some of her own, across the outside of the Jeep.

"Right." It was past midnight; they would need an early start tomorrow. "I'll pull off."

Steph parked behind the restroom structure in a spot not visible from the highway. Eric talked frenetically for five minutes —fingerprints and Mexico and whether or not Tom Petty's stuff came free with Amazon Prime—before passing out cold.

Steph lay awake afterward, curled in a crescent on a Eurovan bench bed. Geese honking overheard spooked her, and with every wheezing open of the restroom door, her body worried deeper into the bench's crease.

Doug had killed Trev Larson. She felt this in her bones, but everything else was a mystery. Why? To make sure Larson didn't talk? Had Doug somehow overheard the Skype conversation? Could he have even been in Larson's car? Why hadn't he tried to kill her and Eric while he was at it? She hiked her jacket up her cheeks for warmth and, smelling sour blood on her fingers, knew *that* answer: because the setup was even better now, more physical evidence tying them to a murder.

She fell asleep at some point, only to be jarred awake before sunrise by Eric's phone.

Bzz! Bzz! Bzz!

Her eyelids cracked. Eric was fumbling his glasses, knocking them along the floor, then swiping his cell-phone screen.

"Come on, recognize the gesture already. Crappy low-battery mode..."

He swiped a second and third time, and then, as a cool-splash chime sounded, his face froze.

"What?" Steph said, up on one elbow and eyes fully open now.

Eric waggled his head as though shaking out cobwebs, then looked back to his screen. "Well, this changes the calculus."

"What? What is it?"

He held out the phone so she could read the flashing-red headline for herself:

FISKE AWAKES FROM COMA, AGREES TO INTERVIEW WITH VERONICA KEANE.

It took Steph a moment to process the sentence. Once she did, her spirits soared.

"He'll exonerate us!" She bounced up onto her knees. "He'll expose Doug. Let's turn ourselves in."

Eric scanned the rest of the article. "Wait a second. We don't know what Fiske is going to say."

"Sure we do, Doug tried to have him killed. He's going to tell the world we're innocent!"

"Trev Larson carried out the kidnapping. Fiske may have no idea Doug was involved."

"But he knows what's in the manuscript."

"True." Eric scratched the side of his head. "Well, actually no. Not true. Or at least maybe not true. Who knows what Fiske knows? He just woke up from a coma—for all we know, he's a vegetable."

"If he is a vegetable, he wouldn't be going on *Veronica Keane Live.*"

"Fair enough. Still...it's weird he would do Veronica Keane. Why not just march into a precinct and tell what he knows?"

"Maybe he already did."

"Why isn't that being reported?"

Steph had no answer. They decided it best to wait and see what came out of the interview. Unfortunately, the interview didn't air until ten thirty, and Eric's phone died in the intervening hours. They got back on 290 and cruised for box stores with electronics departments. Neither Walmart nor Meijer carried the right charger. Six exits on, they spotted the hulking blue corner of a Best Buy. Eric was positive they would have it. He race-walked from the van to the entrance—it was already 10:15—but emerged shortly afterward empty-handed.

"Out of stock." He leaned into Steph's window. "Ridiculous. In San Francisco, you get these outta snack machines."

Steph checked the dashboard clock. Less than ten minutes to the interview. "Let's watch it in Best Buy. They have a million flat-screens, right?"

Eric twisted back toward the store. "On an actual TV?"

"Sure."

"Huh. Old-fashioned, but I guess there's no reason we couldn't."

They tidied up their disguises, which wouldn't matter if Fiske cleared their names as Steph expected, and headed in. There were few customers at this hour. A dozen blue polo shirts strode forward offering help. Eric said they were only browsing, wanted to see how reds looked on these new OLEDs. Every one of the fifty-odd screens was tuned to SportsCenter.

Steph picked up a remote. "What is the range on these, roughly?"

As sales associates stumbled over one another answering, she clicked over to cable news. Veronica Keane was sitting on a beige-upholstered armchair Steph recognized from the hospital. Keane's eyes looked tired, the shoulder pad of her ivory suit rumpled.

"Good morning," the host began. "We wake to significant developments in the Autumn Brockert case. Just hours ago, the body of Trev Larson, one of three suspects at large, was found in a downtown parking garage. Larson was shot through the head. Police have not commented beyond this, but sources tell us that trace evidence points to the remaining suspects, Steph Reece and Eric Pinkersby."

Their pictures flashed. The sales associates were busy doing sideways and diagonal flicks of the remote, showcasing its advanced functionality.

"And the truly stunning news of the day, the reason I am sitting here at Cook County General Hospital: Bob Fiske's coma has lifted. The teacher at the center of this drama is awake. And you will not believe what he has to say to me today, exclusively, on a special early edition of *Victoria Keane Live*."

The intro ran—an urgent, thumping score over stills of Keane with various world leaders and pop icons—then the host reappeared in a wide shot with Fiske.

"For the record, sir," Keane said. "Your name?"

"Robert Fiske."

"Your occupation?"

"English teacher at Evanston Township High School."

"Age?"

"Seventy-four years old."

"Place of residence?"

"417 Dearborn, number 12b. Evanston, Illinois."

Victoria Keane paused to glance at the camera—*Perfectly lucid, see?*—then proceeded to the meat of the interview.

Steph steadied herself by a nearby placard, shaken by the sight of Fiske moving and talking regularly. The patient she'd visited in the hospital had been pale and creased, a warm cadaver, but here was the man whose lectures she had lived for. The sturdy jaw. The penetrating gaze that seemed to shrink every object it fell upon. The hair, unfurling white and intricate from the top of his head like brain smoke.

"Mr. Fiske, we'll delve into the substance shortly," Keane continued, "but first, would you mind characterizing your recall of the last nine days for our audience? How much of the ordeal do you remember?"

Fiske cleared his throat. "Everything."

Victoria Keane raised her eyebrows. "The side effects of a coma typically include confusion, or mild loss of—"

"Every detail of my kidnapping and subsequent incarceration is clear. Clear as a buttonhook in well water."

The host clicked and re-clicked her pen, thrown either by Fiske's vigor or the obscure simile. "Which brings us to the events themselves. It was initially reported that you attempted suicide in the woods of Pictured Rocks National Lakeshore. You dispute this account."

"Quite."

"What actually occurred?"

"A man forced twelve pills into my mouth."

"A man?"

"Trev Larson, if information provided me by the authorities is accurate."

"But you survived."

"Correct." Fiske straightened in his armchair. "I tongued half, which accounts for my presence here today, in concert with the exemplary doctors and nurses of Cook County General."

Victoria Keane flashed a warm smile offscreen. "Yes, heroes all, it seems. Now, Mr. Fiske, as you may or may not know, police recovered a suicide note from your vacation cabin."

"A forgery."

"And whom do you suppose penned that forgery? Trev Larson?"

Fiske flicked at his chin. "Not Larson. Larson was a brainless stooge."

Steph braced for Victoria Keane to ask the follow-up, to let Fiske shout her husband's name from the mountaintop and set her and Eric free.

But Keane changed subjects. "Your relationship with Autumn Brockert has drawn scrutiny. Scrutiny which now, in hindsight, may have been premature. Could you describe the nature of your contact with Ms. Brockert?"

Fiske revealed that Autumn was helping him edit a manuscript: no more, no less. The task required intense collaboration. He described his side career as an author and the role of "student-editor," explaining that he had been filling the post from the supremely talented ranks of ETHS since time immemorial.

Keane listened with a steady gaze. "Where is Autumn Brockert now?"

"Regretfully, that I cannot say." And Fiske did look upset, his chest falling in a dispirited breath. "Our captor separated us from the beginning."

"Your captor being Trev Larson?"

"Yes."

Keane looked down at her notepad, one fingernail tapping the cover. "You say Ms. Brockert was helping with a manuscript."

"A novel. She and I were finalizing edits before the book went to print."

"May I ask what the novel is about?"

"You may ask, Ms. Keane," Fiske said, "but you'll not receive an answer."

The host shifted uncomfortably. "You...you'd rather not discuss it?"

"Not with your viewers, no. I believe this tragedy has quite enough sensationalism to go around without adding my fiction."

"Has there been any suggestion, by the authorities or otherwise, that your book's contents may be germane to the case?"

"Indeed. Very much so."

"Yet you withhold them?"

"Not at all. I've revealed everything to the police. Everything I recall; regretfully, the manuscript itself will need to be recreated from scratch. All physical and digital copies were destroyed by Trev Larson and the person who directed his crimes."

Keane waited for more. Fiske drank bottled water off a hospital cart.

Steph realized she had been inching forward and now stood five feet from the screen, which could've been viewed comfortably from Indiana. *How long is it appropriate to watch a show at Best Buy?*

Fiske finished drinking and, with effort, screwed the top back on his water.

Keane prompted, "Do you know the identity of this person?"

Fiske nodded.

"Is *that* information you're willing to share with our viewers today?"

"I see no reason not to. The infamy is quite deserved."

As her own breath stopped, Steph glimpsed Eric in the TV's glossy trim. He stood poised behind her, on tiptoes, eyes urging behind his glasses. Blue polo shirts milled farther back.

Victoria Keane's lips pursed in annoyance at Fiske's dramatic reticence. "If you please, Mr. Fiske: Who is the person behind Trev Larson's crimes?"

Steph was positive her old teacher would utter words now that reversed everything—that would allow her to rip off this stuffy wig, race back to her mother's house, and hug her children until they whined for air.

Instead, he said, "Stephanie Reece."

PART FOUR

CHAPTER THIRTY-ONE

Steph's face remained still, but everything below shook. Knees, chest, the outsides of her wrists. An all-over tremble that fed off her spiraling panic. She stumbled and nearly fell into the life-sized cardboard athlete promoting DirecTV. Eric caught her just in time.

"Your former student." Victoria Keane crossed her legs. "Who is now a fugitive from justice."

"Yes."

When the host asked why Fiske thought Steph had conspired to kill him, he answered obtusely. "To silence me," was as much as he'd say, reiterating his desire not to make a tragic situation more sensational than it had already become.

As the interview wound down, Steph struggled to understand why this was happening. *How* this was happening. Had Doug framed her in Fiske's eyes too? Somehow gotten Trev Larson to slip him false information about who his accomplice was?

In the periphery, she sensed the attention of the blue polo shirts.

"No, yeah—the contrast ratio is ama*aaa*zing," Eric said loudly to a salesman. "We just need to measure the space, make sure it's going to fit. Hate to get 'er home and then have to take out a wall, right?"

He hustled Steph out of the store, chuffling through offers of free delivery and surround-sound bundles. Groups of blue polo shirts hunched together at the registers, at customer service, lips moving but not their eyes. Automatic double doors startled Steph. She flinched. Eric backpedaled into the parking lot. They looked at each other's terrified expression and knew, without question, the game was up.

They sprinted to the van.

"I'll drive." Eric accepted the keys in klutzy handoff.

Steph yanked her seat belt across her chest with unexpected force, popping off the plastic casing. In the short time it had taken to cross the parking lot, her bewilderment had become anger. How could Fiske believe *she* had hired Larson? It was ludicrous. If only he'd answered Keane's question about the contents of the novel. How was she supposed to defend herself when she didn't even know the accusation?

Eric gunned it up the feeder road, whipped across four lanes of traffic for the eastbound ramp.

"Wait, that's east!" Steph cried. "You're going east!"

"I know." Eric pressed the accelerator until the van whizzed like a clip-on fan.

"You *know*? Where are we going?"

"Downtown. Back to the Loop."

"*Why?*"

"Because we need to know what's in that manuscript. Everything flows downhill from there."

"Larson burned all the copies, remember? He degraded the hard drives beyond recovery."

Eric looked ahead to the Chicago skyline, rising under a cold, orange sun. "Maybe. But maybe not."

CHAPTER THIRTY-TWO

They switched cars in Oak Park. If the blue polo shirts had called the police—which one had to assume—the van would be picked up in no time. Eric cruised for a quiet commercial street, stashed the van behind an auto-body shop, then set about checking fenders and wheel wells. Walking the sidewalk in a quarter squat, peeking with a harmlessly curious air. He felt Steph's admiration at this strange new skill, and couldn't help strutting a bit when a Mitsubishi crossover panned out.

They got back on 290 but exited a mile later when Eric saw the name of his cell provider in the window of a wireless store. Now they really *had* to have a charger; to recover Fiske's manuscript off a trashed hard drive, he would need his phone to access the Paladin cluster.

"You're sure this will work?" Steph asked as he tore into the box's plastic overwrap. "Even if we do find a hard drive in that bathroom, it'll be soaked."

"Moisture isn't a deal breaker in the short- to medium-term. But to answer your question, no. Recovery is never guaranteed."

Their range of outcomes kept darkening. After Fiske's TV appearance, the odds seemed even longer of Autumn Brockert's still being alive—which was grim enough on its own, but also meant one fewer person who knew the truth and could vindicate them.

They parked two blocks from Millennium Park, then walked to the Pritzker bathrooms. Michigan Ave was thick with Chicago cops, but most were busy herding tourists. Some arts festival was underway. Earmuffed painters sipped coffee under canvas display tents, lending additional distraction beyond that provided by resident hustlers, fashion plates, and oddballs.

The Pritzker bathrooms lay belowground at the bottom of a ramp.

"Think Larson sent us on a wild-goose chase?" Eric said. "Why stuff a hard drive down a public crapper when you've got Lake Michigan five hundred yards away?"

Steph thought a moment, then said wryly, "You have to know the guy."

She split off to check the ladies' room just in case while Eric dashed for the men's. A trombonist was tooting for coins at the entrance. He skipped over the man's felt-lined case.

Two urinals were in use. He stepped up to the third and, squeezing out a trickle himself, glanced sideways to confirm nothing strange about the basins.

Four drainage holes...nasty yellow deodorizing puck...yep, kosher.

He zipped up and approached the first stall. The toilets had changed. Gone were the tankless steel bowls of sophomore year, replaced by a more conventional porcelain design. The water level seemed low. Eric hit the lever and, after a furious flush that coated his face with a fine mist whose bacterial makeup he refused to contemplate, watched the bowl refill to the same level.

Huh.

There was a tank, but its lid was bolted on. He looked out through the gap between door and floor to see whether anybody was waiting, or close enough to hear. At the sink, jeans cuffs sagged around a pair of unlaced high tops. He made a very fast, very crass generalization about such a person's willingness to overlook loud-and-possibly-felonious noises, found a plunger in the corner of the stall, and swung away.

The wooden handle *doinked* where lid met tank, each impact a smothered firecracker in his hands. After the sixth ineffectual blow, the plunger's rubber cup flew off, exposing a threaded tip. Eric realized the tip, which ended in a point, might serve as a chisel. He rammed it into the sliver of space underneath the lid, wiggled left, wiggled right, dropped to one knee for leverage—ignoring the wetness now radiating from his kneecap outward—and finally heard the *pop* of a screw shearing.

The lid rattled against the tank, loose but still attached on one side. Eric heaved it clear of the tank's lip and managed—by way of banging his thighs repeatedly—to swivel it off the back. Now he could see into the tank. He let go the lid, fingers grimy and weak, and peered down.

Water. Mote-specked water, surrounding a typical ball-float mechanism.

Eric carried his beheaded plunger to the next stall, whose bowl had an identical water level. Probably some water-conservation measure.

Well, hell.

The last toilet was out of order, but the city had done a bad job closing it off. Yellow tape across the stall door had been stretched aside so many times it was now little more than a limp jump rope. He stepped over and into the cesspool he'd expected from the start.

Flies. A watery turd half covered by sock. Toilet paper snaking from its metal dispenser onto the ground, across soppy tile, and up the toilet's base before joining the disappearing-edge brown of the overflowed bowl.

And stench. Unimaginable, skunk-trapped-in-your-sinus-cavity stench.

Eric rolled his pants. When he saw the bowl's muck up close—the lumpy tides and subsurface ridges, the green streaks and white polyps—he gagged. The reflex rippled through his torso, and his Sox cap fell onto the saturated sock.

Where it would stay.

He recovered upright and raised his plunger handle. This tank's lid had already been pried loose and, judging by the stains down all four sides, contained feces too. *People ripped off the lid to poop in there?*

Eric shook off a flashing certainty that the human race would destroy itself—soon, very soon—to nudge aside the lid. The water was brown but less vile than the bowl's. He poked around with the handle. It felt like more resistance than the parts of a ball-float would create. The water being opaque, he tried sloshing it out to see but had little success using the handle.

He looked down at his bare palms.

"*Eric?*" called Steph's voice from outside. "*Are you still in there?*"

Slipping off his coat, tripling it over his forearms in the style of a crude tarp, he did what needed doing. With half the water gone, it became clear that something else was indeed at the bottom of the tank.

He scooped frantically, splattering his chin, rocking the whole toilet so that the bowl sloshed over. His coat caught on the tip of tweezer-like mechanism.

An actuator arm!

Eric forgot himself and reached inside, dredging up a tangle of broken electronics. Black and silver fragments. Dangling sixteenth-inch screws. A tiny, sad circuit board—resistors and capacitors smashed.

The drive had two data platters. One had splintered into a half dozen shards. The other was merely dented. Eric stuffed every part he could find along with half the busted toilet mechanism into a coat pocket. He would've liked to rinse and dry it all immediately, but the coat, the only vessel available to him, was itself sopping with filth.

A young father was changing his infant daughter on a plastic foldout shelf.

"Two squares," Eric said to his questioning look. "Next time I'm using two squares, and if it still feels wrong back there? I'll shower at home."

And blew out of there cradling the coat, careful not to change its orientation and allow a part to spill.

Steph was waiting at the top of the ramp. Her eyes narrowed momentarily—Eric was aware, by a sliver of peripheral vision, of a non-skin color on his left cheek—but swelled at the bundle in his arms.

"You got it?"

He nodded.

They walked briskly to Lurie Garden, a gorgeous and all-but-ignored part of Millennium Park, which provided a maze of hedges where they could work discreetly. Eric unpacked what he had recovered in a shallow boardwalk canal, pulling each component through the water until it swam clear.

"Okay now, *gimme gimme...*" he muttered as he rotated parts in his hand, squinting for letters on the minute surfaces.

He made out *Sea* on a smudged sticker and, recognizing the font, concluded he was working with a Seagate drive. The serial number had flaked off but the first four alphanumerics of model were visible.

Might be enough.

Next, he moved to the platters, fitting together shards as best he could. From the zippered pouch of his wallet, he produced a micro-USB optical scanner, which he carried around for demos. He plugged it into his phone and tapped an icon for the Paladin cluster.

As Droid's activity spinner began circling, it occurred that this was a risk. Unlike those anonymous tower pings he had freaked over earlier, this data traffic really did threaten to give him away. The Paladin intranet was no Fort Knox. Packets—even log-in info —went over plain http, which meant anybody with web-filtering software could peek. The FBI might well be monitoring connection attempts, and if so, the username *e_pinkersby@paladin* was going to trip every alarm in the Hoover Building.

There was just no alternative. Without knowing what *Illusory Greatnesses* contained, they were rudderless.

"Don't you have to be more precise?" Steph asked as he brushed the eye of the USB scanner across the dented platter. "You're just waving it around like a vacuum."

"That's the beauty of it." Eric finished the dented platter, then began scanning shards of the other. "The back end handles any redundancies or discontinuity. It keeps on plugging until the pieces fit."

Paladin had broken no new ground with data recovery. Prior technologies could read any damaged drive it could. What was new was the accessibility of its method. Previously, exhuming a drive like this would have meant shipping your remnants off to some boutique firm, spending tens of thousands of dollars and waiting a minimum three months. Eric's algorithm effectively automated tasks their engineers did by hand.

It wasn't magic, though: to succeed, it needed hints about the expected shape and size of the puzzle pieces. After Eric had scanned the last shard, he found the smudged sticker again, selected "Seagate SATA" for *Drive Type*, and entered the four alphanumerics he had from the model number.

"Now we wait." Eric stashed the phone back in his pants. "An hour."

"An hour?" Steph glanced about as though the Tennessee coneflower surrounding them were bugged.

"Forty minutes, if we're lucky."

Having not eaten all day, Steph and Eric passed the wait at Millennium Park's outdoor restaurant. They scarfed egg brunches (Eric only after a vigorous scrub down) at a table overlooking Crown Fountain, whose twin glass-and-brick towers spewed water during the summer from giant digital faces, but now just cycled through different faces fluting their lips. Tourists still stopped to gape at the fifty-foot screens, and kids still scampered between—in jackets and gloves instead of swimsuits.

Once the elderly couple at the next table left, they were alone in their section.

They talked. About Fiske. About Autumn. About Detective Wright. About what their family and friends must be thinking. At one point Eric looked deeply into Steph's eyes, and the lyrics that came were Hall & Oates.

Pri-iii-vate eyes... They're watching you... (Clap-Clap)... They see your every move, hey-aaaye... Pri-iii-vate eyes...

What thoughts churned there? For all they had endured together, for as much of a Hellenic ideal as Steph Mills represented in his mind, Eric felt plagued by a tiny, stubborn whisper: *How could so many people believe she was guilty, and it not be so?*

Sure, he was facing trumped-up evidence too. But Bob Fiske could not be in on the conspiracy, whatever it was—he had nearly died. Nor could that partner at Steph's firm. Eric wondered about those texts sent from her phone to Larson, hundreds according to media reports. If Doug *had* sent them, wouldn't she have noticed?

Every time she tapped into *Messaging*, all those *T. Larson* entries should have smacked her in the face.

He imagined the last forty-eight hours as the hook-swallowing moments of an elaborate con, wherein Steph feigned the whole world's being against her, tricked him into doing her legwork. Into battling Doug. Into tracking Trev Larson. With a nauseous pang, he realized he had never actually seen a gunman shoot Larson or heard a car speed off—despite the wound seeming fresh. *Could Steph have been hiding a gun? Some sort of ankle holster?* He played the scenario forward and saw himself murdered in some backwoods Arkansas campground, or taking the fall after a phony blaze consumed all Steph's clothes and personal effects.

In the middle of brooding, he perceived an echo of the face in front of him. Over Steph's left shoulder, in the distance. Big. Digitized.

Her image on the glass-and-brick tower.

A bullhorn blasted, *"THESE PERSONS ARE IN THE AREA. IF YOU SEE ONE OF THEM, DO NOT APPROACH THEM. ALERT AN OFFICER IMMEDIATELY! REPEAT: DO NOT APPROACH THESE PERSONS..."*

The tower image changed to Eric, that pale mug shot that'd been all over TV.

Damn! They must have been monitoring requests in and out of Paladin, traced back the IP address.

One saving grace was that Steph and Eric did not much resemble their giant likenesses. The disguises helped, but also the Crown Fountain software was distorting their faces to fit a water-spewing expression. Eric's looked like it was either crying or constipated.

"Let's take our time," Steph said, apparently drawing the same conclusion. "Pay our bill. Fold our napkins. Walk out nice and easy."

Eric placed two twenties in the bill folder, which the waiter had already left. Steph folded her forearms. They stood without looking at the towers, then picked their way through the restaurant area. A family with teenagers had just been seated. The mother glanced at them but was quickly busy telling her kids, *no, nobody was ordering soda.*

The main walkways of the park felt more anonymous. They discussed running in the Mitsubishi, but without knowing what was in that manuscript—Eric kept pinging the cluster and getting back, *PROCESSING*—they couldn't know which direction to run. North to Evanston to investigate some explosive false charge implied by the story? Or south to...well, someplace far away, if nothing in Fiske's book suggested a path to exoneration.

Eric remembered seeing signs for an afternoon concert today at Pritzker, the first of the season. They headed that way and found the expansive lawn filling with blankets, heard violins and trumpets tuning up through the lattice-hung speakers. They staked out a spot near enough to the lawn's edge that they could boogie if necessary. Eric craned his ear around, pretending to ponder acoustics. Steph sat cross-legged, leaning back by her palms like a bon vivant up for whatever.

The music began five minutes later. A rollicking "Frosty the Snowman" had the audience grinning and singing aloud. A twirling toddler fell into Eric's lap. "No no, not at all," he said, waving off the parents' apologies.

When he looked back down at his phone, he saw that the cluster had returned a new message: *RECOVERED 180 OF 290 GB.*

He bolted to his knees. As he was catching his first glimpse of the damaged platter's contents, beginning with the root directory and its arcane subfolders, "Frosty" ended. Applause roared in his ears. A microphone crackled, then an announcer's voice filled the lawn, welcoming the crowd to this special early-spring performance of the Chicago Symphony Orchestra.

Eric tapped, pulled down, swiped back...sorted by date descending...tap-zoomed, pulled...sorted again by date... Several times he had to double back when his jittery fingers performed an unwanted navigation.

Finally, in */users/autumnB/My Documents/MSWord_bak/*, he found it:

IllusoryGreatnesses_10293.doc.

CHAPTER THIRTY-THREE

S teph read while Eric kept an eye out for trouble. As the CSO thundered away, she pored over Fiske's manuscript. Screen after screen after screen, absorbing three lines per sweep of the eyes—drawing from her experience speed-reading undergrad research proposals as a Stanford teaching assistant. She felt her lips curl against her teeth, was aware of a clump of sod in her fist.

By intermission, she had read sixteen of the twenty-seven chapters.

The main character, Amanda Naylor, was clearly Steph. President of the National Honor Society, volleyball captain, prom queen. The credentials were identical. Fiske gave her brown hair, but the "open, sympathetic eyes" and "effortlessly athletic figure" echoed other people's descriptions of Steph. Like Steph, Amanda had had two fender benders on school grounds. Early subplots showed her struggling with an overloaded schedule, weighing romantic overtures from Doug-like Rick Mead and Kevin Pinkerbee (*really?*), and spreading rumors about sexpot Maggie Monroe—a character Steph did not immediately recognize from real life.

Amanda was laser focused, totally oblivious to the fate of anyone but herself. She wore huggy sweaters to entice Kevin into carrying the load for a debate tournament. (So, *so* false.) She bullied a young French teacher into writing her a glowing rec.

(What was she supposed to do; he'd been sitting on it two weeks!) Fiske's depictions of these mini dramas, which had felt so innocent as she had lived them, chilled her. When Steph had imagined her former teacher's beef with her, what might have earned her that number-one spot on his *Disappointments*, it was not this. Not at all. Had she truly acted like Amanda? "I make them better," the character says at one point, of her suitors. "Without me they would be average. U of I material."

And who was Maggie Monroe?

In one scene halfway through the novel, Amanda builds an elaborate pyramid of innuendo against Maggie. Subtle digs about the way her lips wrap around straws, a misleading observation of Maggie smoking with the scuzzy girls after third period: nasty little plants that have the cumulative effect of marginalizing Maggie among the Wissenbaum High elites. The scene ends with Amanda tittering at a male friend's lewd gesture. "I had succeeded," she says. "Now the name 'Maggie Monroe' meant ten minutes in a parking lot. It was trash."

After a rabid stretch of reading, thirty pages without blinking, Steph set down the phone.

"Okay, this...I have to breathe." She spread her fingers wide in the lawn, decompressing. "He told us to Live Big. Right? He *told* us that. And now he's holding it against us."

Eric broke off scanning for police. "Not good?"

Steph explained about the Amanda Naylor character, the story's critical tone. "I feel so betrayed. I can't even describe."

He touched her back timidly, in the neutral region between the shoulder blades. "Who knows what Fiske really believes? He may not ascribe any of this yuckiness to you, right? Maybe he's only using your likeness as a jumping-off point."

"Except we know otherwise." She looked Eric straight in the eye. "He thinks I murdered to cover this up...and you don't cover up a jumping-off point."

As soon as her mind felt able, she returned to the manuscript. The plot of *Illusory Greatnesses* unfurled slowly. Rick Mead prevails over Kevin Pinkerbee. ("Kevin's net worth might be greater in ten years," Amanda reasons, "but there will be plenty of opportunities to switch.") Maggie, after Amanda's slander attack, blows off the popular crowd to form her own group of free-thinkers who care more about art and blood-pumping thrills—skinny-dipping in Lake Michigan, a zip line scene ripped off from *Divergent*—than typical high-school affirmation. Amanda dubs this new clique "Sluts with Crayons."

As Steph read toward what she assumed was some final show-down between the two, Vivaldi's *The Four Seasons* pranced through the Pritzker speakers. The crowd responded to the orchestra's rising vigor, setting down snacks or hot cocoa to cheer the last piece of the performance.

Steph's eyes ached as though someone were prying them out of their sockets, and she wasn't sure her wrist still had the capacity to move—it had been locked in place holding Eric's phone for a solid hour.

Where was the explosive revelation? Would it just be Mean Girls *cattiness all the way?*

The first subconscious pricks hit during Chapter 22 when characters began discussing an upcoming dance. Kevin Pinkerbee makes an overwrought plan to reveal his crush to Amanda, oblivious that she and everyone else in the senior class already know. Maggie and her enlightened slackers create an off-site alternative, a combination rave/skate party that promises "less awkward feet shuffling, more shred." Naturally, Amanda sabotages them, snitching to the principal about huge stockpiles of street drugs being amassed for the event.

One physical detail kept sticking up in Steph's mind: the way the Maggie character's panties showed above her jean skirt. Of course, it felt off for the current day—the trashiness of the "whale tail" had dragged it out of the mainstream long ago—but thinking back, Steph felt like there was one classmate who had really maxed out that look, always carrying the boys' eyes with her down the hall. *Who was that?* Becky Brindle? No: cleavage was more Becky's thing. She had worn her pants tight but not necessarily low.

Chapter Twenty-Four. The night of the dance. Steph propped taller on her elbows, boring into the screen. The fireworks begin in line for pictures, as Rick Mead catches Pinkerbee staring dreamily at Amanda and empties the punch bowl over the geek's head. Amanda feigns anger but secretly relishes the attention. After the cops put the kibosh on Maggie's off-site bash, she storms the dance floor and grips Amanda by her spaghetti straps.

"Nobody else can have anything! If the glory isn't yours, it must be destroyed, right?"

Amanda keeps her cool, glancing superiorly at Maggie's lacy black thong. (*Come on, what was her name?*) They argue over conventionalism vs individuality and debate the true nature of greatness—Fiske's pet themes spelled out in dialogue no high-school kid would ever speak. Maggie departs with a choice zinger that makes the ETHS gymnasium roar with raucous *We-ain't-gonna-take-it-anymore!* applause. She is strutting through the parking lot, tweeting directions to a mellow after-party spot—having realized her own hypersexuality is merely a different flavor of Amanda's disease—when a car slams into her.

Her head bounces sickeningly off pavement. Amanda saunters around from the driver's side, looming over the lifeless body.

"Shame," she says. "The girl should've been happy with her place."

Steph didn't feel immediate dread reading this. Besides the comically evil portrait of herself, which resembled less and less any real person, the accusation was clearly false. She might have a history of minor fender benders, fine, but she had never backed over anybody.

She kept swiping, reading, swiping, reading, into the penultimate chapter. As the cover-up of Maggie's death unfolded, Steph began to understand. Rick Mead comes searching for Amanda and, discovering her crime, drops to his knees.

"She's dead, dead!" he says. "What are you going to do?"

Amanda corrects, "What are *we* going to do."

They drag the body back inside. Rick wants to find a teacher and explain that it was a terrible accident—he dares not ask Amanda how the collision really happened—but Amanda vetoes.

"She needs to be discovered. It has to be an overdose, or suicide—you know the autopsy is going to find drugs in her system. So let's think. She got high...she ends up in the wrong place...somewhere dangerous..."

Amanda trails off, but her eyes stop on a sign: a stick figure raising its arm above two wavy lines.

The pool.

"*Nora Brockert!*" Steph exclaimed. "Maggie is Nora—he thinks I killed her at prom."

The group ahead of them whirled around.

Eric made a phony chuckle, patting her shoulder. "Alright hon, better get moving and beat the rush."

They shuffled off with bent backs, ostensibly out of courtesy for those still watching, and headed for the east end of Grant Park —nearly deserted this time of year—and Lake Michigan. Steph read as they walked, Eric guiding her at crossings or when she was about to run into a statue.

Amanda, having chosen the pool for a dump spot, returns to the gymnasium, leaving the dirty deed to Rick. Rick hikes Maggie's body over one shoulder and staggers through the locker rooms, bumps his way backward through swinging glass doors to the impressive (eight-lane, twenty-five-yard) Wissenbaum pool. He is just easing her onto the gutter tiles when heels clack behind him.

The Fiske character.

"What in God's name," he demands, "have you done?"

Rick stutters and sweats and slips, soaking one tuxedo shoe in the pool. Facing his coach and mentor, the Great Man himself, he cannot lie.

"She told me it was an accident," he says, confessing all. "Amanda's always been a careless driver, but I—I just have no way of knowing the truth."

The Fiske character agonizes for several pages, referring to Amanda Naylor as his "favorite of favorites" and likening his decision to a dominant lion pondering the fate of a firstborn cub who murders the pride's most-honored matron. He goes back and forth. *Could I have lain at the pool's bottom with boulders on my chest and undone this evil, I would have.*

Finally, with body and mind utterly hollowed, the Fiske character goes along with Rick and Amanda's cover-up. He helps Rick push the body in. Rick, sobbing violently, turns and apologizes for the umpteenth time. Fiske will not look from the water.

"Go," he orders his former quarterback. "I will bear this. I, and I alone."

The last scene was familiar. Flashing lights and the wail of sirens. An EMT cart. Mancini's hasty address, followed by Fiske striding across the gymnasium, dripping wet, broken.

What Steph and everybody else in the class had believed was grief—during the real-life version, ten years ago at ETHS—was actually more. Guilt. Regret. Profound sadness at "what he'd learned tonight about the one in whom he had believed above all others."

Steph read the last page, feeling the lakeshore's harsh pebbles through her shoes.

"So Nora Brockert..." Eric stared up the coast. "This is about her death somehow?"

She filled him in.

He said, "Where does Fiske get the idea you backed over Nora in the parking lot?"

"From Doug. Think about it: from Fiske's perspective, whatever Doug told him there by the pool was true."

"Then who really killed Nora?"

"Doug! Doug, Doug, *Doug*!" Steph growled her husband's name like some newly invented curse. "He killed her, got caught, and pinned it on me."

"Why? We were all just kids—what possible motive could Doug have had to kill Nora?"

Steph had no clue.

She felt tugged by conflicting emotions. Anger and shock at her husband's crimes but also a bizarre kind of relief. Clearly Fiske's disappointment all these years stemmed from prom night, this lie of Doug's. No wonder he'd shunned her in the stands of that homecoming game. He thought she was a murderer. Given this, it was no surprise he would write a fictional Steph as a royal bitch. A character capable of offing her rival, then foisting the cover-up onto her boyfriend? She would have to be ruthless.

But Steph was not ruthless. She had not done what Fiske thought she had.

Still, they couldn't simply waltz into the police station and say so. All that phony evidence from Pictured Rocks and Steph's cell remained. Even if they could convince anyone to care about the contents of *Illusory Greatnesses*, it would be her word against Doug's as to who had really killed Nora.

"We have to learn the truth about Nora Brockert. If we could prove she and Doug were mixed up in some trouble, or"—a gulp choked her words—"involved somehow, leading up to prom, we might have a chance."

"Well, Nora's dead," Eric observed, "and Doug is turning out to be something less than a fount of honesty. Who else is there?"

Steph thought wide and hard, trying to conjure up her old classmate's social circle. Nora had been brash, unfiltered. She had welcomed friends from all walks of the school, but this—whatever it was—did not seem like something a casual acquaintance would be trusted with. Who might she have told? Who would've had her ear? A locker mate? A counselor?

A sister.

CHAPTER THIRTY-FOUR

They crossed Michigan Ave several blocks north at the Water Tower, where the police presence was minimal, then slinked their way back down to the Mitsubishi. Eric took I-90 to avoid the park, exiting fifteen minutes later at *Hyde Park/U of Chicago*. If Lydia Brockert was not at her office, they would sleep in the back seat and catch her in the morning.

The psych department was housed in an imposing brick building that spanned its entire city block. They parked on the sleepiest of three surrounding streets. Most of the entrances—gorgeous stonework doors retrofit with key card readers—were locked, it being a Saturday, but Eric found one propped with a plywood shim.

"Grad students," he explained. "Too lazy to bring keys on a munchie run."

A directory listed *L BROCKERT* on the sixth floor, office 617. They hunted for the elevator bank, passing tear-tab math tutor flyers and solicitations for research participants. A kid shuffled past with fizzing earbuds and his nose in a fat, flopped-open binder.

Steph stalked the halls with purpose. Her intensity spooked Eric a little. He couldn't help recalling that Steph, ten years ago at prom, really had fought with Nora Brockert. Not *fought* fought, and it hadn't been a school-wide scene like Fiske had portrayed in *Illusory Greatnesses*...but they'd certainly exchanged words.

Nora had shown up drunk. (At least.) She said something to the photographer, kindly Mr. Ackerman, the retired US history teacher who still pitched in at dances. Whatever it was—Eric had been farther back in line with Tara Pinney—Steph found it disrespectful. She suggested Nora go find her date. Nora, who'd come solo, took this as an insult and cracked that Steph's dress was "the color of my grandmother's bathroom." After a few more tight-lipped exchanges, Doug and Steph got called up for pictures.

Now, was this motivation enough for Steph to *kill* Nora? No way. Right? Surely, she was not at this very moment considering that gun on her ankle, plotting to make it a clean trifecta of Brockert-sister murders, then turn the barrel on Eric before jetting off to Montenegró. Surely not. That was crazy talk.

Right?

Two bends off the elevator, they found office 617. The door was leaning shut. Eric glanced in by a crack.

Lydia Brockert sat reading behind a desk. Wires of thin brown hair escaped a ponytail. Her skin looked nearly blue. Eric motioned for Steph to come look.

Steph did, then nudged inside. "Lydia? Hi there, could we trouble you for a word?"

Lydia flinched at the intrusion. Once her surprise cleared, a dozen emotions struggled for control of her face. Shock, skepticism, fear, curiosity.

The one that finally won was hate. She said, "Get out."

"We didn't do this," Eric said. "We were framed, it's all a frame job! Give us a chance."

Lydia said nothing. Her glare seemed to originate from some deep, righteous core.

Steph tried, "You know us. You were with us at the cabin— you know we're on Autumn's side."

Lydia moved one finger to her office phone. "Perhaps the police should sort this out."

"No! No, they shouldn't," Eric said, "because they'll throw us in jail and ignore all this stuff we've learned..."

He argued they had information pertinent to Autumn's whereabouts. Steph asked her to consider the extraordinary risk they were taking. If she and Eric were truly guilty, why would they come here?

Across the desk, Lydia's anger yielded to an air of calculation. It seemed to Eric that she watched more than listened.

"We read the manuscript, the one Fiske is saying was destroyed. That's the key!"

"We need your help," Steph added. "Please. We had nothing to do with this awful thing happening to your sister."

Lydia's finger inched off the phone. "I believe you."

"*You do?*" Eric asked—Steph nudged him with her shoe.

"Your heads." The academic seemed to look through them, as though channeling some extrasensory vibe. "They're still. People who lie move their heads. Or touch their mouths. On the drive, Eric, you touched your mouth when Becky asked what music you liked. Embarrassed. You aren't touching your mouth now."

Eric raised his eyebrows. He didn't know how he would feel relying on this magic-decoder-wheel approach to truth detection at a Vegas card table, but if it bought them fifteen minutes here? Heck, sign him up.

"But you're wrong," Lydia said. "You do have something to do with it."

"Honestly we don't, I know how it probab—"

"Winners. Live Big. You. My mother. This *whole...rotten...thing*." Each word, poison through her lips. "It's all phony posturing."

Eric and Steph stopped talking. Lydia was silent for another long stretch, which Eric perceived in a completely different way from previous silences. This wasn't shyness. Lydia Brockert wasn't fragile. Maybe she never had been, even at ETHS.

She was fed up.

At last Lydia said, "If you aren't the killers, who is?"

Steph dropped her head. "Doug. We think he orchestrated the whole thing."

Again Lydia seemed to enter an intense state, churning unseen data.

Eric asked if she had ever picked up cues from Doug. Did *he* touch his mouth? Or blink a lot, whatever?

"No. I could never read anything off Doug. He was a sphinx."

Quickly as possible, they explained the sequence of events—about Trev Larson, and what Steph had found behind Doug's vintage *Sports Illustrated*s, and their harrowing escape at ETHS, and Marna's account of Jesse Weams's last days, and dredging up *Illusory Greatnesses* from the nasty Pritzker bathroom.

"Remember at the cabin," Eric said, "you told me Becky said prom was important?"

Lydia nodded.

"Now we understand. This manuscript portrays Nora's death, how it really happened."

Eric recounted Fictional Steph's murder of Fictional Nora, which they knew to be false. "Doug must have murdered your sister himself. What we're trying to understand is why, what really took place that night. Prom night. Do you have any ideas?"

Lydia said, "No."

But her voice had hitched, some doubt or swallowed footnote.

"Please," Steph said, "if you know anything—what Nora had been thinking, or dealing with leading up to that night—it could be important."

Lydia shook her head.

Eric urged closer. "This is our chance to find Autumn. Maybe our last chance. If we don't figure this out quick? She's a goner. She'll stay wherever she is, and nobody finds her, and she's a goner."

This was cruel and possibly disingenuous, but it did seem to budge Lydia. She snapped her arms closed as though suddenly cold.

Steph: "What do you have to lose? If you know something about that night, why not tell? Why not tell *the world* if it improves the odds of finding your sister?"

Pressure built in Lydia's face. The point of her chin became pronounced. "Because it wouldn't be fair. Not to Nora."

Eric and Steph shared a guarded look.

"We would never say a word against Nora," Steph said. "We just want the truth."

"None of this goes beyond us." Eric made an X of his hands—a severe, not wholly logical gesture. "Guaranteed, thousand-percent confidential."

They assured and assured and assured, and eventually it was enough.

Frowning, Lydia began. She insisted on explaining Nora's inner life first, how she'd arrived at her Party Girl persona, before delving into prom night. Steph and Eric did not object. Nora had defined herself in opposition to Jane Brockert. Sex, clothes, her boisterous egalitarian social style—all this grew from Nora's inherent need to push their mother's buttons. The more Jane objected, the larger became the cutouts in the thighs of Nora's jeans. She dated boys from the vocational school in Skokie. Signed up for remedial math. Whenever Jane Brockert mentioned Fiske or his Winners list, which she did often, Nora would stick a finger up her nose until the subject passed.

"Life was a game at seventeen," Lydia said. "She never got to decide for herself, in an affirmative way, what things mattered to her."

"Of course, *of course.*" Eric winced. "Whatever this is, who would blame her? Who would say she deserved to die at her senior prom?"

"Everyone," Lydia said. "Everyone judged her then, and if I reveal what I know now, she'll be judged all over again. Not just in the halls of high school. On television, the internet."

Her eyes throbbed forward, aimed at some point beyond them.

Steph said, "I understand your instinct to protect her memory. But for Autumn's sake, I think we have to consider possibilities that're...well, hard. For me anyway. Did Nora ever mention Doug? Did they have a, um, a—some kind of relationship?"

The emotion in Steph's voice seemed to bring Lydia back. She swallowed. Her fingers splayed on the desk before her.

"Nora loved him."

Steph's eyes bugged, and she said, awkwardly upbeat, "Oh—uh, okay. A sort of crush?"

"No. An obsession." Lydia bit her lip. "Doug was her blind spot. She was otherwise avowedly antiestablishment, had no interest in conventionally desirable boys at ETHS. But Doug she wanted like...an *animal.*" She whispered the word. "She described it to me once. She said it was sick and absurd and wonderful, and unstoppable. She texted him at three a.m. Stole liquor for him. Kept his scholar-athlete photo from the *Tribune* in her underwear drawer, wrapped inside her favorite bra."

"And they—if they texted like that," Steph said, "then I suppose..."

Lydia studied her lap. "At Lighthouse Beach. In our front yard, against the trunk of the big willow."

As Eric listened, he thought of how un-Steph-like it all sounded. Steph, who had never wanted to do debate prep in the courtyard because the debris might ruin her cards' stack edge. Nora's audacity must have intoxicated Doug. It reminded Eric of his own breakup with Ramona, how desperate he had been for someone different than himself, a whiff of impulse or unconsidered glee.

Steph took Lydia's hand. "You said it yourself: Nora was seventeen. Nobody was married with kids. Seventeen-year-olds are supposed to make mistakes."

Lydia's fury had given in, or at least made room for, sadness. She squeezed out tears, turning away, rounding her back.

Steph circled the desk to hug her from behind. Over top of Lydia's head, Steph looked at Eric. He returned her gaze with solemn—if slightly impatient—eyes. Now they knew Doug and Nora had had a relationship, which was something, but did not explain murder. They'd yet to hear about prom night. Had Nora been pregnant? Or threatening to reveal some deep, dark secret about Doug?

Eric was just querying his mental Scott/Drew Peterson database of motives when a knock sounded on the door. He turned expecting a janitor or student needing a signature for some form.

Instead, he saw Jane Brockert.

CHAPTER THIRTY-FIVE

J ane Brockert pounced into the office, bulldozing toward all
three occupants at once. The tails of a leather trench coat beat
in her wake, and her knuckles looked ready to burst through
shiny dress gloves.

Eric stepped up with palms raised. "Jane, listen, we're here to
help find—"

"Shut it, Cyber Perv." She plowed through him to Lydia's desk
and roared, "*Are you with them?*"

Lydia twisted to face her mother, grimacing as though into a
heavy wind.

"Are you with them?" Jane repeated. "*Are you part of the
conspiracy?*"

An ugly smile played across Lydia's lips. Her lungs filled with
air, and Steph—fearing what might be said—stepped in between.

"Hear us out," she said. "Let us present our side."

Jane whipped her cell phone from a coat pocket. "I don't need
to hear a damn thing."

"We're being framed. And Lydia is not with us—we just
walked in off the street."

But Jane wasn't listening, ripping off one glove, poking at her
phone. Steph extended an arm to dissuade her. Jane brushed it off
with a jutting elbow.

Steph poised to...what, take the woman by force? Stash her somewhere against her will?

Before it came to that, Lydia spoke.

"Put down the phone, Mother. We need their information to find Autumn."

Her conviction affected Jane. A voice answered her call, but she started the cellphone back toward her pocket.

"What do they know?"

Lydia straightened up in her chair. "They know who killed Nora."

Jane Brockert had not expected this. She drew breath to speak and then swallowed it, glancing aside like she had been stung. For several seconds, she cut her eyes between Lydia and Steph, seemingly about to ask a question, then thought better of it.

Eric said, "This whole fiasco is about Nora, covering up what happened on prom night. It was no accident. Nora was murdered."

Slowly Jane began nodding.

"I knew it. I knew it. I knew it." Her crimson-painted lips snarled. "Who?"

"Doug. He killed Nora and then got caught dumping the body by Fiske. But he cooked up some story about Steph backing over her in the parking lot—that's why Fiske thinks Steph is behind everything happening now."

Jane moved her gaze to Steph. Hostile, searching. "How? Why? Doug Reece was apple pie and baseball. Stinking bald eagle on his shoulder."

"That's why we came," Steph said. "To ask Lydia."

The middle Brockert repeated what she had already told of Nora's and Doug's "animal" attraction. Jane listened unflinchingly but clearly did not enjoy hearing about her late daughter's exploits. Every so often, she would sniff violently as though trying to eject phlegm out the back of her head.

Eric waited until Jane was caught up, then asked, "Did anything change leading up to prom? Anything that might have caused Doug to wish her harm?"

Lydia hesitated.

"Was she pregnant?" Steph jumped in, breath short. "She wasn't pregnant, was she?"

"No." Lydia's upper lip firmed. "Not pregnant, but..."

Jane said, "Stop dithering, Lydia. Tell us now. Whatever it is, however unflattering."

The academic's face stormed over at her mother's bossing—Steph had a feeling their dynamic was going to change drastically after this—but Steph reached for her hand.

Lydia resumed, "There was something that I—er, at the time, that I found distasteful. But it passed, and I didn't imagine it meant anything. Not until ten minutes ago." She rubbed her temple. "Nora told me that Doug wanted to do something big at prom. 'Senior prom is seminal,' he told her. 'We should remember forever. It has to be epic.' She told him, great, he should feel free to have some epic fun—but seeing as how he was taking somebody else, she didn't have much control.

"At the same time, his demands were becoming wilder. More daring settings. Other...types of intercourse. Nora started to feel like Doug only wanted her for kinky sex, that he didn't value her. For Nora, sex fit into a greater ethos. She believed physical pleasure plugged you into the universe in a way that books and logic couldn't. She rejected the morality of self-denial, of not doing things because they devalued you in the eyes of others, or might prove harmful absent necessary precaution.

"But she still deserved to be loved." Lydia smeared her cheeks. "To be loved, and enjoy basic tendernesses. Just because you covet a carnal pleasure, you don't forfeit that right."

Listening, Steph burned with shame at what Doug had done. *He was only a kid,* she had to tell herself. Otherwise it was unbearable—the idea that she'd lived so much of her life beside this man.

"For Doug, it seemed all about the thrill," Lydia said. "She confronted him once. Why couldn't they just go to dinner, hang out? 'Because I'm QB1. And QB1 only eats at Applebee's on Friday Night Lights.' Nora didn't like it, but she didn't want to lose what they had together either. So she kept saying yes. She drank more heavily with Doug—it made complying with his requests easier. Her first experimentation with heroin came shortly after being blindfolded by Doug in a movie theater, then feeling an extra hand up her thigh.

"He harbored one fantasy above all others, and it ate at him, Nora said, because it kept eluding them." Lydia's eyes turned inward. "Water. He wanted it underwater. They tried in our upstairs bathroom but couldn't make it work. Doug insisted they try again. *Tub's too shallow.* When the lake worked no better, he decided the problem was excitement—they needed more excitement for him to...well, apparently cold water has certain detrimental effects on male anatomy. But Doug had an idea about what might provide the necessary stimulation." Her gaze moved onto Steph. "A third participant."

Steph reared back. "Me? What? Not in a million years would I agree to—"

"Not you," Eric said.

He looked frankly into Lydia's face, and they agreed without speaking a word.

"Wet hair. I barely remember—this is dredging serious subconscious ROM here—but that night, in the gym, a girl had wet hair. Nobody noticed with the ambulances and Mancini's address, and Fiske being a wreck. She was shivering off in a corner." Eric sighed. "Becky Brindle."

Lydia nodded. Jane Brockert's lips were busy, but no sounds came out.

Steph was still numb from Lydia's account of her husband's depraved sexual tastes. It was like being shown photos of some abscess you knew existed but had not brought yourself to glimpse. Doug had been pushy about sex but not recently. In the early days, especially drunk, he would nudge her and nudge her and nudge her toward things that repulsed her. Once he had gripped her shoulder, forearm barred across her upper back, and she had thought a brutal thing might happen.

Her shout and heel to the groin had stopped him then, and over the years the incidents had waned. All her girlfriends dished about bedroom acts their husbands wanted but weren't getting; was Doug really an outlier?

But as soon as she thought the question, she knew the answer. Yes. Doug's desires contained an element that her girlfriends' husbands' did not. Privilege. There were hints in Lydia's tale—the Applebee's crack—and Steph had felt it just days ago at poker night, the confidence in his grip under the table. He *deserved* those parts of her. Sexual satisfaction came part and parcel with his place atop the pecking order.

Bob Fiske hadn't been the monster, the one who believed his own greatness entitled him to whatever spoils he could get his hands on.

Doug had.

The room was quiet. While nobody especially wanted to vocalize them, the basic parameters of the deed seemed clear. Doug had bullied the two girls into teaming up for his fantasy. Something went wrong in the pool and Nora Brockert drowned. Becky fled upstairs, and Doug was discovered dragging the body away by Fiske. He fabricated the story about Steph backing over Nora in the parking lot, betting that if he invoked the name of Steph—widely known to be Fiske's cherished favorite (and a careless driver)—Fiske would play along.

Jane Brockert paced. "What's the *so what*? That's a lotta icky stuff, but how do we move forward? What gets my daughter back?"

These words shook Steph from her doldrums. Her and Eric's goals, she realized, did not perfectly align with Jane's. Proving they were innocent of these crimes might shed light on Autumn's location, but it might not. The instant Jane Brockert thought dialing 911 was the quickest way to find Autumn, she would do it.

"Take a step back," Steph said. "We've identified one more person who was involved. Becky. Each additional conspirator is a possible source."

"Becky died." Jane kept pacing, hands on hips. "Not helpful."

"Yes, but maybe she told somebody. Or wrote a note, or searched the internet."

As soon as she said it, Steph wanted it back.

"You're right—we need the police." Jane reached for her phone again. "They can get subpoenas, they have manpower to canvass Becky's acquaintances."

"No, not yet!" Steph tried. "We can't prove any of this, we need proof before we—"

"*You* need proof," Jane interrupted. "I need the cavalry."

As faint rings came through her phone speaker, Steph turned imploringly to Lydia, who rose from her desk resolutely but found no words. Eric took a halting step. *What could they say?*

Steph's thoughts went into overdrive, fanning out in all possible directions at once. Jesse Weams, Principal Mancini, *Illusory Greatnesses*...the muscle-head trainer out in Kankakee, a coma, that phrase "tonguing pills"—the matrix of possibilities was dazzling.

She reenvisioned every scene of the last week in a flash, a dumped-water-bucket of sensory detail crashing through her skull. She felt powerfully that whatever they needed was right here. Some nugget, some whispered admission or sideways glance. All it needed was context.

Think. Think, think...think.

Finally, from the chaos, it stood apart: a conversation from the lodge.

CHAPTER THIRTY-SIX

The front of the building was a no-go. Eric drifted toward the curb, preparing to enter the circle drive, but braked at the sight of three silhouettes in the main hall.

"Looks like they beefed up security," he reported to the others. "Cruise around back?"

"How is that less suspicious?" Jane Brockert said.

"They'll figure we're just kids making out."

"Yes. Then they will tap on our windshield, and then we will be toast."

They decided to park a block away and approach by way of the track and football practice fields. Lighting was nonexistent. Eric kept his fingers in the mesh of a chain-link fence for balance. Lydia's shoes crunched over frozen grass behind him, while Jane and Steph charged ahead. After shimmying through a staggered-gap exit, they lowered themselves into a shallow trench twenty yards from the parking lot.

"Can't see a thing," Jane said, her clipped tone adding, *And I blame you entirely.*

She wasn't just being difficult (though clearly she enjoyed this mode); you really could not see the back of ETHS. Eric squinted through the night and made out the garage bay, the second-story ridge line, but nothing more.

Steph was for throwing caution to the wind and walking

straight through the lot. Her second step out of the trench, though, found a divot.

"*Ow!*"

Her ankle had turned. She staggered another step, but the bad foot wouldn't bear weight. Eric helped her back to the trench.

"I have an idea." He took out Droid and searched the app store for *Night Vision*. Though it returned plenty of apps, none had review scores higher than 3.5 out of 5. Possibly this meant that night vision on a cell phone inherently sucked, no matter how good a code monkey you threw at it. Still, it was worth a shot. Night Vision Camera!! had the least-bad score—better than one-exclamation-mark Night Vision Camera!—so he downloaded it.

Wasn't awful. He oriented Droid horizontally and aimed at the school. Through the slow-twitch static, in that weak green tint everybody recognizes from the movies or *Call of Duty*, a single figure patrolled the back. He (must've been a "he": large, block shouldered) walked the middle third of the building, pivoting at the third or fourth classroom from either end.

Eric passed the phone around.

Steph, still gripping her ankle, said, "He's blind to the science wing. If we're quiet, we can sneak around that side."

She crouched and began hobbling that way through the trench. Jane followed. Eric dimmed his screen and was about to do likewise when Lydia cleared her throat.

"The Bio-Dome," she said. "We're going to run into the Bio-Dome."

Eric groaned. Of course. The Bio-Dome: the large, spherical, "self-sustaining ecosystem" ETHS had constructed in 2004. (It turned out to need plenty of sustaining.) The Bio-Dome spanned the south face of the school and would be locked up tight. Tighter than tight, thanks to numerous snake-, ferret-, and salamander-related pranks over the years.

"Mr. Glanville's class is on that end." Steph waved them on. "He always left his windows open."

"Yeah, open into the Bio-Dome," Eric said.

"Not the top ones. Remember how the chemistry rooms had those high ceilings for ventilation?"

"Those windows are twenty feet off the ground!"

Jane had taken Droid ahead, was surveying the green screen. "It's round, right? The bio-thingamajig?"

The others nodded.

"Somebody could scale it. Create some traction, pull themselves up. Looks doable."

Eric was dubious, but when Steph volunteered—grimacing at the pain of merely standing—he knew what had to be done.

"I got it," he said. "I'll give it a whirl."

Steph spotted a coil of rope in the track infield. "Once you're up, tie this to the window frame. Then the rest of us can use it to get ourselves up."

Jane retrieved the rope while Lydia hunted up something for traction, settling on a pair of gritty strips from the starting blocks. Lydia pried off the strips—the outburst in her office seemed to have doubled her physical strength—and fitted them onto Eric's shoes. The group then circled south through the trench.

They lost cover where the sophomore parking lot sloped to meet the terrain, but by then they'd made the corner, beyond the guard's line of sight. Eric crept ahead through the lot, meting out steps, carrying the rope coil. Cold rang in his ears. Saliva flooded his mouth.

Up close, the Bio-Dome was not so impressive. Its actual height was closer to ten feet than twenty. The original design had called for all essential systems to run off solar, but now the panels lay stacked against the base like busted screens. Inside, dimly visible through the condensation-smudged glass, were ferns, beakers, wire-mesh hutches. A walkway of mossy stones led from the inner classrooms to a NASA-worthy entrance boasting rubber airlocks and a ship-wheel hatch.

Eric gripped the hatch, hoping that whichever god was in charge of keeping innocents out of the slammer was on duty tonight.

Nope. The hatch didn't budge.

So he planted one tread-augmented sole against the dome, dug his fingernails into the seam between the second and third panes, and started his billy-goat ascent. It took five minutes to manage the next seam. He kept hiking his foot too far up, torquing his knee up beside his ear and stumbling. He experimented and found that by dropping his hips away from the dome in small steps, he could stagger high enough to gain another hold. Reaching the next seam was easier, the slope less severe, and by the fourth he could crawl with knees contacting glass.

He was actually digging it a little, notwithstanding the slightly woozy, balanced-on-a-marble sensation. He peeked down into the Bio-Dome and saw a tree frog watching with red, protruding eyes.

"*Eric!*" called a hushed voice below. Steph's. "The window, *try Glanville's window!*"

He gave the tree frog a shrug, then cinched the rope coil tighter and crawled on. The Bio-Dome met the brick building at an arced-steel lip, above which lay a row of classroom windows. Eric thought he remembered Mr. Glanville's being smack in the middle. The *Mission Impossible* theme twanging in his head, he planted both palms against the sash. Scanned for wires or infrared doodads, saw none. Gathered himself. Pushed.

It gave.

He knotted the rope around both hinges, tugged until he felt satisfied. *That'll do,* he thought with a Schwarzenegger sneer. Stout shouldered, he was walking the loose end of the rope out to the others when his feet began sliding apart. He bowed backward at the waist, then forward, fighting for balance like a honeymoon surfer, before losing it altogether and crashing down.

His butt slammed the glass. A second later, a pulsating alarm rang through the Bio-Dome.

The rope had slipped from Eric's hands and unspooled to the ground. Lydia grabbed it and scurried up, followed quickly by Jane and Steph—whose one-legged ascent looked excruciating. Eric, ignoring his own aches and pains, joined them at Glanville's open window. He dropped the rope down into the classroom and himself almost as quickly, sliding five feet per clench, landing in a tangle of chairs. In no time, he'd freed a nearby table of its microscope and dragged it underneath, allowing the others to descend more easily.

The alarm kept bleating. You'd have thought a missile launch was imminent.

"Game's up." Jane Brockert reached into her coat. "Better call the cops before they get here, put a frame around this."

"No, no—we're okay," Steph said.

She limped to a door in the corner of the classroom and opened it to a panel of flips, buttons, and gauges. Steph had been Glanville's lab assistant. Her eyes raced until she found a scrap pinned to the inner door, off which she read and entered a four-digit code.

The alarm stopped.

In the sudden quiet, a cautious look passed through the group. They all stood with toes poised inward, as though a wrong step might set off more bleating.

Shuffling sounds. Faint, but coming closer.

"Footsteps," Eric said.

"Hide in the bathroom!" Steph said. "Close that window, bring the rope."

Standing on the table, on tiptoes, Eric could just untie the rope. He pulled the sash flush and gathered the rope. He, Lydia, and Steph raced into the hall, the bathrooms right next door, but Jane Brockert hesitated.

Uh-oh, Eric thought. Steph had managed to convince her to come along on this jaunt by arguing the police would take too long: they would insist on verifying accusations, and obtaining warrants, and who knew what other red-tape nonsense. For Autumn's sake, they simply could not spare the time.

But now, if Jane figured they were on the brink of getting caught anyhow...

Steph took the older woman by the arm. "It's there. If it's anywhere at all, it's on those tapes."

Jane Brockert breathed sourly out her nose, but followed.

Both restroom doors were propped open to air out that sharp, weed/bleach/urine smell that no high-school janitorial crew ever truly conquers. They kicked the stops away and dashed into *Women's,* all four cramming into a single stall. The overhead panels were dark, but a scant light came through an oblong window to the Bio-Dome. Jane and Lydia flattened their backs against the stall. Steph fit herself around the TP lockbox.

If I never set foot in another public restroom, Eric thought as he straddled the toilet's crotch.

In another minute, security guards entered the adjoining class-room. Boots pounded, intercoms crackled—at least two and as many as five. Eric held his breath and listened. A groan. Some code being input, then a similar tone to what Steph had produced from Glanville's control panel. The rattle of keys around a ring. The slurping pop of a door seal disengaging.

"It's the woodchuck," one guard said, his voice audible through the wall. "Trust me."

"He can trip the alarm?"

"He can trip the alarm, he can nibble those oxygenator tubes until the koi die off. That's one sneaky varmint."

They entered the Bio-Dome and could not be heard for the next two minutes. Eric made out a few rodent-like squeaks. At one point, wings flapped furiously.

Then the guards' footsteps were back, followed by another pop.

"So what, he was asleep," the guard said. "He knows how to play possum."

"God's sake, Hank. You need a vacation."

Eric saved a chuckle at the top of this throat. Jane glared at him.

There were beeps, then several impatient breaths, then: "What was the disturbance code again?"

"1492-B."

"What's that?"

"Uh, lemme see..." Pages rustling, snapping. *A manual?* "Here it is. 'Impact.'"

After a silence, a new voice said, "What're you supposed to do for that?"

"Same as the rest," said the guard who had done most of the talking. "Silence the alarm. Confirm boundary integrity. Investi-gate possible root causes."

"All of which we did."

"Yup."

The guards wisecracked about previous false alarms. Appar-ently, during the summer, between humidity and fewer students around to scrape filters, the algae had gotten so bad the newts' color had changed from green to gray.

It was sobering to hear this dirt about the Bio-Dome, which had been such a coup for ETHS in Eric's day. The science department had partnered with an education start-up in Raleigh on the proposal. Initially, the school board had rejected the idea on budgetary grounds. Even after halving the square footage and nixing the "extremophile lava alcove," it seemed a long shot. Principal Mancini saw the writing on the wall and proclaimed the money better spent on at-risk students. The one who turned the tide was Bob Fiske. "The Bio-Dome elevates this school," he testified. "Its sheer ambition is beautiful. The rest of us cannot but gain from such imprimatur of scholarship."

The guards left.

Once their footsteps dissipated, Eric, Steph, Jane, and Lydia unpacked themselves from the stall and took stock. The counselors' offices' recent move to the fine arts hall was a stroke of luck, as it meant they could be reached without passing the security concentrated in the central admin hall.

Steph led despite the bum ankle. They hugged walls and corners and froze at the slightest noise—mop squeaks, a distant car horn. Eric took up the rear, making sure Jane didn't bolt.

The door to Becky Brindle's office was swinging wide. They hurried in. Neither the desk nor file cabinets seemed picked through—possibly because nobody else suspected her involvement. The space felt like Becky, effusive, excitable. A corkboard spanned one wall and featured a smorgasbord of tacked-up, over-lapping items: scribbled reminders, digits, an Ethiopian take-out menu, sticky notes with rudimentary happy faces.

Lydia stood guard, one foot in and one out of the doorway. Eric rifled through drawers and swiped clear bookshelves and yanked up rugs. Steph was running her fingers along baseboards.

Jane was on her knees beside the desk. "Found something. Metal box."

The others hurried over, Lydia abandoning her post, and bent to see the underside of Becky's desk. Mounted low on the front face was a device, four by six by two inches high. Eric immediately recognized the casing and dimensions as those of an optical drive. He spun loose four wing screws and unfastened two cables, jiggled the drive from its sleeve—delicate tasks made difficult by adrenaline surging through his fingers.

The drive was out. It had no screen or terminal for accessing the data, but there was a USB slot. Eric filched a connector from his Paladin demo travel kit and plugged into Droid.

Seconds later, he was looking at a file directory.

CHAPTER THIRTY-SEVEN

Eric tapped through the top-level system folders, investigated a few audio-ish entries like /wav and /sounds, before stumbling onto /rec_live, which contained nested year/month/date subfolders. For each date, there was a single large file, ten megabytes or more.

Steph's chin was sharp against his shoulder. "How far back do they go?"

He spread-pinched the screen. Droid stuttered, took a while loading. "I see 2013, 2012...here's 2011 now. Doesn't look like they ever get erased."

Jane Brockert asked, "Are the conversations labeled? Can you tell who's talking?"

Eric shook his head. It was a letdown, but minor: if Doug and Becky had discussed their plot here, the audio had been preserved. That was the important thing.

Mid-August, they decided, was about the earliest a conversation could've occurred. Eric tapped into /8/15 and played the file. The audio sounded tinny through Droid's speaker, but voices were clear enough. The first conversation was a whiny discussion about the college options of a junior named Hugo, who refused to accept Becky's assessment that Duke and UVA were stretches. "That GPA is bogus—I didn't even try my first year." Becky cheerily suggested Loyola, or one of the Texas state schools if weather was his driving factor.

"Too slow," Jane said. "Skip to the next."

"It's an unbroken file," Eric explained. "There aren't demarcations per student."

"Founded a $50 million tech start-up, and you can't fast-forward a lousy tape?"

"Well yeah, I mean, I *can.*" He squinted at Droid's audio controls. "You can either jump thirty seconds or take your chances using the slider, which is dicey. Without a feather touch, you're liable to end up in the FAT tables."

The others looked at him as though he were quoting Klingon verse, which Eric supposed he deserved. He began skipping ahead by thirty-second intervals, pausing long enough to identify Becky's visitor before moving on. They came across no dead air, so the recorder must have been voice activated, switching off whenever Becky stepped out or left for the day.

August yielded nothing. Ditto September. Eric made liberal use of the slider into October, the first part of which was dominated by talk about a scandal involving cross-country. In an effort to cut to the chase—they had been here nearly an hour—he bypassed large chunks of audio, stopping just two or three times per file.

He began to worry he'd missed something important, some quick phone call or powwow with Doug. *Should he backtrack? How many days?*

Before he could decide, the voice of a girl on the October 17 file stopped him.

"Is it me," he said, "or did that sound like—"

"Autumn!" Jane elbowed to the fore. "Back up, let's hear the start of it."

Eric went back thirty seconds, then another thirty. They heard the tail end of a freshman needing Becky's signature to take physics without prereqs before Autumn's voice returned. The group of four huddled near the phone, their heads a rapt circle. It occurred to Eric they ought to close the door, but nobody pulled themselves away.

Becky and Autumn exchanged pleasantries, talked about the

yearbook staff's progress. Becky sounded extraordinarily happy for the visit. Having just listened to two-plus months of her life's work, Eric could understand why; 99.9 percent of a counselor's time was spent on kids with problems.

Of course, Autumn had one too.

"I'm working on a joint project with this guy, Jesse Weams? The project is for Mr. Fiske. It's supposed to be completely secret —I hesitated even coming here because Mr. Fiske said confidentiality was so vital. I just have nowhere else to turn."

"I understand, Autumn. What's the issue?"

"Jesse. He's not...er—at least, I don't feel he's being discreet enough."

"He talks about the project?"

"Well, his girlfriend knows. Marna Jacobs. She came up to me and wasn't very nice about it. 'You and Fiske shouldn't be messing with Jesse's head.' We were in the hall. Anyone might have overheard."

"I see," Becky said, repeating her go-to phrase when processing a student's concern. "And what is the nature of the project?"

There was a pause.

"A manuscript," Autumn said. "We're helping Mr. Fiske with a manuscript."

"Wow, a manuscript!"

This exclamation of Becky's came out loud—an involuntary yell barely channeled into words. To cover herself, she giggled and complimented Autumn on the honor.

"I probably shouldn't have told you," Autumn said. "I always disguise my work—my mom thinks I tutor Jesse in reading. But Jesse isn't that careful. I feel like I should say something to Fiske, but I'm afraid he'll kick Jesse off the project. And that would devastate Jesse. At the same time, what if he compromises the manuscript? What if Marna blabs it around?"

Becky spoke haltingly for the rest of the discussion. *Probably it would all come to nothing*, she advised with a brittle chuckle. *Steer clear of Marna. Worry about honoring your own obligation to Fiske. Jesse was a big boy; Fiske had placed his trust in him for a reason. What was the manuscript about, by the way?*

Autumn did not say and finally had to take off for a multivar calc exam.

After ten seconds of dead air, the audio clicked back with another student.

Eric looked around the group. Lydia had not moved a muscle, all her intensity aimed at the cell phone as though—with enough will—her missing sister might be pulled back into the room by her voice. Steph likewise reacted little. What she was feeling? Chilled by the affirmation? Angry at a friend's betrayal?

Only Jane Brockert seemed uncowed. "Forward, *forward*! When do they talk next?"

Eric obeyed, zipping through a week's worth of files before next finding Autumn's voice. This conversation felt immediately different. While Autumn again sounded frazzled, Becky didn't stutter or fumble as before.

"Tell me," she said evenly, "how have you been?"

"Honestly not good. I—I have tried not to worry, but it's just impossible."

Becky listened to Autumn's fears. Jesse had been keeping pages of Fiske's manuscript loose in his locker—*where anyone could happen by and see them!* So is that how Jesse got the manuscript, in paper form? Yes: only Autumn was allowed to keep the file electronically, on her laptop.

Becky sighed her concern. "It's very hard to counsel you without knowing what's in that manuscript."

That usual percolating quality of her voice—eager, apologetic in advance—was nowhere. When Autumn balked at telling, Becky kept at it. Maybe the situation was grave, maybe it wasn't. She hated to give bad advice, but without all the facts—the contents of the manuscript, what exactly Jesse was jeopardizing— she feared doing exactly that. The secret(s) would be safe with her, she promised. Autumn needed an ally. Becky wanted to *be* that ally, but first she needed Autumn's trust.

"Doug." Steph gritted her teeth. "She talked to Doug. He put her up to this."

Gradually Autumn yielded. In a strained whisper, she revealed that Fiske's book centered around a crime. She described Maggie and Amanda, and the "accident" in the parking lot. She did not mention the pool or speculate about the characters' real-life counterparts.

"She has no clue," Eric said. "No clue at all that Maggie is Nora. How's that possible? This is a smart girl—how can she not recognize her older sister's story?"

Jane Brockert answered without looking away from Droid, "Because she was seven. We kept it simple. 'Your sister is gone, now finish your broccoli.'"

The audio rolled on, Becky following with low gasps and muttered, *Of course, sure's.*

"That is one wild story," she said when Autumn finished. "But really, Autumn, I wouldn't worry. It's fiction. Harmless, made up."

The audio went silent.

Becky added, "Now I'm trusting *you* with secrets, but know this: you aren't the first student-editor of Fiske's I've advised."

"I'm not?"

"No. Issues have come up over the years. This secrecy Fiske demands—it's because he doesn't want the administration to know he uses students for personal work. Which I absolutely promise not to mention."

With Autumn's information extracted, Becky played out the conversation with further assurances. *Ah, what would anybody make of stray papers in Jesse Weams' locker? Had Marna approached her again? See, there you go—it was forgotten. Go to class. Eat. Sleep. Don't worry. Namaste.*

(*But if new developments came to light, by all means report back at once.*)

Becky and Autumn did not meet again in October. As Eric scanned files, he kept an ear tuned for the cocksure voice of Doug, praying he had spoken in Becky's office about his mind-screw of Jesse. That might be sufficient proof to shift the presumption of guilt off him and Steph.

But no. By mid-November, kids were coming into Becky's office lamenting their classmate's death, saying it was surreal and impossible and could they have an extension for their European history term paper?

Steph said, "Remember how nervous Becky acted, heading to the UP?"

Eric nodded. What all had been whirring through her head? He looked around the counselor's office now—the giant messy corkboard, economy-size box of tacks, sports bra draped off her coatrack—and heard the opening chords of "Candle in the Wind." Back on prom night, she'd been a pawn. Doug had called the shots. Probably he had wanted it rough, wild. Dangerous. Becky and Nora sought to please. When things went to pot, she felt trapped. Doug surely told her she would go to jail forever just for being present, and threatened the same a decade later when *Illusory Greatnesses* came to light, bullying her into being his eyes and ears—and puppeteer—for Autumn Brockert.

That night had destroyed Becky. Everybody thought her life had flipped upside down in Cancun. But it wasn't spring break. It was the week before at prom.

Still, for all they had heard, Eric realized nothing here exonerated them. They were catching downstream ripples of what had incited last week's events, but not the dirty truth itself. They scanned through the December audio, the January, the February. At no point were the words "Doug Reece" uttered. Doug was simply too good. Eric should quit fooling himself; this guy was not going to leave a door unlocked or window propped. Doug Reece had beaten him. Outsmarted him. The nerd would not be tandem-biking away with the jock's girlfriend, or watching him be shoved into the back seat of a cop car.

The jock had won. The jock was better.

Eric had almost fully reconciled himself to this when, the slider near the end, a new voice came through Droid's speakers.

Male. Adult.

"We have a problem, Becks. A big one."

CHAPTER THIRTY-EIGHT

Doug visited Fiske his first evening awake. He would've rather waited a couple days, let the press calm down, avoid being seen with his former coach. But there was too much to chance. Fiske's version of the crime did not match Doug's. Not exactly. Doug had offered up the MetroBuild deal as motive—with the help of Rich Hauser, who would've sold his own mother to get on TV—along with the Eric love triangle. He had said nothing about the manuscript, hoping Fiske would die and *Illusory Greatnesses* with him, but in Fiske's telling, the manuscript was central. Already he'd commented on the discrepancy: "I've no reason to doubt Mr. Reece's voracity. I expect he was confused or misled."

Possibly this could be papered over. After all, both their fingers were pointed at the same culprit.

"How goes it, Coach?"

Doug approached, just fine without the wheelchair, and offered a bottle of 18-year Glenmorangie. Fiske accepted with raised chin.

"It goes," he said. "Forever and anon."

"All the pistons firing upstairs?"

"That is the doctors' estimation, yes."

"And yours?"

Classical music played over the hospital sound system. Fiske nodded at a speaker. "I still find Wagner saccharine. So the touch-stones of sanity remain."

Doug chuckled. The eyes were bleary but responsive. Skin tone fine. Hair frizzed way up—crazy, how he wanted it. He was sitting up, a hospital gown tied loosely over the clothes he had worn on *Victoria Keane Live*.

"If I were a fearful man," Fiske said, "I would request a guard be present."

That answered that. The coot was sharp as ever. While this meant there was work to be done, Doug actually preferred it. Cards on the table. Now he didn't have to guess what might dribble out in some brain-dredging therapy, or plan visits in infinitude to monitor Fiske's mental state.

"You know, I was the one who found you. Did they tell you?"

Fiske nodded. "Together with your wife."

"Yeah she fooled us all," Doug said. "Believe me, I've been kicking myself."

"For mentioning our conversation?"

"No—God no, I didn't say a word about that."

"How do you suppose she became aware of the manuscript, then?"

Doug was prepared for this. "From Becky. They were close— Autumn Brockert must've confided in Becky, who as you know was her counselor, and then Becky passed the info to Steph." Feeling the answer had come across a bit too pat, he added, "Seems like the simplest link. Pure speculation, obviously."

Fiske considered him for a while. The adjacent bed, separated by sliding blue curtain, was empty—Doug had confirmed on entering—and the door was closed. The corner-mounted TV was off. Fiske stared. Kept staring.

Is he trying to sweat me out? Half of Doug felt galled, the other half amused.

The old man had contacted him two weeks earlier, wanting to "speak on an important matter." They arranged to meet at Fiske's condo. The fact that he insisted on hosting the tête-à-tête instead of doing it somewhere public was trouble. Huge red flag.

At that point Doug had known about *Illusory Greatnesses* from Becky but had hoped it was contained. Jesse Weams had been neutralized. Fiske would publish his potboiler based on Nora's death, cash in, and move on to his next. Doug didn't love the idea of such a fictionalized account loose in the world but felt he could weather it. It was a novel. Wasn't evidence. Proved nothing. Even if the events portrayed somehow came to the authorities' attention, they would tarnish Steph and not him.

But if Fiske wanted to talk...

At the condo, six days ago now, Fiske had clapped his arms staunchly across his chest and said he was going to the police.

He explained that he'd been publishing novels under the name Vance Tietjens, and had recently undertaken one based on the events of prom night. The experience of writing the Nora character, of "inhabiting her head," had affected him deeply. For years, he'd suppressed the terrific guilt he felt for covering Steph's role in her death, but no more. He could not bear it. He would confess all. Let the chips fall where they may.

"Perhaps I'll be prosecuted. I care not." Fiske's seamed face fell. "As I wrote the tale, I recalled the pallor of the Brockert girl's skin. The wasted slackness of young muscles. It was Vietnam all over."

Doug listened in silence. Stunned silent, it would have seemed to Fiske. In fact, he'd known about the Tietjens novels for years and half expected this was the reason he had been summoned.

Fiske continued, "Clearly, the implications for you are significant."

Though he kept his breaths even, Doug felt his pulse pound in his neck. He scanned the condo for sources of accidents. Window. Pill cabinet. Kitchen knife. It was seven a.m. and both men were dressed for work.

"Wow, that...that is news...guess that turns us both into accessories," he said, stalling for time. "Something like that?"

"Yes."

"Probation. Short jail term maybe."

"I am a single man near retirement," Fiske said. "No one depends upon me. You have a family, and I do not believe it honorable to foist a thing like this on a family without notice."

"So Steph..."

"Would be exposed. Fully."

Doug, deciding the odds of subduing Fiske there without leaving behind major evidence were poor, considered the *do-nothing* scenario. The scenario where Steph took the fall. Best case, Doug's life would be shattered—his wife in jail, screaming her innocence. Worst case, somebody (Pinkersby?) vouches for her whereabouts that night and the whole thing boomerangs back on him.

"Thanks, Coach." Doug sighed. "You're right. The kids, I—I have a lot to figure out. Course they're young, they'll recover. Hopefully." Trying to sound desperately resigned, he asked, "When?"

"Tomorrow."

Fiske said he could wait no longer. Tomorrow morning. First thing.

Doug had matched his manful expression with one of his own, feeling relief. Good: he could wait. Even better: he didn't have to do the thing himself. Already he had mentioned to Trev Larson that he had a "dark mission" in mind, a job perfectly suited for Trev's unique skillset. Trev had eaten it up.

Doug did not relish the idea of killing. Not then, nor at any point in the following days as events spiraled beyond his control and the body count grew. It was his life or theirs. A straightforward optimization.

Did he wish this domino chain had never been set in motion, that one night ten years ago he hadn't been horny and stupid and drunk and reckless? Sure. But he had been. All that, plus fatefully ignorant about the difference between ecstatic underwater moans and a person drowning.

No point bemoaning it. You find yourself in a situation, you deal with it. Like Jesse Weams.

What a close shave that'd been. If Autumn had not gone to Becky the week she did, the kid might've ruined them. By the time of their "random" meeting at the climbing gym, Jesse had already figured out that Fiske was writing about real-life ETHS scandals, had even dug up the archived police report, hell-bent on impressing Fiske.

"Something's weird," he had confided in Doug. "They never found a mark on Nora's body—*that's why nobody investigated*!" He was eager to show Fiske his discovery, thought maybe it would inspire some sweet plot twist.

Doug had argued for holding the police report in reserve. "Don't go to Fiske with some half-baked theory. *You* investigate, *you* write that twist. Be a Winner. Finish the job."

Jesse, by then fully under Doug's spell, had agreed. And when he agreed two weeks later that the best way to improve his bona fides before Winner selections would be something legendary, something only Jesse—over and above his classmates—could pull off to demonstrate his worthiness? The report died with him.

"I am curious," Fiske said now, his blood-pressure monitor blipping off the time, "about the sequence of events. I read of your confrontation at the school parking lot, and the wounds to your person are manifest. But what of that search party you and Steph joined? Were you not suspicious then?"

"Becky organized that," Doug said. "I thought it was legit. Thought maybe you, uh...decided to take a different course."

He manufactured a sober expression. As Fiske propped himself higher in the hospital bed, Doug felt sure he would conclude Steph had acted alone. So long as the original lie—told a decade ago in humid, chlorine-stinking air—held up, he was golden. After all, why would Doug risk kidnapping and committing multiple murders to conceal a mere accessory role in the crime?

"It's difficult to know a person," Fiske said.

This annoyed Doug. The coyness. What was he, probing for cracks?

"You can know a person's character. Character endures, through time and circumstance."

Doug had no taste for this brand of rumination, but Fiske did —and it was important that he see them as belonging to the same exalted tribe.

"Indeed," Fiske said, then out of nowhere: "What role did you play in Cade Ruckert's arrest?"

"Which one?"

Fiske did not smile. "The one that made state champions of us."

Doug's jaw worked in place. The tale of his takedown of Cade Ruckert—the non-punching version—was famous among ETHS students, but he hadn't known whether the tale had reached faculty ears. Apparently so.

"I orchestrated it," he said, calculating that Fiske wanted a show of honesty. "Guy had no redeeming qualities. I'd do it again."

"So twenty-seven-year-old Doug Reece is the same as seventeen-year-old Doug."

"No, not the same. I've done plenty of stuff I regret."

True statement, 100 percent.

Fiske steepled his fingers. A blue hospital band slipped down his wrist. "As do we all."

Doug could not tell if this referred to Fiske's initial cover-up of Nora Brockert's death, or his own, or the decision to write *Illusory Greatnesses*. Or something else. Who cared? He'd learned what there was to learn. A vegetative-state Fiske would have been better, but this one was workable. The frame job on Steph and Eric still held, so long as Doug managed to eliminate them before they got their own stories out.

He stood. "Let's get together when you're out. Gotta hear where you come down on the new Franzen."

Fiske smiled. Jonathan Franzen was the only contemporary author he read. "Certainly. Until then."

Doug saluted, two fingers off the forehead, and headed for the door. His mind had already moved onto where his wife and the dweeb could be hiding. Shame Fiske hadn't woken up a day earlier. He could have taken them out at the same time as Larson in that garage. He had left them alive to take the rap, but now, with Fiske awake and telling Nora Brockert's story, that wouldn't fly. Now he was stuck with half wins. Rotten options all around.

He had one lucky loafer in the hall, the tile cold through his sock, when Fiske stopped him.

"She won't get away with it."

Doug ducked back in.

Fiske said, "If your supposition that Autumn told Becky

Brindle about the manuscript is correct. If they spoke of the salient points."

For a second, Doug thought the old man was confused or else hadn't gotten the full story in the media. *Didn't he know Becky Brindle was dead? And Autumn Brockert...*

It must have shown in his face because Fiske said next, as though in response, "Every conversation that occurs in the office of a counselor at Evanston Township High is recorded, and preserved in perpetuity."

Muscles locked in Doug's throat. A hot hammering began in his chest.

"That right?" he said.

CHAPTER THIRTY-NINE

Hearing Doug on tape bullying Becky into going along with his plan, Steph literally could not unflex her calves. Even though she knew more or less what she would hear and how things would shake out, she felt anxious for each speaker's response. At one point, the audio beeped as the voice activation decided they were done talking. Becky cried and protested and might've been talking into her sleeve, the microphone picking up her voice clearly one moment and muffled the next.

Doug's was clear as ice. "We have no choice."

"We do, we totally do," Becky said. "It happened ten years ago —so what if he goes to the police? Statute of limitations, right?"

"Murder, Becks. No statute of limitations."

"But was it really *murder*? I mean she drowned, we were all—"

"She died. We covered it up. In the eyes of the law, it's murder."

A silence. Steph could imagine Doug perfectly, kneading the corner of one eye.

For several minutes, Becky pushed back against Doug's plan. *Okay, they had done a bad thing, but they shouldn't compound it with more bad things. What if they walked into the police station with Fiske, and all three of them told the truth? Couldn't that work?*

"Yeah," Doug said, "and the two of us go jail. Maybe they'll give you a furlough to put Kensia and Ana on a boat back to Haiti."

Becky caved at the mention of her twin girls. She sobbed for nearly a minute, then asked softly what Doug wanted her to do.

"Nothing hard," Doug said. "The hard stuff we're taking care of."

He and "his guy" had Fiske holed up at a U-Store near the lake, and planned to lure Autumn there with a text from Fiske's phone. Fiske and Autumn would then disappear to Fiske's cabin in Pictured Rocks, which Doug had stumbled upon years ago doing due diligence after the Tietjens novels began appearing. It was perfect: Fiske and Autumn had already established a pattern of secret communication while collaborating on *Illusory Greatnesses*. The script was half written.

"Sorry I'm so stupid," Becky said, "but what script?"

"Male teacher absconds with female student. Bad stuff happens."

To Steph's left, Jane Brockert glared about the room as though hoping for a ghost to punch.

Becky asked, "To the male teacher?"

"Sure."

But something in Doug's face must have been less than reassuring.

"Because Autumn, she—she doesn't know about prom! She told me all about the manuscript, and she never once connected it to Nora."

"Can we rely on that?"

"I think so!"

"And how would you take care of Fiske without..." Doug considered. "You need suicide at a bare minimum. Murder-suicide feels more natural."

"Why? Fiske could kill himself and then, you know, it would just be Autumn—and as long as she didn't, like, see you guys..."

Doug made squishy sounds with his mouth. "How do we manage that?"

Becky had no answer.

"This guy helping you," she said. "He isn't, like, a pervert?"

Doug said, *no, no, nothing like that*. He answered Becky's questions with scant details, giving off the general impression—always his strength as a husband and father—that all sails were full, nothing could happen he wasn't prepared for.

The role he had in mind for Becky involved the formation of the Winners' search party. His guy had discovered, after nabbing Fiske and pocketing his phone, that the old man had called Eric Pinkersby earlier in the day—after talking with Doug. They needed to know what Eric knew, if anything, about *Illusory Greatnesses* and Fiske's plan to confess. They should also draw out Lydia Brockert. Had Fiske ever let slip some hint about Nora's true fate? Clearly Doug would need to be present to do the probing, and if he was in, it would seem weird not to include Steph too.

As Eric thumbed the *Skip Forward* and *Play* buttons, and the plot's details emerged, the mood was grim. Steph felt hollow. Cored out. The way Doug worked Becky, presupposing his own requirements, comforting and belittling her in the same breath —"Don't worry, nobody will believe you're capable of this"—a hundred small moments from her own marriage leaped from memory and demanded reconsideration. Buying the convertible. Vacationing in Cozumel instead of Whistler. The day-care decision, how cunningly he'd dispatched her wish to have the girls attend Montessori. *Want them going into Kindergarten scared they'll hurt the ball if they kick too hard at recess?* Effortless manipulations. So damned cool and rational.

He heard what you were saying. He understood. But one way or another, once the dust settled, it didn't matter. *You* didn't matter.

Only him.

Near the end of the conversation, Becky got cold feet. "Doug, I —I can't go through with this. Autumn's sixteen years old. It's despicable."

Doug answered without hesitation, "Of course it's despicable. Jesse Weams was sixteen too. What's different?"

"You did that on your own—I didn't know! I would have never helped."

"Becks. Horse is outta the barn. As we speak, my guy has Fiske bound in duct tape."

"So...so make him eat those pills. You said you got pills, right? Suicide. Then it's done."

"We've been over this. We need the Winners' group. Plus, if Fiske dies mysteriously, Autumn Brockert is going to tell somebody about *Illusory Greatnesses*."

"I don't think she would! Really, I don't!"

"Becks."

"She has no idea the book is about her sister. I would swear on my mother's—"

"Too many loose ends. Discussion over."

There were a few competing breaths—sharp, hiccupy versus long and nasal.

"In that case," Becky said in a quavering voice, "count me out. I won't send the FedEx."

Doug tried talking her down. *Focus on jail: on not being there for those twin girls you promised to protect.* He appealed to his own situation, how screwed up Ella and Morgan would be growing up father-less. He berated through gritted teeth, *You know how you always apologize for being stupid? Well you are—you are stupid, you're being stupid now, this is me trying to save you from your own stupidity.* At one point, it sounded like he swept a pile of papers off Becky's desk to the floor.

She held firm.

"Fine," Doug said. "Whaddaya want, huh? What's it going to take?"

"Autumn," Becky said. "I guess Fiske—you guys are, like, committed there. But not Autumn. Autumn lives or else I'm out."

Doug took a while answering. "Jesus Becky, I explained this. We need the teacher/student angle."

"What if you kept her somewhere? You could still lure her away, but...but you could stash here somewhere!"

"Where."

"A hotel? Or something?"

"Right. Then she IDs my guy, and knows Fiske didn't kill himself."

When Becky reiterated her stance, Doug walked back his arguments and said maybe they could stash the girl. What was that place he and Steph had camped, Illinois Beach State Park? Little ways north. Abandoned nuclear facility. Heck, in winter you could probably hideout six months without raising an eyebrow.

Jane Brockert ripped car keys from her purse. "Straight up I-94. Forty-five minutes tops."

Through Eric's phone, Doug and Becky Brindle were still talking. Steph motioned for him to pause.

"Wait," she said. "I'm not sure Doug was being sincere. Sometimes when we argued, he would do that. He would tell me what I wanted to hear, then—"

"No matter," Jane said. "It's plausible, it's straight outta his mouth. We go."

Lydia, too, was standing, already in her coat. She gave Steph a curt nod—thankful, resolved—and mother and daughter took out.

Now the office felt barren. Just Steph and Eric again, as it had been through most of the last forty-eight hours: the most absurd of Steph's life. She felt shoots of hope—a small, fleeting warmth of affirmation—but mostly despair. When all this evil had been opaque, Steph could concentrate on running. On not letting it catch her. Now, it was inescapable—grotesque, oppressive.

"They won't find her. Not alive."

Eric resumed the audio. "Probably not."

Doug and Becky talked through the final preparations, their cover story to the Winners group, how they might adapt if one or more didn't show. "If the geek hedges," Doug said on tape, "tell him we're thinking about divorce." Eric sniffed and looked sideways. Doug coached Becky on how to handle the initial meeting. It should feel like her gig. "Don't worry, Steph will take over soon enough. She always does." He predicted they would quickly seek out Autumn—an obvious first step. He didn't want either Becky or himself present for that meeting.

Eric looked up from the phone. "This has to be enough, right?"

For a second, Steph thought he was making a larger statement about pain and adversity, and how much one should be expected to endure.

"Enough?"

"For the cops. We walk in and play this for them, we're safe, aren't we?"

Steph considered. They had not heard Trev Larson's name, but they did have plenty of particulars about the plot. No way Detective Wright could hear this and believe anyone but Doug had been the mastermind.

"Yes. We've got him."

The audio had moved on, Becky listlessly consoling a kid who'd missed National Merit Semis by a single point. Eric scooped up the school-district drive and raised his eyebrows. Steph nodded. No point staying here and torturing themselves scanning for another meeting, for further details of Doug's scheme. They needed to get this evidence into the hands of the police.

Eric and Steph pivoted to go.

"Here they are," a voice said. "The murdering lovebirds."

After hearing it on tape—scratchy, flat—Doug's voice sounded powerful incarnate. Steph faced him. He wore a car coat over khakis, cashmere gloves, and those lucky loafers. In his right hand, he held a gun.

"How do you live with it?" Steph said. "How do you fall asleep every night?"

"Naked, on my side. You know that."

"You're a snake. Where did you come from? Was any of our marriage real? Ever?"

"Oh, come off it." Doug waved them farther inside with his weapon. "I didn't want this anymore than you."

"What does that *mean*? You did it—all of it! We just heard."

"Had no choice."

"Sure you did. You could have turned yourself in. You could have taken responsibility for whatever happened in that pool. *For God's sake!*"

"And destroyed us. The girls' lives."

"Don't wrap yourself up in the family flag. You did this for you, all the way."

Steph knew these kinds of statements—which she hadn't been able to make two nights ago, in front of the kids—might anger Doug, and harm whatever slim chances they had. She didn't care. This man had destroyed her world. Stolen her adulthood. For all her angst about career trajectory, look at the personal failure that had slipped in right under her nose.

Seven years invested in a sham.

"What can I say? I apologize. It's my fault. But I have to keep living."

"But not me, right?" she said. "Not Eric and me, we don't get to keep living."

The trace of a smirk crossed Doug's face. Steph was reminded of their honeymoon, a particular off moment that stuck in her brain. They had arrived at the parador late, around midnight, after their transatlantic flight had sat on the JFK tarmac for six hours. The woman who cracked the ochre-hued stone door in a nightgown could not find their reservation—and besides, check-in closed at nine. There was a hostel up the coast; they could sleep there and telephone in the morning, sort everything out.

Doug, the Spanish speaker of the two, had flashed the same smirk—at once courteous and ruthless—before explaining that he ran an American travel website. If he and his new wife did not spend tonight "sleeping on a horsehair mattress, smelling the rich brine of the Balearic Sea," as promised online, he would be forced to expose the parador's clear structural issues, rampant bedbugs, and mold-flecked tomatoes in its salads.

Relieved as Steph had felt dropping her luggage in a corner, she had also experienced a twinge of unease. That woman must have been seventy. A single tooth along her gumline. Had it been easy for Doug to speak to her like that? Where had the gall come from? She had told herself he was only looking out for her, doing his best with a lousy situation.

She realized, dimly, that he was doing the same thing now.

CHAPTER FORTY

Eric said, "There is no way you get away with this. It's out in the open. Shoot us if you want, but your problems aren't going away."

"Yeah?"

"It's all on tape. Every twisted detail."

Doug nodded to the drive. "What if that disappeared."

"I'm thinking that would look suspicious. Every other office in the school has audio recordings, and miraculously Becky's doesn't? How's that going to look?"

"Like you two destroyed them. Covering your tracks."

Eric's eyes, which had been pulsing intensely through his glasses, now dulled. "I'm sure everything gets backed up to the cloud."

"District's six million in the red." Doug glanced around the beige office. "Their IT must be cutting edge."

"So what, another murder-suicide? How many of these can you fake before the act goes stale?"

"Exactly one, I figure."

"And why am I killing her? You told the whole world we ran away in love—how does that jibe?"

Doug advanced steadily, his lucky loafers drilling the tile. Eric and Steph shuffled backward and retreated behind Becky's desk. Steph, searing pain in her ankle, scanned for a weapon. Scissors, fork, heavy plaque. Anything. Her hands spread wide in the search, sliding, gripping, pushing papers around.

"You heard the audiotapes," Doug said. "You were devastated. Couldn't believe your beloved was capable of that."

"Where'd I get the gun?"

"The street. Some hood in Grant Park."

Eric scoffed, head ticking back and forth. "Please. Your life is torched, do you know that? Even if you get away with this. You burned everything down."

"True," Doug said. "It sucks, coming and going. No argument there."

Having finally won a point, minor though it might be, Eric stood taller. "This is Fiske's fault. He pounded it into our heads— Live Big, this idea we had to be heroes. Remember how he used to play us off each other? He told me once I could get Steph 'if I made it the sole organizing principle of my life.' Verbatim! It was a game for him, man, dividing up the world into winners and losers. No wonder we fell so hard."

Steph wondered what he was going for. Sympathy? Some kind of flash camaraderie?

"Whine if you want," Doug said. "Life *is* winners and losers. To deny that is asinine. I messed up. Did a dumb thing when I was seventeen. Now I pay the price. That's not on Fiske.

"Now you, Pinkersby," he kept on, "you might have a beef. The old man convinced you, pathetic sniveling tool, that you had game with the crown jewel of the class. Nobody's made that lame movie in twenty years."

Doug gripped the gun overhand and yanked Eric forward, began smearing his palms and fingers across the weapon as Eric had described him doing in the ETHS parking lot. Eric squirmed, kicked, flailed. Doug deflected blows with the meat of his forearms.

"Jane and Lydia know!" Steph blurted. She hadn't wanted to give them up, but the situation was desperate. "They were here— they heard the tape. They're on their way to Illinois Beach State Park right now to search for Autumn."

Doug finished planting fingerprints and forced Eric down,

kneeling on his head. "Only place they're searching is the trunk of my car."

He stood—small, choppy movements, keeping his foot on Eric's neck—and aimed the gun at Steph. She thought she understood Doug's plan: he would rush forward and shoot her before Eric could rise, then whirl and take him out second. They had to attack. *Now*—simultaneously, so Doug couldn't handle them both. Maybe they could pry the gun away or manage a groin shot. Maybe he'd shoot one and the other would escape.

Steph lowered her eyes to Eric's. One was squished closed, but recognition shone in the other.

She lunged to one side off her good foot. Eric spun on his back, propelling himself with frantic, spasmodic legs. He bowed his neck forward and dislodged Doug's foot, managed to flop over, but a second later, his chest was pinned. Instinctively Doug extended his arm, open-fisted, and knocked Steph back.

"Piss-poor effort. Was that breakdancing, Pinkersby? Maybe you need to go first. If you can't stay still."

Again, he lowered himself down onto Eric, knees on his chest, wrestling the gun toward his mouth. Eric huffed and heaved and smashed his own glasses with the back of his head—*crunch*—in the effort to get free.

"*Stop it.*" Doug's voice trembled. "*Stop squirming now, wimp.*"

"Screw you, you're deranged!" Eric screamed. "You're a maniac! Get off me!"

Methodically, Doug subdued each of Eric's limbs, fixing his shin across both thighs, gathering two wrists in his off hand. Then he worked the barrel of the gun between Eric's lips. Eric snapped his head violently side to side, spitting against steel, eyes alternately bulged open and pinched closed. They got spun around in the struggle. Doug's back faced Steph.

She took a soft step forward.

"Not a chance." Doug pivoted on his haunches. *Did he have ESP?* "Five feet is plenty close for what I need to do. You want to try me? Go ahead."

Steph stopped. Pinpricks up and down her spine. Eric continued to worm against Doug's grip, but his motions were slowing. *Was Doug on his windpipe?* After Doug was satisfied

Steph wasn't coming, he thrust the gun back into Eric's mouth. The whites of Eric's eyes flashed. With new, panicked energy, he freed one hand and slugged Doug above the right ear.

Doug growled—rasping, feral—and responded with a brutal headbutt. The back of Eric's head thudded against the office floor. His body wilted.

"Better," Doug said, straddling his docile target.

Steph felt her calves boosting her up to tiptoes and her fingers gripping air. *How to stop him?* Her thoughts surged. Again she turned to Becky's desk and scanned for something, anything useful. Stapler. Block of sticky notes. Computer mouse.

What was that box? Right here at the corner, about the size of a wipes container? She squinted at the label. The print was too fine to read, but the graphic on the side showed a rounded end attached to a sharp point. In the same blink, she sighted Becky's huge corkboard in her periphery.

Tacks!

Steph spun back to her husband. *Please let him be wearing those obnoxious loafers.*

He was.

She snatched the box and, in a single motion, flicked the top and sprayed them forward. Doug flinched at the sound. When he rocked back on his heels, a tack or two must've found the holes. He grabbed for his shoe.

Eric hopped to his knees. He shoved Doug: a wild, crooked-armed blow with zero leverage. It was a distraction, though. Steph came on a furious sprint, biceps pumping, rage overcoming her injured ankle. She plowed into Doug's gun arm, tackling his wrist and elbow joints. The gun tumbled away.

Steph's momentum propelled her on top. She pinned his shoulders with either knee and glared down, seething, thirsty to inflict pain. The advantage only lasted a second—quickly, he had bucked her off and gained a pulverizing grip around her neck.

"Let her go!" Eric commanded.

He'd crabbed over to the gun while they were struggling, held it in two shaky hands.

Doug smiled.

"Now!" Eric said. "I've never shot a gun. I'll just squeeze and see what happens."

Doug jerked Steph between himself and the pointed gun, so violently her spine crackled. "Take your shot, boss. Fifty-fifty."

Eric, without glasses now, screwed up his face. Gripped and re-gripped the gun. Doug slithered left, right, forward, using Steph as a shield, his breath hot on her ears. She swung and kicked backward at him. His flexed body was rock. He winced a few times stepping over tacks but, being prepared for them, never surrendered control of her.

"Help, *help!*" Eric looked skittishly to the hall beyond. "We're in here!"

Doug's voice was a night crawler at the back of Steph's skull: "You're the one with the gun."

With dread, she realized he was cornering Eric, shrinking his angles. Forcing a decision. She stiffened and planted her feet, but he bulled through the small of her back to keep them moving. Eric's eyes spun. He aimed over Steph's right ear, then her left, then cringed and drew back the gun. Steph felt Doug gathering behind. An intake of breath, a coiling of muscles. His fingers spread over her shoulder blades.

"*Eric, shoot,*" she called. "He's just about to shove me into—"

"But—but I can't hit you."

"He'll get the gun and we both die, Eric. Just go, do it now!"

The distance between them had closed to three feet. Eric squeezed his eyes. Doug ducked lower—his forehead brushed Steph's neck—and staggered his stance for leverage, one knee wedging between hers.

He's about to push.

The instant his grip loosened, as his arms exploded forward, Steph dropped. Her legs went limp; her butt crashed to the floor. Doug staggered forward, stomping awkwardly on her thigh, his weight like a cleaver lodging and then twisting into bone. He'd lost balance but kept chopping his feet, reaching ahead for Eric.

A blast sounded.

Steph, sitting in a heap, watched all strength leave her husband's body. He sank. His eyes closed. Blood gouted from his right armpit.

She picked herself up, head passing through wispy gun smoke. Eric stood propped against two walls in the corner. Shaking. Eyes uncomprehending ahead. Steph moved to join him slowly, thinking it best not to startle, and laid the flats of her palms on his shoulders. The shaking slowed, then stopped.

Eric still held the gun. There was a file cabinet. He set it down on top.

Doug lay at their feet, motionless but for respiration in his chest. Viscous blood leached into his hair. The clothes of his right side were shredded, white fibers from an undershirt showing through his coat.

Footsteps thundered from the hall. The audio was playing through Eric's phone, had been playing throughout the struggle. Only now did Steph start processing the tinny sounds again.

"...just wanted to be one *so bad*, Miss Brindle," said a student whose identity she didn't know. "How does he decide? What's the most important factor...?"

CHAPTER FORTY-ONE

From the highway, in the black of night, Illinois Beach State Park looked like those arcane psychiatric facilities Lydia Brockert had studied at MIT. Barbed wire, fortified gates. Flattop buildings. A broad silo—the former reactor, she supposed—rose from the grounds, rimmed by revolving red lights that died over Lake Michigan.

"Don't get your hopes up," Detective Wright said from the driver's seat. "This is a long shot. Doug Reece is a bad guy. Bad guys lie."

He wheeled through the gravel lot and parked at a chained entrance. Jane Brockert had planted a stiletto outside before the cruiser's motor stopped. Lydia refused a paramedic's hand and fell in alongside. The twine had left purple marks on both wrists, and her head still rang from Doug's slammed-down trunk.

A uniformed officer snapped the chain with bolt cutters. Wright led them to the first structure. Despite his warning, Lydia perceived excitement in the detective's body language. His gloved hands flexed, and his pupils showed unprecedented activity as he drew his weapon and radioed for a thermal-scan helicopter.

The front buildings contained only fixtures and stacked municipal furniture. Searching the last, they heard the roar of the police chopper overhead. A telescoping whinny at first, then quite loud. Then deafening.

Wright took a phone call moments later. *"Yes...right, northeast corner...gotcha..."*

With a look to his deputies, he started for an exit.

"Detective," said Jane, "should one of your men stay back with Lydia?"

"No." Lydia stepped forward. "I'm going."

The pressure that had been building these last days, her resentment at Winner-dom and all it had cost her family, had ebbed. Telling Nora's story had pierced something in Lydia. Nora had always been bigger than grudges, too exuberant about the world to get bogged down by hate. She had made it her mission to draw Lydia out. "You're amazing, Sis, let people know!" Reliving their last months together, Lydia had felt Nora's presence —back whispering encouragement at her pillow after lights out, urging her to live for, never against.

Lydia stalked over stiff grass beside her mother and Detective Wright. They bypassed a row of buildings to the one the pilot had indicated. A path was beaten between it and a pulled-back section of fence.

Jumbled, muddy footsteps. A bucket. Two shovels. Red slush.

Wright kicked the door and thrust his gun inside. Deliberately, with his free hand, he found the light switch. The air was assaulting. A sickly-sweet organic smell.

"AUTUMN! AUTUMN, WE'RE HERE FOR YOU!"

The voice boomed through the cold and stench, making the police flinch.

It belonged to Lydia.

Wright joined in, *"Autumn Brockert, call out if you're able! We are here to rescue you!"*

Jane and Lydia ran ahead—if anyone cautioned them, they didn't hear. Around a corner, through a propped door. Chasing a scrabble or scream in a range only they could hear, or shared intuition. Lydia lost all awareness of self. Oxygen blitzed her muscles. Dread and hope filled her brain. She wanted to hold her little sister like she had watching *Watership Down* when they were eleven and five, to feel Autumn's nose in her side.

Finally, they reached the source of the smell. A classroom-sized space. Wright had caught up and now plowed inside with gun

317

poised, but Lydia caught the first glimpse. The scene was demeaning and horrific—a water bowl, filth, cruel black tape—but also lovely.

Because Autumn was moving. In a fetal position, gently rocking on a slate floor.

CHAPTER FORTY-TWO

Eric deplaned and made his way through the terminal. His joints groaned—Southwest really ought to rename economy *contortionist class*—but he felt buoyed the fresh spaces of San Francisco International Airport. Airy, challenging sculptures hung from cathedral ceilings, and scents of cilantro, vinegar, and sushi rice were a welcome change from O'Hare's grease smoke. He boarded a moving walkway feeling weightless.

He had a four o'clock with the investment bankers to discuss raising the IPO's eight-dollar launch price into the low teens after all the positive publicity; Eric's Johnny-on-the-spot recovery of the trashed manuscript file had made the rounds on cable news. He spent the hours until then unwinding in his apartment, breathing live Marina air, watching Windsurfers cut back and forth underneath the Golden Gate Bridge.

The week-long phantasma was over.

Coming through cylindrical silver speakers, a mellow John Legend tune perfectly echoed Eric's inner state. Unconcerned that he couldn't get to the salon and his hair had grown into that nether region where bangs have discernible direction. Unmoved by what restrictions public ownership could force upon Paladin, or glitches the SEC filing process might expose in their back end: potential flies in the ointment that had plagued him before that fateful FedEx.

Something brushed his shin. Eric flinched violently. An orange-white flash tumbled across the hardwood.

"Sorry, Joss—I forgot!" He rushed forward and smoothed the cat's sides. "How's it going? How ya been?"

She flicked her tail and allowed herself to be comforted. Eric glanced down the hall to where the litter was, noting the complete absence of odor. In the kitchen, the automated feeder was still half full of kibble, same as when he had left. He ran his finger along Joss's ribs.

Huh. Didn't feel malnourished.

From his quad-overclocked Xeon workstation, a chime sounded above the radio. Skype.

Who in the world wants to video-chat me? His parents he'd filled in last night from the hotel. His sister, in Bolivia with the Peace Corps, had missed the whole ordeal—her response to his reassuring text was, *did u fall off your bike again?* The press should not have his user ID, and his New York publicists—the only business contacts who had ever insisted on video, in order to assess the viability of his gray patches for the IPO press packet—he had mollified yesterday by e-mail.

There was another possibility. He *had* given her his ID only hours earlier.

Steph.

She realized she'd made a terrible mistake, parting without bold action. Yes, it was crazy to start something in the midst of tragedy; sure, she and her children needed time to "find a new normal" (her words); fine, they both ought to square up their own lives before even thinking of embarking on some new configuration—but heck, fate was fate. Stop overthinking. When angels talk, listen. Don't fret about the shape of their wings.

He skipped to his computer, checking his fly, pinning down a cowlick. Tapped *Answer* and waited for the incoming caller to materialize.

At first the periphery disoriented him, all stucco facades and Magnolia trees—exactly like his own neighborhood. He had the fleeting notion the image came from his own webcam, knocked askew and pointing out the window.

Then he saw Ramona's face.

"The prodigal son." Her voice characteristically indifferent. "Thought you might be back."

"Hey...Ramona."

"The excitement in your face, wow. Like you're chewing cardboard."

"No, no—I was confused," Eric said. "I didn't know who would be calling."

"Righto. Well anyway, I thought it ill-advised to show up unannounced and potentially freak you out, having no desire to get shot today."

"Please, Ramona—I would never shoot you." What universe was this that he needed to vocalize this sentiment?

Her plucky figure bobbed up and down as she turned the corner onto Bay Street. Eric flashed back to Trev Larson, the way his image had zagged as they had pressed him for info in that Loop-district garage. Eric steadied himself by the spare, acrylic desk, dizzied by the memory. Had he really tracked down a murderer using LookyLoo? Broken into ETHS by the Bio-Dome roof and foiled Doug's plot? Shot Doug—with a gun?

"Only from the heights of crisis do we find our own," Fiske used to say.

"I wouldn't have come," Ramona said, "but I thought she might need me today."

"She?"

Ramona raised her eyebrows. "Joss? The feline over whom the county of San Francisco granted you guardianship?"

"Oh! You took care of her this whole time?"

"Who did you think did it?"

"I—well, I didn't know. I guess I figured the automated feeder would..."

At his building's gate now, she tilted her head with mock curiosity. "Would walk itself to the litter and scoop her fecal and/or urine clumps? And provide five minutes of daily human contact to alleviate stress?"

"Obviously my trip took longer than anticipated. It's not like I was off riding gondolas in Venice."

Ramona shrugged. "I am relieved that you're not, in fact, a

sociopath who teamed up with his high-school crush to murder half the city of Chicago."

Eric shrugged back. "Thanks for helping out with Joss. That was really"—he almost said *sweet* but caught himself—"you know, cool of you."

Her video flickered, then froze altogether as she boarded the elevator.

On the radio, a ballad Eric didn't care for, one of those whiny/soulful Brits currently undermining the adult-alternative space, ended. New lyrics began. He recognized the also-British-but-never-whiny sound of Duran Duran.

Cannot forget from fallin' apart...at the seams... Who do need, who do you love...when you come undone...?

The song was not, if Eric was being strictly honest, a high-school bellwether, having been released a full decade before his time at Evanston Township. But it had gotten some airplay, and now he found himself helpless as images of Steph raced through his brain.

Steph smiling. Steph in jeans. Steph bending close to dab blood from his neck, smelling lovely. Steph waving goodbye through security-checkpoint glass.

"Earth to Pinkersby."

Ramona, outside his door, turned her phone around and showed him his unit number. Instead of hanging up like a normal person, she now tilted her phone and drew it slowly back from the decals, which Eric recognized as a recreation of the *Star Wars* opening crawl.

"A long time ago," he said, "in a galaxy far, far away..."

Simultaneously, they began humming the Emperor's Theme. Eric allowed one last remembrance of the girl in Shipley's door well, then let his visitor in.

Steph sat working at her desk. Dashing off last e-mails, tying off a presentation. Meetings had consumed her day. Accounting meetings, strategy brainstorms, a client hoping to spend less, a client itching to spend more. Already it was five thirty, and she had a dinner date at six.

"You needed me?" Chad Nimms asked, ducking a shoulder inside.

Steph pursed her lips at the clock. She had wanted to touch base about Comcast, which was her account now that Rich Hauser had been dismissed for his false public statements regarding Steph and MetroBuild.

"Thanks, Chad, but it can wait," she said. "Let's catch up in the morning."

He knuckled the door twice, grinned, and disappeared down the hall.

It had been strange at first, returning to the office. The secretaries were over-helpful. *Did she need a conference room blocked off, or their teenage daughter to sit for her?* Everybody else avoided her gaze, not in a hostile or judging way, but because they didn't seem to know what she wanted. Privacy? Space? Time to ease back into the flow?

When her new VP scheduled a Nike check-in without her, Steph wondered if regaining a normal role at the firm was even possible. Who could blame Chuck for leaving her off the invite? Every eye in the meeting would be on her, that woman from the news with the diabolical husband, instead of the slides. She would always be a distraction. A liability.

That Saturday she labored deep into the night after the girls went to bed and had her mom watch them Sunday. She walked into Chuck Grayson's office Monday morning with a sharp, clean, compelling eight-pager. Hours later, he led her into the big-boy conference room and said in an uncompromising tone, "This is Stephanie Mills, she's the best we have. I want her working for you."

Nike bought in to the tune of $18 million: the largest RFP Dunham & Prior had ever received from the Swoosh. The next day, Steph was back on the staffing call.

Now she closed her laptop and slipped into her coat. Confirmed the address of the restaurant where she was meeting her date, then drove home.

Ella galloped in from the family room, squealing, "Mommy, Mommy, we saw your car!"

Morgan came crawling in next, all shuffling elbows and beamy eyes. Steph scooped her up.

"You did? Were you spying out the window?"

"*I* was." Ella swiveled about proudly. "*I* saw you from around the corner, before *anyone* else."

"I see." Steph tickled Morgan with the lapel of her coat. "How was your day today? Did you go to Mandarin class? Did Grandma string beads with you?"

From the kitchen, Steph's mother appeared carrying several baggies between her fingers. Each contained a different color of glass beads.

"Oh, we strung." She smiled. "They're eager to show you their best work."

Ella produced a jangly necklace from behind her back. Steph slipped it over her head.

"I love it—thank you, sweetie, it's beautiful."

Her mother had moved in. She had been over so much anyhow since Doug's arrest. One evening over dinner, Steph had just asked. By morning, her mother had installed the bread machine beside the spice rack and secured her medications on a high shelf of the guest vanity. The home was forty-two hundred square feet, and her mom's presence at least began to fill the superhero-sized void left by Doug. Steph had taken the girls out of day care, which she loved; in the past week Grandma had taken them to the Shedd Aquarium, the Field Museum, and Navy Pier.

Steph worried her mother might be overdoing it, compensating for the awful situation. She had texted Marna Jacobs, who said she could watch the girls Tuesday afternoons—the day she wasn't manning the new ETHS peer-counseling hotline.

After necklace showings, Steph led the brigade into the kitchen and dumped her laptop bag. Dinner was ready: meatloaf, broccoli, Ore-Ida fries.

"There's plenty," her mother said. "If you're hungry afterward."

Steph said thanks, puffing her cheeks. She had no idea how

she was going to feel afterward. After this date. But it was something she needed to do.

"Alright girls, eat good for Grandma now," she said, working cheer into her voice. "I have to go out for fancy food. Snails, frog legs."

"*Ooooh* gross," Ella said.

"I know, super yuck." Steph gave her mother a wry look. "I didn't pick the restaurant."

Morgan's expression was stuck between fear and wonder at what the Big People were saying. Steph leaned close with a silly grin and tickled her ribs. Morgan folded in, half laughing.

The tickle was pure Doug. Already Steph had pivoted to backfill his roles, to be the comic release valve in addition to the boundary setter she had always been. The girls had responded amazingly. Rarely whined, did not refuse to put on mittens without his Thumb Monster game.

To his credit, Doug had cooperated. Even while he and his legal team spun preposterous theories publicly to get him off the hook, with the kids, he did right. He told them he had made a bad mistake. Was going away for a long time. *For a whole day?* Longer. *For ten hundred years?* Yes, about that. Maybe eleven hundred.

As he'd brushed Ella's bangs behind one ear—jumpsuited, two guards watching from the door—Steph cried. She buried her face in her sleeve and crunched her eyes against it, but sorrow overwhelmed her. Doug looked between his daughters' faces and asked them to look out for their mother. Morgan would not remember. To her, he would simply disappear. Ella would accept their vague cover story the same way she accepted logistics of Santa's Christmas Eve flight. When they got older, Steph supposed, she would have to give them the truth.

Ten years, she thought. *Give them ten good years of not knowing.*

She kept picturing Doug in his football jersey. Tall and robust. Mechanized by shoulder pads and helmet but graceful as a deer. Leading the Wildkits onto the field. Grin handsome through the face mask. Bursting with promise. Dauntless. If he had ripped a goalpost one-handed from the earth, nobody would have batted an eye.

It broke her heart.

Parking was tight in Wicker Park. Steph drove up Damen Avenue six times before spotting brake lights. She flipped her blinker and waited on the departing driver, mindful of her mirrors. The fact that her driving was so notoriously bad Fiske had believed Doug's poolside lie had been a wakeup call.

Gourmand occupied the top floor of its building, a new renovation whose lower levels housed condos and another, lesser, restaurant. Steph passed by the boisterous burger/bistro crowd to board an elevator. As the gold-plated car accelerated, her stomach tingled. In downtime at the office today, she had tried imagining the conversation. Her mother wished she wouldn't go. Chad Nimms had offered her Valium.

Off the elevator, in a spidered-glass mirror, she took a final bracing stock of herself.

Here goes nothing.

He sat near the window, the skyline giant and centered before him. Approached from behind, he looked every bit the Einstein or Hemingway figure he had cultivated. Hair sprawling above the chairback, white and wiry. The collar of a jaunty sports coat flared up. A leather-bound volume open beside his menu. Oblivious—seemingly—to the peeks of fellow diners, he licked his thumb and turned the page.

"Hello, Mr. Fiske."

"Ah, Stephanie." He closed his book and formally pulled out her chair. "Please."

A waiter materialized with a second menu: lowercase, cardstock big as a chessboard.

"How are you?" she asked. "On the mend?"

"Quite. *Et vous?*"

"*Comme ci, comme ça,*" she replied without missing a step. "My injuries were minor. Physically."

His chin raised in acknowledgment. He did look well, vigorous, his face a lusty pink.

"The chef is revolutionary." He nodded to her cardstock. "The first to pair poutine and kimchi, though she has been copied to the point of banality now."

The waiter, in topcoat and skinny jeans, returned. Fiske quizzed him on the house vinaigrette before ordering duck confit and a bone marrow appetizer for the table. Steph said she would try the poutine.

Relinquishing the menu, Steph laced her fingers before her. She faced her old teacher with an unwavering expression. Not quite challenging but clearly expecting something. And expecting him to begin.

Finally, after the fitness of a sauvignon blanc had been confirmed and each had received a tray of utensils resembling medieval torture instruments, he did.

"You're owed an apology. Manifestly." He laid one hand upon his chest, extended the other like an imploring poet. "I erred tragically in assuming Trev Larson was your agent: a thing he told me, it's true, but which I never should have taken at face."

Steph tipped her head. "Doug deceived everyone. He was pathological."

"Indeed. It shakes me to the core that a man I thought I knew could possess a character so radically different from my own assessment."

She didn't respond. She wanted more. She wanted to hear about the self-published books, or the years he had shunned her, or why exactly he had believed Doug's version of prom night—both ten years ago and, again, waking from his coma. Fiske showed no interest in these topics. Instead he picked out his marrow spoon and gouged the cylindrical cavity of a cow shank.

Steph sipped her wine. "I visited Autumn Brockert yesterday. She's itching to get back to school."

"So I understand," Fiske said. "Remarkable."

"How about you? Surely Principal Mancini would reinstate you under the circumstances."

Fiske finished a bite, concentrating on the small, fine chews. "I shan't ask it."

"You're done teaching?"

"I am."

"Why?"

"Given the publicity, I could not imagine class succeeding. An English course is about texts. The curriculum must inspire awe. A continuous procession of wonder at what literature can do, at the thread of human consciousness weaved from Homer, through

Joyce, through Roth; at its democratizing power to bring the world—any world—to the individual brave enough to simply read. The moment students become preoccupied with their guide, the spell breaks."

"What's next for *Illusory Greatnesses*?"

"A rewrite. Naturally focused around the Rick Mead character." Fiske set aside his marrow spoon, having scraped his shank clean. "My publisher wants a summer release ahead of the new Jack Reacher."

"Competing with the bestsellers now? Great."

He shook his head. "Fortune has found me as a direct result of others' misfortune. In that, there is nothing great."

Leading up to this dinner, Steph had not known what to make of Fiske. He was saying the right words now, more or less, but a certain gleam in his eye made her wonder. Was his retirement truly for the good of students? Or was he seizing an entrée to fame? (His survival tale had been told by *20/20*; the verb "tongue," as in "tonguing pills," was firmly in the zeitgeist.) It would be a completely ordinary response.

To Steph, the person whose actions in this ordeal most qualified as beyond ordinary was Becky Brindle. Becky, always saying she was stupid and deferring to "the smarties," had stood up to Doug. The full investigation had turned up texts from Becky to Trev Larson—time stamps corresponding with the Winners' initial drive north, hours before her death—in which she claimed to be Doug and told him to keep Autumn Brockert alive. *Steph's watching my phone, ignore any messages you get from it.*

Doug had overpowered or outwitted so many. But not Becky.

"Eric and I read blurbs on your previous books when we were on the run." Steph would never ride another Barnes & Noble escalator without thinking of Vance Tietjens. "You really took advantage of your perch."

Fiske's brow creased. "Beg pardon?"

"All your plotlines, your characters. It's all borrowed from ETHS."

"'Borrowed'?" he huffed. "Did you take nothing from my course? We recycle, every last writer among us. We write what we see every day."

"And in me, you saw Amanda Naylor."

Fiske glanced uneasily into his lap. Outside, the sun was nearing the horizon, winking behind and between different Loop skyscrapers. "You were merely the starting point. Bear in mind, I was writing under the misapprehension you'd killed Nora Brockert. That colored all else. I saw false motives. I retrofit a worldview onto a character—selfish, uncaring. Not for nothing is it called fiction."

This was just what she'd hoped to hear, of course. What Eric had said in Millennium Park, what she had tried convincing herself of as she speed-read *Illusory Greatnesses*. Amanda Naylor was not her. Fiske had dreamed her up for effect.

So why didn't she feel relief?

Fiske asked whether she was planning to write a book of her own.

"Me?" The question surprised her. "Oh, I'm swamped just putting my life back together."

"Last spring, you told me you saw marketing not as an end point but as a beginning." He tapped his chin. "Might this be your opportunity?"

"*Opportunity?*" Steph could think of few more offensive words for her situation.

"Elizabeth Warren's public life began in the embers of the financial crisis. Perhaps you could transition into public advocacy of a sort."

"What, raising awareness for people whose spouses lie and attempt to murder them?"

Fiske sniffed off the remark. "You'll soldier on in advertising, then, I suppose."

Steph noted his word choice: "advertising" rather than the more strategic "marketing." "That's the field I'm trained in. I have seven years' experience with Dunham & Prior."

"Do you love it?" She was drawing in breath to speak when Fiske amended, "Can you be great within its confines?"

"I enjoy the work," Steph said. "Mostly I enjoy my coworkers. It allows me to provide for my children, which I have to consider now."

Fiske's mouth puckered mildly. He looked past her, chest full, to the sunset. "You are special, Stephanie. I pegged you right the first time—before that abominable night. Your actions have been lionhearted. The loyalty you showed when I was at large. Your resourcefulness tracking me down, then having the wherewithal to slip your husband's trap and ferret out the truth. Naught short of amazing. You must write the tale. Consider it your final English 411 assignment."

He smiled, but only for a moment.

"You are a Winner." His eyes firmed. "I cannot conceive an obstacle beyond you. Your talents compel you to greatness. They demand it. I demand it. A world without you at the fore is bankrupt—utterly, tragically."

Again, this was exactly the sort of praise she'd yearned for. And although Steph did feel superficially soothed by the words—a thrum on the ego, an automatic rush of gratitude—they did not touch her deeply.

With a flourish, the waiter lifted two domes simultaneously off their food. The duck confit sat in a shallow pool of orange glaze among herb-flecked fingerling potatoes. The drumstick jutted up at forty-five perfect degrees, the nubby hock crisped to a gorgeous caramel. Steph's poutine came beside a purple-asparagus salad, crème fraîche, and fiery kimchi layered on top like white and red armies in a melee.

"I'm in the wrong mood for this," she said, fingering Ella's necklace through her shirt. "I think I'll find something less marvelous at home."

She left, embracing Fiske where he sat with both arms, wishing him the best.

21833615R00186

Made in the USA
San Bernardino, CA
05 January 2019